Chance and Circumstance

by

KARA LOUISE

Copyright © 2017 Kara Louise

All rights reserved.

ISBN-13: 978-1976544286
ISBN-10: 1976544289

Cover
Image by Cheryl Wallace
Design by Kara Louise

Published by Heartworks Publication

Printed in the United States of America

All rights reserved. No part of this publication may be reproduced, stored in a retrieval system, or transmitted in any form or by any means -- for example, mechanical, digital, photocopy, recording -- without the prior written permission of the publisher. An exception would be in brief quotations in printed reviews.

Library of Congress Cataloging-in-Publication Data

Kara Louise

Chance and Circumstance

Dedication

This book is dedicated to my two granddaughters,
Aisley and Emery,
who have brought an abundance of joy to our lives.

Thanks

Thanks to Mary Anne Hinz and Gayle Mills for their
willingness to read through my manuscript and
for offering their excellent suggestions and critique to
improve both the story and your reading experience.

I also want to thank my sister, Cheryl, who painted the lovely picture for me for the cover. It means so much to me to have an original cover made by someone who I love and admire deeply.

And finally, thank you, Jane Austen, for your original inspiration.

KARA LOUISE

Chapter 1

"My dear Mrs. Bennet, a letter from Jane has arrived." Mr. Bennet stepped into the drawing room where his wife sat quietly with their daughter, Elizabeth. The tall, lanky gentleman, who was in his early fifties and had thinning grey hair, beamed a rather youthful, teasing smile.

Mrs. Bennet squealed as she quickly pushed her plump body out of her chair and rushed to her husband's side. She snatched the letter from his hands. Elizabeth, also eager for news from her sister, felt like doing much the same but restrained herself.

"It has been far too long since we heard from her," Mrs. Bennet whined. "I have been quite despairing that something dreadful had happened to her."

"Well, now you may rest assured that all is well," her husband said, as he looked at Elizabeth and winked. "I do hope, however, that it does not contain news that something has befallen your brother and his wife."

"Oh, do not be ridiculous!" She walked to the bottom of the stairs and called out while gesturing nervously, "Girls! Come quickly. We have a letter from Jane!"

Elizabeth smiled as she heard the commotion of hurried steps coming down the stairs. Such an eager response by her three younger sisters might not have occurred had a persistent rain not kept them indoors the past week; consequently, they were all quite eager for news of any sort. Usually, that news would come from Mrs. Phillips, their mother's sister in Meryton, and involve all the neighbourhood gossip. Elizabeth, on the other hand, would heartily welcome news from Jane over anything else. The two sisters were very close, and Jane had been gone over a month. Elizabeth missed her terribly.

They gathered in the drawing room and surrounded Mrs. Bennet.

"Oh, I hope they are having a good time. I so love the Lake District." Mrs. Bennet wore a broad smile as she tore open the letter, bouncing her shoulders up and down in anticipation. "It has been many years since I was there. I was a little younger then than she is now, however, and attracted many a gentleman's eye."

Mr. Bennet rolled his eyes and let out a huff.

"Do you suppose they are on their way home already?" Mrs. Bennet asked.

"Well, my dear, I suppose you can read it and find out for yourself." Her husband folded his arms across his chest.

"So what do you think, Lizzy?" he leaned over and whispered. "Would your mother consider it better news if she finds out Jane is about to return home directly or if she is to remain with the Gardiners a little longer?"

"I think she would likely find something equally good and bad with either," Elizabeth laughed.

"Read it aloud to us!" Lydia exclaimed. "I so wish I could have gone to the Lake District with them."

"You shall have your turn once the other girls have had theirs," Mrs. Bennet replied, carefully unfolding the stationary. "Lizzy goes next year, and then Mary, Kitty, and finally, you."

Lydia slouched and let out a groan. "It is not fair being the youngest! I have to wait for my four sisters to have their share of everything before I have my turn!"

"Someone has to be the youngest, Lydia, and it happens to be you." Elizabeth knew there was little sense in trying to get Lydia to see reason, but she could at least make an attempt. "We all will have waited an equal amount of time as you when it is our turn to go."

"I shall likely be married by then," Lydia retorted. She crossed her arms as if defying anyone to refute her claim.

Elizabeth laughed and looked at her with a raised brow. "Do you really think so? You have to wait for your four elder sisters to marry before you do that."

Lydia shrugged. "I shall not wait if the right man asks me!" A smile then formed, and she remarked to Kitty with a giggle, "I am certain I shall be married first, before any of you! La! It would be a great deal more fun to go to the Lake District with my husband than with our aunt and uncle."

"Then we need hear no more about it," Mr. Bennet said, prompting Lydia to look up surprised, as if she had not thought anyone could hear her – or had paid attention to her. He then looked at his wife. "Read the letter, my dear."

They all turned their attention to Mrs. Bennet and listened silently as she began to read.

Dearest Father, Mother, and Sisters,

I hope this finds you all well! We have been having a wonderful time in the Lake District, and will have so many stories to tell when we return.

Although there has been some rain of late, we have been able to see so much, and have greatly enjoyed the scenery. The lakes are beautiful. One day in particular dawned perfectly clear, and we set out to for Lake Windermere. The water glistened with all shades of blue and green as the sun shone upon it, and a slight breeze travelled across it, creating playful ripples. I do not think I have ever seen anything so beautiful.

We walked across green meadows that overlooked the lake and took in the view as we enjoyed a picnic lunch. We had two chance encounters that afternoon. The first happened as we were eating our lunch. We were sitting on a hill overlooking the lake when we heard a noise off to the side. We turned and beheld three large sheep standing shoulder to shoulder on the path, staring at us. We stared back in astonishment. I think we were as startled to see them as they were to see us. We remained very still, and, at length, the sheep moved on. I suppose they wanted to graze in peace, as much as we wished to eat our meal in peace.

Later that day, we strolled along the lake, looked in the shops, and met some long-time friends of the Gardiners whom they had not seen in over ten years. They invited us to join them at a soiree they were hosting the following evening. We were delighted to be able to go and were entertained by some very talented musicians and singers. We had a wonderful time.

I have to confess that I had been thinking how nice it would be to remain here for a while. Well, just this morning, Aunt Gardiner asked me to write to see if our return could be delayed a few weeks. The unusually poor weather we have had has hampered several of our outings, and we wish to spend more time with these friends. Please write and let us know if this is acceptable to you. I hope you do not mind.

I miss you all and send you my love. Aunt and Uncle Gardiner send their love, as well.

Lovingly, Jane

"Well! That was rather short," Mrs. Bennet lamented, turning the stationary over several times to ensure she had not missed something. "I suppose they are so busy with these friends that they have forgotten all about us! So they are to stay longer!"

"I know my trip will not be extended when it is my turn," Lydia complained. "They shall be so tired of taking this trip for the four previous years that I will be lucky if it is even half as long!"

Elizabeth leaned over to her father and whispered, "I do not doubt that when Aunt and Uncle Gardiner take Lydia, they shall be ready to return with her before they even set out!"

Mr. Bennet folded his arms across his chest. "Perhaps we ought to pray that Lydia *does* get married before it is her turn to go!"

Elizabeth chuckled and followed it with a sigh. "I also wish Jane had written more, but I suppose she is too busy. It sounds as though she is greatly enjoying the trip."

"Perhaps," her father replied with a twinkle in his eyes. He reached into his pocket and pulled something out. "But then it just might be that she saved her more detailed observations for you." He furtively handed Elizabeth another letter. "For you, Lizzy. I would assume you will want to read it on your own without interference from your mother or sisters."

A smile brightened Elizabeth's face, and she said in a fervent hush, "Oh, yes! Thank you so much!"

Mr. Bennet nodded in acknowledgement. "You are more than welcome, but in turn, I expect a little report on what she writes. Not all, mind you, but enough to satisfy my curiosity."

Elizabeth smiled. "Of course, Papa."

As the others talked about what little Jane said and did not say, Elizabeth announced over the din that as the rain had stopped and the sun was finally shining, she was going out for a stroll. She turned to walk away when she heard her mother.

"Heavens, Lizzy! Do you know how muddy it is out there? Why would you want to do such a thing?"

Elizabeth stole a glance at her father and smiled. Turning back to her mother, she answered, "I shall take care and try not to step in the mud or fall into any puddles." She walked over to the chair, where she had last placed her shawl and threw it about her shoulders. "I will see you later."

Before waiting for a reply, she left the room, patting her pocket where Jane's letter safely resided. She was eager to read what Jane had intended only for her eyes.

She walked in the direction of Oakham Mount, attempting to avoid the puddles of water by jumping over them or skirting around them. Her mother had been correct. It was quite muddy, but she was determined to read Jane's letter in solitude. She knew none of her sisters would have wanted to accompany her out on a walk, and if she had taken it up to her room, there was the likelihood that at least one of them would intrude on her solitude and alert the others.

Elizabeth drew in a breath as she reached the well-worn path that would take her to the top. A slight, cool breeze whipped up the ties of her bonnet, tickling her neck. The hot days of summer were over, and September had bid them farewell with several days of a light, but steady, rain. She stopped, closed her eyes, and lifted her head, allowing the rays of the sun to warm her. She smiled, as it was the first day in over a week that she had been able to get out and breathe in the fresh air.

If Jane were here, she would have joined Elizabeth on her walk, and they would be enjoying warm conversation and frequent laughs, while sharing the deepest secrets that made the two sisters close. They certainly would not have walked to the top of Oakham Mount, as Jane was not an avid walker, but they would have enjoyed their time together away from the others. Elizabeth let out a sigh. How she missed her and looked forward to her return!

Being confined to the house for the past week had been a trial on Elizabeth's nerves. She would likely have taken a walk today in the midst of a flood if it was the only way to spend some guaranteed time alone to read Jane's letter! She was grateful the sun had risen to a perfectly blue sky, dotted with a few clouds left behind from the storm.

She opened Jane's letter and was pleased to see that it was longer than the one written to the whole family, and she eagerly began reading.

Dearest Lizzy,

I cannot begin to tell you what a lovely time we are having. As I told everyone in my other letter, we have had rain, but that has not deterred us from enjoying our stay. The meadows are so green, and the water is so blue. When the sun shines, it dances off the surface of the lakes like sparkling diamonds.

Oh, Lizzy! I do not know where to begin! I wrote about the friends of the Gardiners whom we encountered. They had known the Marshalls in London, and the family now resides in Ambleside in a lovely manor. You can actually see Lake Windermere from one of the windows if you stand up on your toes when you look out.

The Marshalls have been very gracious to us, taking us out sailing in their boat and inviting us to a soiree in their home. But the one thing I did not mention in my other letter was that their son, Jacob Marshall, has been exceedingly attentive to me, and we have gotten along quite well. I know I am not overly expressive of my feelings, but there have been times when we have been together that I have been almost overcome with emotion. I sometimes think I might just burst out in song.

And perhaps the reason I say that is because Mr. Marshall sang several songs for us at the soiree. He has the most pleasant voice I have ever heard. There were times when he sang that he looked directly at me, and I felt as though I might swoon. My heart feels as though it might burst! I know you are wondering if this letter is truly from me, but believe me, Lizzy, I have never felt this way!

Please do not mention him to Mother or our sisters, as it would likely cause unwarranted speculation. I wanted to share this with you, however. He is the real reason that our stay was lengthened. His family inherited the manor in which they live from an uncle, his father is the magistrate here, and they have a good standing in the county.

You will likely want to share this with Father, and I will allow you that. I know you and he will look at this as it should be, and not conjecture what may or may not happen in the future between the two of us. I have to admit, however, that Mr. Marshall is a most handsome and proper gentleman, and I fear it will prove to be difficult for me to leave when we return home. It is my dearest hope, however, that he will come to Longbourn soon so you can meet him. I hope you will like him as much as I do.

I look forward to getting back home and seeing you and the family. I miss you and especially our long talks. If you were here with me now, I know we would not get a minute of sleep at night due to our talks and giggling.

I hope you are in good health and that all is well at home. Our plan now is to return in two or three weeks. As much as I look forward to seeing you, I will greatly miss Mr. Marshall.

*All my love,
Jane*

Elizabeth smiled as she read the letter and pressed it to her heart when she finished.

"So Jane has a beau," she whispered softly and smiled. "Oh, how I wish we were not separated! I would want to know everything about him. Is he as kind and generous as you are, Jane? Does he have a good opinion of everyone he meets?" Chuckling, she asked, "But most importantly, is he a man to whom you can ardently attach your affections?"

She pinched her brows as she thought of the gentleman who once tried to woo Jane by writing her poetry. "I do hope he is not a poet. He must have some qualities and accomplishments that will not only endear him to you, but endear him to me, as well!"

She glanced up the path and saw that she was almost at the summit. From there she would be able to look out over the whole neighbourhood. In one direction she could see the little town of Meryton, and in the other direction she could see Longbourn, her home. If she walked to the other side, she would see several large country manors, including Netherfield, the grandest of all, which apparently had just been let.

The breeze was brisk at this height, and she hugged her shawl tightly about her. She did a little side-step around a mud puddle and then began to laugh as she looked down at the hem of her dress which was now caked with mud. "Mother will be quite displeased when I return!" She shrugged her shoulders slightly. "At least it is unlikely I shall encounter anyone!" She smiled as she considered that no one with good sense would venture a walk up here in the mud.

Elizabeth looked at the letter again. "Oh, Jane. I am so glad I had the opportunity to read your letter in peace and solitude." She hugged her arms about her. "I love sharing secrets with you." She chuckled softly. "Especially secrets such as this one."

She came to another, much larger puddle, which covered the whole path, and she puckered her mouth in thought. "I do want to get to the top to see the view." She shook her head. "I refuse to let this puddle stop me!"

She lifted her dress slightly, and just as she readied herself to jump, a noise behind her startled her, causing her to lose her balance. She began to tumble head-long to the ground. Her hands flew out to break her fall, but the slick mud caused one foot to slide, and she landed on her side. At least she had been able to keep her head up.

She looked back to see what the noise was, and was startled to see an unknown, but well-dressed, gentleman, quickly dismounting his horse. Curly blond hair framed a round pleasant-looking face, and warm and cheerful blue eyes looked down at her with concern.

"I am so sorry! Are you all right?" he asked as he hurried over.

Elizabeth looked down at herself, feeling her face warm in a blush. "I have been better, sir, but I am not injured."

"I am relieved to hear that. I would have been deeply grieved if you were hurt."

She sat up and looked about her, wondering what she could say to this young man that would excuse her appearance. "Perhaps only my pride is injured, having been discovered in such a state!"

He reached out his hand with an apologetic smile. "It is solely my fault that you stumbled; the sound of my horse startled you. Pray, allow me to assist you."

"Oh, no. I do not think that is a good idea, sir." She put up a hand to stay him and added, "And have no fear; it was all my doing. I have been confined to our house this past week by the incessant rains, and when the sun began shining this morning, it beckoned me to come out and enjoy the day. I had to step out for a walk, despite the mud." Elizabeth slowly extricated herself and stood up. She wiped her hands together to brush off some of the mud, but to little avail.

"Yes," he said with a cheerful laugh. "I know what you mean. I wondered if the skies would ever clear."

Elizabeth looked down at her dress and laughed. "I do look a fright, do I not?"

The gentleman shook his head and smiled. "On the contrary, I think you look… charming."

Elizabeth felt her cheeks warm again. "You are too kind, but I fear you must be blind!" Elizabeth drew in a breath. Was he flirting with her or was this his usual manner of behaviour? "I hope you do not mind my asking, but are you new to the neighbourhood or merely visiting? I do not believe we have met." She smiled. "My name is Miss Elizabeth Bennet. My home, Longbourn, is down there, through the trees." She pointed in the direction of her home.

"I am very pleased to make you acquaintance, Miss Bennet. And yes, I am new to the neighbourhood!" he announced joyfully. "I recently let Netherfield. In fact, I came up here to see if I could get a good view of the land surrounding it. My name is Charles Bingley."

Chapter 2

"It is a pleasure to meet you, Mr. Bingley. We heard Netherfield had been recently let." She smiled and looked up at him with a raised brow. "And, I might add, we have heard all about you."

"From your father perhaps? Mr. Bennet? I met him the other day when he came by during a slight lull in the rain."

"No, we did not gain any intelligence from him. My father is a man who loves to tease, and while we all wanted him to tell us about our new neighbour, he conveniently deflected our questions with answers that were not at all informative."

A surprised look crossed Mr. Bingley's face. "As I have not yet met many people in the neighbourhood, from where could the account come?" He grimaced teasingly. "I hope you have not heard anything too dreadful."

Elizabeth looked ahead and smiled, thinking it was nice to have a new face in the neighbourhood – particularly one who was handsome and agreeable. Standing alongside him, she acknowledged that he was tall, had a medium stature, and a ready smile. In the short time since encountering him, she had sketched his character to be quite amiable, lively, and altogether charming.

"Mr. Bingley, I fear we would have heard about you even if you had not met a single person here. You must understand that any time someone new moves into the neighbourhood – or even just passes through it – there is always a great deal of conjecture about who the person is, what they are like, and anything else of interest." Elizabeth shrugged. "So you see, what we heard was likely not based on someone having met you at all, but merely speculative rumours."

"I understand completely," Mr. Bingley said, looking down as

CHANCE AND CIRCUMSTANCE

he scuffed the dirt with his boot. He glanced up at Elizabeth with a twinkle in his eye. "But pray, do I want to hear the stories that were circulated about me?"

She waved a hand through the air. "You have no reason to be concerned, I assure you." She dared not mention the gossip circulating the neighbourhood about his fortune of four or five thousand a year.

Mr. Bingley let out a reassured breath and said with a chuckle, "I am greatly relieved!"

Elizabeth smiled. "We did hear that you came down from the north. Would that be accurate?"

"Partially. My family is from the north, but I came here directly from London."

"I see. And are you here by yourself or did you bring others with you?"

"I arrived last week with two gentlemen and two ladies."

"So small a party?" Elizabeth laughed. "We heard it was a much larger party, of seven ladies and four gentlemen. You know how people love to exaggerate."

"The two ladies are my sisters, one of the gentlemen is my sister's husband, and the other gentleman is a good friend, although he had to return to London on business. I had hoped he would come out with me this morning to see the view of Netherfield from up here, but he took his leave at daylight when he saw the weather had improved."

"I look forward to meeting them all."

"And indeed, you shall."

Elizabeth looked out at the view below and turned back to him. "Mr. Bingley, as it is a delightful day and since you were on your way up to see the land surrounding Netherfield, I shall leave you to continue on." She pointed off towards the left. "You are almost to the summit, and then you need only walk around a little to the left."

"I will not hear of you walking home unaccompanied! I can see the view at any time. Please allow me to escort you so I can meet the rest of your family. I planned to return your father's visit, and what better time to do it than now?"

"I thank you, Mr. Bingley, but it is truly not necessary to

accompany me. If you knew how often I walked up and down this mountain by myself, I fear you would be shocked."

"Not a great deal shocks me, Miss Bennet. Come, let us walk."

"Thank you. I know my family will be delighted to meet you." Elizabeth could not have asked for a more good-natured and delightful gentleman to escort her home.

The two began walking as Mr. Bingley led his horse behind him.

"If I recollect correctly, your father informed me you have four sisters."

"Indeed. You have an excellent memory."

"I shall look forward to meeting each of them."

"And so you shall, but my elder sister is from home visiting the Lake District with our aunt and uncle. You will have to make her acquaintance another time, as it may be a few weeks before she returns."

"So it shall have to be!" he said with a smile.

The two had a pleasant conversation as they walked, and although it appeared Mr. Bingley thought nothing of how dishevelled she looked, every time Elizabeth's eyes caught a glimpse of the mud on her dress or shoes, she chided herself for not taking care to stay out of the puddles. What would her mother say?

Mother! Elizabeth suddenly stopped, her eyes widened, and she took in a quick breath.

"Is anything amiss?" Mr. Bingley asked.

Elizabeth took a moment to organize her thoughts and pressed her fingers to her lips. "You may find this an odd request, Mr. Bingley, but when we reach Longbourn, would you allow me to return indoors alone? Could you possibly wait a few minutes before coming to the door? I fear my mother would be quite horrified if she knew that the new gentleman in the neighbourhood had come upon her daughter in such a state." Elizabeth chose *not* to inform him that despite her mother's mortification, she would likely be ecstatic that he had accompanied her down the hill and in her mind would have them married by Christmas.

He smiled and nodded. "I shall be more than happy to oblige

you. Shall I wait long enough to allow you some time to make yourself presentable? Perhaps, fifteen minutes?"

Elizabeth looked down at herself, winced, and shook her head. "Perhaps twenty would be best." She laughed and looked up at him. He was still smiling at her, and it warmed her. She could not help but feel truly pleased by his company.

When they reached the base of Oakham Mount, Elizabeth thanked Mr. Bingley for his chivalry and graciousness, and hurried off to the house. As she walked, a smile lit her face, and she thought that perhaps she might have a handsome gentleman about whom she could also write to Jane.

~~*

Elizabeth was grateful no one saw her step inside through the back door. She slipped off her dirty shoes and hurried up the stairs, entered her room, and closed the door behind her. She went to her closet and perused her dresses, suddenly feeling as though none would be stylish enough for the wealthy and single gentleman from the north.

She finally selected a pale blue muslin dress, one that Jane often said suited her quite well, as it brightened her eyes and complimented her skin. She carefully removed her soiled dress, taking care not to get any mud on her face and trying not to dishevel her hair.

She went to the mirror and felt another wave of mortification when she saw that there was a fairly large smudge of mud in the centre of her forehead. She took a handkerchief and dipped it in a basin of water. She hoped it had found its way there when she removed the dress, but considering how dry it was, she was fairly confident it had been there the entire time she had been walking down the mount and talking with Mr. Bingley.

"And he did not mention it at all!" she said, shaking her head. But a smile immediately appeared. "I think Mr. Bingley has just improved in my estimation of his person!" Then she pinched her brows. "Or would I have preferred it if he had mentioned it?" She shrugged and laughed. "I feel as though I am a silly young girl who has developed her first crush!"

Elizabeth heard a commotion downstairs and determined the gentleman had been let in. He had perfect timing! She took one last glance in the mirror, tidied a few strands of wayward hair, and then stepped from her room.

She hurried down the stairs to find her sisters and mother gathered in the drawing room.

"What is all the commotion?" she asked innocently.

"A gentleman has just been shown into your father's study! We believe it is our new neighbour, Mr. Bingley," Mrs. Bennet said.

"I know it must be him, for it is someone we have never seen before!" Kitty cried. "Lydia and I saw him through the window when he came up with his horse. I think he is quite handsome."

Lydia tossed her head. "I have seen much handsomer men. Perhaps if he were in regimentals, his appearance would be much improved."

Mary looked up from her needlework. "I doubt that we shall ever see him in regimentals, Lydia." She shook her head. "Men of fortune have no need to join the military."

"Well, I can hope, can I not?" Lydia asked.

"Do you think Father will introduce him to us?" Kitty asked. "I hope he does. I will be most disappointed if he leaves after their meeting without an introduction."

"Mr. Bennet had better introduce him to us, or I shall be most displeased!" Mrs. Bennet said loudly and then let out a soft chuckle. "I want to meet him as much as you girls do."

The ladies waited – some of them more impatiently than the others – and they finally heard the study door open.

Mrs. Bennet gave her daughters a look that demanded they be on their best behaviour. She turned expectantly towards the door as the sound of approaching footsteps and low conversation could be heard. Just before the men reached the door of the drawing room, the matronly woman smiled, clasped her hands, and then rested them in her lap.

The two men stepped into the room, and Mr. Bennet began to make introductions. Mr. Bingley looked at Elizabeth and smiled furtively, and then very politely greeted her mother, herself, and each of her sisters, acknowledging each one with a kind word. He seemed truly pleased to make their acquaintance, as were all the ladies of Longbourn delighted to make his. His manners were impeccable, and everyone seemed well pleased with their new neighbour.

"Mr. Bingley," Mrs. Bennet cried. "It is with great joy we welcome you to our little neighbourhood. We are quite certain you will be delighted with all your neighbours. But please, you must join us for dinner one day this week. We would be honoured to have you dine with us."

"Why, thank you, Mrs. Bennet. I…"

"Shall we plan on Thursday?" she said. "Our cook prepares the most delicious meals. I am certain you will enjoy it."

Mr. Bennet stepped forward. "Mr. Bingley presently has his two sisters and a brother-in-law residing with him. Shall we extend the invitation to them, as well, Mrs. Bennet?"

"Of course!" she replied. "Pray, you must invite your whole party. They are all welcomed to join us, as well."

Mr. Bennet patted their new neighbour on his shoulder. "Now, ladies, I am certain Mr. Bingley has business he must see to, so let us not keep him any longer."

Mr. Bingley nodded to Mr. Bennet and turned back to the ladies. "Indeed, Mr. Bennet is correct, and as much as I regret it, I must take my leave." He addressed Mrs. Bennet. "It has been a pleasure to make your acquaintance, Mrs. Bennet, as well as your daughters. I shall see you on Thursday." He stole a glance at Elizabeth, smiling briefly, before he stepped from the room.

Mr. Bennet accompanied the gentleman out, while the ladies remained silent until the men had stepped through the door. Once they were outdoors, there was a gleeful squeal as the first impression of this gentleman had been quite favourable. Elizabeth remained subdued outwardly, but on the inside she felt a great deal of delight.

Later that day, Elizabeth went to her room and pulled out some stationary. She would have preferred to have Jane here to talk to, for they would have much to say to each other about Mr. Bingley *and* Mr. Marshall, but writing to her about him would be the next best thing.

Elizabeth held her quill above the stationary as she thought about all she would say. She finally dipped it into the ink and put it to the paper.

My dearest Jane,

How delighted I was to receive your letter. Mother read your letter to all of us, and I confess I was disappointed (as was she) that it was so short. But when Father presented me with your letter, I could not have been happier.

I immediately sought privacy by walking up Oakham Mount, much to Mother's distress, for we, too, have had a lot of rain. I knew our sisters would not wish to join me, and I would have the pleasure of reading your letter in solitude.

Oh, Jane! I could not believe the news you shared with me. How fortuitous it was to have encountered this gentleman and his family, being as they were long-time friends of our aunt and uncle. He sounds absolutely wonderful, and I am delighted for you! I hope that as you remain in the Lake District and spend time with him and his family, that the two of you will grow in your attachment towards one another — if that is what is meant to be.

But now I have news of my own. I also had a chance meeting just this morning with the gentleman who recently let Netherfield. When I took the path up Oakham Mount, I was startled by the approach of a man on horseback as I was attempting to jump over a puddle. Needless to say, I ended up in the puddle instead of clearing it on the other side.

This gentleman, Mr. Bingley, was grieved that he had caused my stumble. I had to assure him that I was quite well and was solely at fault, but he insisted on escorting me back home. Dare I tell you that my dress and shoes were covered in mud, but he seemed not to notice at all? We talked and laughed, and I found myself greatly enjoying his company.

He even obliged me and waited twenty minutes before coming in to meet the family so I could make myself more presentable. Father had met him a few days earlier, and Mr. Bingley had planned to repay the visit. I knew Mother would be vexed at me if she saw me walking back to the house with him in my state of disarray.

So, just as you wished to keep news about Mr. Marshall from her, so I did not want her to know about my encounter with the new gentleman in the neighbourhood who is worth four or five thousand pounds! She would have been mortified by my unkempt appearance and that he had encountered me in such a state, but at the same time she would have begun planning our wedding! So you see, Jane, you and I are now both conspiring to keep our news from

Mother for the very same reason. We know her well, do we not?

Oh, how I wish you were here so we could both laugh and giggle as we talk to each other about these two gentlemen we have just met. I do not know Mr. Bingley well enough to have lost my heart to him or to even believe he is everything I want in a man I might marry, but it certainly is a nice change having a new, handsome face in the neighbourhood – someone who is gentlemanly, kind, and altogether charming.

I know you are busy, and quite enjoying your time, but I do look forward to your next letter. Please write soon. I am eager to hear more about you and Mr. Marshall!

With much love,
Lizzy

Elizabeth folded up the letter and pondered the similar circumstances in which she and her sister found themselves. She had readily noticed her rapidly beating heart as she had pondered how to describe Mr. Bingley to Jane, and felt a grand sense of delight that she and her sister were likely experiencing very similar feelings.

Whether or not the outcomes would be the same she could not say, but right now she could not be happier.

Chapter 3

Elizabeth made every attempt to remain calm as she waited for Thursday's dinner, which Mr. Bingley and his family would be attending. She kept telling herself that it was far too early to have formed an attachment to the gentleman, but she looked forward to his coming, anyway, as it would be a pleasant diversion.

She was also eager to meet his two sisters, brother-in-law, and his friend, if he had returned. She wondered whether they would all be as agreeable as Mr. Bingley. She hoped and expected they would be.

Elizabeth was slightly disappointed, then, when he sent word early in the day that his sisters and brother-in-law had to return to London unexpectedly, and his friend had not yet returned. He expressed his regrets, but assured them he looked forward to dining with them.

On Thursday, Mrs. Bennet repeatedly checked on the meal Cook was preparing. She wanted everything to be perfect, for certainly Mr. Bingley would form an attachment to one of her daughters. Both Kitty and Lydia claimed that he had likely found one of them completely irresistible. Lydia, however, continued to insist that he would be more suited for her if he were to wear military attire.

Elizabeth merely smiled at the folly of her two sisters, grateful that her brief, prior meeting with the young man had been kept from them all.

That evening, Mr. Bingley arrived and was ushered into the drawing room where the Bennets were gathered, waiting expectantly. Elizabeth was pleased when she observed how he was steadfastly polite in the midst of Kitty's and Lydia's silly antics and her mother's foolish outbursts. The conversation was all about

Netherfield, what changes he might want to make, and whether he was pleased with the neighbourhood.

"I shall not make any changes until I determine whether I want to purchase it."

"Oh!" exclaimed Mrs. Bennet. "You will definitely wish to purchase it, for our neighbourhood is one of the finest in all of England."

Mr. Bingley chuckled. "I am certain it is," he said, as he looked at Elizabeth and smiled. "I have met a good number of the families here, and everyone seems..." Bingley paused and a finally added, "delightful."

Elizabeth gave her head a slight shake as the thought crossed her mind that he was much like Jane in that he seemed pleased with everyone and everything. You could not ask for a finer quality than that in a gentleman.

"It is a shame your family could not join us tonight," Mrs. Bennet said, looking quite dejected. "What could they have to do in London that would draw them away from here?"

Mr. Bingley's mouth twitched, and he said, "They were sorry to leave and wanted me to express their deepest regrets to you." He shrugged. "My sister and her husband have a home in town and something needed their immediate attention." He shrugged his shoulders. "They needed to see to it directly."

"Oh, but certainly they did not..." Mrs. Bennet began, but Elizabeth interrupted her.

"Oh the joys of owning and maintaining a home," Elizabeth laughed. "Shall they return shortly, do you think?"

A wide smile appeared on Mr. Bingley's face. "I believe they shall return in a few days, as well as my good friend. I think... I hope they shall be here in time for the Meryton Assembly."

"Oh, you must write them directly and insist they be here in time for that. I know they will enjoy it immensely!" Mrs. Bennet declared.

"How can they not?" Lydia asked incredulously. "With all the music and dancing."

"And all the food!" Kitty added.

Lydia looked pointedly at their guest. "Do you enjoy dancing, Mr. Bingley?"

"I do, very much!"

"Oh, wonderful!" exclaimed Mrs. Bennet. "We have enough daughters to keep you dancing the whole evening."

"Mother," Elizabeth said. "I am certain Mr. Bingley will wish to dance with other young ladies in the neighbourhood. We are not the only ones for him to choose from."

"I shall insist on dancing with each of your daughters," Mr. Bingley assured Mrs. Bennet as he looked at each one. "If they will be so kind to accept."

"Oh, but Jane is not here," Mrs. Bennet lamented. "I do not think she will make it back in time for the Assembly."

"Jane? Would that be your eldest daughter who is from home?"

"Yes," Elizabeth said, with a knowing smile. "She has been in the Lake District with our aunt and uncle."

"She was expected back by now," Mrs. Bennet said, "but we recently received news that they have been delayed in their return. Such a pity. I know you would like her. Everyone says she is quite the prettiest young lady in the entire neighbourhood."

Kitty and Lydia rolled their eyes at their mother's claims. Elizabeth, however, readily recognized her sister's beauty and looked upon it with no hard or jealous feelings. There could be no two sisters closer than she and her elder sister, and none kinder than Jane. She wholeheartedly agreed with her mother's assertions, and believed Jane was at least five times prettier than herself.

The conversation continued as they moved into the dining room for dinner. They talked about the Meryton Assembly and the people of the neighbourhood, while Mr. Bennet seemed to enjoy talking with their guest about the joys and pitfalls of home ownership and property management.

Mr. Bingley proclaimed several times throughout the meal how delicious it was, which greatly pleased Mrs. Bennet. Elizabeth was certain this was an exaggeration on his part, for to her it was nothing exceptional, but she attributed his praise to the kind of man he was – kind and gracious.

When Mr. Bingley finally left that night, Elizabeth was confident that everyone approved of the young man. While her two youngest sisters claimed that he was amiable and certainly attractive, it appeared their infatuation with him had lessened.

Elizabeth attributed it to the news that soon the militia would be coming to Meryton and a young man in uniform was more to their liking. Her other sister, Mary, rarely said anything about the desirability of a young man, but agreed he was certainly a fine and respectable addition to the neighbourhood.

That night, as Elizabeth lay in bed, she thought back to the evening. Mr. Bingley was certainly a fine young man. She could not find a single fault with him, but the thought kept reappearing that her heart was not yet touched. "It is best," she said softly. "I barely know him."

She curled up under the coverlet, wrapping her arms about her bended knees. "He is handsome and respectable, everything a young lady would want in a man," she said. "But…" She could not shake off that thought, or even finish it.

~~*

Netherfield – Two Weeks Later

"I am so glad you have returned, Darcy!" Bingley exclaimed. "I thought you had left me for good. But I will have you know I have thoroughly enjoyed getting to know my new neighbours!"

"I am certain you have," Darcy replied drearily. "That surprises me not one bit, but *you* are the new neighbour, not them! I am sure everyone in this little country neighbourhood lavished you with their gentility and hospitality. Far better for you that I was not here to hinder you in your pursuit of country acquaintances."

Bingley let out a huff. "Between you and my sisters conveniently having business taking you all back to town, I only hope no one was the wiser."

"I am certain they were not. They are all likely simple folk with simple country manners."

"I have enjoyed every new acquaintance I have made." An odd smile appeared, and Darcy shot him a questioning look.

"I have seen that look before, Bingley." Darcy crossed his arms at his chest. "If I can trust my intuition, I would say you have met a young lady for whom you now think you have a grand affection… again!"

His friend's smile widened. "I have! Miss Elizabeth Bennet is wonderful, Darcy! She is witty, intelligent, clever, and quite pretty."

"As were all your previous affections."

"No, she is different!"

"Of course, she is," he replied with little enthusiasm. "I shall reserve my judgment until I meet the young lady in question."

"And you shall! There is an assembly on Saturday."

Darcy brought his fingers up and rubbed his forehead. "An assembly? In this neighbourhood?"

Bingley nodded. "I am quite looking forward to it."

Darcy clenched his jaw and fisted his hand. His friend was too eager to throw himself into the life of this neighbourhood and possibly into the life of one of its ladies. He did not want to discourage his friend, but neither did he want to boost his already heightened delight. "You certainly do not expect me to go, Bingley."

"I do, and I expect my sisters and Hurst to go, as well."

"They will not be happy attending such an affair."

"What of you?" Bingley stood in front of his friend and propped his hands on his hips. "I know you dislike being in places where you know few people, but remember when we were at Cambridge? You remember the favour you always asked of me?"

Darcy drew in a breath. "That was a long time ago." He turned quickly away. "This is different."

"Yes, it is, as this time I am asking the favour of *you*." Bingley looked down at his feet, and then glanced back up. "I know this is a *simple* country neighbourhood, but I want you… I ask you to join me at the assembly."

Darcy muttered, "I shall consider it. When do you expect your sisters and Hurst?"

"They arrive on the morrow."

"Have you informed them of this assembly?"

Bingley shook his head. "No, not exactly. I requested that they return by Friday, but did not tell them why."

Darcy began to rub his jaw. "Bingley, you know what they thought about your taking this house. I cannot imagine they will want to attend an assembly held in a neighbourhood such as this."

"Well, I am tired of everyone's complaints. I am perfectly

satisfied with the house, its grounds, and even its neighbours." He grew silent for a moment. "I only wish Caroline and Louisa had not decided to return to London when the Bennets had invited us for dinner. I knew what they thought about having to dine with them, and I was quite put out."

"You wanted them to meet these Bennets because of the young lady?"

A smile again appeared.

Darcy took a seat and indicated his friend to take one, as well. "All right, Bingley. Tell me all about her... this Miss..."

"Miss Elizabeth Bennet!" Bingley hurried over and sat down. "I met her when she was out walking and I was riding up Oakham Mount to get a bird's eye view of the land around Netherfield, as we had discussed ought to be done. My horse startled her, and she fell into the mud."

Darcy dropped his jaw. "Goodness, Bingley! She was out strolling in the mud?"

"Well, certainly you recollect how much rain we had received. She had been just as eager to get out and walk as you were to get out and ride back to London!" he replied and laughed.

"Who was with her?"

"No one; she was alone."

Darcy looked at his friend incredulously. "No one was accompanying her?"

"Now, I can see what you are about, Darcy, but I found her adventurous spirit quite endearing."

"Imprudent, if you ask me." Darcy shook his head, as he was not impressed with this young lady. "Those are not the manners of a well-bred and refined lady, Bingley. You need to take care in a neighbourhood such as this."

"Wait until you meet her. I have never met anyone so delightful."

"I have heard you say that before," Darcy grumbled. "What are her connections? Who is her family, and what fortune do they possess?"

Bingley shrugged. "Mr. Bennet owns a manor on a small estate. They have several servants, and while they do not have a grand fortune..." His voice trailed off as he caught his friend's expression of disapproval.

"I doubt she would be considered suitable, Bingley."

"No, my friend, trust me. I honestly believe you will think highly of her."

"I shall reserve judgment until I meet her, but I hope you have not paid her any particular attention. A lady from this neighbourhood is likely desperate to marry a man of fortune and will interpret any such attentions as a sure sign of his attachment."

"Have no fear. She has three sisters and I treated them equally the same." A sly smile appeared. "Except, of course, when we came down from Oakham Mount." He looked at his friend earnestly. "She was…" Bingley paused and merely sighed.

"Delightful is how you described her, I believe."

"Yes, you shall see. Wait until you meet her, and that will be at the assembly… on Saturday."

"As you have said." Darcy let out a frustrated breath. "So be it."

~~*

On Saturday afternoon, the Bennet ladies hurried to ready themselves for the Meryton Assembly. While this was an event that Elizabeth usually looked forward to with a reserved enthusiasm, today she found herself filled with eager anticipation. She credited it all to Mr. Bingley.

She took extra care with her dress and hair, asking Sarah to help her weave some flowers through her upswept curls. She looked at herself from every angle in a mirror, adjusting her sleeves, bodice, or anything else that she felt could use improvement. When she was at last satisfied, she went downstairs and joined her father in his study.

"You are not going to accompany us this evening?" Elizabeth asked.

He looked up from his book and frowned. "You know I take no delight in these affairs where the women all compare themselves and their dresses to one another, and the men stand about trying to make idle conversation and look engaged." He shook his head. "No, I shall be perfectly content to remain here, reading in peace and quiet."

Elizabeth smiled, already knowing her father's thoughts on assemblies.

"And you, Lizzy? Are you looking forward to a dance or two with Mr. Bingley?"

Elizabeth's eyes shot up, and she felt a blush warm her cheeks.

"Ah, just as I have suspected all along. Ever since seeing the two of you come down from Oakham Mount that first day he came to Longbourn, I have had my suspicions." He wore a sly smile.

"You saw us?"

"Oh, yes. I was quite amused with how you both feigned unfamiliarity with each other when you were first introduced." He let out a chuckle. "I assume you did not want your mother to know you had already encountered him on your walk as you were quite covered in mud when you arrived home. I was amazed at how quickly – and pleasingly – you tidied and cleaned yourself up."

Elizabeth looked down at her clasped hands. "His horse startled me when I was trying to jump over a mud puddle. I did not want Mother to know that Mr. Bingley had seen me in such a state. She would have been quite displeased with me."

"So I suspected." Mr. Bennet leaned back in his chair and began tapping the table. "And I suppose you also did not want her to know you had already met him for she would likely have you married – in her mind, at least."

Elizabeth nodded. "Yes, just as Jane did not want Mother to know about her beau."

Mr. Bennet looked confused. "Jane has a beau? What news is this?" He clasped his hands and looked up at his daughter.

"Did I not tell you about the contents of her letter to me? Mr. Bingley's unexpected appearance must have made me quite forget that you wanted a report of what she wrote."

"So Jane has a beau?" He leaned forward on his elbows, his bushy brows lowered over his eyes.

"According to Jane, he is a very fine gentleman, the son of Aunt and Uncle Gardiner's friends. He is the main reason they delayed their return." Elizabeth's shoulder rose as she drew in a breath, and she watched for her father's reaction.

Mr. Bennet pressed his lips together and brought his clasped hands up to his chin. "This is significant news, Lizzy. Imagine that! My two eldest daughters entertaining the notion that a gentleman they have just met might be the one who captures their hearts." He looked back up. "Does Jane know of your Mr. Bingley?"

"He is far from being my Mr. Bingley, Papa, but yes, I did write to her to tell her about him. I truly cannot say that he is everything I want in the gentleman who will one day be my husband. I hardly even know him." She gave a slight shrug of her shoulders. "But I am more than willing to find out."

"He seems to be a friendly and polite enough gentleman, to be sure," Mr. Bennet said with a nod. "I cannot say that he has your intelligence and wit, Lizzy, but then, like you, I have not spent a great amount of time with him."

"I appreciate your candour, Father. Mother would not be so cautious in her opinions if she had a notion of anything between us."

"Then it shall be our secret, Lizzy, until you are certain."

"I appreciate that." They both sat silently for a moment.

"I understand his friend has arrived, and possibly his sisters, as well," Mr. Bennet said.

"I hope they are as agreeable as he is."

"No reason why they should not be," he replied.

"Girls! Girls! Hurry along! We do not want to be the last ones to arrive!"

At the sound of her mother's shrill voice, Elizabeth sent her father a resigned look. "I must leave you now. Enjoy your evening, Father."

He nodded and smiled. "I know I shall. Now, get along, and I hope you enjoy yours."

Chapter 4

Elizabeth endured the ride to Meryton with her mother and three younger sisters, as the two youngest were plotting and scheming how to ensure they danced every dance. Mr. Bingley was mentioned a few times, but Kitty and Lydia no longer spoke of him with excessive praise; their thoughts were on the militia that would soon be stationed in Meryton for the winter. Elizabeth was grateful for her sisters' distraction, for that would make it easier if Mr. Bingley began to show her particular attention... and if she were to welcome it.

When they stepped inside the Assembly Hall, Elizabeth searched for her friend, Charlotte Lucas. At least, that is what she told herself. In truth, she was looking for Mr. Bingley and his party. When she did not see him, but instead saw her friend, she hurried over to her.

"Charlotte!" Elizabeth said, reaching to take her friend's hands. "How have you been?"

"I have been quite busy, but we are all well." She tilted her head at Elizabeth. "What news do you have of Jane? I thought she would have returned by now."

"Their trip has taken an unexpected turn, as our aunt and uncle encountered friends they had not seen in many years." She bit her lip as she pondered whether to mention Jane's beau. Despite being a confidential friend, Charlotte also tended to tell her mother everything, who would then pass the information on to everyone she encountered. Elizabeth knew her mother would be displeased if she was the last person to hear about her own daughter's admirer. "We expect her home within a few weeks."

"I imagine you are looking forward to her return."

Elizabeth laughed. "I am. You know me well, Charlotte!"

Charlotte nodded her head toward the main door. "Look. Our new neighbours have arrived."

Elizabeth turned to see Mr. Bingley flanked on either side by two very fashionable ladies. They both stood erect, but the taller one regarded those in the room through squinted eyes and lips turned down in a frown. The look of disapproval was readily evident in her features. The other lady, wearing a solemn expression, was murmuring something to the gentleman at her side. It was evident to Elizabeth they were not pleased with what they saw.

Another gentleman stood on the other side of the taller lady, and Elizabeth tried to determine which one was the husband of Mr. Bingley's sister and which one was his friend. Both gentlemen were tall, but one had a portly build. That gentleman's gaze seemed focused on a nearby food table rather than the people; he barely acknowledged the shorter lady's words to him. The other gentleman, decidedly handsome and slimmer, cast his eyes down and away from anyone who might look his way.

Charlotte grasped Elizabeth's arm. "Look, my father is going over to greet them. Am I mistaken, or does it appear as though Mr. Bingley is the only one pleased to be here?"

"I was thinking the very same thing, Charlotte. Have you met them?"

"Only Mr. Bingley, when he returned my father's call." She turned to Elizabeth. "I understand Mr. Bingley has already dined with your family at Longbourn."

"Yes, he did. We had invited his whole party, but his family and friend had business that took them back to London." Elizabeth shuddered. "If their disapproving looks indicate what I think they do, I am glad they did not come for dinner." She shook her head. "They do not seem at all pleased with what they see here."

"I agree. If only Jane were here to temper our opinion," Charlotte said with a soft chuckle. "She would tell us they are very pleasing women and that we are much mistaken."

"That she would, Charlotte!" Elizabeth said with a laugh.

Elizabeth's mother stepped up behind her and spoke in a fervent whisper. "Look, Lizzy, it is Mr. Bingley and his sisters. Do you not think the ladies elegant and quite fashionable?"

Elizabeth pondered what to say to her. "They are certainly wearing gowns that are unlike anything that would have been made around here."

"They must have been made at one of the finer millinery shops in London," Charlotte added.

Mrs. Bennet nudged Elizabeth. "Smile, girls! Mr. Bingley and his party are coming this way. We are about to be introduced to them."

Elizabeth heard her mother squeal softly as the party approached. Despite being eager to make the acquaintance of his family, she did not have high expectations that they were as eager to meet hers.

Mr. Bingley came up to the three ladies and gave a slight bow. "Good evening, ladies. What a pleasant affair this is. May I introduce you to my family and good friend?"

Mr. Bingley made the introductions. His sisters, Caroline Bingley and Louisa Hurst, her husband, Reginald Hurst, and Bingley's friend, Fitzwilliam Darcy, did not seem particularly affable, as they extended only the barest civilities. Despite being polite in their words and manners, Elizabeth sensed that she was being scrutinized by the four of them.

But for the scowl that seemed etched on his face, Elizabeth could have considered Bingley's good friend handsome. He finally lifted his eyes, and Elizabeth saw that they were on her. She attempted to smile, but his response was only to lower his brows and press his lips tightly together. She turned her attention back to Mr. Bingley and his sisters, who were engaged in conversation with her mother.

It was at that moment that Kitty and Lydia hurried over, out of breath.

"Mamma?" Lydia tugged on her mother's sleeve.

"Oh, and here are my two youngest daughters, Kitty and Lydia."

The two girls gave a small curtsey, and Lydia turned back her mother. "Mamma! Aunt Phillips has told us the militia will be here any day now!"

Elizabeth noticed Mr. Bingley's sisters share a look of disgust between them. Her mother, fortunately, seemed unaware, or at least she did not acknowledge their disdain as she shooed her youngest daughters away.

Mr. Bingley's smile, however, was genuine, and he turned his gaze to her. "Miss Bennet, if you are not already engaged, may I have the next dance?"

"I am not engaged. I thank you, yes." As Elizabeth spoke those words, Mr. Darcy glowered and turned away.

Mr. Bingley joyfully expressed his appreciation to Elizabeth, and he walked away with the rest of his party to await the next dance.

Mrs. Bennet, unable to contain her feeling of triumph, walked away and laughed with great mirth.

Elizabeth turned to Charlotte. "What say you, good friend? Do you think Mr. Bingley's party is at all satisfied with those they must now consider as their neighbours?"

"It was quite apparent in their manner and expressions what they think of us," Charlotte replied. "Not too highly, I would suppose." She shook her head. "Considering their family fortune was made in trade, I fear they must have very short memories!"

"Or convenient lapses! If they are to settle here, they shall be quite lonely, for there are few here that they would consider their equals." Elizabeth lowered her brows in thought. "It seems odd that Mr. Bingley is so completely unaffected by those his sisters and friend consider to be beneath their notice." Her brows pinched in consternation. "And how is it he is such good friends with Mr. Darcy?"

"That I cannot answer." Charlotte turned towards the small orchestra and nodded her head. "But we shall have to contemplate that later, as it appears the next dance is about to begin, Lizzy."

"So it is, and I shall quite enjoy dancing with Mr. Bingley."

Charlotte laughed. "And I shall quite enjoy watching his party as they watch you dance with him." She squeezed Elizabeth's hand. "He pays you an honour to single you out for his first dance."

Elizabeth smiled. "Whether that was his intention or not, I am quite honoured he did."

Elizabeth enjoyed her dance with Mr. Bingley. He was an excellent dancer and a delightful conversationalist. She was, however, slightly distressed when the movements of the dance forced her to take her neighbouring partner's hand, which happened to be that of Mr. Darcy. He was dancing with Miss Bingley, and Elizabeth readily noticed him scrutinizing her frequently, as if watching for a misstep or for her to do something that did not meet his expectations. Fortunately, those moments with him did not last long, but each time she met his solemn glare, she was more determined to enjoy Mr. Bingley's company.

"Tell me, Mr. Bingley," she said as she stepped around him with a backward glance. "Are you settling in well at Netherfield?"

A wide smile lit up his face. "Indeed! I feel as though I have lived there forever, and yet it has been less than a month."

"I am glad. I have lived at Longbourn all my life, and I can only imagine what it must be like to get used to living in a new place."

"I have lived several places and found that, in each one, I settled in quite well." He laughed. "I have often been told I am easy to please."

Elizabeth considered this a good trait for a gentleman to have. She let out a soft laugh as she turned to take Mr. Darcy's hand, her smile quickly fading. The fact that he did not speak to her did nothing to improve her opinion of him. She felt as though he was looking at her only to find fault.

When she and Mr. Bingley came back together, he said, "I hope you will allow my sisters to pay you a call at Longbourn. I do wish them to become better acquainted with you and your family."

It was easy for Elizabeth to smile as she looked into Mr. Bingley's hopeful face. "We will welcome them warmly."

When the dance concluded, Elizabeth thanked Mr. Bingley and walked over to sit with Mary. Charlotte was now taking the dance floor with Mr. Bingley. As her eyes swept across the room, she noticed Mr. Darcy sitting out, as well.

As the evening progressed, Elizabeth danced about half of the dances, as there were not enough gentlemen in attendance to partner all the ladies. She often found herself talking with Charlotte, her mother, Mary, or her aunt, Mrs. Phillips. Towards the end of the evening, Mr. Bingley came up to her and addressed her.

"Miss Bennet, would you do me the honour of standing up

with me for a second?"

Elizabeth felt honoured, but was somewhat surprised that he would ask for a second dance. She was about to claim fatigue and decline, as she truly did not want to dance anymore this evening, but her mother answered for her.

"Oh, such an honour, Mr. Bingley! Lizzy would be delighted!"

Elizabeth shuddered at her mother's outburst, especially since Mr. Darcy stood nearby and it was apparent he had heard her, for he turned his head towards them. She continued to smile, however. "I look forward to it."

When Bingley walked away, Elizabeth pursed her lips tightly together, knowing that she would soon be the object of gossip amongst their neighbours for having danced two with the new occupant of Netherfield.

Despite her fatigue, she enjoyed her second dance with him, as well. Mr. Bingley had such a lively personality, laughed frequently, and was always gracious in his manner of speaking. She also preferred this dance to her first one, as Mr. Darcy stood this one out. But even though he was across the room, she could readily see the censure on his face as he watched them.

When the dance ended, Elizabeth again thanked him and excused herself, saying she needed to freshen up. She hoped that in doing so, it might discourage any gossip relating to her and Mr. Bingley.

She picked up a drink and stepped outside to join Charlotte in the back courtyard. It was a delightful evening, with a mild breeze, and she enjoyed being able to get away from the crush of people. The two ladies stood in a corner near the door and watched as people came in and out.

As they talked, Elizabeth noticed Mr. Darcy step out with Mr. Bingley.

"I cannot approve of your asking Miss Bennet for a second dance, Bingley. It is far too soon to be declaring yourself in such a manner, and you must realize she is completely unsuitable for you."

"Declaring myself! Darcy, you are too old-fashioned, and besides, what if I do find Miss Bennet's company enchanting and delightful?" He shook his head. "Why should I not dance two dances with her? I cannot help it if you refuse to dance with anyone here but my sisters."

"You know I detest dancing unless I am acquainted with my partner. To dance with anyone else at an assembly such as this would be insupportable!"

"Darcy, you are too fastidious for your own good!"

The two men stepped further out, and Elizabeth could hear no more. She nudged Charlotte to urge her back inside before the men turned around and saw them. Once they stepped through the door, Elizabeth turned back with a glare, only to see that Mr. Darcy had turned and witnessed their retreat.

Elizabeth was outraged, and once they were inside, she let out a huff. "Did you hear what Mr. Darcy said to his friend?"

"I did, Lizzy. I was not certain whether you had."

"He has no right to tell him what he ought or ought not do!" Elizabeth said angrily.

Charlotte took Elizabeth's hand. "Lizzy, while Mr. Bingley likely meant nothing by it, two dances with a young lady is significant. I can assure you people in Meryton will be talking."

Elizabeth drew in a long breath and let it out slowly. "I know you are right, Charlotte, but it irritates me that Mr. Darcy thinks he has a right to direct Mr. Bingley's actions." She laughed. "What kind of friend does that?"

Charlotte shrugged her shoulders. "I suppose it depends on whether he feels he must look out for his friend's best interest or merely wants to use his influence on him for his own purposes."

"Well, I shall know which one I think it is, and he is certainly not someone I would want as *my* good friend!"

Charlotte laughed. "I suppose he never will be, either!"

"I would imagine not!" She shook her head. "It is a pity, then, that he is so handsome."

"He is both rich and handsome – a deadly combination that often makes one think they can do and say whatever they please and not be questioned about it."

"As he most likely has done all his life!" Elizabeth attempted to calm herself, and then said softly, "Charlotte, when we stepped back indoors, I looked back and saw that Mr. Darcy turned and saw us. I am certain he will not tell his friend we were out there and likely overheard what he said!"

"He saw us?"

Elizabeth turned to look in the direction of the gentleman. "He did." She gave her head a determined shake. "That man has no idea who he is dealing with. I shall show him!"

"How do you intend to do that, Lizzy? The man has a fortune greater than we can ever imagine, and with that, he likely has a good deal of influence."

"I am not quite certain, but the more he insists that I am not suitable for his friend, the more I shall convince Mr. Bingley that I am."

Charlotte placed her hand on Elizabeth's arm. "You have no need to try too hard, Lizzy. I believe the admirable Mr. Bingley is quite fond of you already."

~~*

Later that night, when the ladies returned home, Mrs. Bennet could not stop talking to her husband about how Mr. Bingley danced two with Lizzy and only one with every other lady.

"He favoured my Lizzy, did he?" Mr. Bennet laughed. "He is obviously a man of good sense!"

"Papa, there is no need for you to add to the speculation. Enough of our neighbours in Meryton will do that for us!" Elizabeth smiled. "But I do find him quite agreeable."

Mrs. Bennet clasped her hands together. "I doubt Mrs. Lucas will want to add to the gossip. I saw her looking with disapproval during that second dance of yours. I could see on her face that she wished it would have been her Charlotte."

"Well," said Mr. Bennet as he folded up his newspaper. "Let us all go to bed and sleep on it. Perhaps on the morrow we shall wake up and find it was all a dream!"

Elizabeth was glad to retreat to her room. She had much to think about concerning Mr. Bingley and his particular attention towards her, and how Mr. Darcy discouraged such attention. She pondered what her feelings for Mr. Bingley really were. He was certainly amiable and a very well-mannered gentleman, although she did not particularly care for his sisters and friend. It was quite unfortunate, indeed.

Elizabeth sat down and looked at a letter she had been penning to Jane. She had left off when she had departed for the assembly, assuring her she would give her a detailed account of the evening. As she wrote about the charming Mr. Bingley, she paused as she wondered if she was being more effusive in writing about her feelings for him than she actually felt. She tapped the end of the quill on her chin as she pondered what her true feelings for him really were.

She bit her lip as she questioned whether she felt true affection for him or merely wanted to spite Mr. Darcy and his attempt at interference. She gave a slight shrug of her shoulders. "Whatever my feelings for Mr. Bingley are, he is worth writing about to Jane." She tapped her fingers a few times on the table.

"So it shall be," she said softly. "Jane can extol the new gentleman in her life, and I can extol the new one in mine!"

~~*

The following morning, Elizabeth was grateful no one seemed inclined to speak any further about her and Mr. Bingley. Her two younger sisters would not stop talking with great enthusiasm about the officers who were coming, and her mother seemed equally eager for them to arrive. That appeared to replace her excitement over her daughter dancing twice with Mr. Bingley.

A few days later, Mr. Bingley's sisters visited Longbourn. The ladies displayed civil manners and engaged in friendly conversation, but Elizabeth could readily detect condescension in their exchanged looks, rigid comportment, and even the stilted tone of their voices. As one who loved to sketch a person's character, she was more attuned to the small mannerisms that conveyed – or betrayed – one's true sentiments. Her mother did not appear to notice their disdain at all. She doubted the youngest ones would, as Kitty and Lydia had stayed but a few minutes, as they were determined to set out for Meryton to hear the latest gossip.

Elizabeth determined that Miss Bingley and Mrs. Hurst had paid the visit to Longbourn at the urging of their brother. She was certain he had persuaded them to call.

She was speaking of this to Charlotte, who came to visit the next day. "I cannot help but be wary of the motives of Mr. Bingley's sisters. While they appear in every way gracious and courteous, there is an underlying animosity that I find distressing."

"Perhaps it is due to all the talk about your second dance with Mr. Bingley, "Charlotte said as they strolled through the garden. "It is as I expected."

"I wish people would not talk so much about it," she replied.

"His sisters likely wish they would not, as well. I doubt they will say anything to promote the gossip!"

Elizabeth laughed. "And neither will his friend, I would imagine."

Charlotte tilted her head and looked at Elizabeth. "Mr. Bingley is a good man. It is a shame he has such sisters and friend as he does. I heard that Mrs. Long attempted to engage Mr. Darcy in conversation, and he said very little. When he did speak, he almost seemed angry that someone imposed upon him by conversing with him."

"Oh, that we could choose our family, as well as our friends." She shook her head. "There is nothing to be done about family, but I do not see how Mr. Bingley and Mr. Darcy are such close friends. They are so very different."

"There must be some reason," Charlotte said. "Perhaps you might discover it this Friday at the party we are hosting at Lucas Lodge."

"A party?"

Charlotte nodded. "My father thought it would be a good way to welcome our new neighbours, as well as the officers who have arrived."

"They have arrived, then?" Elizabeth said.

"Yes, they arrived just yesterday."

"I am certain Kitty and Lydia will look forward to meeting them at the party." She let out a huff. "If they have not already met them by then."

"And do you look forward to seeing Mr. Bingley again?"

Elizabeth only smiled.

"You need to make up your mind, Lizzy. I can see that you are not yet decided about him."

"It is true, Charlotte. He has so many fine traits and yet…"

Charlotte shook her head and took her friend's hand. "Must you always so painstakingly evaluate one's character? You will never find a gentleman who fits every standard of the man you want to marry." She sighed and looked down. "I know I am more practical than you, but if a good, kind gentleman began to single me out, I would welcome it. Neither of us can afford to be too particular."

"I do welcome his attentions, Charlotte." Elizabeth laughed. "But it is still too soon for me to have developed a strong feeling of love for him."

"Do not wait too long, my friend."

Before Charlotte left, she informed the rest of the Bennets about the party and the arrival of the militia. This excited Kitty and Lydia to no end, and the two young girls set out immediately for Meryton, hoping to meet some of the officers.

When the girls returned, having also stopped in the milliner's shop to purchase ribbons and lace for their bonnets and gowns, it was evident they had succeeded in their mission. They could not stop talking about the handsome officers in regimentals they had met.

In all their effusions over the officers, Mary gave them a look of stern disapproval, Mrs. Bennet squealed with delight, and Mr. Bennet rose and stepped from the room. Elizabeth listened quietly with more than a little concern that the girls were far too young to be so interested in these men. She hoped she could trust her sisters to act with restraint and decorum around them. She inwardly sighed. Or was that asking too much?

Chapter 5

A few days later, Elizabeth received another letter from Jane, who informed her that she and their aunt and uncle would soon be returning home, and that Mr. Marshall was going to accompany them. He had an acquaintance who lived in Hertfordshire and had been long hoping for an opportunity to visit him. Coming to Longbourn would provide the perfect opportunity for him to meet the Bennets as well as visit his friend. Jane had also written to her parents to inform them about Mr. Marshall and their forthcoming arrival.

"I shall finally meet Jane's Mr. Marshall!" Elizabeth exclaimed. "And she shall meet my... she shall meet Mr. Bingley." She giggled softly. "Poor Mamma. How will she handle two gentlemen showing particular attention to her daughters? She has not had reason to hope for a suitable and favourable match for any of her daughters since Jane was fifteen, let alone two such matches at once."

Elizabeth frowned and bit her lip. *If only Mr. Bingley's sisters and friend were not so intolerant of everyone,* she thought. *It would be so much easier to enjoy his particular regard.*

On Friday, the Bennet household was filled with anticipation for the party that evening at Lucas Lodge. Kitty and Lydia could hardly wait to dance with the officers, and Elizabeth looked forward to seeing the amiable Mr. Bingley again. Mrs. Bennet hoped that nice young gentleman would continue to single out her second eldest daughter and could not wait to inform everyone about Jane's new beau who would be arriving soon. She had been ecstatic when she read Jane's letter, and with the possibility of two of her daughters marrying well, she was certain nothing would ever vex her again.

Elizabeth attempted to curb her mother's conjectures in both quarters, but to no avail.

As she readied herself for the party, she gazed into the mirror. She could not help but wonder whether Mr. Bingley had taken Mr. Darcy's admonition about her to heart and whether his sisters would continue with their disapproving looks towards her, her family, and essentially the whole neighbourhood. She pondered this as her fingers tapped her lips. How would she feel if his attentions waned? She stood up and snatched her shawl, throwing it about her shoulders.

She turned back and looked at her reflection again. For some reason, the only strong feelings she felt were anger and resentment towards his friend and sisters. She pressed her lips together, shrugged her shoulders, and walked out of the room.

That evening, many from the neighbourhood gathered at Lucas Lodge, ready to meet, welcome, and dance with the newly arrived officers. It was apparent to Elizabeth that Kitty and Lydia had already become acquainted with several of them, and they soon introduced her to some of those whom they had met.

Elizabeth was talking to Colonel Forster and a few of the officers when Mr. Bingley and his party stepped in. She saw both him and Mr. Darcy glance her way, and the expression on each were as opposite as one could imagine. Mr. Bingley's face lit up with a broad smile, but Mr. Darcy frowned, and his eyes darkened, provoking Elizabeth to such a degree she felt she had hackles raised along her back.

Mr. Bingley approached her with a wide smile. Mr. Darcy followed grimly, and she watched with humour as Sir William Lucas stepped up, intercepting Mr. Bingley's sisters, who seemed not at all pleased with his intrusion.

She continued to talk to Colonel Forster about the regiment being stationed in their small neighbourhood. "Are the militia here because we are suspected of having spies among us?" she asked with a laugh.

"Oh, heavens no!" the colonel replied. "At least I hope not!" He laughed. "It seems to be a most civil and… peaceful neighbourhood."

"Did they perchance hear of our populace rising up in protests and riots, or do they hope to incite a riot here so they may then subdue it?"

"Of course not!" Colonel Forster replied.

Those around her laughed, and she excused herself from the colonel and those with whom she had been talking. She turned to Mr. Bingley and smiled.

"Good evening, Mr. Bingley. It is good to see you… and your sisters and friend here." She glanced briefly at Mr. Darcy, who stood behind his friend.

"Thank you!" he said with a grin. "I have been looking forward to it. There is nothing like delightful company, delicious food, and exceptional music and dancing to round out a good day." He continued to smile as he looked about.

Elizabeth lifted her brows and gave him a rueful smile. "I can assure you the food is delicious and hope the company is delightful, but I cannot guarantee that the music will be exceptional."

"I am certain I will enjoy it." He extended his arm towards some empty chairs. "Would you care to sit down?"

As Mr. Bingley guided her towards two vacant chairs in the corner, she noticed Mr. Darcy turn away and walk to the fireplace. He stared into the fire, and then turned, propping his arm up on the mantel as he slowly looked about the room with a displeased look on his face.

She and Mr. Bingley sat down and began conversing. He was very attentive to her, asking about her family, friends, and what she enjoyed doing. To his credit, he did not seem at all put off by – or that he had even noticed – the behaviour of her family across the room. Unfortunately, it appeared Mr. Darcy had noticed.

Lydia was openly flirting with the officers, laughing with such abandon that the boisterous sound filled the room. Mrs. Bennet stood nearby watching, but instead of admonishing her youngest to behave properly, seemed to be enjoying it, and at times joined in with her own laughter. She then nodded her head towards Elizabeth and Mr. Bingley as she spoke with some ladies, likely pointing out his continued attention to her daughter while exulting in the fact that her eldest had met a suitable gentleman from the Lake District who would be accompanying her party on their return.

After Sir William left Mr. Bingley's sisters, Miss Bingley walked over to speak to Mr. Darcy. He wore that same scowl Elizabeth now believed was permanently etched on his face. His and Miss Bingley's gaze shifted between her, her mother, and her two youngest sisters. She knew they were displeased both with the behaviour of her family *and* that Mr. Bingley was sitting with *her*.

"Miss Bennet?"

Elizabeth started. She had not been attending to his conversation. "Pray, forgive me, Mr. Bingley. Of what were you speaking?"

"The neighbourhood. I find the people so very pleasant. Is everyone truly as amiable as I have found them to be?"

Elizabeth smiled, silently chiding herself for not paying attention to the gentleman who was being so attentive to her. "It is a fine neighbourhood indeed. While there are the occasional conflicts and frustrations, most everyone gets along quite well."

"Splendid! In the short time I have been here, I have come to like it very much." He gave her an encouraging smile. "I have found everyone quite amiable."

Elizabeth looked around the room. In addition to the glaring eyes of Mr. Bingley's sisters and friend upon them, the eyes of the people in this very fine neighbourhood were on them, as well. She was certain their wagging tongues were doing a great deal of unwarranted speculation. This would not do.

"Mr. Bingley, if you do not mind, I see my good friend Charlotte. If you will excuse me, I would like to visit with her." She gave him a sympathetic look. "Would you mind if we continue our conversation later?"

"Not at all!"

Elizabeth walked away, grateful to have a small respite from Mr. Bingley's company. She approached Charlotte and greeted her.

"Good evening, Charlotte. It is a lovely evening. How are you?"

"I am well." Charlotte stole a glance at Mr. Bingley. "It appears as though you are also doing quite well, Lizzy. Mr. Bingley is again singling you out and spending a good amount of time with you." She paused and smiled at her friend. "There can be no doubt that he admires you." She tilted her head. "And what of you? Have your feelings for him deepened?"

"Oh, Charlotte, I still feel as though I hardly know him."

"I wonder if one can ever really get to know someone, no matter how much time they spend with one another."

"Well, of one thing I am certain. I am currently not making any plans to marry the man."

"Do you not feel as though you could love him?"

"I know I would be treated with kindness by *him*. But love?" She shrugged her shoulders.

"You know my opinion on the subject. Happiness in marriage is entirely a matter of chance. There are always things about the other person we cannot find out before the wedding, and then there is always the possibility that a person will change."

"You make marriage sound like it is destined to fail from the start." Elizabeth laughed and then sighed. "But he certainly seems to be one of the finest gentlemen I know."

Charlotte gently placed her hand on Elizabeth's arm. "I have said many times that I am more practical than romantic, but I cannot help but wonder what reservations you may have about him. We are, both of us, from families of little fortune with only a small dowry. Do you think another opportunity will present itself – one with such an esteemed gentleman with a more than acceptable fortune?"

"Charlotte, my feelings are not yet deep, my affections not secured. He is handsome and kind, and I certainly enjoy his company, but I need more time getting to know him."

"Well, since he needs to get to know *you*, as well, come. I insist you play for us." Charlotte smiled at her friend. "Let Mr. Bingley see you are a lady of musical accomplishments."

"I hardly think I..."

Charlotte waved her hand and lifted her voice to the crowd. "How delightful! Elizabeth has agreed to play and sing for us this evening." She gave her friend a nod and extended her hand towards the pianoforte.

Elizabeth sat down at the instrument after casting an admonishing glare at Charlotte.

She was flattered when Mr. Bingley came and stood by her, a smile on his face. Out of the corner of her eye, however, she espied Mr. Darcy, who appeared displeased as she performed. She determined he was most likely used to listening to only the finest performers, and had judged her playing as deficient in comparison.

When Elizabeth stepped away from the pianoforte, Mary sat down to play. Unfortunately, it was not a song conducive to dancing or even enjoying.

Mr. Bingley looked at Elizabeth. "Do you think we shall soon have music to which we can dance?"

Elizabeth nodded as she watched her mother hurry over to Mary. "If my mother has her way, my sister has most likely been told to play something suitable to dancing."

After watching Mary struggle through her piece, Elizabeth said, "Pray, excuse me, Mr. Bingley, but if you do not mind, I believe Mary is in need of someone to turn the pages for her."

"Certainly! But if she plays a song suitable to dancing, may I request the dance with you?"

Elizabeth smiled. "You may, sir."

As she walked away, she noticed several pair of eyes following her. She let out a soft huff. Speculation about her and Mr. Bingley was likely getting out of hand. When her gaze fell on Mr. Darcy, she made no attempt to stifle her chortle and the quick shake of her head. He looked as if he were a statue, with his arm propped up on the hearth's mantel and his head held high. She could readily detect, however, the movement of his eyes following her as she moved across the room.

She took her place beside her sister at the pianoforte and read the music as Mary played, turning the page when needed.

"Thank you, Lizzy," Mary said. "No one else seemed inclined to help me this evening."

"Unfortunately, Kitty and Lydia are preoccupied with all the officers here," Elizabeth said with a shake of her head.

Mary frowned and pounded the keys a little more severely than written. "They are far too young to be consorting with them."

Elizabeth gave a resigned shrug. "Hopefully the officers will have the sense and discipline to refrain from indulging those two silly, young girls."

Mary let out a disgruntled groan. "They are men, Lizzy. I strongly doubt it."

When Mary finished her song, Elizabeth moved away. Her brow lifted when she saw that Mr. Darcy had moved to stand beside his friend. She strongly suspected he was giving his friend more unwanted and unwarranted advice.

The ire she felt at his continued interference overruled all thoughts of prudence and caution, prompting her to return to Mary to ask her to play a country dance. She looked forward to dancing with Mr. Bingley just to spite his friend.

"Mother just requested I do the same," Mary said solemnly. "And so I shall."

As she began the introduction, Elizabeth watched Mr. Bingley jump to his feet and hurry over to her, hopefully leaving his friend with an unfinished sentence or thought. *Good for you, Mr. Bingley*, she said to herself. *Defy his admonitions!*

Mr. Bingley was very attentive and talkative during their dance. Elizabeth could not help but notice the stark differences between him and Mr. Darcy, who stood up with Miss Bingley. He was neither talkative with his partner, nor with *her* when they occasionally came together in the movement of the dance. She suspected both he and his partner were silently conspiring against them with their rigid looks of censure and disdain displayed on their faces. As usual, Mr. Bingley was completely oblivious to their expressions. Or perhaps he did not care.

That was certainly in his favour – and yet not. Elizabeth did not mind that he cared nothing for their critical judgments of her, yet she would have preferred him to display a little more backbone and take a stance in defending her to them. She tried to convince herself that he did it when he was with them in private instead of a public place.

For the remainder of the party, Mr. Bingley and Elizabeth danced and conversed with others, but when he was not with her, he often smiled in her direction. She hoped that by spending time with others, people would cease their staring and gossiping about the two of them.

When Mr. Bingley took the floor with Charlotte, she looked at Elizabeth with an apologetic shrug, followed by a smile. Elizabeth shook her head and laughed, wondering what, if anything, her friend would say to him as they danced. She hoped Charlotte would not misrepresent her feelings to him. She turned away and collided with someone. She looked up into Mr. Darcy's face.

"Pray, excuse me, Miss Bennet."

Elizabeth waved her hand. "It was my fault. I was not looking where I was going."

Mr. Darcy drew in a breath as if he were about to say something, but he did not. The two stood silently staring at each other when Sir William Lucas stepped over to them.

"Miss Elizabeth! I see that Mr. Bingley is engaged in dancing with my daughter, but that is no reason why you should not be on the dance floor, as well!" He turned to Mr. Darcy. "Miss Elizabeth is an excellent dancer. You have likely seen how well she dances."

"I have. She is indeed a fine dancer."

Sir William turned to Elizabeth. "And Miss Bennet, you have likely seen how well Mr. Darcy dances. He is…"

Elizabeth smiled. "Indeed, I have seen him dance, but if you will excuse me, I am fatigued and am in need of some refreshment."

Darcy simply nodded as she walked away.

~~*

As the Bennet ladies returned home in the carriage, Elizabeth found herself at odds with her mother. Mrs. Bennet was delighted at how the esteemed and quite wealthy Mr. Bingley was continually singling her out, and she was certain an engagement would be announced directly.

"Really, Mamma, it is too soon to speculate on such a thing. I am not even certain he is the right man for me."

"Right man? Why do you speak so? Everyone in the neighbourhood has been saying how they believe it is already a decided thing!" Mrs. Bennet let out a huff. "He is a most amiable gentleman, quite wealthy, and gets along splendidly with you. How could you even think such a thing?"

Elizabeth drew in a slow breath and turned her head towards the window in the carriage, glancing out into the darkness. Just as she had suspected, she and Mr. Bingley had become the topic of gossip and speculation. Her mother was likely the one encouraging it all. She turned back to her. "He is indeed amiable, but there are other things that I must consider."

"Other things? Heavens, Lizzy. You could not ask for anyone finer. I would be honoured to have him as a son in our family. Oh, yes, indeed! I would be more than delighted!"

Elizabeth pursed her lips, knowing there was no sense in trying to convince her mother otherwise. After a while, she said, "Indeed, he is amiable, but it is far too soon for him to ask for my hand. Pray, do not further the neighbourhood gossip that has already decided the two of us will marry before Christmas. Let us patiently wait and see how things transpire between us."

That seemed to appease her mother for the duration of the ride home. Kitty and Lydia spoke of the officers and their delight with how many handsome gentlemen had come into the neighbourhood. Mary tried to voice warnings about the two younger girls' behaviour, and while Elizabeth believed her to be a little severe, she could not argue with her caution. Mrs. Bennet was inclined to allow the girls a little fun and not be so harsh. Their father, who had not accompanied them, would likely have done nothing to check their behaviour, either.

As Elizabeth continued to stare out into the darkness, the accusatory looks of Mr. Darcy and Miss Bingley further inflamed her. Would they have sway over Mr. Bingley and persuade him out of what they likely considered an imprudent marriage? Marriage? Was she really concerned that they might do that – when she was not even certain that was what *she* wanted?

She slowly turned to her mother and sighed. At present, there were no other prospects for her in their neighbourhood. There were available gentlemen, to be sure, but none that she found attractive and appealing to her sensibilities. It was apparent that Mr. Bingley was the most suitable gentleman for her among all her acquaintance. She might never meet another so pleasant. Perhaps Charlotte was right.

She leaned her head back and closed her eyes. The bright smiling face of Mr. Bingley appeared, bringing a smile to her lips. But his image slowly faded, and before her was the proud and brooding Mr. Darcy. She shook her head briskly, opening her eyes to quickly rid herself of the image. Once it was gone, she breathed a sigh of relief.

She began to finger the fabric of her gown as she thought about Jane. While she missed her terribly, she was envious that her sister had remained at the lakes. She considered her fortunate to have been able to spend the time getting to know Mr. Marshall away from their mother and endless speculations on a forthcoming engagement.

It was not difficult to imagine Jane having a beau. She was at least five times more beautiful than anyone she knew, and there was no one kinder or more generous. She was certain Mr. Marshall was likely already very much in love with her.

~~*

As Bingley's carriage returned to Netherfield, Darcy sat rigidly staring out the window into darkness. Bingley continued to praise Miss Elizabeth Bennet to the other occupants, while his sisters continued to disparage everyone and everything in the neighbourhood. Darcy remained quiet, thinking about the evening.

So lost was he in his thoughts, that he had not heard Bingley call his name out several times.

"Darcy, have you fallen asleep?"

"No. Pardon me. What were you saying?"

"How did you find the party tonight?"

Darcy expelled a quick breath. "It was tolerable, but nothing exceptional," he replied with an edge in his voice.

"I thought it was delightful!" Bingley's voice resonated with a hint of laughter.

Darcy leaned forward and rested his arms on his knees. "Your description of everything is *delightful*, Bingley. You really must learn to expand your vocabulary."

"I found the whole thing pathetic," Miss Bingley said. "There was no music to speak of at all, and the behaviour of *some*..." She looked at her sister. "...was inexcusable."

Darcy shifted on the seat. He had actually enjoyed Miss Bennet's playing and singing. While she had not sung and played with flawless proficiency, she had performed with heartfelt emotion, which he truly enjoyed.

He had closely watched her this evening to determine if she was suitable for Bingley, and he found that the more he watched her, the more he became intrigued by her. The night of the Meryton Assembly, he had cautioned his friend that he ought not to have shown her such particular attention, for it was too soon. But even then, at his first meeting with her, he had taken great delight in observing her. He shook his head when he realized he sounded like his friend.

What is there about Miss Elizabeth Bennet that has me so captivated? And what am I to do about these burgeoning feelings when my good friend is already so fond of her?

What is it about her? He closed his eyes and leaned his head back. He instantly saw an image of her laughing. *She does not stifle her laughter, as do some ladies who feel it is impertinent to laugh out loud. She is not flippant, as Bingley is, nor boisterously loud as her younger sisters are. Her figure is light and pleasing, and her eyes...*

Darcy suddenly opened his eyes. Her eyes were very fine indeed. While he would never have considered her beautiful, he was drawn to her dark eyes that either had a twinkle in them when she smiled or a piercing glare when she was displeased. He grimaced when he considered that was often how she looked at him.

He had listened to her converse with several people that evening. She seemed to have an intelligence that likely came from reading and studying, perhaps she had received an education under one of the finer masters.

What a foolish infatuation I have developed! Miss Bennet is not only someone whom Bingley seems to greatly admire, but she is also so far beneath me! This is absurd, and something I need to conquer directly!

He found himself unwittingly shaking his head, and he stifled a grumble. His eyes turned to the others in the carriage. Gratefully, none of them seemed aware of the turmoil in which he found himself. For that, he was grateful.

Chapter 6

A few mornings later, Elizabeth threw back the coverlet of her bed when the first rays of sunlight began to light the room. She stretched out her arms, stood up, and walked to the window to pull back the lacy curtains. Gazing out, she smiled at the day awaiting her. She looked forward to enjoying a brisk hike up Oakham Mount again.

The house was quiet as she came downstairs, but she stopped at the door to her father's study and gave it a soft tap.

"Come," her father said.

Elizabeth opened the door and peeked in. "Good morning, Papa."

Mr. Bennet looked up from the book he was reading and removed his glasses. He leaned back in his chair and gave her a smile. "You are up and dressed early, Lizzy. I believe I know what that means."

Elizabeth gave a slight shrug. "You know that once the sun comes up announcing a new day, I must rise with it." She laughed. "And as it is such a lovely morning; I am going to walk up Oakham Mount."

He lifted a brow. "Ahh! Do you hope for another unexpected encounter with Mr. Bingley?" He tapped his fingers on the desk. "Or perhaps it will not be unexpected as the two of you made plans for a clandestine meeting while talking at Lucas Lodge, eh?"

"I know you are teasing, Father. I am merely looking forward to a pleasant walk. Whether I encounter Mr. Bingley or not will have no bearing on the delight it will provide me."

Mr. Bennet waved his hand. "Then be off with you, Lizzy, and enjoy your time."

"You know I shall! Nothing shall deter my pleasure."

"Make certain you return in time to break your fast with the rest of us."

"I will." Elizabeth left the study and walked to the front door. When she stepped outside, she drew in a deep breath, filling her lungs with the cool, fresh air.

She took brisk steps to the path that led to Oakham Mount, shielding her eyes from the glare of the sun on the horizon. As she looked up at the bright blue sky, she brushed a wayward strand of hair that blew across her face. The morning was cool, but the bright sun warmed her. She could not have asked for a more perfect morning.

When she came to a small lookout along the path, she stopped and gazed at the beauty below. The greens of summer were beginning to fade into shades of bronze, gold, and an occasional red. Soon the leaves would drift lazily down, leaving the trees barren through the long months of winter. She loved this time of the year, especially from the lovely prospect atop Oakham Mount!

She continued up the path, humming as she went. When she finally reached the summit, she ambled about, looking at the view before sitting down on the trunk of a fallen tree. She clasped her hands and looked towards Netherfield and smiled. This was the view Mr. Bingley was on his way to see when they first met. She wondered whether he had ever made it back up here.

It was a beautiful property that extended even beyond what she could see from her lofty vantage point. As she thought about him, she had to admit he was kind, gentlemanly, enthusiastic, and… she chuckled. He was also very attentive to her – to the great displeasure of his family and his *friend*. Her shoulders rose as she took in a breath and then let it out briskly.

As she rose to her feet to begin the walk down, she felt a tug at the back of her dress. She turned her head and saw that it was snagged in a branch of the tree upon which she had been sitting. She reached around to untangle it, but it was thoroughly caught, and she did not want to pull it and risk ripping her dress. She stamped her foot and turned the other way. She could not untangle it from either direction.

She gave one more unsuccessful pull, and when she looked up, she started, for she was staring into the face of Mr. Darcy!

"Mr. Darcy!" she said, with a hitch in her breath.

The gentleman walked towards her and gave a quick bow. "Miss Bennet." He looked at her with an amused smile. "Do you find yourself in a predicament?"

Elizabeth shook her head. "Nothing that cannot be remedied by a good pull!" She turned in aggravation and reached behind her, giving another tug at her dress, but again to no avail.

Darcy reached out and stopped her. "There is no need to put a tear in a perfectly good dress." He lifted his brows and asked, "Would you allow me?"

Elizabeth swallowed hard and acquiesced with an extended hand. "I thank you, sir." She turned away while Darcy came near, and she felt her face warm when he reached down to untangle the cloth. As she waited impatiently for him to announce he had loosened it, she heard him grumble. "Is there a problem, sir?"

"It is firmly caught. I am attempting to take care and not do further damage to the gown."

"Further damage?" she asked.

"There is a slight hole where the branch snagged it, but I think it will be easily repairable." He abruptly stood up. "There! You are free!"

"Thank you," Elizabeth said softly.

His shoulders rose as he took in a deep breath. "I am rather surprised to see you walking so early in the morning."

Elizabeth lifted a brow. "Are you? I do not think there is a finer time to walk." She forced a smile. "And what brings you out so early?"

Darcy looked down. "I am of the same mind as you." He shifted from one foot to the other. "Do you walk often?"

Elizabeth nodded affirmatively. "I take every opportunity."

Darcy looked about. "Alone?"

Feeling her ire rise and her body tense, she glared at him and announced determinedly, "As you see." She forced herself to relax. "Unfortunately, I seldom find anyone who is interested in climbing to the summit, particularly at the break of day." She wondered whether Mr. Bingley had informed him of their meeting up here when she was walking unaccompanied, as she was this morning.

Darcy walked to the edge of the path and looked out over Netherfield, crossing his arms across his chest. "It is a good prospect of Bingley's home from up here."

"It is indeed," Elizabeth replied. "As well as of the whole neighbourhood." Elizabeth wondered whether he suspected she had come up here to look at the large country manor she hoped would one day be hers.

When he did not seem inclined to say anything further, she said, "If you will excuse me, sir, I will let you continue on your way, and I shall go on mine."

"No, I shall accompany you back." He returned to her side.

"You really have no need, sir."

He turned abruptly. "That may be true, but I shall, nevertheless." He extended his arm for her to join him.

Elizabeth let out a soft sigh and reluctantly put her hand through it, barely touching it. "If you insist, Mr. Darcy."

As the two walked silently, Elizabeth waited for her unwelcomed walking companion to say something. When he did not seem inclined to talk, she said, "I would assume you do not approve of a young lady walking unaccompanied."

"I would not tolerate my sister walking such a distance unaccompanied."

Elizabeth stopped. "You have a sister?" She suddenly felt sorry for this unknown sister that was likely forbidden to go anywhere by herself. Darcy stood rigid, his frame unbending, much like his strict views on propriety, Elizabeth thought.

"I do." A small smile appeared, and Darcy's comportment suddenly relaxed. "She is fifteen."

"So young?" Elizabeth was surprised, as she had suspected her to have been older. "I suppose at fifteen your parents are committed to ensuring she is being raised as a proper and accomplished young lady, and she goes nowhere without a companion."

Darcy's expression sobered. "Both my parents have died, Miss Bennet."

"Oh, I am sorry for your loss." Elizabeth felt a touch of regret and knew not what more to say.

Darcy gave a nod. "Thank you, but it has been many years. My cousin and I share guardianship of my sister – and yes, we are doing everything in our power to ensure a proper upbringing." He extended his hand forward, and they began walking again. "Including always having a companion with her," he said after a moment's silence.

Elizabeth stole a glance up at him. Knowing this man had guardianship of his sister made her feel even more sorry for the young girl. She could not imagine how much influence he likely exerted over her life.

"Does she give you many worries or is she exceedingly obedient to your wishes?"

Darcy did not answer immediately.

Finally, he said, "She has... she gives us no worries." He drew in a deep breath. "Since you live around here and enjoy walking, can you give any other recommendations for places to walk in the area?"

Elizabeth sensed he wished to change the subject. "There is a stream that flows between the Gouldings' property and Meryton that has a lovely stone bridge crossing it. In the spring, it is a delightful walk when the flowers are budding and the trees blossoming. In autumn, some of the trees turn vivid shades of orange and red." She chuckled.

Darcy looked down at her. "What do you find so amusing, Miss Bennet?"

Elizabeth closed her eyes briefly as she now wished she had not given thought to that day four years ago. What would he think of her? She gave her head a little shake. It mattered not what he thought of her. He would likely despise her more, but she was certain if she told Mr. Bingley what had happened, he would laugh along with her.

She straightened her shoulders. "Four years ago, I found myself in quite a predicament." She laughed again and looked up at Mr. Darcy. She was somewhat surprised to see that he was looking at her with a smile, albeit a very slight one. "A little more severe than my predicament in which you just found me."

"And what was that?"

Is that a genuine smile or a mocking smirk?

"It was a beautiful spring day, and nature had beckoned me for a walk." She drew in a breath. "I wanted to walk to the bridge, but at the age of sixteen, my mother had some reservations about my walking alone, so I talked my elder sister Jane into accompanying me."

"I see."

Elizabeth shrugged. "It was a rather long walk for Jane. She grew weary before we reached the bridge, and I told her to sit and wait for me to return while I continued on."

"I assume she is not quite the walker that you are."

Elizabeth briskly shook her head. "Heavens, no! She will walk short distances with me, but this was…"

"Too far?"

Elizabeth winced. "I should never have pressed her."

Darcy folded his arms across his chest. "So, I assume your predicament occurred after you continued on without your sister?"

Elizabeth closed her eyes. "I made it easily to the bridge, walked across it and sat on its wide ledge, dangling my feet over the side. It was a beautiful day, and I was enjoying the trees, blossoms, and birds singing." She smiled. "Merrily, merrily shall I live now. Under the blossom that hangs on the bough."

Darcy looked at her with widened eyes. "Shakespeare?"

Elizabeth nodded.

"Do you read Shakespeare?"

"I have read several of his works that my father owns. I hope someday to read them all." She looked up at him. "You seem surprised."

"No, I…" Darcy shrugged. "I really had not considered whether you had read Shakespeare, or anything, for that matter."

"I will have you know I am an extensive reader."

"Indeed?"

Elizabeth watched him press his lips tightly as an indecipherable look quickly flickered across his face. "Continue."

"This large tree, with the brightest pink blossoms I had ever seen, spread its branches over the crystal blue water. Whenever there was a slight breeze, I watched some of those blossoms drift lazily from the branches and begin floating down the stream." Elizabeth chuckled. "I was rather mesmerized, and before I knew it, I leaned over to watch them float under the bridge, and I…"

"You fell off the bridge into the water?" Mr. Darcy's voice resonated with a touch of laughter.

Elizabeth was surprised at how his slight smile softened his features. "I did. Everything would have been all right if I had not twisted my ankle when I landed in the shallow water."

"What did you do?"

"I waited for Jane to begin worrying as to why I had not returned, and for her to come look for me. I *hoped* she would come look for me. When she finally found me, I sent her to the Gouldings' home for help. Mr. and Mrs. Goulding and their son brought her back in their carriage to get me. The men helped me in, and they took us back home."

Darcy was quiet for a moment. Finally, he asked, "Did you learn anything from this accident?"

Elizabeth laughed. "Oh, yes! Never worry about what others think of you." She stole a glance back up at Mr. Darcy. "There are some people whose opinions are too severe, and you will never please them no matter what you do."

"Do you refer to the Gouldings?"

Despite believing Mr. Darcy's opinions were too severe, she nodded. "Their son had often spoken of Jane with great admiration, but it was quite apparent that he and his parents did not look upon our adventure with approval. Thankfully, they gave us the assistance we needed, but as they took us home, Mr. Goulding admonished us about the hazards of young ladies walking unaccompanied." She shrugged. "Young Mr. Goulding ended up marrying another young lady from the neighbourhood the very next year." Her eyes and nose crinkled in a smile. "I would consider that his loss."

Mr. Darcy drew in a breath and stopped, as they had come to the fork in the path that would take her to Longbourn and Mr. Darcy in the other direction to Netherfield. "There is no need to walk me further, Mr. Darcy. Longbourn is just around the bend."

"I do not mind."

Elizabeth shook her head. "It is truly unnecessary, but I thank you."

Mr. Darcy stood quietly for a moment, shifting from one foot to the other. He looked at Elizabeth intently and said, "Miss

Bennet, Mr. Bingley is my good friend, and I would not wish him to be hurt in any way." He looked down and scuffed the dirt with his boot.

"I have no intention of hurting him, if that remark is intended for me," she replied tartly.

He gave his head a brisk shake. "I would not wish for *you* to be hurt, either." He bowed and quickly turned away, leaving no opportunity for her to respond.

Elizabeth stood watching him for some time, perplexed by his last words. She gave a shrug and continued on to Longbourn. Unfortunately, her walk had not given her the delight she had anticipated at the start, but... She suddenly stopped and looked back at Mr. Darcy's retreating figure. Her lips turned up into a wide smile, and she laughed as she realized that she had taken great delight in vexing him.

~~*

As Darcy walked the three miles to Netherfield, the image of Elizabeth Bennet's face, brightened by the exercise and suffused in delight and mischief as she relayed her story, seemed imprinted in his mind. Her lilting voice seemed always to have a hint of joy and laughter in it. He found her truly captivating, even in her perfect indifference to what others thought of her – and her apparent disregard for him!

He clenched his jaw as he considered his dilemma. Each encounter with this young lady evoked a stronger conviction that she was more suited to him than he could have imagined possible. She had a clever and well-informed mind, pleasing and engaging manners, a lively animation to her features, and he considered her as one of the handsomest women of his acquaintance.

He clasped his hands behind him and trudged with his head down. She was also unlike any other woman he had ever met. She did not attempt to use arts and allurements to attract his attention, and he had never noticed her use them around Bingley, either. He believed his friend had been the force behind their mutual attachment since the beginning. He felt at a loss to know what he ought to do with such burgeoning feelings, when he had no right to entertain them because of Bingley's previous attachment to her. He shook his head as he considered her family and how he would normally consider them beneath his notice.

He kicked a rock, sending it flying off into the bushes. He had to conquer this! There was no reason he should not be able to. He merely had to keep from being in her presence, and when he was, he had to remind himself that Bingley was well on his way to falling in love with her – as wrong as he felt they were for each other!

Chapter 7

A week after her encounter with Mr. Darcy, Elizabeth received a letter from Miss Bingley inviting her to join her and Mrs. Hurst for tea while the men visited the officers in Meryton. Elizabeth was surprised and could not help but wonder if she had extended the invitation solely because her brother had suggested it.

Mrs. Bennet was convinced this was a sure indication that a marriage proposal was imminent.

Elizabeth was not as confident as her mother that this invitation was even a hint of such an intention, but she was curious how Mr. Bingley's sisters would treat her. She hoped she would find their company agreeable and they would treat her with the civility that was her due as their guest.

The evening before the tea, rain seemed to be threatening. As the Bennets sat down for dinner, Elizabeth asked for the use of the carriage on the morrow.

"You shall not use the carriage!" her mother cried. "You will take the horse."

Elizabeth eyed her mother suspiciously. "With the threat of rain you will have me take a horse? I will not be presentable when I arrive!" She looked down and stirred her food around on her plate. "Besides, you know I detest riding."

"Your father needs the carriage horses," Mrs. Bennet said adamantly.

Elizabeth frowned and glanced up at her father. "Certainly, Father, you must see this is absurd!"

"Your mother is correct. I did have plans for them."

"But if it rains, you will have no need for them."

Mr. Bennet looked at his wife, who was shaking her head. He then looked back at Elizabeth. "I am sorry, Lizzy."

Elizabeth shrugged her shoulders. "Well, then, I shall walk, for I shall certainly not ride."

"You shall do no such thing!" Mrs. Bennet cried. "If it rains, only imagine the mud that will be on your dress, shoes, and stockings."

Mr. Bennet looked at his daughter with a sly smile. "If Mr. Bingley were to be there, I wager he would not mind it if there was a little mud on you!"

"Oh, heavens, Mr. Bennet! He would most certainly mind!"

"So it is settled," Elizabeth said as she dabbed her mouth with her napkin. "As I do not think Mr. Bingley's sisters would approve of their brother continuing to attach his affections to a lady who arrives for tea with six inches of mud on the hem of her dress, I shall insist upon taking the carriage!" Elizabeth looked at her mother with a victorious lift of her brows. "Or I shall not go at all."

Mr. Bennet drew in a long breath. "Mrs. Bennet, I suppose I can do without the horses for such a good cause."

Mrs. Bennet grumbled. "Oh, if you put it that way, you may take the carriage!"

"Papa, I will send the carriage home once I arrive at Netherfield, and you can send it back to retrieve me after a few hours. Or perhaps Miss Bingley will see fit to send me home in their carriage."

~~*

Elizabeth was grateful she had secured the carriage, for she doubted she would have been able to walk even a mile in the deluge that began shortly after she set out. As she was helped out of the carriage at Netherfield, she was grateful for an umbrella which shielded her from the rain, but she still entered the house slightly damp.

Miss Bingley and Mrs. Hurst politely welcomed her and then apologized for the inclement weather, as if it was their fault. Elizabeth assured them that she would not hold it against them. When they looked at her with expressions of confusion, she realized they did not understand she was teasing and thought it best to watch what she said to them in the future.

As they conversed over tea, Elizabeth endured an interrogation by the two sisters. Who were her relatives? Where did they live? Had she been presented at court? Why not? Had she been taught by a governess or any masters? She felt their questions were much like the rain outside – increasing in intensity as the afternoon passed, with little intention to cease.

Elizabeth wondered if Mr. Bingley knew his sisters would be asking such personal questions, and, more importantly, what would they do with the answers she gave them. It was apparent they were not impressed with her responses. Having had no formal education and having relatives who were not well connected, she readily noticed their disdain.

After tea, Elizabeth could not help but be concerned about the conditions outdoors. She wondered whether she ought to send for her carriage before it was impossible to traverse the roads.

Her thoughts were interrupted by the return of the men.

Mr. Bingley was elated to see that Elizabeth was still there. He greeted her and immediately declared, "I must say, the roads are unfit for man or beast." He looked at her apologetically. "I would be remiss if I sent you out in this storm, Miss Bennet. Our carriage barely made it home."

"Is it truly that bad, Charles?" Miss Bingley asked in a whimper. She looked at Mr. Darcy. "What is your opinion, Mr. Darcy? Certainly the short distance to Longbourn would not be treacherous for Miss Bennet."

"No, Bingley is correct. I am grateful we took our leave when we did. The officers wanted us to stay, but we were uncertain how the roads would fare under these conditions."

"Yes, better safe than sorry," Mr. Hurst said, as he walked over to the table still laden with tea and cake. "Insufferable out there!"

"Miss Bennet, if it is acceptable to you, I will send a rider to Longbourn to let them know you will be staying the night." Mr. Bingley gave her an encouraging smile. "It should be easy enough on a horse, but would be almost impossible in a carriage."

"Thank you. I appreciate your hospitality." She laughed. "I know James, our driver, will be relieved he does not have to return for me. I am certain it is raining as hard at Longbourn as it is here."

"Indeed, it must be!" Bingley smiled and clapped his hands. "I shall have the maids make up a room for you directly!"

"Thank you, Mr. Bingley." She looked down at herself. "Unfortunately, I did not bring a change of clothes."

"Caroline or Louisa can loan you something to wear for the remainder of your stay." He looked at his sister. "Would you be able to provide her with something?"

"We would be happy to oblige you, Miss Bennet," Miss Bingley said with a forced smile. Despite her words, her tone reflected much the opposite.

"Thank you," Elizabeth said as she looked from Miss Bingley, who was several inches taller than her, to Mrs. Hurst, who was several inches shorter. Hopefully they would find something suitable for her.

They continued to talk, and Elizabeth readily noticed that Mr. Darcy was not as engaged in the conversation as he had been when they met the other day on their walk. Although he had said little that day, now he sat with one hand rubbing his jaw and the other hand resting on his knee, his fingers tapping incessantly. He seemed distant, observing more than participating in the discussion.

If Elizabeth was correct in her estimation of his demeanour, he was not pleased that she was staying at Netherfield. It was apparent that Mr. Bingley's sisters were not, either. She felt he was studying her and consequently determining that she did not meet the strict expectations he held for his friend.

Later, the men excused themselves to freshen up, and Miss Bingley had a maid take one of her gowns and a nightdress to Elizabeth's room.

After more idle talk, the ladies went to their rooms to prepare for dinner. A maid accompanied Elizabeth to show her to her room and help her dress. When she saw the gown Miss Bingley had sent, she stifled a laugh. She had been occasionally amused by the clothes Miss Bingley wore, but this was unlike anything Elizabeth had ever seen. She wondered if it was something the woman had actually ever worn.

It was a bright gold voile fabric that had the modern style of an empire waist, but the neckline was much higher than currently fashionable. The sleeves were puffed, then continued down the arms, where an abundance of lace extended over her wrists. When she slipped into the gown, it seemed to suffocate her with warmth. This was going to be a very long evening.

She thanked the maid and sent her away, then went to look at herself in the mirror. She felt the gown's colour made her look pale; it completely hid her natural figure as it was too large and bulky, and she feared that she would trip over the hem, as it was several inches too long. She wondered how she would eat without getting a mouthful of the lace. As she looked at her reflection, she widened her eyes and gave a shrug of her shoulders. There was little she could do about it.

When Elizabeth joined the others in the parlour, she took care to lift the gown's hem so as not to stumble. Mr. Bingley joyously declared she looked lovely. Mr. Darcy covered his mouth with his hand, and she was certain he was hiding a smirk. She thanked Mr. Bingley for the compliment and his sister for the use of her gown.

As the party conversed before the meal, Mr. Bingley spoke enthusiastically of their meeting with the officers. He had never met a finer group of men and enjoyed hearing their stories of places they had been.

"Have they seen much fighting?" Miss Bingley asked.

"These men are not the Regulars so they have seen very little action," Mr. Darcy said indifferently.

"Do they intend to crush any French sympathizers we may have here in Meryton?" Elizabeth asked with a teasing smile.

Mr. Bingley leaned in towards Elizabeth. "Oh, I am certain nothing like that happens here."

"At present," Darcy said, "things are rather calm on the home front. They chose Meryton because it is close enough to the amenities in London, while at the same time it is far enough away from its temptations." He picked up a book he had brought in and opened it.

Elizabeth laughed wryly. "The militia need not travel to London to find dissolute diversions. Unfortunately, they likely can find those same temptations in any village such as ours here in Hertfordshire."

"Heavens! I would hope this neighbourhood is not so corrupt as to indulge in questionable behaviour!" Miss Bingley cried. She turned to her brother. "If that is the case, Charles, we must give up the place at once!"

"But I…" he began.

Darcy put up his hand. "I am certain Miss Bennet means that in every city, town, and country village one might find those who behave in an imprudent manner. It is not just in London." He looked at her. "Am I correct?"

"Yes," she replied, turning to Miss Bingley. "I hope you do not think I speak from seeing first hand that kind of behaviour in the neighbourhood."

"You see, Caroline? All is well here!" cried Bingley. His sister gave a small, tight smile.

"I do not see the reason for their being here and do not think it good at all," Caroline complained.

"Their presence here is, in equal parts, both good and bad, depending on one's perspective and expectations in relation to society and commerce, I suspect," Elizabeth said.

Caroline looked at her with a blank look, while Mr. Darcy turned his eyes down to his book with a small smile.

They were soon called to their meal, and Elizabeth was grateful to sit down to dine. She was hungry and was looking forward to the meal.

The conversation around the table was friendly. Mr. Bingley and his sister lead the discussion and spoke more than anyone else. Elizabeth answered politely when asked a question, but again, Mr. Darcy said little, seemingly more intent on observing than conversing.

After the meal, the ladies repaired to the drawing room and waited for the men to join them. Elizabeth was feeling quite overheated in Miss Bingley's gown and could only think of throwing it off as soon as she could. She wondered whether the nightdress provided for her would be just as stifling.

She had begun to sense that Mr. Bingley's sisters were not enthusiastic about having to offer her refuge. She did not feel quite like an unwanted trespasser, but more like someone they were resigned to entertain because of their brother's partiality.

When the men finally joined the ladies, Mr. Darcy was not with them.

"Where is Mr. Darcy?" Miss Bingley asked.

"He went to the library," her brother answered. "You know how much he likes to read. I am certain he will join us directly."

"I would enjoy seeing your library," Elizabeth said.

"It is nothing like Mr. Darcy's library," Miss Bingley said with a long sigh. "I have never seen anything that compares to the library at Pemberley."

"You are an avid reader, are you?" Mr. Hurst asked.

"I do love to read, although I do not have access to a large selection of books." Elizabeth smiled. "Perhaps I can visit the library later to see if I can find something diverting. I did not bring a book, and I enjoy reading before going to sleep."

"Good luck finding something interesting!" Mr. Darcy announced as he entered. "Bingley, you simply must address your lack of books."

Bingley let out a groan. "I need you to help me decide which books to buy for it. The next time we are in London, we shall go to one of your favourite book stores."

He shook his head. "Bingley, what good is having a library filled with books if you do not read them?"

Elizabeth saw that he turned and looked at her, and then back to his friend, who merely shrugged.

"But if you insist, Bingley, I shall help you fill your library." Darcy waved his hand through the air. "The books you now have in there are..." He did not finish, but only shook his head. "This one will suffice," he said, as he held up the book he was carrying.

Darcy sat down and opened the book. Mr. Hurst made a futile attempt to gather everyone around the table for cards, and Elizabeth was grateful no one seemed inclined.

She noticed a chess set across the room and walked over to it. Picking up one of the intricately carved ivory pieces, she said, "Mr. Bingley, this is a beautiful chess set. Do you play?"

Bingley laughed. "To own the truth, I am still learning. That was my father's. Darcy has tried several times to teach me, but..." he shrugged. "One of these days I am sure the strategy of the game will suddenly make sense to me." He shook his head. "It takes too much analytical and anticipatory thinking."

Elizabeth sent him an encouraging smile. "I am certain you shall learn eventually."

Darcy looked up from his book. "It has been almost four years now, and you still do not fully understand the rudimentary strategy." He slowly shook his head. "You only need to apply yourself, Bingley."

Bingley sheepishly shrugged his shoulders. "I suppose, although I feel as though I have not the superior mind that you have, my good friend. There are other things I would much rather do."

Darcy let out a huff. "You ought to learn, Bingley. It is a thinking man's game…"

"I beg your pardon, Mr. Darcy," Elizabeth said. "A thinking woman's game, as well, if you please."

Darcy turned and looked at her with a surprised glimmer in his eyes. "Do you play, Miss Bennet?"

Elizabeth nodded. "I do. My father taught me a few years ago. I do not often have the opportunity to play, however, as none of my sisters took the time to learn. My father does not have the leisure time for it now as he used to."

"Would you care to play now?" Darcy stood up and walked to her side.

Elizabeth had been looking down as she replaced the chess piece she was holding and was surprised when she saw him at her side. She knew not what to say.

"Oh, please do not agree to play against him, Miss Bennet, for Darcy has little compassion for his opponents."

Elizabeth was grateful for the diversion and laughed. "Are you saying he is ruthless and plays only to win?"

"Oh, yes, he is merciless!"

Darcy began to protest, but Elizabeth interrupted.

"I thank you for the offer, Mr. Darcy, but no. Perhaps… perhaps some other time." She turned back to Mr. Bingley, who wore a somewhat relieved smile.

Mr. Bingley quickly stood up and extended his arm. "Come, Miss Bennet. I shall show you the library before Darcy tries to talk you into playing a game of chess against him."

Elizabeth smiled and slipped her hand in his arm. "Thank you,

Mr. Bingley. I would enjoy seeing it."

"I think I shall join you," Miss Bingley said. "I am in need of something to read, as well."

As they walked, Mr. Bingley said, "I wanted to let you know, Miss Bennet, I was informed that the rider has returned from Longbourn. Your family expressed their gratitude for your being in such good care."

"I am glad to hear that, sir. I also appreciate your kindness."

He smiled. "It is the least we could do." He pointed to the right. "Here it is."

Elizabeth stepped into the library and smiled politely at the large expanse of the room with beautifully polished wood shelves, but felt an inner disappointment that most of the shelves were empty.

"I shall fill it with only the best books," Mr. Bingley assured her. "I have just had so many other things to tend to." He shook his head. "I hope you will find something that suits your taste."

"I am certain I shall." Elizabeth walked over to the one shelf that had a good number of books. She looked at the titles, and finally, not wanting to appear to Mr. Bingley that she was disappointed in his selection, found a book she had read many years ago and took it off the shelf. "*Evelina*, by Frances Burney!" she said. "I shall enjoy reading this very much."

"Good! I am glad you found something." He turned to his sister. "Do you see anything to your liking?"

Miss Bingley looked at a few titles and seemed to choose one at random.

They returned to the drawing room, where Darcy was reading. He looked up. "Did you find anything?" he asked as he eyed Elizabeth curiously.

"Yes, I did, thank you," Elizabeth said, lifting the book up for him to see.

"And I did, as well," Caroline said. "I cannot wait to begin reading this." She casually tossed the book down.

They continued to talk, and Elizabeth appreciated Mr. Bingley's kindness and ebullient temperament. He was paying a good amount of attention to her, and they could readily laugh over any and all subjects. Despite those things in his favour, she realized

CHANCE AND CIRCUMSTANCE

there were many ways in which they were very different.

At length, she thanked the Bingleys for their gracious hospitality, and said she would retire for the evening. She was eager to slip out of Miss Bingley's smothering gown.

"It has been a delight, I assure you," Miss Bingley said as she stood up to usher Elizabeth out of the room. "Let us know if you have need of anything. I shall send up a maid."

"Thank you. Good night, everyone."

Elizabeth returned to her room and was determined to remove Miss Bingley's gown directly. She did not wait for a maid and slipped into the nightdress and robe she had been given. They were definitely more comfortable, but not something she would want to wear every night. When the maid came, Elizabeth thanked her, but told her she had no need for her assistance.

She walked to the window and looked out. The sky was dark, but she could see flashes of light from the storm far off into the distance. She propped her elbows on the window sill and rested her head in her hands, looking out into nothingness. Mr. Bingley had many fine qualities, and she would praise him to anyone who wished to know what he was like, but…

She let out a sigh and sat down in the chair. Elizabeth looked around her and pounded her hands down into her lap. "I left the book downstairs!" She groaned, looking at the dress she had just taken off. "I am sorry, Miss Bingley, but I refuse to put that back on." She went to the dressing room and pulled out the dress she had been wearing earlier when she came to Netherfield. "This will have to do. It will certainly be more comfortable."

She slipped it back on and took the stairs down. As she neared the door of the drawing room, she heard Miss Bingley's shrill voice.

"Charles! You are being unreasonable!"

"On the contrary, I am being quite reasonable. You cannot deny that she is delightful!" Mr. Bingley said.

"Only consider her family. You certainly saw how they behaved at Lucas Lodge. And her uncle is in trade and lives in Cheapside!" She let out a long sigh. "You must be aware of her obscure family connections and lack of fortune! You should not be entertaining thoughts of a young lady so beneath us! Tell him, Mr. Darcy!"

Elizabeth clenched her fist in anger and strained to hear what followed.

"Bingley," Mr. Darcy said. "I cannot give my full approval of this attachment. She is... she is completely unsuitable for you!"

"I care nothing about those things! I find her charming and agreeable in every way, despite what you both think!"

"Bingley, there are more things to be considered about her than her being charming and agreeable," Darcy said firmly.

"Charles, singling Miss Bennet out is the most foolish thing you have ever done!" Miss Bingley cried. "I do not know what you see in her!"

Elizabeth could bear to listen no longer and turned to hurry back to her room. She decided to forget about the book, for she would not be able to read, as angry as she was.

She walked into her room and closed the door. "The nerve of Miss Bingley and Mr. Darcy!" She stamped her foot and wrapped her arms tightly about her. They were obviously conspiring together to convince Mr. Bingley of her unsuitability. She shook her head and pursed her lips. "They will not be successful!" She would not allow them to win.

Elizabeth sat down on the bed and then fell backwards. "Oh, Mr. Bingley, what am I to do about this?" She pounded her hands down. "I have never met a kinder, more generous gentleman, but..." Her voice trailed off softly. After a moment, she added, "I cannot allow them to get away with this!"

She slowly sat up. "You are certainly one of the most agreeable gentlemen I have ever met, and I think of you with a great deal of fondness, but...." She drew in a breath. "Would it be terribly impertinent for me to continue to display admiration for you a little while longer... just long enough for your sister and friend to writhe in agony and defeat?" She smiled. "But you can rest assured, dear Mr. Bingley. I will make certain you do not lose your heart to me." She winced. "At least I hope you will not."

Chapter 8

Later that evening, Darcy watched as Miss Bingley and her sister left for their rooms. Mr. Hurst was prone on the sofa, already asleep.

Darcy leaned forward in his chair with his hands clasped, wondering what more he could say to his friend. While he had agreed with Miss Bingley regarding the unsuitability of Miss Bennet, it was not for the same reasons. She had felt Miss Bennet's obscure family connections, lack of fortune, and having family members in trade were all decidedly against her – and she should be far beneath his notice.

While she had a right to her opinion about Miss Bennet's position in society, Darcy did not consider her unsuitable for those reasons. In his opinion, it was due to the difference in their interests and intellect. He let out a groan as he considered that as he listened to each of her conversations, he discovered something new about her that tugged at his heart. She seemed to be exactly the type of lady who would make him happy.

It was something he had found himself fighting from the moment he first saw her. It grieved him that he felt the need to discourage this infatuation Bingley had formed with her. He had seen it happen before, however, only to have him enjoy a lady's company for a short while, believing himself hopelessly in love, and then moving on when someone prettier came along. He did not want Elizabeth to be hurt.

It grieved him even more that Miss Bennet had heard his remark at the Meryton Assembly when he had stepped outside with his friend. Did he really believe he could dissuade his friend from his affection for Miss Bennet only to step into his place? Did he even have a right to do so?

He slowly turned his head and looked at his friend, who sat quietly after receiving such a pummelling. "Bingley, I know what you must be thinking."

"Do you?" Bingley shook his head. "I feel as though I have been ambushed by my sister and my good friend, and I find it hard to justify your opinions. I could care less about her family, her connections, her fortune or lack thereof. She is a delightful lady, lively, intelligent…" He paused and looked at Darcy. "I am rather surprised you are so set against her when I would expect you to think highly of her."

Darcy's head shot up. "What do you mean?"

"I thought you would find her intelligence and wit appealing." He shook his head. "She is nothing like the other ladies who have turned my head."

Darcy clenched his jaw. "I do admire that in her." His voice cracked as he considered just how appealing he found her, and more than just her intelligence and wit! How could he ever tell Bingley that in truth he felt Miss Bennet would be the one making the mistake if they married? As long as his friend felt this way towards her, he could not – and would not – allow himself to do the same.

"Darcy, I have been doing a lot of thinking, and feel she would be good for me. I know you think I am going to see another pretty face and shift my attentions, moving them on to someone else. I will have you know I have no such intention."

Darcy bit back his response, which would have been to say he actually wished he would. "I do not wish for either of you to be hurt."

Bingley shook his head. "Have no fear, good friend. My intentions are honourable, and my hopes are high that she might be the right one." He gave his friend a broad smile.

Darcy was grateful his friend seemed to harbour no ill feelings against him. It would grieve him to lose Bingley's friendship. His chest tightened as he considered that to keep that friendship, he might have to rid himself of all the ardent admiration he had begun to feel towards Miss Elizabeth Bennet.

~~*

Later that night, Darcy paced about his darkened room. He stopped and braced his hands on his desk, seeing the intelligent, sparkling eyes and lively smile of Miss Elizabeth Bennet. His heart pounded in his chest as he wondered how this could have happened. How was it that he finally found a woman he felt he might just be able to spend the rest of his life with, but Bingley happened to meet her first and had also formed the same opinion of her?

He sat down in the chair, put his head back, and closed his eyes. Dare he hope that Elizabeth would come to the realization that Bingley was not suitable for her? He could only hope she would, for Bingley seemed more determined than ever. He hoped that Elizabeth would see that his friend was not suited to her, as Bingley was not a good reader, did not play chess, and – as he had so conveniently informed her as they had walked up Oakham Mount – was not an avid early morning walker.

Darcy pressed his lips together as he considered she might be inclined – obligated, perhaps – to consider and accept any offer of marriage if it was favourable in terms of fortune. The Bennets had little wealth, and Longbourn was entailed along the male line. Having only daughters, it would one day go to someone else. Would she accept an offer of marriage solely to provide for the family even if the gentleman was not completely suitable? He shuddered and hoped she would have more sense.

A wave of guilt passed through him as he considered how critical he was being of Bingley. He had no right to think so poorly of him, and assert that he was not good enough and would not measure up to the expectations Miss Bennet may have regarding the man she would marry.

Bingley was a good man – an excellent one – and he would be a very suitable match for Elizabeth in terms of how he would treat her and what he could do for her and her family. Darcy knew there was nothing he could do if she did not care that he took little pleasure in the things she enjoyed.

For her sake, he hoped she would ponder long and hard about those differences and deficiencies before an offer of marriage was made. He dropped his head and thought how foolish he had been to allow his heart to be so easily touched! There had to be something he could do about it.

~~*

In the middle of the night, a fierce thunderstorm developed. Elizabeth had been sleeping fitfully, and she rose and walked to the window. She looked out, and could tell by the flashes lighting up the sky that the storm was on the south side of the house. Unlike her sisters, who took shelter under the blankets during a storm, she loved to get up and watch it.

She put on the robe Miss Bingley had given her and stealthily opened the door and stepped out. There was a large window in the drawing room that faced south, so she set out for that part of the house.

The house was quiet, and as she came into the room and walked towards the window, she could readily see the bright arcs of light in the distance. Thunderous booms followed.

She peered out and smiled at one that was particularly large, with fingers of light streaking from the clouds to the ground. "Oh, my!" she said in an excited whisper.

"That one was quite breath-taking, was it not?"

Elizabeth abruptly turned, startled by the voice behind her. Mr. Darcy was seated in a chair, which he had turned to face the window.

"Pray forgive me for startling you. I came out to watch the show. I believe this is the best seat in the house." He stood up and extended his hand to the chair. "Would you care to sit down to watch from here? I can pull up another chair."

Elizabeth would have found his chivalry charming, if not for what she had overheard him say earlier. "No, thank you. I had not..." She turned back and looked out as lightning lit up the room again, followed almost instantly by more thunder. She swallowed; her mouth was suddenly dry. "I do not plan to stay long."

"That one looked – and sounded – fairly close," Darcy said.

Elizabeth nodded and closed the robe more snugly about her. She had no wish to have a conversation with him, but she could attempt to be civil. "Yes, it did."

"Do storms... do they frighten you?"

Elizabeth laughed. "On the contrary, I love to watch them."

Darcy let out a breathy chuckle. "Why does that not surprise me?"

"Pardon me?"

He shook his head. "Nothing."

Elizabeth continued to stare out, but a sudden realization came to her. If she could hint to Mr. Darcy of her admiration for Mr. Bingley, she doubted he would inform him. Knowing what he thought of his friend's attachment to her, he would undoubtedly not wish to encourage those affections by revealing to his friend how she felt – or supposedly felt.

She could readily cause *him* distress without blatantly – and deceitfully – encouraging Mr. Bingley's affections. "Do you think Mr. Bingley will come out to watch the storm? I would... I would greatly enjoy his company. It has been such a delight to get to know him better." She turned and looked at him and forced a smile.

Darcy let out a huff. "I highly doubt Bingley would leave his bed for anything, particularly to watch a thunderstorm."

Elizabeth looked at Mr. Darcy with surprise. "Are you saying thunderstorms frighten him?"

Darcy shook his head. "No. I believe he does not wish anything to disturb his precious sleep." He laughed. "Even a marvellous thunderstorm display."

"I see," she said softly. She gave her shoulders a slight shrug. "He has so many other fine qualities; I suppose one ought not to judge a man by whether or not he arises to watch a late night thunderstorm."

"Indeed," Darcy said with an edge to his voice. "Or whether or not he arises early to take a walk and enjoy the sunrise or reads several chapters in a book before going to sleep, or for that matter, any book," Darcy said softly. He pointed to the table. "You left your book here when you retired."

"Yes, I... I realized it too late." She walked over and picked it up, feeling somewhat perplexed by his words. "I should get back to my room. Pray, excuse me."

"There is no need to leave on my account. The window in my

room faces this direction. I can watch the storm from there. Please excuse me."

He bowed, and Elizabeth watched him step from the room. When another boom shook the house, she jumped and turned back to look out the window. She glanced at the chair in which Mr. Darcy had been sitting, and she moved to take his place. When she sat down, she became very much aware of the warmth emanating from it. She pushed herself up from it and returned to the window.

She shook her head as she pondered the many differences between her and Mr. Bingley. It was unfortunate that she agreed with Mr. Darcy on that subject, but she certainly did not have to tell him that she did.

~~*

Elizabeth awakened the next morning after a restless sleep. She had spent her waking hours either weighing Mr. Bingley's suitability or considering the words Mr. Darcy and Miss Bingley had spoken about her.

She had remained in the drawing room only a short time after Mr. Darcy had left. Surprisingly, she had found it more diverting to watch a storm with someone else, even if it had been Mr. Darcy.

She despised the thought of causing Mr. Bingley any intentional pain by using arts and allurements to secure his affection. She suddenly remembered Mr. Darcy's words to her that he would not want to see his friend hurt. She winced. Despite not really caring for what Mr. Darcy said, she did care about Mr. Bingley's feelings.

She walked to her window and gazed out. The sky was just beginning to lighten, and it appeared the rain and storm had moved on. She actually felt that some of the anger she had felt last night had moved on, as well, but only because she had set into motion her plan teach Mr. Darcy and Miss Bingley a lesson.

She retrieved her dress from the dressing room and slipped it on, pondering what she might say to Miss Bingley about her partiality towards her brother that might unsettle her. She hoped she would have some time alone with her this morning.

She let out a sigh. She was eager to leave Netherfield and return to Longbourn. She hoped Mr. Darcy and Miss Bingley would fret about her and Mr. Bingley for a few days, but the next time she saw him, she would kindly discourage him in his attentions towards her.

When she came downstairs, she found it quiet. The delicious aromas coming from the kitchen teased her nostrils, and she could almost taste the bread and meats that were baking in the oven.

She came to the drawing room door and peeked in, almost expecting Mr. Darcy to already be there. She had encountered him without warning so often, she was certain he would be around every corner she turned or in every room she entered. Knowing he was an early riser added to that expectation. When she was fairly confident he was not in the room, she stepped in.

She sat down and began to read her book, occasionally glancing up when she heard a noise. A maid brought in tea and freshly baked bread, warm from the oven, and offered some to Elizabeth.

Although Elizabeth had already read *Evelina*, it had been many years. She had forgotten much of it, so she was enjoying rereading it. She was lost in the action of the story when out of the corner of her eye she noticed someone standing at her side, and she jumped in surprise.

"Again, I have startled you, Miss Bennet," Mr. Darcy said. "I have no idea how to make my presence known to you. Pray, forgive me, again."

Elizabeth shook her head. It was difficult not to smile at the contrite expression on his face. "I was merely caught up in the story, so I imagine any manner of alerting me to your presence would have startled me." She looked down and began reading again, thinking that, in truth, she was not so much startled as vexed.

Darcy stood at her side for a moment, and she was relieved when he finally walked over to the sideboard for coffee and something to eat. Perhaps if she kept her eyes on the page, he would realize she did not wish to talk.

He came back and sat down across from her. He took a sip of his coffee and then asked, "You are enjoying your book, then?"

Elizabeth inwardly groaned, but looked up and forced a smile.

"Yes, even though I read it years ago. I have forgotten much of it, so yes, I am enjoying it."

Darcy's brow lifted. "You read that book many years ago?" He seemed surprised. "That looks to be at least five hundred pages."

She shrugged her shoulders. "True, but if a book is well-written and keeps my interest, it matters not how long it is." She smiled and lifted a brow. "Or how young I was when I read it."

"I am actually surprised Bingley had that book in his library. Or any book, for that matter." Darcy shook his head. "Reading is not something he particularly enjoys. He even had difficulty at Cambridge finishing the required reading."

"You were with him at Cambridge?"

"I was in my final year there when he first came, but we became good friends."

Elizabeth was curious how two men who seemed so different from each other could have become such good friends. Instead, she asked, "And what was it that drew the two of you into such a close friendship?"

Darcy looked at her, and he appeared to be carefully choosing his words.

"Bingley is intelligent and applied himself well, however..." Darcy began to rub his jaw. "There were a few areas that held little interest to him, and I agreed to help him out."

Elizabeth lifted up her book. "And reading was one of those areas?"

Darcy silently nodded.

"I see." She turned the book back to the inside cover. "Well, this might explain why Mr. Bingley has this book in his library." She pointed to the page. "The name inscribed is Wellingsford. That was the name of the family who previously lived here."

"That would certainly explain it. They must have left it behind," Darcy said with a wide smile and a quick lift of his brow. "I wonder if all the books in his library belonged to the Wellingsfords."

Elizabeth waved her hand through the air, intent to convince him that it made little difference to her. "Either way, Mr. Bingley has so many other excellent traits. The fact that he is not an avid reader means little to me." She feigned a wide smile. "He is an exceptional gentleman, and from what I have seen of him, he is a man with very few faults."

Darcy's eyes narrowed as he looked at her. "Indeed?"

She could not meet his gaze and looked back down to her book. Hopefully she had been able to convince him that she did not care whether Mr. Bingley read or not, although, in truth, it mattered greatly to her. She just wanted him to hear enough praise for his friend to make him believe she was on her way to falling in love.

They sat quietly, each reading their own book, as they waited for the remainder of the household to waken and join them. At length, Mr. Bingley came downstairs, looking tired.

"Good morning!" he said as he poured himself a cup of coffee. "For some reason, I feel as though I did not sleep well."

"It was likely the thunderstorm that kept you awake."

"Thunderstorm? Did we have a thunderstorm?" He shook his head. "I must have slept through it."

"If you slept through it, I would wager you got enough sleep," Darcy said. "Having seen you often in the morning, however, I can guarantee this is the way you often look – and feel – when you waken."

Bingley laughed. "I suppose that is the truth. That is why I need my coffee before I talk to anyone!" He looked at Elizabeth. "How are you this morning, Miss Bennet? Did the storm keep you awake?"

She unwittingly looked at Darcy, who was watching her. "It did waken me. In fact, I came in here for a short while to watch it."

"Oh, you are one of those," he laughed. "Just like Darcy. I am surprised you did not encounter him."

Elizabeth felt her cheeks warm as Bingley sat down. She was certainly not going to say anything, and she hoped Mr. Darcy would not, either.

"Bingley, you make it sound as if there is something wrong with people who get up to watch a storm."

"In the middle of the night? Yes. It makes no sense to me," he said with a laugh. He took a long sip of his coffee.

Elizabeth gave Mr. Bingley a warm smile. "I cannot tell you again how grateful I am for your kindness and hospitality in allowing me to stay here last night. I have enjoyed getting to know you and your... family."

Mr. Bingley leaned forward in his chair. "It has been a pleasure and a delight getting to know you better, as well, Miss Bennet. I could not have asked for a more delightful houseguest."

Elizabeth could readily see an expression of joy in his eyes. She felt a slight stab of caution that he might truly be forming an attachment to her, and if it were not for Mr. Darcy eyeing them with an expression of displeasure, she would have discontinued this charade at once.

"You are too kind, Mr. Bingley," she said with an appreciative smile.

Miss Bingley came downstairs about fifteen minutes later, followed by her sister, and then Mr. Hurst. Elizabeth was grateful for the foods that had been set out for them, for she would have been starving if she had been required to wait for everyone to come down to breakfast.

As they finally gathered around the table, Elizabeth hoped to have some time alone with Miss Bingley to convince her of her growing attachment to her brother. Then she could return to Longbourn and imagine the frantic discussions she and Mr. Darcy would have about her.

It was later that morning that she had the opportunity. The men had gone to the billiard room, and Mrs. Hurst had stepped away.

Elizabeth looked at Miss Bingley. "I want to tell you again, Miss Bingley, how much I have appreciated your hospitality. I admire your brother, and I do not think I have ever met a gentleman who is so kind and considerate, and oh, so generous. You are so fortunate to have such a brother." She smiled at her and tilted her head.

Miss Bingley practically sputtered out the tea she was sipping. "Charles? Kind and considerate? Oh, Miss Bennet, you must be mistaken. And generous? If only you knew!" She shook her head vehemently.

"You have no idea how often I must sit down with him and give him a good scolding about his behaviour."

"Truly?" Elizabeth was surprised to hear such harsh words

from Miss Bingley about her brother, although she had her suspicions why she would say such a thing. "I find that hard to believe."

"Well, he is a complicated man and so difficult to understand." She let out a snicker. "I have lived with him my whole life, and he is still a mystery to me!" She looked at her with a pathetic smile. "One moment he is generous and charming, and the next…" She shuddered. "He can be a fool and even a tyrant at times!"

"A tyrant? Surely you jest." Elizabeth shrugged. "I have never seen that in him. He seems… quite well-mannered and proper. He is… everything a young man ought to be."

Miss Bingley attempted to smile, prompting Elizabeth to smile back. *There! Let her and Mr. Darcy suffer a bit under the misapprehension that I consider Mr. Bingley a most favourable match!*

Elizabeth did not believe a single word Miss Bingley said about her brother and wondered what he would have thought if he had heard her. Despite Elizabeth's uncertainty about his suitability, he was certainly not deserving of such a critical appraisal.

~~*

Mrs. Bennet sent a note to Netherfield saying she and her two youngest daughters would come later that day to get Elizabeth. This surprised her, as she would have expected her mother to have made some excuse for her to stay longer. She finally determined her mother likely wished to see Netherfield for herself, imagining it would soon belong to her second eldest daughter.

Elizabeth sighed. She hoped her mother would make no inappropriate remarks or speculate about any match between her and Mr. Bingley. It was one thing for her mother to express her hopes, wishes, and expectations to her own family, but it would be totally imprudent to express them to those in this household.

Chapter 9

Mrs. Bennet arrived at Netherfield later that day with Kitty and Lydia. They were shown into the drawing room where Elizabeth and the others had gathered. As the guests walked in, Elizabeth's mother spoke effusively of the fine home, elegant furnishings, and its most esteemed occupants.

Elizabeth could readily see Mr. Bingley's rapt interest in her mother's ramblings, in sharp contrast to the expressions of disgust on the faces of the others. If Mr. Bingley was not earnest in how warmly he received her verbosity, he was very good at disguise. In truth, Elizabeth felt he was genuinely interested in all she said.

Miss Bingley politely invited them to have a seat, and they talked of the neighbourhood and last night's storm. Mrs. Bennet told of the excitement in the Bennet household over the news from her eldest daughter Jane, who would be returning with her new beau in a little over a week.

"I cannot wait to meet Mr. Marshall!" Mrs. Bennet declared. "I am certain he must have been taken by her great beauty. You will see when you meet her. Everyone in the neighbourhood says she is by far the prettiest young lady around."

Mr. Bingley smiled. "I will be delighted to meet your daughter and Mr. Marshall. I am certain you must be pleased she will be home shortly."

By the manner in which Mrs. Bennet spoke, Elizabeth was certain that if there was not yet an understanding between the two of them when they arrived, her mother would make certain there would be one directly.

"You must give a ball when they return!" Lydia pleaded with Mr. Bingley. "We so long for a ball!"

Mr. Bingley smiled. "That is a splendid idea." He looked at his sister. "Caroline, what do you think?"

Miss Bingley smiled sweetly, muttering an affirmative, but she gave Mr. Darcy a pained glance. Elizabeth smiled, as well, knowing the two were not pleased by this *splendid idea.*

After a bit more idle conversation, the party took their leave, as Mrs. Bennet profusely expressed thanks and appreciation for all they had done for Elizabeth.

As the carriage pulled away, Mrs. Bennet clasped her hands and turned to Elizabeth. "Now, you must tell me all that happened! Mr. Bingley is such an excellent man, Lizzy. I could not be more delighted by the way things have turned out for both you and your sister!"

Elizabeth turned her head to glance out the window. *I fear she will not be delighted when I tell her Mr. Bingley may not be someone I consider suitable for me, but I shall wait until later to enlighten her with that news.*

~~*

Darcy stood at the window watching the Bennet carriage pull away from Netherfield. His shoulders rose and then quickly lowered as he saw Bingley wave joyfully, while Miss Bingley abruptly spun around to return to the house. His chest tightened and his throat constricted as he considered the predicament in which he found himself. How could he have formed this misplaced affection for a young lady who had such questionable family connections, a lowly fortune, and who was completely unsuitable for him? *But was she truly unsuitable?*

He let out a groan. In his estimation, her only true unsuitability was that his friend had met her first and was well on his way to being in love with her. He inhaled deeply. And worse, she seemed inclined to return that affection and seemed to have little regard for him.

He pondered all he had discovered about her since their first meeting, and it had become very apparent to him that she was an exceptional young lady, one who shared his enjoyment of many things. This would be easy enough to overlook, however, had she not unwittingly penetrated his heart.

His gaze was solemn as the carriage made a turn and disappeared from view. He felt a pang of emptiness flare within him. His head dropped as he wondered if there was anything he could do to discourage his friend from this attachment... or to rid himself of the ardent affection he felt for the same lovely woman – a rare woman who took delight in walking in the early morning, playing chess, reading a five-hundred-page book, and watching thunderstorms.

Brief as the lightning in the collied night, that, in a spleen, unfolds both heaven and earth, And ere a man hath power to say 'Behold!' The jaws of darkness to devour it up: So quick bright things comes to confusion. Darcy gave a quick shake of his head. "Confusion, indeed! Shakespeare's words have never seemed so significant!"

Miss Bingley stepped into the room. "I beg your pardon, Mr. Darcy; did you say something?"

Darcy quickly shook his head and turned away from the window. "No."

"I did hear you, and I can surely guess what you were saying under your breath. What are we to do about this, Mr. Darcy? Miss Elizabeth Bennet may be lively and intelligent, but certainly you can see that her family is vulgar with no fortune or connections. She speaks her mind too freely for my taste, and I am of the opinion she is not at all suitable for Charles. He can do so much better. You must talk some sense into him!"

Darcy rubbed his chin. "I would agree Miss Elizabeth Bennet is unsuited for Charles, but perhaps not for the reasons you think." He shook his head. "All we can do is to wait to see what happens. You know your brother. Once a prettier face comes along, he will suddenly shift his affections to her." He could only hope!

Miss Bingley smiled. "I am delighted you concur with me on her unsuitability, no matter the reason. It is true my brother might be swayed by a prettier face. I wish I knew of someone suitable that I could bring to Netherfield. I would do it in an instant." She turned to Darcy. "Certainly, you must think of something we can do to bring this nonsense to a stop."

"I will give it some thought." On that, he could definitely agree to Miss Bingley's request.

"Why could he not have formed an attachment to someone

who is of consequence in society? Perhaps the daughter of an earl or baronet." Miss Bingley collapsed into a nearby chair.

"Bingley could care less about those things."

"*He* might not care about them, but *I* certainly do!" Miss Bingley drew in a few breaths to calm herself, bringing her fingers up to massage her temple. "Oh, I can barely tolerate this." She shook her head slowly. "Mr. Darcy, you must know that my brother considers you an invaluable friend. You only need to say a few words to him to steer him in a more proper direction!"

Darcy turned away. How could he persuade his friend of Miss Bennet's inferior standing in society when he could not even convince himself of it? And even if he did talk Bingley out of this infatuation, could he follow that by stepping in and declaring his own intentions regarding her?

"Heavens! I know I will miss having Miss Bennet around!" Mr. Bingley announced jovially as he walked in. "Is she not delightful?"

Darcy did not answer directly, but unwittingly looked at Miss Bingley, who met his gaze with a glare. He was suddenly aware that he was clenching both his fists and his jaw. He forced himself to relax and swallowed to moisten his dry throat. "Indeed, Bingley. That she is."

~~*

Elizabeth looked forward to seeing Jane and the Gardiners, as well as the addition of Mr. Marshall and a family member no one had ever met. Her father informed the family of the forthcoming arrival of Mr. Collins, a cousin, who was to inherit Longbourn when Mr. Bennet died.

Mrs. Bennet lamented that this cousin was only coming to survey what would one day belong to him. Mr. Bennet, on the other hand, assured his wife that he had no plans to die any time soon, and he informed her that Mr. Collins only wished to mend the breach that had occurred years ago between him and his father.

The cousin was a clergyman from Kent, and the day before he was to arrive, everyone conjectured about what he might be like.

Kitty insisted he would be handsome, since he was a cousin of theirs. Lydia, however, protested that he would never be as handsome as the soldiers in red coats. Mary scolded the girls for talking so, but seemed excited to meet him. Elizabeth listened with good humour, for the only thing she looked forward to was the arrival of Jane, for then, she would finally meet Mr. Marshall.

About four hours before Mr. Collins had said he would reach Longbourn, the sound of a carriage alerted the household that someone had arrived.

Kitty rushed to the window. "It is Aunt and Uncle Gardiner's carriage! Jane has returned!"

"Oh! They are here! They are here! Mr. Bennet, come quickly! Jane is here with Mr. Marshall!"

They rushed outdoors to greet the travellers, who stepped out of the carriage to squeals of delight.

Mrs. Bennet rushed towards Jane with outstretched arms. "Oh, Jane! You have returned!" She gave her a hug and then pulled back. "And my, you are glowing with beauty!" She leaned in with a sly smile. "Could there be a particular reason for this?"

Jane blushed and shook her head. "It is mainly due to the joy I feel at finally being home."

Once everyone had welcomed Jane and the Gardiners with hugs and kisses, Jane introduced Mr. Marshall to her family. He had been standing back to allow the family time to greet each other.

"We are so delighted to make your acquaintance, sir!" Mrs. Bennet exclaimed. "We welcome you to our home!"

"It is a pleasure to meet you, Mr. Marshall." Mr. Bennet extended his hand. "It will be nice to have another gentleman in the home."

Mr. Marshall grasped the offered hand. "Thank you, sir. I have heard so much about each of you."

"Hurry along! Let us get inside. We have refreshments for you." Mrs. Bennet led the way.

As they returned to the house, Elizabeth took Mrs. Gardiner's arm. "I am so pleased Mr. Marshall was able to accompany you on your return trip."

"Yes. I think it will be good for him to get to know the family."

Mrs. Gardiner squeezed Elizabeth's hand. "Hopefully you will not be too upset at us, but your uncle and I plan to freshen up and then we need to leave for London directly."

"Must you? You cannot stay at least until the morrow?"

"Our children have been left with their nanny far too long. While they are in good hands, we are eager to get home to them. A short visit, quick bite to eat, and something to drink, and we will be on our way."

Elizabeth stopped and tugged her aunt's arm. "Tell me, what are your thoughts on Jane and Mr. Marshall?"

Mrs. Gardiner looked at the couple. "One could not ask for a finer gentleman. He is kind, polite, and very attentive to her."

"And?" Elizabeth asked.

Mrs. Gardiner chuckled. "Neither of them are particularly expressive in the display of their feelings. It may be good that they are both reserved in that way, but I hope in time they will exhibit more enthusiasm in their interactions."

Elizabeth glanced over to the couple. Mr. Marshall was speaking earnestly with her father. "I do hope I shall like him. I would not wish for Jane to marry anyone but a man who is the very best for her."

Patting Elizabeth's hand, her aunt said, "He is everything that is good and honourable. He is very practical and considerate. Indeed, I find nothing objectionable in his character."

"And he is handsome, as well," Elizabeth laughed. "Perhaps not in a striking way, but rather in a very… how should I say this… acceptable way."

"Now that, Lizzy, is an interesting observation." Mrs. Gardiner laughed, and her niece joined in.

~~*

After the weary travellers freshened up, they gathered in the drawing room for much needed refreshments. The Bennets were in rapt attention as they listened not only to the Gardiners and Jane give an account of their trip, but also to Mr. Marshall as he discussed living in the Lake District.

"Oh, the beauty of the place! Every time I visit, I am in awe of it," Mr. Gardiner declared.

"The scenery is forever changing," Jane said. "Under a dark, cloudy sky, all the blues and greens of the water and trees were subdued. Then suddenly, there would be a break in the clouds, and a ray of sunlight would dance atop the shrubberies and treetops, lighting them up in a brilliant display of colours as the cloud sauntered across the sky."

"And how the lakes glistened like silver when touched by the sun," Mrs. Gardiner said.

"We could have watched it for hours," Jane said.

Elizabeth turned to Mr. Marshall. "It must be wonderful to live in such a place."

He nodded. "Indeed, it is. The lakes provide a perfect environment for fishing, which I greatly enjoy. If I could, I would weather storms, wind, and even snow just to fish."

Elizabeth narrowed her brows as she looked at Jane, knowing her sister was not particularly fond of fish. She hoped she could learn to like it.

"But the scenery..." she continued. "Certainly, you must never tire of looking about."

"Perhaps I have grown accustomed to its beauty, although I am certainly not insensible of it. It was delightful seeing it afresh through the eyes of Miss Bennet and the Gardiners." He chuckled. "I am no William Wordsworth; no one can describe the lakes better than he does in his poems." He turned to gaze upon Jane and then looked at the Gardiners. "Yet, I was surprisingly moved by their words of admiration as we walked about."

Elizabeth sat back and pondered the possibility of living in a place of natural beauty like that, knowing she would forever be in awe of it. For now, she was content to walk up Oakham Mount and enjoy the prospect from the summit whenever she had the opportunity.

The Gardiners departed after a short visit, and the Bennets continued to enjoy Mr. Marshall's company. Elizabeth carefully observed Jane, and while it was true she did not overtly display her admiration and affections, she had a ready smile whenever he addressed her.

"Now that we have heard all about the lakes, you must tell us about your family, Mr. Marshall." Mrs. Bennet smiled at the young man.

"We understand that your family was acquainted with the Gardiners in London," Elizabeth said.

"Yes. My father was a barrister in town and did quite well there. We had a distant uncle who owned a small manor and some land in the Lake District, and we visited often over the years. When he died, my father inherited it, as this uncle had no children of his own."

"Is your father still practicing as a barrister?" Mr. Bennet asked.

Mr. Marshall shook his head. "He received a commission to be the magistrate in the county."

"And do you aspire to follow in his shoes?" Elizabeth asked.

"Hardly," he said with a laugh. "When I was younger, of course, I wanted to be just like him. My interests are now in managing our small manor and the tenants and farmers we have on our land." He drew in a long breath. "I do enjoy doing that." He turned back to Mrs. Bennet. "But as I said earlier, I enjoy taking the boat out to do some fishing. The lake is teeming with perch and trout."

Mrs. Bennet clasped her hands tightly together. "Ah, a small manor and a boat to take out on the water. That does sound lovely!" She waggled her brows as she looked at Jane.

Mr. Marshall smiled. "It is not as grand as some of the manors in the country, but it does serve its purpose."

The Bennets were so captivated by Mr. Marshall and learning more about him, they had completely forgotten about their other guest who was to arrive.

When they heard the sound of another carriage, Mrs. Bennet looked with surprise at the others. "Now who can *that* be?"

Mr. Bennet walked to the window. "I believe it must be Mr. Collins!" He turned back to the others. "Excuse me while I go see to him."

"Who is Mr. Collins?" Jane asked.

Mrs. Bennet waved a handkerchief through the air. "He is your father's cousin, the one who is to inherit Longbourn when your father dies." She turned to Mr. Marshall, suddenly mindful of his presence. "Oh, but you have no need to worry, for Mr. Bennet has informed me he is in the best of health and has no plans to die any time soon!"

"Why is he coming here?" Jane asked.

Elizabeth could see that her mother regretted having blurted out about the entail and most likely did not want to risk saying anything else, so she answered. "According to Papa, he wants to mend the breach that was between him and his father."

"I see," Jane said. "Have we met Mr. Collins before?"

"No, we have not." Mrs. Bennet leaned towards Mr. Marshall. "He is a clergyman in Kent. Apparently, he has a very prestigious patroness."

Mr. Marshall merely nodded, and then all heads turned to the door as voices were heard approaching.

"Longbourn is delightful, Mr. Bennet. I am certain I will find your family as charming as the home."

"Well, Mr. Collins, you shall now meet them. They are in here."

The two men entered. Mr. Collins wore a stiff smile on his face and gave a deep bow.

Mr. Bennet extended his hand towards the others. "May I present my cousin, Mr. Collins?"

Kitty and Lydia whispered something to each other and giggled, prompting Mary to send them a chastising look.

Mr. Bennet made the introductions, and polite conversation ensued. Elizabeth readily observed that the young clergyman's gaze rarely moved from Jane. As he spoke of Rosings Park, the home of his patroness, he often glanced in her direction with a smile. Jane was considered at least five times prettier than any of her sisters, but Elizabeth determined this would certainly not do. Especially as Mr. Marshall seemed to have noticed it, as well.

Elizabeth looked directly at their cousin. "Mr. Collins, you must tell us more about Rosings Park. You have mentioned it several times. I am certain my mother would love to hear about it."

"Oh, certainly!" gushed Mr. Collins. "It would be difficult to find a more magnificent home. Inside and out, it is superior to any home I have seen."

Elizabeth was glad he had turned to her mother as he spoke, although he still stole quick glances at Jane. He continued to speak effusively not only about the home, but about Lady Catherine de

Bourgh, his patroness, and her daughter, Miss Anne de Bourgh.

"And how old is Miss de Bourgh?" Mrs. Bennet asked.

"She is not yet seven and twenty, and although somewhat frail, a finer lady one will never meet."

"She is out, I suppose?" Mrs. Bennet asked.

Mr. Collins gave a slight wave of his hand as he shook his head. "No, but she truly has no need." A triumphant smile emerged. "She is engaged to her cousin, the illustrious Mr. Darcy."

Elizabeth gave a start. "Mr. Darcy? Do you mean Mr. Darcy of Pemberley?"

Mr. Collins smiled. "The very one! Are you acquainted with him?"

"Yes, we are, but only recently. He is the good friend of our new neighbour, Mr. Bingley." She pinched her brows as she asked, "You said he is engaged to his cousin?"

Mr. Collins nodded enthusiastically. "Indeed! It is an engagement that was the wish of his aunt and his mother, made in their infancy."

Kitty and Lydia giggled at the absurdity of such an announcement, and while Elizabeth wished she could laugh at it, as well, she remained silent. Her mind, however, pondered this surprising revelation.

Mr. Collins sat up erect, and his eyes widened. "Is Mr. Darcy perchance in the neighbourhood now?"

Mrs. Bennet clasped her hands. "Indeed, he is!"

"I have never met the man, but I have heard much about him." He gave a simpering smile and clasped his hands. "Lady Catherine will be delighted when she hears about this good fortune."

Elizabeth leaned back in her chair as their cousin continued to describe Rosings and the parsonage, which Lady Catherine had much improved before his arrival. Elizabeth found it difficult to attend to his conversation, however, as she pondered the unexpected news about Mr. Darcy. It surprised her, due to Miss Bingley's apparent interest in the gentleman. She assumed Mr. Bingley would know of his friend's engagement and would have informed his sister of it. Perhaps Miss Bingley considered it only a minor obstacle that she could readily overcome. Elizabeth silently chuckled. The woman would likely be willing to do anything to secure his affections, and most likely felt completely able to do so.

Mr. Collins continued to speak in a wearisome and droning manner, and it was apparent he was completely unaware of the stupor that had overcome his audience. Kitty and Lydia whispered between themselves, giggling occasionally, her mother had grown quiet, and her father tapped his fingers on his legs restlessly. Even Jane, who was always so generous towards others, was politely trying to stifle a yawn. Mr. Marshall stared straight ahead with little evident emotion on his face. The only one who seemed enraptured was Mary, which Elizabeth did not find surprising.

At length, Mr. Collins excused himself, saying he wished to go to his room to freshen up. This delighted Elizabeth, as she wanted some time alone with Jane and Mr. Marshall. She wished to get to know him better and see if she could witness the effusive admiration for Mr. Marshall that Jane had spoken about in her letter.

Elizabeth stood up. "Jane, Mr. Marshall, as it is such a pleasant afternoon, I wondered if you would care to take a turn in the garden. I would imagine after several days of sitting in a carriage you would enjoy some exercise. Would you care to accompany me?"

Mr. Marshall looked enquiringly at Jane, and she nodded. "Yes, Lizzy. I would like that very much." She turned to Mr. Marshall. "Would you care to join us in the garden?"

"I would, indeed!" He rose and offered his arm to Jane as she stood.

When they stepped outside, Elizabeth turned to them both with a frustrated look. "I did not think Mr. Collins would ever stop talking about Rosings. I wanted so much to spend some time with both of you." She addressed Mr. Marshall. "I do not know if Jane told you, but she and I are extremely close." She leaned in to give Jane a hug. "I missed you so much and am delighted you are returned."

"I am, as well, Lizzy."

"What did you think of Mr. Collins?" Elizabeth asked with a laugh.

"Mr. Collins is…" Jane paused and shrugged. "I suppose you might call him an interesting character."

"As to that, there can be no doubt!" Mr. Marshall said with a laugh. "I would think he would have had the sense to see that none of us were interested in the windows and fireplaces at Rosings."

Elizabeth laughed. "He did go on and on about the home *and* his patroness."

"Do you think perhaps that he may have been nervous?" Jane asked. "He was likely uncertain how we would receive him."

Mr. Marshall shook his head. "I did perceive that he was nervous when he first arrived. After receiving such a warm and gracious welcome, however, he seemed intent on making a good impression of his situation to your family."

"Well, whatever his reason," Elizabeth said, "I thought his descriptions of Rosings, Lady Catherine, and her daughter would never cease!" She shook her head. "To think she is Mr. Darcy's aunt!"

"Who is this Mr. Darcy?" Jane asked. "You wrote about Mr. Bingley in your letter, but not about Mr. Darcy."

"There was nothing to write about *him*," she answered. "He is supposedly a good friend of Mr. Bingley's, but..." she paused as she considered what she ought to say. "I find him a little too officious, for my liking."

"From the way Mr. Collins spoke of his aunt, it sounds like they are very similar." Mr. Marshall pressed his lips together and nodded. "I find there are certain familial traits that extend even beyond the immediate family."

"Tell me more about Mr. Bingley, Lizzy." Jane turned to Mr. Marshall to explain. "He is a new neighbour of ours."

Elizabeth decided she would talk about him as though he were merely an acquaintance, as is seemed Jane had not told Mr. Marshall about him. "He is very kind and generous, lively, and almost always has a smile on his face. I have never heard one word of complaint out of his mouth. He seems to enjoy everything and everyone." She shook her head. "One could not ask for a finer neighbour."

"He does sound agreeable," Jane said.

Mr. Marshall rubbed his jaw, and with a teasing smile said, "He sounds a great deal like someone with whom I just recently made an acquaintance."

Jane looked up at him. "Truly? Who is that?"

Mr. Marshall let out a hearty laugh. "It is you, Miss Bennet." He turned to Elizabeth. "I have never heard a critical word from her since first making her acquaintance."

"Although you have not known her very long, Mr. Marshall, I have known her my whole life and have yet to hear her speak an unkind word to anyone or about anyone."

The trio laughed, and they continued to walk in the small garden until it was time to return to the house to ready themselves for dinner. As Elizabeth went to her room, she pondered Mr. Marshall. He was a nice-looking gentleman and very kind, but as her aunt claimed, he was also very practical, seeing things as black or white. Jane, on the other hand, tended to be more lenient in her appraisal of people and situations. Elizabeth sat down at her dressing table and looked in the mirror.

She toyed with a wayward strand of hair as she considered the two prominent men in her and her sister's lives. She was fairly certain she knew how things would turn out between her and Mr. Bingley, but she could not help but wonder about Jane and Mr. Marshall. She hoped things would turn out well for both of them.

Chapter 10

Later that evening, when Elizabeth and her sister were alone, Jane asked her to tell her more about Mr. Bingley.

"Oh, Jane, as I said, I have never met a kinder, more amiable gentleman. He is…" Elizabeth drew in a deep breath.

"Yes?" Jane leaned in with a smile.

Elizabeth tucked her hand through Jane's arm. "He is a man possessed of open and inviting manners, is very polite, and his appearance is greatly in his favour." She chuckled. "I am certain you would approve of him."

Jane took her sister's hand in hers. "I am very happy for you. I approve of him already."

"Now you sound like Mother, assuming there is something between us when there really is not."

Jane smiled. "Pray, forgive me, Lizzy, but he does sound charming and delightful."

Elizabeth's smile faded. "Indeed, he is, but I do not know what to think about his sisters. They are so different from him. While they treat me with kindness outwardly, I felt they were silently looking at me with disdain and contempt." She let out a sigh as she shook her head. "And Mr. Darcy, who is supposedly such a good friend of his, may even be worse."

"Oh, certainly not, Lizzy."

She shrugged her shoulders. "I know they are not pleased with the partiality he seems to be displaying towards me." She paused. "And I am not…"

"What is it?"

Elizabeth shook her head. "It is nothing."

"Lizzy, I know once they get to know you better, they shall love you as much as I do."

Elizabeth's lips turned down in a frown. "I strongly doubt it. I was with them for a full day and night." She patted Jane's hand. "I am certain they do not consider our family good enough for him – or more particularly, for *them*."

~~*

For the next few days, Elizabeth struggled to avoid Mr. Collins and keep him away from Jane and Mr. Marshall. He seemed intent on joining in on their every conversation and every walk, and barging in whenever Elizabeth and Jane wished to be left alone in privacy.

Mary, however, showed an interest in everything Mr. Collins said, but unfortunately for her, he was not particularly attentive towards her. Even when Mary directly complimented him or Elizabeth hinted to him that he might prefer her company to theirs, he remained at their side.

On one particularly pleasant day, Elizabeth sat outdoors, grateful that Mr. Collins was nowhere in sight. She sat on a bench making every attempt to keep her eyes from watching Jane and Mr. Marshall walk about. They appeared to be enjoying each other's company, but as her aunt had said, neither displayed an outward show of emotion, other than an occasional warm smile.

She gave her head a slight shake as she considered that Jane had never been one to reveal her true emotions. Whether it was excitement, fear, anger, or frustration, one would rarely see an outward sign of it. She always seemed serenely content.

Her attention on the couple was drawn away when she heard Kitty and Lydia's squeals as they rushed towards her.

"Lizzy! Just try to guess what Mr. Collins and Mother were just now talking about," Lydia prodded.

Elizabeth shook her head. "He is in with Mother? I wondered where he was. I imagine he was saying something about the spectacular lace window coverings in the drawing room or the imported rugs in the parlour at Rosings."

"No!" Lydia said as she clasped her hands. "The reason he came to Longbourn was to select one of us as a wife!"

Elizabeth drew back. "Truly? And has he selected you, Lydia?" she asked with a teasing smile. "You did say you wished to be the first of us to marry."

"Ha! I would not marry him for anything, but I have no worries. This is one time I am grateful I am the youngest!"

"Why is that?" Elizabeth asked.

"Because Mother told him he was not to consider her youngest daughter because I am... *too* young."

"Well, good for her." Elizabeth's stomach tightened. "And what else did you hear?"

Kitty answered. "You and Jane are safe. Mother hinted that her two eldest were likely to be very soon engaged to other gentlemen."

Elizabeth let out a sigh of relief. "Did she?" Elizabeth silently gave thanks for her mother's haste in coming to that conclusion! For once, it served a beneficial purpose! "So... it is to be Mary?"

"Or, of all people, me!" Kitty cried with a groan. "Can he not see how perfect Mary is for him? But he does not seem interested in her at all! You must do what you can to make sure he does not single *me* out!"

"What do you expect me to do, Kitty?"

"I do not know." She shrugged. "You must somehow make him realize how perfect Mary is for him!"

"I shall think on it, but I make no guarantees."

"Thank you! I know you will be able to do something!" Kitty squealed and gave Elizabeth a quick hug.

Elizabeth looked at Jane and Mr. Marshall and then back at her sisters. "Do not say anything to Jane. I will tell her later how she escaped a fate worse than death thanks to Mr. Marshall."

"You can thank us any time, Lizzy," Lydia said triumphantly as she jutted her chin and drew her shoulders back.

Elizabeth looked up at the exuberant faces of her young sisters and obligingly said, "Thank you."

"You are welcome!" Lydia grabbed Kitty's arm and pulled her away.

"I am counting on you!" Kitty cried. "Do not let me down!"

Elizabeth watched them leave and drew in a deep breath, letting it out in a whisper. "Oh, thank you, Mr. Bingley and Mr. Marshall, for being unwitting participants in thwarting what could have been a most awkward – and disagreeable – situation." Elizabeth laughed. "You have no idea how you just saved Jane and me."

She shook her head. She could not allow anyone to know of the doubts she had in regard to Mr. Bingley's suitability. At least not yet. She would have to make her mother and Mr. Collins believe that her affections were as deeply engaged as were his for a little while longer.

An idea suddenly came to Elizabeth. Mary had never made an effort to make herself look pretty. Perhaps all she needed was a little help in that area for Mr. Collins to notice her. The only difficult part was for Mary to agree. It was for an excellent cause, and it might actually prove advantageous for her, as well as the rest of her sisters.

~~*

The next day it was decided that all the young people would walk into Meryton. While this was not something Mary normally would choose to do, Elizabeth took her aside and encouraged her to join them, as Mr. Collins seemed intent to go.

"You know I dislike walking that far just to look into the windows of the shops," Mary protested, "or to meet up with the officers in the militia, as Kitty and Lydia are wont to do."

"Yes, I understand that, but there is a reason of greater import here."

"Of greater import? What would that be?"

"Mary, you must promise not to say anything, but apparently Mr. Collins has come to Longbourn in search of a wife."

Mary's eyes lit up. "Has he?"

"Yes," Elizabeth said as she took Mary's hand and brought her to sit at the dressing table. "Now, a man wants a lady who makes an effort to look pretty for him."

"Lizzy, you know I do not care for that sort of thing. Vanity is…"

"Yes, I know, but there is something I would ask you to consider." She paused and tapped her lips. "Tell me, what does Mr. Collins enjoy talking about?"

Mary glanced down at her dress, fingering the worn fabric of a gown passed down to her. "He talks about the church, his patroness, and…" Her voice trailed off.

"And what else?"

"And Rosings."

Elizabeth smiled. "Yes! He is a man – a gentleman – who appreciates finer things." She leaned in to Mary. "Do you not also think he would appreciate a young lady who takes the time to make herself attractive?"

Mary shook her head. "There are more important qualities a lady must possess."

"Certainly, there are, Mary, and you do possess all those inner qualities a gentleman – and especially a clergyman – requires. But let him notice your outer beauty, as well."

Mary let out a long sigh. "How do I do that?" She waved her hands in front of her face. "I only have what the good Lord has given me."

Elizabeth took her hand and gave it a squeeze. "And what He has given you is so worth taking good care of." She fingered the fabric of her sister's gown. "I believe if I rearrange your hair a little and find you a nicer gown to wear, it will be a good start."

Mary gave a futile shrug. "Do you really think so? I suppose you can try…"

"Thank you, Mary! Just sit back and let me see if I can find you a more flattering gown."

She hurried to her room and picked a dress that she thought would look nice on Mary, and then returned to work on her sister's hair.

When she was finished, Elizabeth stood back and smiled. "There! You look very nice, indeed. Just remember to smile often." Elizabeth chuckled softly. "And be sure to let him know how fortunate he is to live just across the lane from such a fine home, provided to him by a most generous and kind patroness."

"I suppose I can do that," Mary said. "At least, I will try."

Elizabeth hurried to get herself ready and then came downstairs to find everyone commenting on how nice Mary looked. Mr. Collins said little, but she felt that, at least, he noticed. She hoped it was just the beginning.

As they walked into Meryton, Elizabeth made certain Mary was always close enough to Mr. Collins to comment on his ongoing discourse. Jane and Mr. Marshall followed behind Lydia and Kitty, who talked of nothing but which officers they might encounter in Meryton.

Elizabeth, however, was more interested in watching Jane and Mr. Marshall. They occasionally conversed, not excessively, but when they did, Jane smiled sweetly. It was apparent they enjoyed each other's company, but were their hearts engaged? She was not certain.

When they arrived in Meryton, Lydia and Kitty hurried off to look in the window of the millinery shop, while glancing about looking for officers. Mary and Mr. Collins stood back silently. As Elizabeth pondered whether that was a good sign or not, Jane and Mr. Marshall came and stood alongside her.

"Lizzy, Mr. Marshall and I were discussing the militia's presence in Meryton. Has their being here had much effect on the neighbourhood?"

"The officers have added an interesting diversion, particularly for Kitty and Lydia." She nodded her head in their direction. "Look, I believe our sisters have spied someone they know."

"They look like decent gentleman," Jane said.

"I imagine they are typical officers," Mr. Marshall said. "Your sisters need to take care."

"I wonder who that gentleman is with the officers," Elizabeth said. "He is not in regimentals."

"Your sisters seem particularly pleased to be making his acquaintance."

Elizabeth's brow lifted. "Perhaps we ought to join them and make sure they are behaving properly."

When they reached them, Lydia was delighted to introduce officers Denny and Chambers, and a newly arrived officer, Mr. Wickham, to everyone.

As they chatted with these new acquaintances, a cheery greeting came from behind Elizabeth. She turned to see Mr. Bingley riding his horse towards the group and then dismounting. "How fortunate! We were just on our way to Longbourn to visit."

"Mr. Bingley! It is good to see you!" Elizabeth said cheerfully.

CHANCE AND CIRCUMSTANCE

His smile was wide as he walked to Elizabeth's side. "We have decided to host a ball at Netherfield on the twenty-sixth of November. The invitations are not yet ready, but I wanted to apprise you of the date."

"We will certainly look forward to it very much." Elizabeth said. "Mr. Bingley, there are several here with whom you are not acquainted. May I introduce you to them?" When he nodded, Elizabeth introduced him to Jane, Mr. Marshall, and Mr. Collins.

Mr. Bingley addressed Jane. "It is a pleasure to finally meet you, Miss Bennet. I have heard so much about you." He drew in a deep breath. "I hope... I hope you will be able to attend the ball."

"Thank you, Mr. Bingley. I am certain I shall."

As Mr. Bingley became immediately engaged in conversation with them, Elizabeth turned and noticed Mr. Darcy seated on his horse behind them. His eyes were on the small group consisting of her youngest sisters and the officers as they moved away. When Mr. Wickham turned towards them and then to Mr. Darcy, he stiffened and gave his horse a kick, leading it away.

Elizabeth glanced back at Wickham, noticing that the smile he had been wearing since first being introduced had disappeared. He appeared distressed and unsettled. After a moment, however, he turned back to his small group and became engaged in conversation with the others, his smile reappearing. She could not help but wonder what prompted such a response between the two men.

She turned back to Mr. Bingley, who was asking Jane about her trip.

"We had a wonderful time, thank you."

"I am delighted you enjoyed yourself and would love to hear more about it sometime." Mr. Bingley clasped his hands. "I am very excited to be hosting our first ball at Netherfield. I do hope you shall be able to attend." He nodded several times, looked behind him, and then turned to Elizabeth. "Where did he go?"

Assuming he was speaking about Mr. Darcy, Elizabeth pointed up the street.

"Oh... well, I ought to join him. Good day." He gave a quick bow. "It was a pleasure to make your acquaintance." He looked at Jane and then Mr. Marshall, and then promptly turned to mount his horse and set off after his friend.

Elizabeth walked over and took Jane's arm.

"Mr. Bingley seems quite nice," Jane said softly. She leaned over and whispered, "I can see why you are partial to him."

"Miss Elizabeth, did I hear your sister correctly?" Mr. Marshall asked with a wide grin. "You are partial to Mr. Bingley? I am delighted to hear that."

Elizabeth smiled and looked down the street after him. "He is quite amiable and a delightful gentleman."

"I readily noticed that," Jane said softly.

"Who was that gentleman who was with him?" Mr. Marshall asked.

"That was Mr. Darcy. For some reason, he did not seem inclined to stop and be introduced," Elizabeth said with a tone of disgust.

"Mr. Darcy was here? I did not see him," Jane said regretfully. "I am sorry I did not get the opportunity to meet him."

Elizabeth laughed. "Well, I am certain you shall have plenty more opportunities, although..." She paused and shook her head. "That was quite ill-mannered of him."

"He must have had a good reason," Jane said.

Mr. Marshall shook his head. "Whatever the reason, it is quite unpardonable for him not to extend even the basic civilities, especially since he is already acquainted with you, Miss Elizabeth."

Elizabeth agreed with Mr. Marshall, but then looked over at Mr. Collins, who was now walking down the street with Mary. She assumed that with the time she was spending with him, Mary would now have a complete account of the parsonage, Rosings, and Lady Catherine. She chuckled as she considered that he had apparently not been aware that the nephew of his esteemed patroness had been only a few steps away from him.

~~*

A few nights later, a party was to be held at the home of their Aunt and Uncle Phillips in Meryton. They had heard that several of the officers had been invited, and Kitty and Lydia spoke of little else, displaying a great deal of impatience for the evening to arrive.

The night of the party, the five sisters, accompanied by Mr. Collins and Mr. Marshall, crowded into the carriage and set out for Meryton. As they entered their aunt and uncle's home, men's voices could be heard, and Kitty and Lydia rushed off to the parlour to see which officers had come.

A large number of people, including officers, filled the modest home. Kitty and Lydia seemed acquainted with many of the soldiers. Elizabeth saw Denny and Carter, as well as Mr. Wickham. She hoped her youngest sisters would conduct themselves properly. She would not want Mr. Marshall to witness any impropriety in their youngest sisters' behaviour.

As she watched Mr. Wickham speaking to the others in the room, she tilted her head. She thought he might be someone she could shift her attentions to if... no, *when* she discouraged Mr. Bingley's affections. Mr. Wickham was handsome and appeared gentlemanly and kind. She believed he had the look and manner of a man of consequence and a respectable upbringing. He also seemed to have a lively disposition. She hoped to discover if his interests were similar to hers.

Different games were set up in the various rooms, and while eager to join in playing, Mr. Collins did not prove to be proficient at any of them. Elizabeth smiled as she considered this would be most suitable for Mary, who disliked playing and was sitting out. There were some things she refused to do.

At length, Mr. Wickham approached Elizabeth. He had been spending most of the evening with Kitty and Lydia, so she was rather surprised... and somewhat pleased. She greeted him with a warm smile.

"Pray, excuse me, Miss Elizabeth, I was talking with your sister, Miss Lydia, and she informed me that you were fairly well acquainted with Mr. Darcy, whom I saw the other day in Meryton."

Her expression sobered at the mention of the gentleman. Recollecting the uncomfortable response between the two men when they had noticed each other, she was curious about their connection. "I am only slightly acquainted with him. He is a good friend to Mr. Bingley, who recently moved into the neighbourhood. I have seen him on a few occasions." She tilted her head and shrugged. "For some reason, he did not seem inclined to stop and chat the other day as we were walking in Meryton, while his friend was more than happy to."

"No, he did not, and it was likely because he noticed me."

Elizabeth drew back in surprise. "You are acquainted with him, then?"

Wickham nodded. "My good father was his father's steward. I grew up at Pemberley."

Elizabeth's eyes widened. "Did you? I am surprised he did not stop to acknowledge you."

Wickham nodded. "While Darcy and I were always the best of friends when we were young, things changed, and our relationship is now... strained."

Elizabeth's brow furrowed. "To own the truth, I had wondered whether something happened between you." She shook her head. "I noticed that he appeared rather unsettled when he saw you."

Mr. Wickham shook his head and cast his eyes down. "I really ought not to say anything about it, as it was a personal matter between the two of us, and I would not wish to blacken his name to those who might esteem him in this neighbourhood."

"Esteem him?" Elizabeth laughed. "He has presented himself as very proud and above us all."

"He is a man full of pride in the Darcy name and fortune, but it is that very name and fortune that I had counted on to help me out in my life, as his father had promised." He laughed derisively. "Not that I expected anything, but I wished to be a clergyman. A living had been promised to me by the late Mr. Darcy." He looked down and began to rub his jaw. "After Mr. Darcy's death, the son decided not to bestow it on me when it became available."

Elizabeth's hands fisted tightly. "He had no right to go against his father's promises."

A satisfied smile appeared. "I did not think so, either."

Elizabeth readily recollected the words of caution Mr. Darcy had given to Mr. Bingley regarding his attentions towards her. "I have witnessed him trying to control his good friend in a way I found quite distressing."

"Did you?" Wickham leaned in and gave her a pointed look. "The man has only two goals in life. He either wants to run your life… or *ruin* it."

Elizabeth looked intently at the gentlemen. "That does not surprise me, Mr. Wickham." She slowly shook her head. "That does not surprise me at all."

Chapter 11

Elizabeth returned home from her aunt and uncle's home in a restless and unsettled frame of mind. Despite having seen evidence of Mr. Darcy's officious behaviour, it was difficult to fathom him going against his own father's wishes and promises to Mr. Wickham.

How could he have acted in such a malicious manner? She crossed her arms and stamped her foot as she considered his inexcusable conduct.

She sat on her bed and picked up her pillow, wrapping her arms tightly about it. She knew Mr. Bingley and Mr. Darcy had met at Cambridge, but she wondered how such a strong friendship between them continued. Was there something beyond Mr. Darcy's assisting his friend in some of his classes while at Cambridge?

Was Mr. Bingley aware of what Mr. Darcy had done to Mr. Wickham? Her eyes widened as she pondered how Mr. Bingley felt about Mr. Darcy's interference in regard to *herself.* Did Mr. Darcy have some sort of control over him?

She fell back on the bed, causing a rattle. She winced as she hoped it would not waken anyone, but a moment later there was a tap on her door.

She rolled over and looked up. "Come in," she said.

The door opened, and Jane walked in. "I wondered if you were awake. I wanted to know if we could talk."

Elizabeth sat up. "Of course! You may have been gone a few months, but nothing has changed between us. I welcome your visits any time." She tilted her head and looked at her. "What is on your mind?"

Tears came to Jane's eyes. "Oh, Lizzy, I am not quite certain what I should do."

Elizabeth reached out and took her hand. "What is it?"

Jane wiped away a tear that rolled down her cheek, and then began fingering her handkerchief. She drew in a deep breath. "It is Mr. Marshall. I began to realize on our journey here that he and I are very different." She cast her eyes down. "And then tonight, while playing the games at Aunt and Uncle Philips's, I found him to be so..."

Elizabeth smiled. "Intent on winning?"

Jane nodded and let out a nervous laugh. "Almost ruthless in his desire to win." She shook her head. "While he is a very kind and proper gentleman, he has some..." Jane paused and shrugged. "I do not know why I now have so many doubts." She lifted her hands in frustration. "But I just do."

"Jane, there are times we can only listen to our heart and believe what it is telling us, even if we are not certain why."

Jane nodded. "I do not know what to do. He came all this way with me..."

"Jane, there is no understanding between you, is there?"

Jane shook her head and wiped her tears again.

"Then all is good in that respect." Elizabeth clasped her sister's hand. "But Jane, there is something I must tell you. You may not fully understand at first, but it is imperative that you not say anything to anyone else about your doubts. Not just yet."

"But I need to let him know."

"Yes, but you must wait a little while longer."

"Why?"

Elizabeth pressed her lips tightly together and looked at Jane intently. "Apparently Mr. Collins has come to Longbourn with the intention of selecting one of us for his wife."

Jane's eyes widened. "He has? How do you know?"

Elizabeth sighed. "Kitty and Lydia overheard him speaking with Mamma. Fortunately, our dear mother informed him that you and I were *almost* engaged, and he would need to look elsewhere. When Mother suggested Mary, he did not seem particularly interested, but Jane, I believe she would be ideal for him. Of course, Kitty and Lydia are adamant *they* will not have him."

"So you and I are spared because of Mr. Bingley and Mr.

Marshall?"

Elizabeth nodded and then tilted her head, looking at her sister with a twinkle in her eyes. "Do you think perhaps I can help Mr. Collins see Mary in a different light?"

"He did spend a good amount of time with her today."

"Yes, he did. I gave her a little advice on how to gain his interest and make herself a little more attractive to him."

"Did you? Did she welcome your advice?"

Elizabeth let out a breathy chuckle. "Surprisingly enough, she did, but reluctantly. Jane, you are by far the prettiest of all of us, and I had readily noticed how often our cousin's gaze went to you when he first arrived. If there was any indication that you and Mr. Marshall were not on the path to an engagement, I believe he would shift his attentions back onto you."

"So what should I do?"

Elizabeth shrugged. "The Netherfield Ball is only a few days away. Let us wait until then. I plan to transform Mary into a most desirable looking young lady that night and hope it will be all that is needed to secure his affections."

Jane pursed her lips in a smile. "Oh, Lizzy, only you would think of doing such a thing. I would have never thought of trying to convince Mr. Collins that Mary is for him."

Elizabeth's brows narrowed. "Jane, it will not be *me* influencing him! Heavens, it will be Mary herself."

Jane leaned over and kissed her sister on the cheek. "You are the dearest sister one could ever have." She walked towards the door, and then turned back. "Mr. Marshall is pleasant enough that I am certain I can enjoy his company a little longer."

"Just do not accept an offer if he makes one!" Elizabeth whispered with a laugh as Jane walked out and closed the door.

Elizabeth suddenly frowned and slowly shook her head. "My trying to influence Mr. Collins's affections is not at all similar to Mr. Darcy trying to influence his friend!" She drew in a breath. "Not in the slightest!"

~~*

For several nights, Elizabeth slept fitfully. The account Mr.

Wickham had given her concerning Mr. Darcy, as well as wondering about Mr. Bingley, Jane, and Mr. Marshall, weighed on her mind. She also fretted whether there was anything she could do to help Mary attract Mr. Collins's attention. She tossed and turned, pounded her pillow, and got up and paced into the early hours of the morning. Nothing helped her form any conclusive answers for any of her concerns.

A few days later, Mr. Marshall set off to meet his friends in southern Hertfordshire with the promise that he would return the day before the Netherfield Ball.

Once he departed, Mrs. Bennet began to question Jane persistently about his intentions and whether she believed he would be asking for her hand when he returned.

Elizabeth felt sorry for her sister, as she could readily see the distress apparent on her face. She gave her smiles of encouragement, for she hoped she would say nothing about her reservations, especially when Mr. Collins was sitting nearby. *Just a little while longer, Jane.* She turned to see Mary seated close to Mr. Collins, but unfortunately, they were not conversing. *Will Mr. Collins ever see how perfect Mary is for him?*

Later that afternoon, Elizabeth inquired whether anyone wanted to walk with her. It was an unusually warm November day, and the sunshine beckoned her.

Jane was tired and said she preferred to stay at home. Lydia and Kitty agreed to go with her but only so far as the path that would take them into Meryton.

Neither Mary nor Mr. Collins wished to join her, as they had both become quite fatigued when they had walked with everyone to Meryton.

Once Elizabeth and the two youngest sisters had left the house, it grew very quiet. Jane concentrated on stitching a small piece of needlework, Mrs. Bennet rocked in her chair resting her eyes, Mary sat in a far corner reading, and Mr. Collins had repaired to his chamber. When there was a knock on the door, Mrs. Bennet was startled awake.

"Who can that be?" she asked, fluttering her hands. "We were not expecting anyone." She looked at Jane. "Are we expecting anyone?"

Jane shrugged. "I cannot say."

She suddenly frowned. "Oh, dear. What if it is Mr. Bingley? I am certain it must be Mr. Bingley! With Elizabeth gone, what are we to do?"

"Mother," Jane replied calmly. "We do not know who it is, but if perchance it is Mr. Bingley, we can still invite him in and visit with him." Jane ran her hand over her dress to smooth it. "Besides, I should like to get to know him a little better."

"Yes, but it would be so much better if Lizzy were here!"

A maid stepped in and announced Mr. Bingley.

The young man stepped in, and Mrs. Bennet welcomed him warmly. "What a pleasant surprise, Mr. Bingley. We are glad you have come, but unfortunately, Lizzy has gone out for a walk. Perhaps if you stay long enough, she will return." She waved her hands through the air. "Or perhaps if you set out directly, you can catch her." She shook her head. "But then, I do not know where she was planning to go."

Mr. Bingley smiled. "She does enjoy walking. I had not planned to stay long, but... since Miss Elizabeth is not here, perhaps I can get to know Miss Bennet better." He looked at Jane and smiled. "If you do not mind."

Jane returned his smile. "I do not mind at all."

"That would be splendid," Mrs. Bennet said cheerfully. "Mr. Marshall departed this morning for a few days to visit friends. With him away, I am certain Jane would welcome any company." She extended her hand inviting the gentleman to sit.

Mr. Bingley sat down and clasped his hands. Turning to Jane, he asked, "Are you enjoying being home, Miss Bennet?"

Jane nodded. "Yes, indeed. I missed everyone, although my aunt and uncle are very dear to me and it was a delight to travel with them."

He smiled broadly. "I am certain they enjoyed their time with you, as well."

"Oh, they most certainly did!" Mrs. Bennet exclaimed. "Jane is the sweetest girl and never causes any trouble." She shook her head. "I know Mr. Marshall has enjoyed getting to know her and most likely misses her already."

Jane blushed. "I am certain he is enjoying visiting with his friends, Mamma."

"He seems an amiable gentleman," Bingley said. "Although I only met him briefly in Meryton."

"Oh, he is, he is!" Mrs. Bennet said. "We are delighted with him and so pleased that Jane seems to have become an object of his admiration."

Jane's cheeks turned rosy. "Please, Mamma."

Bingley looked around him and then back to Jane. "I have enjoyed getting to know your sister, Miss Elizabeth, as well. She is lively, witty, and such delightful company." He laughed. "And she loves to walk!"

Jane chuckled. "That she does. She loves to read, as well. She takes after our father in that regard. If she finds herself with any idle time, she immediately picks up a book." She inclined her head. "She has learnt a lot about the world that way."

"And are you and your sister alike?"

"No, we are not," Jane said with a smile. "While we are as close as any two sisters could be, we are quite different. I do not have such a voracious desire to read, I am content to walk if only to spend time with her, and I am much more… subdued." Jane let out a breathy sigh. "I regret that I am not like her at all."

Bingley laughed, and his eyes sparkled. "Miss Bennet, there is no reason to feel any regret over the differences between you and your sister." He looked down and smiled. "I must confess that I am not as good a reader as I ought to be." He shook his head. "I know I ought to read more than I do, but I find there are so many other things I prefer to do."

Jane smiled. "Then you ought to do the things which you prefer."

"Yes, but my friend Darcy claims a person should always make time to read a good book to improve their mind."

"I have heard about Mr. Darcy, but have not yet met him," Jane said. "Lizzy said he had ridden into Meryton with you the other day. I did not notice him, and apparently he did not stop to be introduced."

Mr. Bingley's face clouded. "I cannot account for it. He is always so very proper."

"I am certain he had his reasons," Jane said.

Mr. Bingley leaned in towards her. "Yes, those were my thoughts precisely."

At length, Mrs. Bennet cleared her throat and said, "Mr. Bingley, I wish to thank you again for your generous hospitality towards our Lizzy when she stayed at Netherfield. She could not stop talking about how kindly she was treated and how she was made to feel so comfortable."

"It was our pleasure," he replied. "I know…"

"She has assured us that she experienced no ill treatment. She was quite at ease being there and owes it all to you… and your sisters."

"I am greatly relieved to hear that." His voice held a hint of laughter, and his eyes shone with amusement as he turned to look at Jane. "I would be terribly distraught if she felt she had been treated poorly."

"She could not stop talking about how kind and generous everyone was," Mrs. Bennet added. "She was…"

"Mother, I am certain Mr. Bingley is assured of her gratitude," Jane interjected. "And yours."

"We were happy to do it. The rains that day were ferocious!" Bingley looked at Jane. "We have had quite a bit of rainy weather since I moved here in September. Did you have much rain while touring the Lake District?"

"We had some rain, but we were there long enough to have had many pleasant days, as well." Jane looked down as her hand ran across the fabric of her dress. "We could not complain about the rainy days at all."

"Oh, but I am certain you did not endure what we did here!" Mrs. Bennet cried. "For three straight days no one could venture out. And then the day Lizzy went to Netherfield, I thought for sure our home would be washed away in a flood!"

"Was it truly that bad?" she looked from her mother to Mr. Bingley.

He nodded. "The roads were getting quite impassable as Darcy, Hurst, and I returned from being with the officers in Meryton. I am grateful Darcy suggested to me that we have Miss Elizabeth remain at Netherfield for the night."

"Yes, that was very wise," Jane said.

They further discussed Jane's trip to the Lake District, with Mr. Bingley expressing his desire to see it, as he had never been there.

There was silence in the room for a moment, and then Mr. Bingley said, "Oh, I almost forgot the reason I came. I wanted to offer my carriage to you the night of the ball. I know that with nine people, it would be impossible to fit into your carriage, and I thought it might help to have another one at your disposal."

"Oh, Mr. Bingley," Mrs. Bennet waved her handkerchief through the air. "That is so kind and generous of you. I do not think any of us even considered how we would get to Netherfield in our finest attire in only one carriage. You are too kind."

Jane looked at him and smiled. "Thank you, Mr. Bingley."

He drew in a slow breath. "You are very welcome, but the idea was actually…" He did not finish. "I am pleased to be able to do it."

"On many occasions we have squeezed all seven of us into the carriage, have we not, Jane? But nine?" Mrs. Bennet winced. "It is very good of you, sir."

Standing, he brushed off his breeches and gave a quick bow. "Again, there is no need to thank me, but I fear I have taken up too much of your time. Thank you both for allowing me to visit."

"Oh, there is no need to leave so soon. Lizzy ought to return shortly," Jane suggested.

He quickly sat back down. "If you insist. I do believe I can stay a little longer." He turned to Jane. "Tell me, Miss Bennet, what is your favourite thing to do in the neighbourhood?"

Chapter 12

Elizabeth set out towards the path that would take her to Oakham Mount as her two sisters hurried ahead. When they reached the road that would take them into Meryton, she called goodbye to them, but they were so engaged in giggling and talking, she doubted they heard her. As she looked up at the hill, she suddenly changed her mind.

When she told Mr. Darcy about the stream between Meryton and the Gouldings' home, she realized she had only walked there a few times in the four years since that fateful day. It was not terribly far, and she decided that was where she wanted to go. She hurried along, eager to enjoy some time walking along the stream in the warmth of the sun.

Despite looking forward to a little respite from her thoughts, her mind played Wickham's words over and over as she walked. With each recitation of his accusations, she grew angrier at Mr. Darcy. Her steps became more forceful, and she clenched her fists and jaw. She occasionally let out a frustrated moan and kicked an innocent rock lying on the path.

"How could he have behaved in such a despicable manner?" she asked aloud. She could not determine any sound reason for him doing so, other than to exert his authority over Mr. Wickham and make his life miserable. *He either wants to run your life or ruin it*, was what he had said. She fully agreed!

She shook her head as she again contemplated the friendship between Mr. Darcy and Mr. Bingley. They were so completely different, and she wondered if Mr. Darcy had some self-serving control over his friend. Was Mr. Bingley so naïve and easily persuadable that it was possible he was not even aware of Mr. Darcy's power over him?

She pondered whether it had something to do with Miss Bingley, that perhaps there was an understanding between her and Mr. Darcy. "No, that cannot be," she said. "Mr. Collins said he is to marry his cousin."

She came to an abrupt stop when a new thought crossed her mind. "If he has no qualms going against his father's wishes, he certainly would not think twice about going against the wishes of his mother, especially as it was expressed by her in his infancy!"

She thought about that for a moment and then let out a sigh. Truth be told, she would likely not abide by her parents' wishes regarding an engagement they had arranged when she was born. She pursed her lips and shook her head as she considered she would certainly not agree to it if her mother had expressed the wish, although she might consider it if her father had, for she trusted his good judgement.

She puffed out a breath and stopped when she came within sight of the stream. It seemed to have an almost magical effect over her, replacing her ire with calm. She hurried over and began walking just along the edge of the stream, far enough from the water so she would not get her feet wet.

The clear blue water flowed briskly, with small white rapids appearing as it cascaded over large boulders. It playfully splashed and gurgled as it made its way towards the stone bridge that arched across it downstream.

She slowly shook her head as she pondered how circumstances concerning both Mr. Bingley and Mr. Marshall had turned out quite differently than either she or Jane had anticipated. She winced as she considered that she had not yet told Jane she was uncertain whether Mr. Bingley was suited for her. It was probably the only thing she had ever kept from her. She did not know why she had not told her, other than wanting to make certain no one came to know of it – especially her mother and Mr. Collins. She bit her lip as she considered that it was also possibly due to her concern that Jane would likely not understand. Mr. Bingley was, after all, a kind, handsome, and most proper gentleman.

As she slowly meandered on, the fallen, dried leaves crunched underfoot. She occasionally picked up a thin, smooth rock and skipped it across the water, smiling as she realized she was no longer kicking them. The soft gurgling of the meandering stream helped soothe her anxious thoughts.

She was almost to the bridge and had reached the large tree that four years ago had been filled with beautiful blossoms. Today, however, it held a small remnant of brown leaves; most had already fallen to the ground. At least she would not be tempted to lean the bridge over and watch the blossoms as they sailed down the river. She would be safe from falling in.

She continued on towards the bridge, stepping carefully to avoid the larger rocks scattered along the shore. Just before she reached the bridge, she stopped, immersed one hand into the frigid water, and sent the water splashing, laughing as she did.

"I would be content with my lot in life if I had a stream like this running past my home." She turned and looked in the direction of the Gouldings' home. "It is unfortunate that young Mr. Goulding married someone else," she said with a laugh. She shook her head and winced. "Not that I would have married him solely to have my own stream!"

When she reached the stone bridge, she walked up to its centre and braced her arms on the wide ledge, looking out. She let out a long sigh, turned around, and sat on the ledge. Then, very deftly and discreetly, she swung her legs around so they dangled over the water.

"I could sit here forever," she said, as the sunlight glistened on the blue water. The swiftly moving stream provided a melodious lapping that was as pleasant to her ears as an orchestra playing. She closed her eyes, swung her feet, and swayed as if she were dancing.

The sound of a horse approaching startled her, and as she turned to look in its direction, her foot came back too strongly against the bridge, and her shoe dropped off into the water. She gasped when she felt it come off, while at the same time seeing that it was Mr. Darcy approaching. She quickly looked back in dismay to see that her shoe had been picked up by the current and was floating away.

"Oh!" she said as she pounded her fists into her lap, and then instantly regretted it.

"Are you in distress?"

Elizabeth felt a tremor pass through her and steeled herself momentarily before turning back to acknowledge him. She could not believe that she encountered him again, in such a distressing state. She turned and saw him tether his horse and begin walking towards her.

"Nothing out of the ordinary, I assure you."

Darcy laughed. "Are you so inclined to tempt fate?" He shook his head as he came and stood at her side, looking out over the water.

Elizabeth shook her head. "I have no intention of falling in," she said as she tried to tuck her now shoeless foot under the folds of her dress. "I am merely enjoying the stream on this beautiful day." She narrowed her eyes as she looked up at him "What are you doing here?"

"If you recall, you are the one who told me about the place. I thought I would come and see it for myself."

Elizabeth shrugged. "I suppose I did."

"I am rather surprised you are here." He sat down on the ledge of the bridge.

She was grateful he was now facing the other way so he would not notice her shoeless foot. "Why does it surprise you that I am here?" she asked.

"Perhaps I am not so much surprised, but I did not expect to see you. I can assure you, however, that Bingley is likely disappointed."

"Why would Mr. Bingley be disappointed?"

"He was on his way to Longbourn. I assume he was going to call on you."

Elizabeth readily noticed the catch in his voice. She could not pass up this opportunity to let Mr. Darcy know how disappointed she was in not seeing his friend. "Oh, dear, I am so sorry to have missed him, but I am certain he is enjoying his visit with my family." She could only hope this was true, and she stole a glance up at him, seeing the slight grimace she had expected to see. "And you chose not to accompany him?"

Darcy shook his head. "I was reading when he took his leave, and he knows I do not like to be disturbed when I am reading. I imagine he decided to go on without me." He looked at her intently. "Bingley reads so little himself. It is a shame. He prefers to be off and about doing something rather than taking time to improve himself by extensive reading."

Elizabeth stiffened, but checked her responses and her tongue. He was continuing one of his tactics to try to convince her that Mr. Bingley was not suitable for her. He apparently had not been able to talk his friend out of the attachment, so he was trying to change her mind. She would not give him the satisfaction!

"Ah, but how considerate it was of Mr. Bingley not to disturb you. He is one of the kindest, most thoughtful gentlemen I know." She then cast a frustrated glance towards the swiftly moving water.

"Is something wrong?"

Elizabeth let out an exasperated sigh as she considered telling him *he* was wrong. Wrong for showing up when he did, wrong for attempting to control people's lives, and wrong for trying to convince her Mr. Bingley was not suitable for her. He was correct in that regard, but she would not give him the satisfaction of agreeing with him. Instead, she turned and pointed downstream. "My shoe…"

Mr. Darcy propped his hands on his hips and let out a laugh. "Did you lose a shoe in the stream?"

Elizabeth rolled her eyes, nodding as she did.

"Miss Bennet, do you often find yourself in such predicaments?"

Was he laughing at her? He must consider her a fool – or perhaps an awkward and clumsy simpleton. She steeled herself and looked up at him.

"No, Mr. Darcy. It is not often – it is on an almost daily basis!" He thought poorly of her already; she did not mind sinking further in his estimation.

"Well, it is a good thing I brought my horse. I had intended to walk but thought that in the unlikely case I got lost coming here, the horse would serve me better."

When Elizabeth looked at him blankly, he added, "You certainly cannot walk all the way back with only one shoe." He shook his head, and a slight smile appeared. "Without my horse, I would have to carry you." He lifted a single brow. "I do not think you would want me to carry you all the way back to Longbourn, would you?"

Elizabeth swallowed to rid her mouth of the sudden dryness. She shook her head emphatically. "No, that would not do at all!" She turned on the ledge and let herself down. "Ouch!"

"Now what has happened, Miss Bennet?"

She lifted her food and exclaimed, "I stepped on a rock." She let out a huff. "It is nothing serious, I assure you."

Mr. Darcy extended his arm. "Allow me to assist you to the horse."

Elizabeth did not wish to be indebted to him and hesitated to take it. "I can manage, thank you." With that, she limped to the end of the bridge, with an occasional soft moan of pain.

Darcy went to his horse and brought it to her. "You do know how to ride, do you not?"

"I... Yes, however I am not particularly fond of riding."

He chuckled. "Is that so? I had not expected that." He shook his head.

Elizabeth propped her hands on her waist. "And why is that?"

"I... I actually love the exhilaration of riding." He paused and looked at her intently. "I would have thought you would, as well."

"No, but then the horses we own have not provided me with particularly enjoyable experiences."

"Well, then, if you would prefer not to ride, I can always carry you..."

"No!" Elizabeth said, a little too forcefully, as his smile broadened. "No, thank you, I shall ride."

"Allow me to assist you up." He turned, and before she could protest, he lifted her up to onto the saddle. He then reached down and gently took her stockinged foot in his hands.

"What are you doing?" Elizabeth tried to pull her foot away but could not remove it from his grasp.

"I am checking to see if it was injured when you stepped on the rock."

The warmth of his hands encircling her foot erased any rational thought from entering her mind, especially when he pressed his thumb against it.

"Is that where it hurts?"

Elizabeth mutely nodded. "But I only... as you said, I only stepped on a rock."

"It is not bleeding." He rubbed it a little more and then suddenly stopped, letting out a huff and giving his head a shake. "There. It will likely be tender for a few days, but I doubt you will have much problem with it."

"Thank you," she said softly, her face feeling warmer than it should.

"I will lead the horse, so you need not fear that he will gallop away. Mercury can be as wild as a stallion when I give him full rein, but he will carry you as gently as a lamb." Darcy leaned in. "As long as you behave properly."

"Behave properly?" Elizabeth asked with indignation.

Darcy crossed his arms and looked up at her. "As long as you do not kick him or startle him in any way." He gave her a condescending smile.

Elizabeth let out a huff. She did not like being at the mercy of Mr. Darcy but decided that as she needed his assistance in getting home, she should not irritate him and would not bring up the subject of Mr. Wickham. There was enough time later for her to let loose her accusations.

They made their way back to Longbourn in silence, with Darcy walking ahead holding the reins. She was surprised at how kindly he was treating her. She did not feel as much disapproval from him, which was unexpected.

At length, she thought of something she could bring up as conversation and was eager to see his reaction. "Mr. Darcy, my cousin arrived recently from Kent."

Darcy turned back. "Did he?"

"Yes," she said, with as much indifference as she could produce. "He is the clergyman in a small village called Hunsford." She lifted her brow to see how he responded.

There was a hint of surprise in his features, and he studied her with a slightly lowered brow, as if to see what more she might say.

"He claims that your aunt, Lady Catherine de Bourgh, is his patroness." She laughed. "It is a small world, is it not?"

Darcy looked down at the reins and began running them through his fingers. "So it would seem. And what... Did he say anything about her?"

"Oh, yes! He cannot stop speaking about your aunt, Rosings,

the gardens..." Elizabeth paused.

Darcy stopped abruptly, and his chest heaved as he drew in a deep breath. "I hope... I hope he only had good things to say."

Elizabeth's eyes widened. "Do you have reason to suppose he might have adverse things to say?"

He shifted his weight from one foot to another as it appeared he pondered his response. "I would have no idea what my aunt's clergyman might have to say about her. I... I have not yet met him."

Elizabeth laughed. "Well, you have no need to worry, Mr. Darcy. My cousin is very effusive about how generous and affable your aunt is, how great her home is – especially all the chimneys and window coverings – and..." She could not stifle a chuckle. "How delighted he was that she had already approved both of his discourses which he had preached to her."

Darcy shook his head as he pressed his lips into an amused smile. "I am pleased; it sounds as though they are both satisfied with their arrangement." He turned back and began leading the horse again.

"Yes, he seems to be, at least." She paused briefly and fixed her gaze on him. "And he had only the most favourable things to say about her daughter." Elizabeth was rewarded with a look of apprehension when he turned back to her.

"He mentioned Anne? What did he say about her?"

"Oh, I cannot recollect all he said, other than she is a charming young lady, most amiable, and drives a little phaeton pulled by ponies." She lifted a brow as he seemed placated and then turned back.

She wanted to question him about his engagement to Miss de Bourgh but thought better of it. She was now content to proceed in silence, as was he. She shook her head as she considered that her reputation with Mr. Bingley and Mr. Darcy was likely settled in stone as each had encountered her in at least one predicament. Mr. Bingley did not seem to mind, but she was certain Mr. Darcy thought her actions quite unfitting for a young lady, having had to rescue her twice.

As they drew near to Longbourn, Elizabeth called out to Mr. Darcy.

"If you please, would you lead the horse over to the grass? From there I can readily walk to the house without too much distress on my foot."

He did as she asked and then walked over to help her down.

She put up her hand to stay him. "I can easily slide down, thank you."

He shook his head. "And land on your sore foot? I think not." He lifted his hands. "Please, allow me."

Elizabeth reluctantly leaned forward and soon felt his arms about her waist, bringing her slowly and gently to the ground. When her sore foot came down, she winced and lifted it slightly, causing her to sway to one side. Darcy quickly steadied her with his hands on her shoulders.

"Take care, Miss Bennet." He drew in a breath. "I shall not always be nearby to rescue you."

She unwittingly shuddered as she met his intense gaze. "Yes, well... thank you." She turned and began to limp away as quickly as she could towards the house. She felt her racing pulse and pressed her hand to her neck, feeling its warmth. She did not understand these unexpected feelings that had suddenly and inexplicably surfaced, but more than anything, she was not pleased with them.

She could almost say she had begun to think well of him and had rather enjoyed his gallantry. *Almost.*

She gave her head a shake as she had to forcefully remind herself how much she disliked him and how much he wanted to control people's lives. What she observed today was not at all who he really was! She had to remember what he had done to Mr. Wickham!

Chapter 13

Impatience reigned in the Bennet household as they waited for the Netherfield Ball. Days of inclement weather prevented them from going out, and Mrs. Bennet fretted that if the downpour did not let up, Mr. Marshall would likely not make it back in time to attend.

The ladies spent their idle time choosing which gowns they would wear, how they could alter them to appear new and improved, and what they could do differently with their hair. Kitty and Lydia could not stop talking about the officers who would be at the ball, and Mary frequently questioned Elizabeth about whether she thought Mr. Collins found her attractive or what more she could do to draw his attention to her.

After Elizabeth's encounter with Mr. Darcy, she was grateful she was thinking more sensibly about him, pushing aside those feelings that had unexpectedly stirred within her that day. She needed only to call to mind how he had officiously treated Mr. Wickham and was currently treating Mr. Bingley. What he had done in coming to her aid that day was all that was proper and kind, but he had only done what any gentleman would have done.

While she knew it was imperative she begin discouraging Mr. Bingley's attentions, she hoped an opportunity might present itself for her to speak with him about George Wickham first. She wondered if he knew anything about the acrimonious relationship between Mr. Wickham and his friend. She had hoped to meet with either of those two men again before the ball to possibly discover more, but the rains had prevented it.

She smiled as she thought of how amusing it would be to watch

Mr. Wickham and Mr. Darcy at the ball to see what – if anything – would transpire between them.

It seemed that Mrs. Bennet's fears about Mr. Marshall came to pass, for despite a slight let-up in the rain, he did not arrive the day before the ball. She was certain some dreadful accident must have occurred on a dark, lonely road, and no one would find him before it was too late.

He finally arrived the afternoon of the ball, quite apologetic, but assuring them he was well, had suffered no mishap, and was looking forward to an enjoyable evening of music and dancing.

There were several anxious and fretful moments in the ladies' quarters as the time drew near to depart for Netherfield. Kitty and Lydia wondered if their gowns would stand out as striking. Up until the last minute, they were making alterations by adding or removing ribbons or lace. Mary fretted over whether she would look better with her hair in one style or another and continually sought Elizabeth's advice. Mrs. Bennet could not decide whether one piece of jewellery would best suit her gown and enhance her appearance, or if another would be more flattering. Jane and Elizabeth were the only two who seemed to be content with their gowns, hair, and jewellery.

Elizabeth walked into Mary's room and found her simply staring into the mirror, shaking her head. "There is nothing to be done, Lizzy. While Mr. Collins has been attentive to me, he has certainly not given me any indication that he has any real affection for me."

Elizabeth placed her hands on her sister's shoulders and looked into the mirror at her. "Then you must let him know where your interest lies." She bit her lip. "Stand up, Mary, and let me see you in your gown."

Mary stood up, although her shoulders sagged and her head drooped.

"No, you must stand tall and erect." Elizabeth pulled her sister's shoulders back. "You must carry yourself like you know you are a beautiful woman."

"But I am not a beautiful woman."

Elizabeth let out a sigh and led her to a full-length mirror. "Look at yourself in that dress. You are beautiful Mary, and if you believe that, others who look at you will believe it, as well."

Mary sat back down, and Elizabeth began to play with her hair, curling some strands and weaving ribbons through them.

"How am I to let Mr. Collins know I am interested in him? I do not know how."

"Mary, if I may be so bold, may I give you one piece of advice?"

Mary solemnly nodded.

"Smile. Smile frequently. Smile and even laugh at what he says... when it is appropriate."

"I could never..."

"Mary, the good Lord made us to laugh. It is an indication of our being joyful and well-pleased." She leaned down towards her. "I would imagine that if you smiled at Mr. Collins and let him know that you find delight in what he says, it will please him immeasurably."

"I do not always feel like smiling."

"Mary, if you do not feel like smiling, think of something that makes you smile." Elizabeth came and stood at her side. "Perhaps you can imagine being married and having a houseful of children that you are holding and rocking. You love children. Only think how that will be."

A small smile appeared on Mary's face. "That does make me smile."

"Good." Elizabeth looked away so Mary could not see the wince she made at the thought of being married to Mr. Collins, but she truly felt her sister would welcome it.

After adding a ribbon and flowers to her hair, Elizabeth stepped back. "Mary, you look beautiful, and I would imagine there will be several gentlemen who will ask you to dance with them this evening."

"Oh, I do not think so, and even if they did, I would not wish..."

Elizabeth put up her hand to stay that thought. "Mr. Collins has already expressed his intention to dance with each of us tonight, so you know you must dance at least one with him, and..." Elizabeth chuckled. "Perhaps you can accept a dance with another gentleman or two in order to promote a bit of jealousy on his part."

"Oh, Lizzy, I could not do such a thing!"

"Not intentionally, Mary, but if a man sees a lovely young lady with another man, it does make her seem more desirable to him."

Mary's eyes widened in frustration. "Must I?"

Elizabeth wagged her finger at Mary. "Indeed, you must!"

Mary began to slouch. "If you think it will help."

Elizabeth pulled back her shoulders again and gave her a hug. "I believe it will, Mary."

As they gathered downstairs, Elizabeth was eager to observe Mr. Collins when he saw Mary. She had to admit that Mary looked lovelier than she had ever seen her. Perhaps she was not as pretty as her other sisters, but Elizabeth was rather proud of her sister's successful transformation.

When Mr. Collins joined them, he greeted the others and then stopped abruptly when he saw Mary. He smiled, looked around at the others briefly, and then went to her side.

Elizabeth had to force herself not to let out a triumphant victory cry. It appeared her hard work had paid off!

~~*

Mr. Bingley's carriage was waiting as they stepped out of Longbourn. With some hints from Elizabeth, Mr. Bennet determined that Mr. Marshall, Jane, Lizzy, and he would travel in Mr. Bingley's carriage, and Mrs. Bennet, Mary, Kitty, Lydia, and Mr. Collins would ride in the Longbourn carriage.

As the two carriages made their way to Netherfield, the moon was full and bright, but small trails of clouds occasionally passed in front of it, obscuring its light. The air was cool, but fresh from the recent rains.

In the one carriage, Kitty and Lydia were their usual boisterous selves, declaring that they would dance every dance, that there would be more officers than they would be able to count, and that it would be the finest affair to ever have been held in the neighbourhood.

In the other carriage, it was mostly quiet, with Mr. Marshall answering questions about his trip to visit his friends. It was the first time since returning that he had been given the opportunity to talk about it. He had not seen these friends in five years, had grown up with them in London, and had an enjoyable time seeing them again.

When they pulled in front of Netherfield, everyone stepped out of the carriage. The candlelight glistened from every window, and several torches lit up the front of the stately home.

Mrs. Bennet let out a joyous cry of exclamation. "Heavens! It looks beautiful!" She clasped her hands tightly. "Will this not be a splendid affair?"

Mr. Bennet shook his head. "I will consider it splendid only when it is over and we are returning home."

"Papa!" exclaimed Lydia. "I do not know how you can say such a thing!"

He huffed. "Very easily, my dear. Very easily."

They greeted friends from the neighbourhood as they walked up to the stately house. Inside, candlelight bounced off the walls, and music could be heard playing in another room. Mr. Bingley, his two sisters, and Mr. Hurst stood just inside welcoming their guests as they arrived.

When the Bennets stepped up to greet them, a wide smile appeared on Mr. Bingley's face. "Good evening! It is so good to see all of you this evening." He turned to his sisters to introduce them to Jane and the two other gentlemen in their party, whom they had not yet met. As Elizabeth stepped up to him, he whispered, "May I ask that you save the first dance for me?"

"I would be pleased to, Mr. Bingley." She hoped she sounded polite but not overly eager.

As their party walked in, it was apparent that the Bingleys had hosted parties before. Everything seemed perfect, from the flowers around the room and the small orchestra, to the tables laden with an assortment of food. It *was* going to be a splendid affair!

Elizabeth looked around and readily noticed several officers in attendance, save for one in particular. She did not see Mr. Wickham. It was possible he was there, but she wondered whether he may have decided not to come. She would be so disappointed if he did not! And all due to Mr. Darcy, whom she noticed standing off in a corner of the room.

She glimpsed Charlotte and hurried over to her with outstretched arms. "Charlotte! It is so good to see you. It seems like it has been forever."

"Yes, it has. I believe I saw you last at the party we had at Lucas Lodge."

"Oh, now you make me feel terrible, Charlotte. With Jane having finally come home, I fear that I have not had the time to visit you."

"And it is just as much my fault, Lizzy. I did not feel it was right to intrude with her having just returned home."

"You need not feel that way," Elizabeth reassured her.

"No, I suppose not. Would you mind introducing me to the gentleman at her side? I have heard from my mother that she has a beau!"

Elizabeth gently patted her friend's hand. "You know how my mother likes to jump to conclusions, Charlotte. Mr. Marshall is most amiable, but Jane does not wish there to be a lot of speculation yet about the two of them."

"Much like you and Mr. Bingley?"

Elizabeth only smiled. "Come. I shall introduce you, but I must warn you. The gentleman next to Mary is our cousin, Mr. Collins, and I fear you must be introduced to him, as well."

Charlotte laughed as they walked over. "You make that sound like a warning, Lizzy."

"You might call it that, my good friend. He is… well, I shall hold my tongue."

"You? Hold your tongue?"

"To own the truth, Charlotte, we believe he is perfectly suited to Mary. He is a clergyman, and I think they would do well together."

They walked over to the two couples, and Elizabeth made the introductions.

"Miss Lucas, it is a pleasure to meet you." Mr. Marshall gave a quick bow.

"Thank you, Mr. Marshall. I hope you are enjoying your stay here."

"I am. It is a delightful neighbourhood." He smiled and said,

"Ah! I believe that the first dance is about to commence." He extended his arm towards Jane. "Shall we?"

Mr. Collins expressed his pleasure at meeting Charlotte, as well, and then hurried Mary off to the dance floor.

Elizabeth turned to see Mr. Bingley walking over. "Miss Bennet, I am here to claim our first dance!"

"Certainly, Mr. Bingley." She sent Charlotte an apologetic look for leaving her by herself.

As Elizabeth walked with Mr. Bingley to the head of the set for the dance, others gathered around. She greeted Mr. Darcy, who took his place with Miss Bingley next to them. She looked down the set and beamed with joy when she saw Mr. Collins smiling at Mary.

With a smile still on her face, she happened to glance over at Mr. Darcy. He smiled back, and Elizabeth realized he likely thought she was smiling at him. She quickly sobered her expression, more from wanting to rid herself of the thought – only a slight thought – that he was much more handsome when he smiled and when dressed in the fashionable, formal attire he was wearing. She looked towards the orchestra, hoping they would begin soon. She needed to keep his true character foremost in her mind.

As the dance began, Mr. Bingley took Elizabeth's hands, and she complimented him on the success of the ball.

"I thank you," he said. "I owe much to my sisters, who planned everything. I care little for all the details, and they are more than willing to make the decisions."

"I see," she replied.

"I was sorry to have missed you the other day when I visited Longbourn."

"Yes, I heard you stopped by. I apparently returned from my walk just after you left."

They separated, and Elizabeth found herself taking Mr. Darcy's hand briefly. "It is good to see you, Miss Bennet. Have you had any need of being rescued lately?"

His smile was more like a teasing smirk; at least, she believed that was his intention.

"You will be pleased to know that I have not, but only because the rains kept me indoors."

Darcy nodded. "Good for the rain."

They parted, and it appeared that Bingley was continuing his conversation with her.

"But I had a delightful conversation with your mother and your elder sister."

"They enjoyed their time with you, as well, and Jane said she enjoyed getting to know you."

"Did she say that? I am glad."

Elizabeth noticed Mary and Mr. Collins, who were just on the other side of Jane and Mr. Marshall. It was apparent that Mr. Collins had taken a wrong step and collided with the person next to him.

Mary did not seem to be dismayed by it at all, which made Elizabeth smile. She suddenly had a thought and turned to Mr. Bingley when they came back together.

"Would you mind if I asked you a favour?"

"Not at all!" he said joyfully.

"Would you please ask my sister Mary to dance when she has finished with Mr. Collins? She rarely gets asked, and... I think it would be nice."

"I would be delighted to!" His face lit up in a smile, "In fact, I shall ask *all* your sisters to dance!"

"Well, I fear Kitty and Lydia likely have the remaining dances already spoken for, but you can certainly try."

"I shall do just that!"

When the dance ended, Elizabeth watched as Mr. Bingley walked over to Mary and asked her to dance. Mr. Collins, who stood by her, appeared somewhat surprised, but when Mary and Mr. Bingley stood up together for the dance, she readily detected a furrowed brow.

Mr. Collins then hurried over to Jane and asked for her hand in the next set, prompting Mr. Marshall to walk over to Elizabeth.

"It appears we are both without partners," he said. "Did I comprehend correctly what just happened, and that you asked Mr. Bingley to dance with Miss Mary?"

Elizabeth widened her eyes in mock innocence and smiled. "You would charge me with doing something as scheming as that?"

"Never, but if you like, I shall ask her to dance, as well."

"Would you? That would please me to no end."

"And perhaps make Mr. Collins a little jealous?"

Elizabeth gave a guilty nod. "You are quite perceptive, Mr. Marshall."

He laughed. "Not really. Miss Bennet informed me of your plans for Miss Mary and Mr. Collins."

"Ah, I see."

"Meanwhile, may I ask you to dance this one with me?"

Elizabeth smiled. "It would be my pleasure."

They took their place between her two sisters and their partners, somewhat disappointing Elizabeth, for she would not be able to quiz Mr. Marshall about his feelings with Jane nearby.

"Are you enjoying yourself, Mr. Marshall?"

"Indeed. There is nothing like a country ball in a fine manor to boost one's spirits."

"I agree," she said, but wondered why his spirits needed boosting. "You are fortunate you were away from Longbourn this week, as a household of females stuck indoors because of the rains and planning their attire for a ball may have been overwhelming if you are not used to it."

He laughed. "I can only imagine. How does your father handle those times?"

"Have you not noticed how much time he spends in his study? That is where he finds rest and solace when our household is in an uproar."

"He has found a very practical way to handle it."

They continued to dance, with Elizabeth keeping her eye on Mary. Elizabeth was pleased with Mr. Bingley in that he conversed readily with her sister, and she often saw both of them smiling.

When the danced ended, Mr. Collins hurried to Mary's side, as if to ensure she did not dance with someone else.

Mr. Marshall bowed and thanked Elizabeth, setting off to the side of the room. She then watched Mr. Bingley approach Jane, and it was apparent he asked her to dance. She began to join Mr. Marshall, but realized he had asked Charlotte to dance.

As all couples lined up in the set to wait for the music to begin, she felt someone at her side.

"Miss Bennet?"

Elizabeth turned to face Mr. Darcy.

"Yes?"

"As it seems you are without a partner, may I have the next dance?"

She was rather surprised he solicited *her* hand and was momentarily without words. Finally, she said, "I... thank you." She could endure one set with him, but she was suspicious of his motives for asking her. She surmised that during their dance, he intended to try to convince her out of any feelings she might have for Mr. Bingley. She swallowed and squared her shoulders, as if defying him to try.

She realized, however, that with Mr. Collins paying so much attention to Mary, she might have to continue with this charade for only a day or two more. She let out a soft sigh, however, as she considered the only reason she would wish to continue feigning a strong admiration for Mr. Bingley was to spite Mr. Darcy and Miss Bingley.

As the prelude to the music began, Mr. Darcy walked Elizabeth over to the set. When he placed them as far away from Mr. Bingley as possible, she was certain it was so he could speak to her without his friend overhearing.

She noticed Miss Bingley's rather surprised and irritated glance at the two of them. Elizabeth thought she looked more disappointed that they were dancing rather than delighted that Mr. Darcy would likely take advantage of the opportunity to discourage her affections towards Mr. Bingley.

As Mr. Darcy had only danced with Mr. Bingley's sisters since coming into Hertfordshire, Elizabeth wondered whether Miss Bingley was feeling jealousy rather than partnership with him in his manipulative endeavour. Elizabeth laughed to herself. At least this was an easy way to irritate Miss Bingley.

As the music began, and they took their initial steps towards one another, Darcy appeared content to merely watch her and seemed uninterested in talking. This was fine with Elizabeth, except she was certain he was trying to formulate an argument against his friend that she would not be able to counter.

Darcy finally spoke. "Your sister appears happy to be home."

"She is," Elizabeth said. "As am I that she has returned."

"Are the two of you close?"

They parted briefly, and when they came back together, Elizabeth said, "Indeed, we are. She is a wonderful sister and friend, and is the perfect example of a proper young lady."

"She seems pleasant."

"Yes. Jane has the good fortune of being exceptionally beautiful, gracious, and generous…" The sound of Lydia laughing boisterously drew Elizabeth's attention.

"But sadly, she has the misfortune to have two younger sisters who are not inclined to emulate her."

"And you?" Darcy asked as they parted again.

Elizabeth took a moment to ponder her answer. When they came back together she smiled and said, "I fear I have tried, but she is far too good for me. I have neither the ability to overlook one's faults as she does…" She looked up at him with an arched brow. "Nor the desire to do so." She hoped her arch look would make him realize she was speaking of him.

They walked down the set with his hand holding hers, and she felt him tense. Perhaps he had taken her words as she intended. When she glanced up at him, however, he was looking towards the side door.

When she turned to look in that direction, she saw that George Wickham had entered the ballroom. *He had come!* Elizabeth smiled broadly just as Darcy turned back to her with a deep scowl etched on his face.

Chapter 14

"I see Mr. Wickham has finally arrived," Elizabeth said cheerfully. "I wondered whether he would come."

Darcy lowered his brows. "You are acquainted with him?"

"We met him in Meryton the day Mr. Bingley stopped to visit. He also attended a party my aunt and uncle hosted." She stole a glance up at him. "He seems to be an amiable young man."

"That might be a matter up for debate," he replied tersely.

Elizabeth could tell his thoughts were no longer on the dance. She had rather enjoyed dancing with him because his movements were so smooth, but since Mr. Wickham's appearance, they had become abrupt and forced.

For some reason, it pleased her that he was so distressed upon seeing Mr. Wickham. She wondered if he feared his contemptible actions would be discovered now that Mr. Wickham had come into the neighbourhood.

The thought of tormenting Mr. Darcy a little more appealed to her. "Well, everyone is entitled to an opinion. I found him very gentlemanly and polite." She paused to let him ponder that for a moment and then added, "Oh, and he told us he has known you his whole life, that his father was your father's steward at Pemberley."

Darcy's face paled, and he glanced back at the man, who was now leaning against the wall staring at the two of them.

"That is correct."

They separated again, and when they came back together, she saw colour in his cheeks and a steely glare in his eyes.

"But there was something..." She shook her head. "He

mentioned that the two of you are no longer on good terms with each other."

Darcy drew in a deep breath and then let it out through clenched teeth. He and Elizabeth stood opposite each other as the dance came to an end, and she wondered if he would say anything to her in his defence.

Instead, Darcy gave a short bow, and Elizabeth followed with a slight curtsey. He took the few steps to stand before her and extended his arm to escort her away from the dance floor. "I am certain that Mr. Wickham has many grievances against me, but allow me to say that the man may not be all he appears to be."

"Are any of us truly who we appear to be, Mr. Darcy?" She gave him a tight smile, thanked him for the dance, and turned to walk away indignantly.

~~*

Darcy watched in disappointment as Elizabeth walked away. He had hoped to engage her in conversation that might endear himself to her, but he felt he had failed miserably. It could not have gone worse. When Wickham entered the ballroom, he could not conjure up any thought other than confronting him about being there. Perhaps that was as it should be. He should not be entertaining thoughts about the young lady his good friend admired.

He glanced about the room again, but no longer saw Wickham. He needed something to drink and walked to the table laden with food and beverage. As he did, Miss Bingley came up to him.

"Mr. Darcy, during your dance, I hope you were able to discourage Miss Elizabeth in her attentions towards my brother," she said in a fervent whisper. "I greatly fear he is about to ask for her hand!"

Darcy turned sharply to her. "Why do you suspect that?"

Miss Bingley's eyes widened. "Because he is constantly humming and wearing a smile." She shook her head and groaned. "Did you say anything to her?"

Darcy took his drink and downed it. "The subject of Bingley did not come up."

"But I noticed you talking. Certainly, you felt the need to..."

"Miss Bingley, it would have been a little difficult to dissuade Miss Elizabeth from her affections towards your brother, when others were so close to us in the set!"

Miss Bingley choked back a response. "Well, I begin to feel it is too late. Look at them talking!"

Elizabeth stood in a small circle with Bingley, Jane, and Mr. Marshall. They were laughing, and it was apparent they were greatly enjoying each other's company.

"I have heard that Miss Jane Bennet and that gentleman, Mr. Marshall, have an attachment, as well. They are likely planning a double wedding."

Darcy closed his eyes. "I would hope not." He wondered if the evening could get any worse. He just had shared a miserable dance with the one woman he felt he could love and most likely already did love. He had watched in indignation as Wickham entered the ballroom. He was accosted by Miss Bingley who claimed she believed her brother was close to asking for Miss Elizabeth's hand, and then watched her laugh as her eyes danced with joy when she spoke with his good friend.

Darcy gulped. It just got worse!

He watched as Wickham, who had just reappeared, approached Elizabeth, apparently asking her to dance. As the two joined the set, Darcy felt his insides begin to churn. He could not watch this! He needed some fresh air.

"Miss Bingley, would you excuse me?" Darcy abruptly turned to step out into the courtyard, not waiting for a response.

~~*

"I thought perhaps you decided not to come," Elizabeth said as she and Wickham walked to the dance floor. "When I did not see you, I thought there was something keeping you away."

Wickham's eyes danced. "Something or *someone*, perhaps?" He laughed.

"Yes," she said. "I thought perhaps you did not want to come because *he* most certainly would be here." She nodded her head in Darcy's direction, unaware that he was no longer there.

CHANCE AND CIRCUMSTANCE

"I own that I considered it. I debated whether to come, but then decided not to forfeit a splendid evening when I have every right to be here."

"And so you do, Mr. Wickham."

The dance began, and Elizabeth was pleased that he was an excellent dancer. He was as friendly as Mr. Bingley but had a more engaging personality. She smiled as she thought he might be better suited for her than Mr. Bingley ever was.

At length, he said, "I noticed you were dancing with Mr. Darcy."

"Well, think nothing of it, Mr. Wickham. It was not an enjoyable dance, and I am quite certain he regretted the dance as much as I did."

Wickham pressed his lips together as though pondering this. "Yes," he said slowly, "but I own I was surprised to see him dancing at all. He rarely dances, and only with those whom he knows well or admires." Wickham looked at her intently, almost as if to judge her response.

Elizabeth laughed. "I suppose I could claim an acquaintance with him that might be considered more than casual, but only because of my association with Mr. Bingley."

"Ah, yes. Mr. Bingley! I have heard rumours from some of the other officers that he seems to be singling you out. I feared I might not even be able to secure a dance with you!" He winked. "I wondered whether these rumours were true."

They separated for a few moments, and Elizabeth debated whether she ought to confirm or deny this. When they came back together, she said, "It is true that Mr. Bingley has been very attentive to me, but..." She wanted so much to tell him that there was nothing between her and Mr. Bingley! "I consider him a kind and considerate gentleman."

Wickham nodded, seemingly satisfied. "And what of his friend?"

Elizabeth's smile left her face, and she shook her head. "You already know my opinion of the man and his officious behaviour. Many in the neighbourhood have expressed how rude he is and have noticed how he ignores almost everyone but Mr. Bingley and his family." She let out an exasperated huff. "I cannot see how someone so kind and generous as Mr. Bingley could have such a close friendship with someone as cruel and ruthless as Mr. Darcy!"

Wickham smiled. "It is difficult to fathom, is it not?"

The dance continued, and they spoke no more about Mr. Darcy or Mr. Bingley. Elizabeth was able to determine in the course of their conversation that he was indeed an avid reader, appreciated intelligent conversation, and even enjoyed venturing out on a good walk. She hoped that they might eventually be able to enjoy some of those things together.

When the dance ended, Elizabeth thanked Mr. Wickham, and they parted. Elizabeth did not think she had enjoyed a dance this evening as much as she had that one.

~~*

Darcy braced his hands on the back of a bench in the outer courtyard. He was grateful no one else was out there, for he was in no mood for idle conversation. He drew in several deep breaths, attempting to ease the constriction in his chest and calm his erratically beating heart. He was unsure if these troubling attacks were due to how disastrously his dance with Elizabeth had turned out or if it was due to Wickham's sudden, unexpected, and most unwelcome appearance at the ball.

He was not certain he could even step back inside with that man present! He could not fathom being in the same neighbourhood with him, let alone the same room. And dancing with Elizabeth! He kicked the leg of the bench with his foot.

"Upset about something, Darcy?"

Darcy clenched his fists and then turned to Wickham with an icy glare. "What are you doing here?"

"Do you mean here in the courtyard or here at the ball?" Wickham lifted his hands. "I believe I am entitled to be in both places. An invitation was extended to the officers."

"You, an officer!" Darcy spat out.

Wickham gloated. "The militia recognizes my qualities... unlike someone I know."

"Oh, Wickham, I recognize your qualities better than anyone."

Wickham sauntered over to where Darcy stood. "I am sure you

do." He crossed his arms and leaned back against the wall. "Speaking of qualities, I understand you have not done well here yourself in that regard."

Darcy's eyes shot up. "What nonsense is this?"

"Word is that you have not made a good impression in this neighbourhood."

Darcy groaned and turned to walk away. "I do not need to listen to your poor attempts to discredit my name."

Wickham began to rub his chin. "No, but I thought perhaps you might be interested in what Miss Elizabeth Bennet had to say about you." He let a satisfied smile touch his lips when Darcy stopped.

He slowly turned back.

"Yes, I noticed the two of you dancing. You rarely dance, Darcy. I was surprised."

"It is none of your business with whom I dance," Darcy asserted.

"But I am curious. Were you dancing with her to talk her out of this attachment with your friend..." He paused. "Or, could it be that she is someone you have come to deeply admire?" He turned his eyes towards the ballroom. "I have to say she is quite the beauty."

Darcy's eyes widened, and he instantly regretted it.

"Oh, Darcy, I can read you so well." Wickham chuckled, a sneer appearing. "Would you care to hear Miss Elizabeth's opinion of you?"

"I am certain Miss Elizabeth has no opinion of me," he grumbled.

"Oh, I beg to differ," Wickham taunted him. "She was quite... effusive in her opinion of you." He gave a soft, malicious laugh. "If I recall... Yes! She said you were officious, rude, cruel, and..." He paused as he counted these off on his fingers. "And ruthless." He laughed mercilessly.

Darcy's whole body felt in turmoil at hearing these words, but he refused to give Wickham the satisfaction of knowing how deeply they hurt. "I am certain you were completely innocent of helping her form any of these opinions," he said sarcastically.

"I think she has a rather realistic perspective of who you are."

Darcy's mouth went dry as his thoughts went to the first night he met Elizabeth and how she overheard him talking to Bingley about her. He unwittingly shuddered and then pointed his finger at Wickham. "You had better make yourself scarce around me and be on your best behaviour, Wickham, because I shall be keeping a close eye on you. If I see any misconduct, I will have no qualms reporting you to your superiors."

Another laugh escaped from Wickham. "Do you plan to bring up your sister? Or should I? From my perspective, you have kept that very quiet."

Darcy felt his blood boil through his veins. "If you say anything, Wickham…"

Wickham put up his hands, whispering tauntingly, "Have no fear, Darcy. I rather liked Georgiana, remember? It was you, who supposed I had ulterior motives when it came to her."

"I did not suppose anything! I knew!" Darcy pointed to the door. "Now get out!"

They both turned and saw that Elizabeth had just stepped outside. Before either could say anything, she turned quickly and returned inside.

Wickham shrugged. "I fear, old friend, that she likely has added another trait to her list – unpardonable!"

Wickham returned to the house laughing, leaving Darcy alone with his thoughts. He could barely breathe and wondered how he would be able to exhibit any self-control with Wickham around. He did not know if Wickham knew for a certainty he had strong feelings for Elizabeth, but it was very possible he would eventually come to see it. Wickham knew him well and could always tell what he was thinking or feeling. Usually it involved anger of some sort directed towards him, but in the past, he had also recognized when he was hurting, jealous, grieving, or even just unsure of his heavy responsibilities. He would not be able to conceal how he felt about Elizabeth, especially if Bingley continued to attach his affections to her or – heaven forbid – made her an offer of marriage.

He closed his eyes and tried to think. The last thing he wanted to do was go back inside and pretend all was well. He had no appetite to eat or drink, did not think he could concentrate on the steps required in a dance, and had no desire to carry on a conversation with anyone. He looked towards the door and wondered how easily he could find Bingley and excuse himself with the pretext that he was feeling unwell. Which was absolutely the truth!

He waited for the music to finish to ensure Bingley was no longer dancing. He slowly stepped inside, caring not that his face was likely red from anger, his lips turned down in a frown, and his comportment rigid. He quickly spotted his friend and walked over to him.

"Bingley, if you please, may I have a word with you?"

His friend had been talking to a small group of people, including Miss Mary Bennet and a gentleman he did not recognize. Darcy was grateful Elizabeth was not there.

Bingley turned. "Darcy, you are unwell?"

He nodded. "I regret that I will be retiring to my room. I am not feeling well."

"I am sorry to hear that, good friend. The ball has only just begun!"

"Yes, and I am truly sorry."

"If you insist, Darcy. Shall I have some food and drink sent up to you?"

Darcy shook his head. "No, I recently had something to drink, and I... I do not think I could eat anything."

"All right. But be sure to let me know if you have need of anything. Anything at all."

"Thank you, good friend." Darcy drew in a breath. "Thank you."

Darcy was grateful that was over.

He began to walk away, but the gentleman who had been with Miss Mary Bennet was suddenly at his side. He stiffened with exasperation when the man called out to him.

With a solemn bow, the gentleman said, "Sir! I am most thankful I heard Mr. Bingley mention you by name, for you must allow me to pay my respects to you."

Darcy blinked, wondering who this man was and what he meant. "Pardon me?"

"I beg your pardon, but it is in my power to assure you that your aunt, Lady Catherine de Bourgh, was quite well when I last saw her in Hunsford. I am Mr. Collins, and I am the clergyman there. Your aunt is my patroness."

"I thank you," Darcy said, with an abrupt nod. As he walked away, he heard the clergyman begin to speak again, but fortunately, the man's prattle was lost as the orchestra began playing.

Darcy returned to his chambers and rang for his valet, Sumner. As he waited, he paced the floor, attempting to sort out his thoughts and feelings. Miss Bennet had a more severe opinion of him than he could ever have imagined. What good would it do him if Bingley – or Elizabeth – finally realized that the differences in their temperaments and interests were too great? From what Wickham said, she would likely never receive *his* addresses with any pleasure.

His valet entered and asked what he could do for him.

"Unfortunately, I am not feeling well and wish to dress for bed, if you please."

"Certainly, sir."

After that was accomplished, Darcy looked at Sumner.

"There is one more thing I need you to do directly."

"What is that, sir?"

Darcy swallowed. "I need my bags packed. I will be leaving early in the morning to return to London."

Chapter 15

As the Bennet party departed Netherfield in the early hours of the morning, the atmosphere in the two carriages was again as different as night and day. One carriage was boisterous and lively, as Mrs. Bennet, Kitty, and Lydia recounted the numerous dances, excellent food, fine gowns, and handsome officers dressed in their redcoats.

Elizabeth was grateful for the quiet in her carriage, for she had much to think on. After hearing Darcy order Mr. Wickham to leave, she was surprised not to see the former again for the remainder of the evening. In making an inquiry to Mr. Bingley about him, he told her Darcy was feeling unwell and went to his room.

Mr. Wickham seemed unaffected by his encounter with Mr. Darcy and satisfied with the man's apparent departure. He danced every dance, laughed and conversed with many, and was being completely amiable. She was glad, for his sake, that Mr. Darcy's foreboding shadow was not darkening the room.

Elizabeth was grateful that Mr. Darcy was not there for another reason, as well. Her mother, younger sisters, and even her father behaved disgracefully during the meal. Kitty and Lydia were shamelessly flirting with some of the officers, Mary had played a very sombre piece on the piano, her skills evidently not sufficient to the task, and was disinclined to give up her place, even when her father reproached her to do so.

Mr. Bingley did not seem to notice, which had not surprised Elizabeth. His sisters had, however, and they were not pleased. Mr. Marshall, who sat at the table with her, Mr. Bingley, Charlotte, and Jane, often looked towards her family members when they were being indiscreet in their actions.

Elizabeth was certain he overheard her mother claiming that both her daughters were very close to becoming engaged to two very eligible men of generous fortune. Elizabeth had cringed and felt that he was not pleased to hear her make that announcement. She wondered if he was having second thoughts, as was Jane. She did not know how he felt about her family and whether their behaviour might influence him in his affections towards Jane. They certainly did not help the matter, for everyone, save Jane alone, had behaved poorly at some point in the evening.

Elizabeth shuddered as she recollected that she had even seen Mr. Collins act improperly. To her chagrin, she watched as he was determined to pay his respects to Mr. Darcy before being introduced to him. He had declared later that it had been a point of duty and that he had only been following the dictates of his conscience. His desire to stand and sing during the meal was a point of humiliation that made her want to grab Mary and talk her out of the growing affection she had for him. She did not, however, as she considered that both Mary and Mr. Collins had behaved similarly.

She dropped her head back against the seat cushion and closed her eyes as she considered that Miss Bingley and Mrs. Hurst, who often sent disparaging looks in the direction of her family, would likely have much to say to Mr. Darcy regarding her family. It was bad enough that her family was the last to leave, but her mother did not seem to know when to stop talking, even though Mr. Bingley's sisters complained of fatigue and seemed not at all interested in what she had to say.

She could not explain why she was grateful Mr. Darcy had not witnessed the impudent behaviour of her family, for she had enjoyed provoking him with her own impertinence. She gave her head a shake as she pondered this. Perhaps she was more concerned with his opinion of her family than of herself. She really did not know.

Elizabeth felt no great sense of loss in her affections for Mr. Bingley, for her heart had never truly been touched by him. She had considered him to be merely an amiable gentleman and respectable acquaintance. She hoped, once he understood that she had no strong inclination for him, he would find another nice young lady to receive his attentions.

Her mother would be another matter. She would not readily get over each of her two eldest daughters throwing away the prospect of an engagement with two very eligible men. She and Jane would likely hear about it for a long time to come. Elizabeth lifted up a silent prayer that her plans for Mary and Mr. Collins would soon be realized. An engagement between them might soften the blow of the loss of Mr. Bingley and Mr. Marshall.

~~*

Darcy's valet awakened him just before dawn. He had not slept well. The music from the ball had drifted upstairs into his room into the early hours of the morning, prompting him to wonder with whom Elizabeth might be dancing, and whether she was laughing with Bingley or – heaven forbid – Wickham! Once the ball ended and all was silent, he could not find the peace he longed for; his thoughts were relentless, his accusations against himself were fierce, and his despair smothering.

Darcy slowly sat up and put his feet on the floor as Sumner handed him a cup of coffee, which Darcy took gratefully. He downed several gulps, almost burning his tongue.

"Do you plan to go to London on horse or in your carriage, sir?"

Darcy said nothing, as he wrapped his hands around the cup and looked down into the dark, steaming liquid.

Sumner stood back, and Darcy knew he was looking at him. He might not know all of what was disturbing him, but his valet likely knew he was troubled. If making this simple decision was difficult for him, what would it be like to make major decisions as he attempted to return to a semblance of normalcy? He shook his head as he considered that whichever means of transportation he decided upon, he would come to regret it.

After a few moments of waiting for his master to answer, Sumner said, "If you do not mind me saying, I believe taking the carriage would be best for you this morning, sir. It will take longer to get to town, but I can send a rider ahead to notify Darcy House you are coming so things will be ready when you arrive."

Darcy nodded. It was a wise decision, although he was still not certain that riding in the solitude of the carriage was what he preferred, for his thoughts would likely go on unabated. If he rode, the pounding of the horse's hooves would help keep his mind distracted, although that same pounding was likely to aggravate the throbbing in his head.

"You might get the rest that eluded you last night."

Darcy blew out a puff of air and nodded. "Yes. You are right. Ready the carriage, but have my horse saddled in case I want to ride as we draw near to town."

"Yes, sir."

Darcy was grateful that Sumner appeared satisfied, saying little as he helped him dress.

Once he was finished, Darcy asked that some bread, cheese, and fruit be put in the carriage, for he would not be eating at Netherfield. He then requested some time alone so he could write Bingley a letter.

When he sat down at the desk, his hand, holding a quill, hovered over the stationary. He closed his eyes as he wondered what and how much to say to his friend. He had decided not to tell him last night he was leaving this morning because he did not wish to answer any questions. He knew Bingley would not arise until almost noon, and he would be able to depart without his knowing.

He was determined to be brief in this letter, which was unlike him. Bingley would not mind, however, for his letters were always brief, misspelled, and smudged from being written hurriedly; in fact, they were often unreadable from not blotting the ink properly when he was finished.

He put the quill to the stationary. He would apologize and be done with it.

My good friend Bingley,

You likely are now aware that I have departed Netherfield. I regret that I was not able to personally take my leave of you and your sisters this morning, but urgent business is drawing me back to town. Please accept my sincerest apologies for such an abrupt departure.

I want to thank you for allowing me to stay with you at Netherfield these past two months and hope to see you again soon.

Again, please accept my apologies and pass them on to your family.

Fitzwilliam Darcy

He stood up and walked to the window, looking out towards Longbourn. "Good bye, Miss Elizabeth Bennet. It was a pleasure making your acquaintance." He expelled a shaky breath. "More than you will ever know." He turned quickly and exited the room, eager to put this place – and her – behind him.

~~*

At Longbourn the next morning, all talk of the ball ceased, for much to Elizabeth's relief Mr. Collins made an offer of marriage to Mary. Although Elizabeth was grateful Mary seemed delighted with the prospect of being married to him, she could not wholeheartedly join in the tumult of praise and exaltations that flowed from her mother.

Her father wished them both a lifetime of happiness, but then came and stood next to Elizabeth.

"So, Lizzy, your scheme in making Mary his choice succeeded. Are you well pleased?"

Elizabeth shook her head. "I did not do any scheming, Papa. I merely helped Mary attract his attention."

"I see." He smiled and took her hand. "I confess I am glad it is Mary. I could not abide having him ask for your hand!"

Elizabeth laughed. "Heaven forbid it if he had! You know I would have never accepted it!"

"No, my dear. I am quite certain of that. Now all that is left is to find out whether you will accept an offer from Mr. Bingley." He smiled and walked away.

It was fortunate for everyone that Mrs. Bennet did not take the opportunity to hint to Mr. Marshall that his turn was next. Perhaps she was content that one of her daughters was finally engaged and the security of her family was established.

Elizabeth knew that talking to Mr. Marshall weighed heavily on Jane, and now that matters between Mr. Collins and Mary were settled, she felt Jane ought to talk with him about her feelings.

Later in the afternoon, as celebrating wore down, the perfect opportunity presented itself. Mr. Bennet was in his study, and Mrs. Bennet had retired to her chambers for a nap. Mary and Mr. Collins were sitting together in the garden, and their two youngest sisters had walked to Meryton.

With Jane and Mr. Marshall sitting in the parlour, Elizabeth excused herself and nodded at Jane, encouraging her to speak to the gentleman honestly about her feelings.

As she began to step out, she almost collided with the maid, who was escorting Mr. Bingley into the room.

"Mr. Bingley, this is a surprise. How are you?"

"Indeed, I am well," he said. "I hope this is not a bad time." He glanced over to Jane and Mr. Marshall, and then back to Elizabeth.

"It is always a good time, Mr. Bingley." Elizabeth hoped her true sentiments on his unexpected visit did not belie the expression on her face. "We were just... chatting." This was *not* an opportune time, but what could she do? As he walked in, she said, "We cannot thank you enough for your generosity to us last night in providing your carriage as well as hosting one of the finest balls we have ever attended."

He smiled. "It was my pleasure. I am glad you enjoyed it."

He greeted the others and sat down next to Jane in the chair where Elizabeth had been sitting. She took the chair on the other side of him. The four began talking, and a few minutes later, Charlotte entered the room.

"I hope you do not mind my stopping by," she said as she walked towards the empty chair on the other side of Mr. Marshall. "I had such a wonderful time at the ball, Mr. Bingley," she said as she looked his way. She folded her hands in her lap. "I wanted to come by and hear everyone's thoughts on it."

"We were telling Mr. Bingley how grand an affair it was," Jane said.

Elizabeth felt her frustration increase. Their friend's arrival would certainly prevent Jane from having an opportunity to talk

CHANCE AND CIRCUMSTANCE

with Mr. Marshall any time soon. Her visits were always lengthy.

They discussed the ball a great deal, and Elizabeth inquired whether Mr. Darcy was still unwell, since he had not accompanied him.

"Heavens! I cannot believe that man! When I awoke and dressed this morning, I discovered he had departed for London at some ungodly early hour!"

Elizabeth's eyes widened. "Did you not know he was going to leave?"

"No! He said not a word to me about it. He merely left me a note with his apologies. It seems he had some urgent business to tend to."

"I am certain he must be a busy man," Jane said.

"He is, and he has so many responsibilities, but..." Bingley shook his head. "I hope he is well; I was concerned about him last night."

"Do you think he will return?" Elizabeth asked, although she felt she already knew the answer. As long as Mr. Wickham remained in the neighbourhood, Mr. Darcy would stay away.

Bingley shrugged and shook his head. "I cannot say. He has been acting in ways so unlike him recently."

The five continued to talk about the ball and other subjects, including the recent engagement between Mr. Collins and Mary. Mr. Bingley and Charlotte were both rather surprised, but they expressed their delight.

At length, Elizabeth excused herself, and later when she returned, she stopped at the door. Looking inside the room, her eyes widened, and after watching a short while, she left again.

She walked to her father's study and tapped at the door.

"Come in," he said.

Elizabeth walked in. "Hello, Papa."

"What can I do for you, Lizzy?"

She shook her head. "I am not certain. Both Mr. Bingley and Charlotte are here, and they are all gathered in the parlour."

"Do you not think you should go back in and spend time with Mr. Bingley?" He laughed. "Another engagement today would certainly delight your mother."

"I... I am not certain I should."

"Why not?" Mr. Bennet asked, a perplexed look on his face.

She motioned with her finger for him to follow her and then pressed it to her lips for silence.

When they looked in at the door, they saw Jane and Mr. Bingley deep in conversation. Both were smiling, and it appeared they were having an avid and captivating conversation. Mr. Marshall and Charlotte were talking with each other, as well. Charlotte was nodding her head in agreement of something he was saying.

Elizabeth and her father watched for some time as the four of them, oblivious to their onlookers, continued talking. Then she drew him away.

"I believe this is the perfect solution! I cannot believe I had not thought of it before!"

"Solution? To what?"

"Oh, Papa, neither Jane nor I were convinced that the two gentlemen everyone else had such expectations for, were suitable to us."

"Well, I confess I am relieved, Lizzy. While Bingley is certainly amiable, I never felt he had those traits that would make you happy in marriage." He looked towards the room where the two couples were. "Now Bingley and Jane just might be a suitable match."

"And what do you think about Mr. Marshall and Charlotte?"

Mr. Bennet shrugged. "That I cannot say, but I had my doubts about Jane and him, as well. Perhaps this is the way things were meant to be."

Elizabeth smiled. "Somehow, we have to assure the two gentlemen that they will not hurt anyone's feelings if they switch their affections!"

Mr. Bennet walked back towards his study and with a chuckle said, "I shall leave that up to you, my dear. You seem to be the expert on relationship machinations."

"I..." She started to protest, but stopped when her father disappeared behind the door.

Elizabeth peeked in again and watched the interactions that were continuing unabated. She shook her head. Mr. Bingley and Mr. Marshall needed no assistance from her to realize that Jane and Charlotte were quite well suited for them. And the same could be said for the ladies regarding those gentlemen. She chuckled as she thought that this had turned out much better than she had ever imagined.

She stepped outside and walked over to the swing, whose ropes had been replaced several times since it was put up almost twenty years ago. The wooden block had weathered storms, five children, and all their friends who wanted to swing. Elizabeth sat down and held onto the rope, rocking and twisting as she pondered the turn of events.

If matters turned out as she suspected they might, it was possible there could be three weddings in their small neighbourhood in the next few months. Despite the fact that she was not one of those who might conceivably be getting married, she was delighted with the prospect.

She sat there, oblivious to the time passing and the air growing cooler with dusk drawing near. She had much to think about, but for some reason, the question of Mr. Darcy's actions continued to taunt her. She shook her head as she tried to convince herself she was not interested in the man at all! He had behaved abominably, and she was grateful she no longer had to put up with him. Let Jane and Mr. Bingley treat him with all the kindness and generosity that they willingly extended to others; she would continue to think of him as she had all along.

As she pondered this, she heard Jane calling her.

"Lizzy! There you are! I have been looking for you."

Jane ran up to her sister, put her arms about her, and started to sob.

"Jane, what is it? What has happened?"

"Oh, Lizzy, I am certain you are angry at me." She drew back and looked at Elizabeth, taking in a few shaky breaths.

"Jane, what makes you think I am upset with you?"

"Because of me and... me and..." She paused. "I do not know what I am going to do. I am so terribly distressed." She released Elizabeth and turned away.

"I can readily see that, but pray tell me what is wrong."

She turned back and wiped her eyes. "I like him so much, Lizzy, but I have no right to him."

Elizabeth smiled. "Do you mean Mr. Bingley?"

Jane nodded mutely. "He is... he is..."

Elizabeth took her hand. "He is everything a gentleman ought to be, is he not? He is kind and generous, and I think he suits you very well."

"He is, indeed..." Jane tilted her head. "What did you say?"

Elizabeth laughed. "I have realized for some time that he and I are not well-suited for each other, and when I saw you talking with him, I suddenly knew the two of you were."

Jane drew in a ragged breath. "Lizzy, you are not just saying that, are you?"

Elizabeth chuckled. "That is the reason I came out here."

"Oh, I have been so troubled since his visit the other day when you were out walking. I felt he was so much more suitable for me than Mr. Marshall was, but I knew there was nothing I could do about it."

"I am sorry you felt that way. Please forgive me for not telling you about my true feelings for him." Elizabeth's brows lowered, and she looked around. "Where is he, by the way?"

"He had to return to Netherfield. He asked me to give you his regrets." She sighed heavily. "Are you certain, Lizzy? You are not just saying that, are you?"

"I am certain! I saw how well you and Mr. Bingley and Charlotte and Mr. Marshall were getting along." She drew back. "And where are Charlotte and Mr. Marshall?"

Jane laughed merrily. "They are still in there talking." She shook her head. "In the few months I have known him, I do not think we talked as much altogether as they have been talking since she arrived."

"I believe, Jane, that perhaps things are now as they were meant to be."

Jane grasped her sister's hands. "But what of you, Lizzy?"

Elizabeth shrugged. "I am certain someone is out there for me." She leaned in to her with a sly smile. "Perhaps it is someone else who is already in the neighbourhood."

~~*

Darcy leaned back in the carriage, rubbing his temple with two fingers as he made a futile attempt to sleep. His head still pounded with pain and assaulting thoughts and images of Elizabeth.

He had hoped that once he was away from Netherfield and had left every reminder of her dancing eyes, sparkling wit, and intelligent conversation behind, he would be able to put her out of his heart and mind.

All he had to do was to think on those things about her that were not to his liking.

He closed his eyes as he tried to bring those points to mind. First and foremost, was her attachment to Bingley — in spite of everything about him that was wrong for her. Could she not see that? Did she continue to receive his addresses solely because marrying him would take away worries about the future for her family? He pounded the seat with his fist.

Why was she so blinded to how well suited *he* was for her? Was Wickham correct in his assertion that she found him unpardonable? Was her opinion of him formed the first night they met when she overheard him cautioning Bingley about singling her out so soon?

He shook his head. While he had known practically nothing about Elizabeth when they met at the Meryton Assembly, he was aware that despite being one of the kindest men he had ever known, Bingley could readily talk himself out of an attachment when someone nicer, prettier, or more to his liking came along. He had seen it happen many times before.

Just outside London, Darcy fell asleep. He was wrong, however, in believing sleep would remove Elizabeth from his thoughts, for there she was in his dreams. What made it worse was that Wickham had also invaded his dreams and was at her side sneering at him in derision.

Chapter 16

Within three short weeks, Elizabeth's assumptions that there might possibly be more than one wedding in the neighbourhood in the near future were realized. The first, of course, the nuptials of Mr. Collins and Mary, was to be held the week between Christmas and New Year's.

Mr. Collins had returned to Kent the Saturday after he asked for Mary's hand to discuss his engagement with his patroness Lady Catherine de Bourgh, and – as Elizabeth suspected – to get her approval.

He planned to return to Longbourn to celebrate Christmas with the Bennets. The final preparations for the wedding would then be finalized.

Mr. Marshall had remained another three weeks at Longbourn, and before he returned to his home in the Lake District, he had asked for Charlotte's hand.

As both of them were very practical in their views on love and marriage, they reasoned their match was an excellent one, and their marriage would have just as good a chance at happiness as a couple who had known each other for years. They decided he would return to Hertfordshire with his family after Christmas, and they would marry in late January.

As all this was taking place, it was a joy for Elizabeth to watch Jane and Mr. Bingley as they became better acquainted. She was convinced the two could not be better suited in their even temperaments, unfettered kindness, and excessive generosity.

Mr. Bingley apologized frequently to Elizabeth for his apparent display of inconstancy. He told her he would be deeply grieved if he had been the cause of her feelings being hurt or her heart broken. She reassured him again and again that she heartily approved of his affection for Jane and felt the two of them were much better suited.

In observing Mr. Bingley's sisters, Elizabeth felt they treated Jane a trifle better than they had treated her when their brother had been seemingly settling his affections on her. She could readily see, however, that they were still not wholly pleased. Perhaps Jane's kind and generous demeanour was more to their liking, but her family, fortune, and connections were still undesirable in their eyes. Elizabeth was grateful it was her sister and not she, who would have to continue to smile sweetly at them, for Jane could do it under any and all circumstances. She, however, could not. She was certain Jane would win them over in due time.

When Mr. Collins returned from Hunsford before Christmas, he was delighted to inform Mary and the rest of the Bennets, that his noble patroness was pleased with his choice of the middle Bennet daughter and she had assured him the parsonage would be improved to make it warm and welcoming for the blushing bride. This statement, followed by an indulgent smile directed at Mary, prompted the youngest girls to groan and shudder.

Wedding preparations soon began. Despite both Mr. Collins and Mary insisting their wedding be small and simple, Mrs. Bennet refused to listen to them, even though her nerves often left her in need of a rest, leaving decisions and chores to Elizabeth. As a result, there were few walks into Meryton, except when her task required it. She had to go several times with Mary to be fitted for her gown or buy additional lace and ribbons and other items her mother insisted they needed.

On the days when Elizabeth was not occupied with wedding preparations, the frigid weather kept her home. She regretted not being able to talk with Mr. Wickham, for she had not seen him since the Netherfield Ball.

Despite all Elizabeth was called upon to do, she was happy to do it for Mary. She could not help but wonder, however, how her mother would handle four more weddings if, indeed, all her daughters married. When Mr. Collins and Mary's wedding was only a few days away, the third engagement Elizabeth had hoped for finally occurred.

On Christmas Eve, Mr. Bingley proposed to Jane, and she happily accepted.

He had joined the Bennets for their Christmas Eve meal. His sisters and Mr. Hurst had returned to London, where they felt the festivities in town would be more to their liking. Elizabeth wondered if they left because they knew what their brother was about to do and were not pleased.

The Bennets and Mr. Bingley ate in the flickering light of the large Yule candle, placed in the centre of their table. A sumptuous dinner of succulent roasted duck and stuffing, creamed squash, freshly baked bread, and mince pie received many compliments from their guest.

After the meal, everyone bundled up to go outside to gather evergreen, holly, ivy, and mistletoe to decorate the home. They stepped out into the blustery air.

Mr. Bingley looked up. "I would not be surprised if it began to snow before we are finished."

Jane laughed and touched the tip of her nose. "I believe you are wrong, sir, for a snowflake just landed on my nose."

"Indeed! You are right!" he exclaimed, touching the single snowflake with his finger. "Could there be anything more delightful than snow on Christmas Eve?"

Mr. Bennet, who had been apprised of Mr. Bingley's intentions, looked slyly at his eldest daughter. "I am certain that Jane can think of nothing finer than a light dusting of snow on Christmas Eve. Am I correct, Jane?"

"Oh, yes! And then to wake up on Christmas morning, look out the window, and behold the ground covered in a plush white blanket of freshly fallen snow!" She clasped her hands and then shivered. "I can think of nothing more delightful."

When they had collected all the greenery needed, and everyone returned inside, hot drinks, cake, and pie awaited them. They enjoyed their refreshments in front of a blazing fire. Once warm, they set to work making garlands from the greenery, adding ribbons, and placing them along the windows, mantels, and around the room.

Jane had been given the task of making the kissing bough,

which would be placed in the doorway of the sitting room. Mr. Bingley hovered near her, watching as she expertly attached small pieces of mistletoe, evergreen, and holly with its berries.

She held it up and asked him, "How does this look?"

"I think it looks wonderful!" Bingley said.

"Do you think so?"

"Let us hang it up and see if it works," he said with a smile.

"See if it works?" Jane asked as her cheeks grew rosy in a blush.

They left the others in the parlour to go to the sitting room. Mr. Bennet nodded to Elizabeth, giving her permission to sneak away and watch.

She stood behind the door watching as Mr. Bingley climbed up on a small ladder to attach the kissing bough by its ribbon to the centre of the doorpost.

He got down and gently moved Jane so she stood underneath it. He looked at her and moved his eyes upward so she would glance up.

"I think it looks lovely," she said, admiring their handiwork.

Mr. Bingley took the opportunity to lean over and kiss her gently. He then went down on one knee. "Jane, you are dearer to me than anything, and more than I could have ever asked for." He reached up and took her hands. "It would make me the happiest of men if you would consent to be my wife." He drew in a deep breath. "Will you do me the honour of marrying me?"

He squeezed her hands, and she returned the grip tightly as he stood. She nodded as tears began to trickle down her face. "Yes, Mr. Bing… Charles. Yes, I wholeheartedly accept!"

Elizabeth clasped her hands tightly and then hurried back to the others, eager to share what she had witnessed, but she said nothing, for she felt the news should come from the newly engaged couple rather than from her.

Her father looked at her, and she merely smiled and nodded.

When the couple returned, Mr. Bingley cleared his throat to get everyone's attention.

"I fear I must make a confession to all of you tonight," he began.

"Confession? Oh, Mr. Bingley, I am certain you have done nothing wrong." Mrs. Bennet wagged her finger at him.

"Oh, but I did. For you see, the kissing bough that Jane made was so beautiful, that when it was hung, I simply had to steal a kiss."

The younger girls giggled. Mrs. Bennet's mouth opened, but no words came out, and Elizabeth said, "Please continue, Mr. Bingley."

"Well, just to ease your minds, I have asked for your daughter's hand in marriage, and she has accepted."

Everyone rushed over to congratulate them. Elizabeth reached in through the crowd and grasped Jane's hand and squeezed it, mouthing, "I am very happy for you, Jane!"

After some discussion about this exciting event, the couple asked for some time alone. They returned to the sitting room.

"This is wonderful news!" Mrs. Bennet exclaimed once they stepped out. She shook her head. "He is so much finer than Mr. Marshall! I cannot imagine how Mrs. Lucas will be able to show her face after hearing our news!"

"My dear, Charlotte and Mr. Marshall make an excellent match, and I do not want to hear you gloating to her or anyone else about how this is a better match."

"Thank you, Father," Elizabeth said. She looked at Mary, who would likely no longer be the object of her mother's exultation. She smiled at her and Mr. Collins and said, "All the engaged couples are perfectly suited, and we rejoice in each one!"

"Thank you, Lizzy," Mary said. "I almost feel as though I have been forgotten, and our wedding is in but three days."

"No one has forgotten you, Mary!" Mrs. Bennet cried. "Goodness, with all I have been doing to get ready for it, how could you be forgotten?"

"Hush now," Mr. Bennet said. "We do not want Bingley to hear us. He might just change his mind!" He stole a glance at Elizabeth and smiled.

"Oh, Mr. Bennet, I know you take great delight in vexing me, but nothing you say will upset me. I shall have two daughters married soon, and I could not be more pleased!"

Charles and Jane returned shortly, and Elizabeth was quite certain they had made good use of the kissing bough in the privacy of the sitting room. Jane's face shone with bliss, and her cheeks had a warm rosy glow.

Mr. Bingley announced that after discussing the details with Jane, they wanted their wedding to take place in the middle of February so it would not conflict with the two other weddings. Everyone agreed it was an excellent idea.

"It has been a delightful evening," said Mr. Bingley with a wide smile as he was taking his leave. "I cannot wait to write to Darcy and tell him."

"Have you heard from him since he left?" Elizabeth asked.

Bingley shook his head. "No, I have not. That actually surprises me, as he is an excellent letter writer." He laughed. "I, on the other hand…, he tells me I need to take more thought and care when I write." He shrugged. "He will be surprised to hear from me."

Elizabeth considered that the word *surprised* might not be the best way to describe Mr. Darcy's reaction. She chuckled softly. He will likely be frustrated and angry at his friend's decision.

~~*

The wedding of Mr. Collins and Mary took place a few days later in front of a few family and friends. It was, after all Mrs. Bennet's intentions, a simple ceremony, as befitting a clergyman and his bride.

Elizabeth had done Mary's hair and felt she had transformed her into a lovely bride. She wore a simple, yet elegant gown, and looked exceptionally happy. During the ceremony, Elizabeth thought how she would never have suspected that Mary would marry before any of her other sisters.

During the wedding breakfast, Mary asked her father if he would be willing to journey to Kent to see her and her husband in the spring. He agreed, and asked Elizabeth to accompany him, knowing his two youngest would never agree to a trip to see them. He also firmly believed he would not be able to endure the foolishness of either of them for the duration of the journey. Of course, he could not ask Jane, as she and Mr. Bingley would be newly married and would not want to be separated. Elizabeth was his logical choice.

Mr. Bennet decided he would remain only a few days in Kent,

while Mary asked that Elizabeth remain with her for three weeks. Her father would then return to accompany her home. Everyone felt this was an excellent idea.

Elizabeth found herself looking forward to it. She had never been to Kent and knew that after the three weddings, she would welcome a restful sojourn. She was also very curious about Lady Catherine de Bourgh and her daughter, who Mr. Darcy was supposedly to marry.

Mr. Collins and his new bride were then sent off with cheerful wishes of joy as they journeyed home to the Hunsford parsonage in Kent.

~~*

Darcy walked towards the parlour at Pemberley, eyeing the boughs of evergreen, holly, and ivy that still lined the hallway, windows, and doors from Christmas over a week ago. Red ribbon bows had been tied to the ends of each garland, and as he approached the door, he stopped.

The one single kissing bough that had been hung at Pemberley was in the doorway to the parlour, and as he looked up at it, it seemed to taunt him.

He reached up to yank it down, spilling some of the evergreen and mistletoe onto the floor.

Mrs. Reynolds entered, stirring him from his reverie.

"Oh, Mr. Darcy. Did the kissing bough fall?" She reached out to take it from him. "I shall dispose of it for you."

"Thank you," he said, placing it into his housekeeper's hand, thinking that disposing of it was the best thing to be done with it.

"It was a very nice Christmas, Mr. Darcy. The staff all greatly appreciated your generosity."

He nodded. "As you and many of them have kindly said several times. It is all due to my mother and father, as I saw them do it often."

Mrs. Reynolds' face grew sombre, and she shook her head. "Such a great loss, and so unfortunate that many here never knew them." Her eyes turned to him with a smile. "I am confident, however, that they can see how good your parents were by how kindly you treat them."

"Thank you, Mrs. Reynolds."

Darcy watched his housekeeper leave and he felt the familiar tightening in his chest as he considered his housekeeper's words. How could she say he was kind and generous when Elizabeth had accused him of being cruel and ruthless?

It had been over a month since the ball at Netherfield. In his mind it seemed as though a considerable amount of time had passed since that fateful night, and yet, the pain in his heart lingered as strong as if it had been yesterday.

When he had left Netherfield for London, his sole intention had been to get Georgiana and set out for Pemberley to spend Christmas there. He had no desire to participate in the season's festivities in town. He longed for the quiet and solitude of his home in Derbyshire.

He had hoped to make it a good Christmas – at least for Georgiana. Despite that, he had not felt his normal joy in watching his sister delight in the season. Unfortunately, her joy had been tempered by events that had taken place in Ramsgate earlier in the year, and his, by what had happened recently in Hertfordshire. He hoped she had not noticed the change in him, but he had often seen her looking at him, as if pondering whether to ask him if anything was wrong. He hoped she did not think his melancholy was due to what had happened between her and Wickham.

He returned to his study and sat down at his desk, picking up his book and reading a page or two before closing it. He had never taken so long to read a book before, and wondered if the story was just not engaging his interest or because his mind was elsewhere. He shook his head – he knew the answer.

He stood up, walked to the window, and looked out. A fresh snow covering the ground glistened in the sunlight. It was a beautiful sight that made him truly appreciate all he had. Unfortunately, when he admired Pemberley's beauty, it made him wish he had someone with whom to share it. Someone like Elizabeth.

He turned and leaned his back against the wall. His fist pounded his chin several times as he considered there had to be something he could do to expunge her from his heart and mind.

His eyes closed, his head fell back, and he could feel his heart pound rapidly. "How long?" he asked himself. "Will this ever cease?"

He heard footsteps and quickly straightened up and returned to his chair. A footman came in with his mail. Darcy thanked him and asked him to leave it on the desk. He let out a sigh as he looked through the few pieces, knowing he would give most to his steward.

He stopped, however, when he saw a small letter with very familiar handwriting. It was from Bingley! He stared at it as a sensation of dread flooded through him. Why would Bingley be writing him? He closed his eyes as he wondered whether his friend was soliciting his advice as to whether to ask for Elizabeth's hand.

What would he say in response? What *could* he say?

His hands shook as he struggled to open the letter.

"This is absurd!" Darcy said aloud. He had no idea why his friend was writing to him, and if Bingley was seeking his advice, he would be honest. He could readily tell him what an excellent woman Elizabeth was and how she would make him an excellent wife. He would not, however, mention how poorly suited he felt his friend was for *her* – or that he wished more than anything that she could have been his.

Darcy opened the letter, immediately noticing its brevity, which was not unusual for his friend.

He began reading, his jaw clenched, and his heart began pounding as he read the first few lines.

Darcy,

I hope this finds you well and that you had an enjoyable Christmas at Pemberley. I must ask if you will be able to return to Netherfield on the thirteenth of February. For you see, my good friend, I have asked Miss Bennet to marry me, and she has said yes! I am the happiest of men, but I must tell you…

Darcy could not read the rest. Even if he wished to, he could not, for the words were severely smeared from improperly blotted ink.

He tried to maintain calm as he put the letter down, but instead, his fist came down hard on the desk.

"No!"

Chapter 17

Darcy abruptly pushed himself up from the chair and walked again to the window, gazing out but no longer seeing the glistening white landscape before him. Instead, he could only see Elizabeth's smiling face as she looked up – not at him – but at Bingley. He shook his head to rid himself of the image and turned away.

He fisted his hands and began to pace about the room. He had assumed Bingley would seek his advice before asking for her hand, as he always sought his advice for any decision of major importance. Perhaps Elizabeth had advised him not to. She knew – at least she thought she knew – his feelings on the matter.

Anger stirred within him. Was he angrier at Bingley for asking her to marry him or at Elizabeth for accepting his offer? Perhaps his anger was directed more at himself for allowing his own heart to be so foolishly taken captive. He suddenly shook his head. No, what he felt was not anger. Anger was what he felt towards Wickham when he had found out his intentions towards Georgiana. There was a burning within him at the mere thought. *That* was anger. This was... grief, disappointment, and regret.

Wickham! He raked his fingers through his hair and then stopped. He let out a sigh – almost of relief – that at least Elizabeth would now be safe from *him*.

He walked over and picked up Bingley's letter again. He narrowed his eyes as he tried to decipher any more of the letter. He was not certain he wanted to know, but he was curious. He was only able to make out a few more words – *you might be, so happy,* and *angel.*

"Angel?" He shook his head and dropped his hand. Perhaps

Bingley's propensity for kindness, generosity, and — he lifted up the letter and looked at it again — his use of endearing terms — prompted Elizabeth to disregard all those ways in which they were different.

In the letter Bingley asked him to come to Hertfordshire for the wedding. He was not certain he could watch the two of them marry. His eyes unwittingly went to the phrase, *I have asked Miss Bennet to marry me, and she has said yes.*

He crumpled the letter and walked over to the fireplace, gazing into the flames. He almost tossed it in, but instead, held onto it tightly. Without thinking, he pounded the wall with his fisted hand.

He lowered his head and let out a long sigh, extending his hand towards the flames. "Perhaps someday I will be able to face the two of you as husband and wife."

"Fitzwilliam?"

Darcy pulled his hand back in and spun around. "Georgiana! I... I did not hear you come in." He pulled himself erect and walked over to his desk. "What can I... what can I do for you?"

His sister walked in and grasped the back of the chair across from his desk. "Is something wrong?"

His heart thundered. *I cannot tell her. I would not want her to feel burdened by my anguish.*

"What... what makes you think something is wrong?"

A worried smile appeared. "It is not often you pound on walls."

"No, I suppose I do not." At once he regretted that he had not regulated his emotions. He could readily see the concern on his sister's face.

Georgiana walked around the chair and sat down, tilting her head and lifting her brows, waiting for him to answer.

Darcy opened his mouth and then closed it.

"I am waiting," she said softly.

Darcy slowly sat and then looked at the crumpled letter in his hands.

"Did you receive distressing news?" she asked.

"It is... it is from Bingley. He is to marry." His voice cracked as he attempted to speak those words.

Georgiana's eyes widened. "How delightful!" Her face grew

sombre. "But you are not pleased. Do you not approve of the young lady?"

Darcy pondered what to say.

"Fitzwilliam, you were not still hoping that there would be an attachment between the two of us, were you?"

"No, not at all."

"But something is wrong." She reached her hand across the desk and placed it on his. "I can see it in your face." She bit her lip. "Has your good friend made an unsuitable match?"

Darcy pulled his hand out from underneath hers and stood up again. "I would prefer not to talk about it."

Georgiana folded her hands and placed them in her lap. "I see." She paused and looked about the room. "Do you remember when we returned to Pemberley from Ramsgate and we sat here exactly as we are now?"

Darcy winced. "Yes."

"Do you remember what you told me?"

When he did not answer, she said, "You told me I needed to talk about how I felt. You told me that even though we do not often speak of our feelings or about things that upset us, there are times we need to talk about it to help ease the burden."

"I said that?"

She gave her head an emphatic nod. "You did." She leaned in towards him. "Even though it was difficult for me, you were right. It did help me feel better." She crossed her arms in front of her. "I am going to sit here until you tell me what is wrong."

Darcy sat down again and began smoothing out the letter. "You asked me if I felt Bingley made an unsuitable match."

Georgiana nodded. "Is that what has you concerned?"

He looked down at the letter and then lifted his eyes to his sister. "On the contrary. I think very highly of the young lady and believe he made an excellent choice."

Georgiana's brows pinched. "Then what is wrong?"

"I... I think I am more disappointed in the lady. I believe she is..." He shook his head. "Bingley is a most proper and excellent gentleman, and I would never say anything against his character..."

She tilted her head. "But...?"

This young lady is intelligent and has excellent understanding. She reads extensively, knows and quotes Shakespeare, loves to walk..." He chuckled and shook his head. "She even got up in the middle of the night and watched a thunderstorm with me."

Georgiana's eyes widened, and her face paled. "Fitzwilliam, that could not have been proper!"

"No, no!" She had to stay at Netherfield for the night due to severe rain and flooding. There was a storm in the middle of the night, and we both unexpectedly encountered one another when we left our rooms to watch it." He gave her a smile. "All was proper. I did not remain with her." *Although I wish I could have stayed longer*, Darcy added to himself.

"And Bingley is not at all interested in these things." Understanding suddenly flooded her face. "Yet, these are all things *you* enjoy doing."

Darcy silently nodded.

Georgiana pursed her lips and shifted in the chair.

There was silence for a moment, and then she finally asked, "Fitzwilliam, did you come to admire her? Did your affections become attached to her, as did Mr. Bingley's?"

Darcy felt his cheeks warm at the question and experienced the familiar tightening in his chest.

"Did you come to... to *love* her?"

He suddenly stood up and turned away. He let out a long breath before answering. Very slowly he said, "I did grow to greatly admire her." He shook his head. "I do not know if it was love, for I have always believed that love needs to be returned."

"I see." Georgiana stood up and walked over to him. Taking his arm, she said, "I am very sorry. I know... I know what a great disappointment this must be."

"I only wish she had come to see how..." He did not finish aloud, but said to himself, *how suited we are for each other.*

"Will you go to the wedding?"

"I do not know if I am equal to the task of watching the two of them marry."

"But he has been such a good friend for many years."

Darcy wrapped his arm about his sister and kissed the top of her head as he blinked away tears that threatened to spill. "I know, and that is what is making this so much more difficult."

"What shall you do?" she asked softly.

"I am not yet certain, but I have been promising Fitzwilliam I would visit his family in Portsmouth. I will apologize and explain to Bingley that I regret that I cannot attend their wedding."

"But you will see him again, will you not?"

Darcy's body tensed at the mere thought. "I am certain that in time I shall be able to look upon her as indifferently as if I had never met her." He could only hope that would eventually be the case.

~~*

With the weddings of the Collinses and the Marshalls behind them, plans began for Mr. Bingley and Jane's wedding. It was to be a much grander affair than the two previous weddings, and that made it much more difficult for Mrs. Bennet to remain calm. Again, Elizabeth was called upon and expected to do most of the work.

She discussed the menu for the breakfast with Jane and went to the milliner's shop with her to finalize fittings on the wedding gown and the other dresses being made. It was a great delight to oversee all of this, for both Jane and Mr. Bingley were easy to please. The only thing that made it difficult was that at times they were unable to make a decision, wishing to relinquish the choice to the other.

When she and Jane returned from Meryton one afternoon after a busy morning of shopping and alterations, they both collapsed into chairs in the parlour.

"Lizzy, I do not know what I would do without you. I am so grateful I had you with me today."

"It has been a pleasure, Jane. It is a joy and privilege to be doing this for you."

The two were discussing the upcoming wedding, when Mr. Bingley was announced.

"Good afternoon, ladies. I hoped I would find you at home."

"We have just returned from Meryton, Charles," Jane said. "Your timing is perfect."

"I know we did not have plans to see each other today, but I could not stay away. I hope you do not mind."

"Of course not," Jane said. "I am pleased you have come." Jane's face suddenly clouded. "You look as though something is wrong. Has something happened?"

Mr. Bingley let out a long sigh. "It is nothing to worry about."

Elizabeth stood up. "If you will excuse me, I need to speak to Mother about something."

"Oh, please, there is no need to leave on my account," Bingley exclaimed. He turned to Jane. "It is Darcy."

Elizabeth slowly sat back down. "Mr. Darcy?"

"I have received a letter from him."

Elizabeth tensed, wondering if he had expressed his objections to the wedding.

"Something has you concerned, does it not?" Jane asked.

He pulled out the letter and slowly unfolded it, looking at it silently for a moment. He began to read aloud.

Bingley,

I wish you and Miss Bennet great joy. I know she will make you very happy. I regret, however, that I am unable to come to Hertfordshire for the wedding. I have family obligations that are taking me to Portsmouth at that time.

Yours, Darcy

Mr. Bingley looked up. "His letter is so brief! It is not at all like him to be so brief." He shook his head. "I cannot believe he will not be at our wedding! Of all my friends and family, he is the one person I want there."

"I only wish I had been able to get to know him before he left," Jane said.

"Oh, I wish that, as well, although I know you will have more opportunities in the future."

Elizabeth was flooded with a strange sensation of regret upon hearing he was not going to come to the wedding. She gave her head a quick shake and blamed it on wanting to see how he would act towards her sister and his friend once they were married. As she had wondered about the long friendship these two men shared, she realized this was the perfect opportunity to inquire about it.

"Mr. Bingley, if you do not mind my asking, I am curious about your friendship with Mr. Darcy. How did the two of you become such good friends?"

Mr. Bingley looked up as if he were thinking back to something, and then he lowered his head, and his shoulders fell. "Grief," he said softly. "We were both grieving the loss of our fathers."

He was quiet for a moment and then began again. "I had just started at Cambridge after my father's death the year before. My father had done well in trade, and I inherited a good fortune, but I had not grown up amongst those who were of high rank and wealth." He shook his head. "I was trying to find my way around, but there were many from the higher classes of society at Cambridge that chose not to associate with me because of my connection with trade."

"Oh, Charles, how could they do such a thing?" Jane asked. "You are such a fine, outstanding gentleman."

"Very easily," he said with a soft chuckle. "Many of them look down on those who made their fortune in trade. But it mattered not to me. I knew I could make friends easily, and one day I happened to encounter Darcy." He gave a shrug. "We were both in the library, and we began talking. He had missed the whole previous year of school because of his father's illness and then his death, and he had returned to finish."

"That explains your age difference," Elizabeth said.

Bingley nodded. "We were both, I think, in need of someone to talk to who would understand what we were feeling."

Jane placed her hand over his. "You must have both been deeply grieving."

"We were. But his grief was so much deeper than mine, for he had the added responsibilities thrust on him of being the master of his estate, as well as suddenly becoming the guardian of his twelve-year-old sister. Despite sharing guardianship with his cousin, I know it weighed heavily on him." Bingley placed his other hand over Jane's. "I had no pressing responsibilities at the time other than acquiring my education, providing for my sisters, and eventually finding a home in town and one in the country." He smiled. "I still have to find one in town, but I shall wait to choose one with you, Jane."

Jane smiled. "I would be pleased with any home if you had already chosen one," she said.

Elizabeth laughed. "I hope one of you will be able to make a decision, for you are both always pleased with everything and find fault with nothing."

"Elizabeth, you know that is not true," Jane said with a blush. "Why, just a few months ago, I..." Jane paused and looked at Mr. Bingley. "Never mind," she said.

Elizabeth chuckled, believing she was going to mention her concerns about Mr. Marshall, but she must have thought better of it.

Elizabeth turned to Mr. Bingley. "Did you ever wonder whether Mr. Darcy would have been like the others and would want nothing to do with you if you had not your grief in common?" She was truly wondering this herself. "He is a man of great fortune and from a distinguished family, after all."

He shook his head. "True, but he has always treated me with the utmost civility and respect. I was honoured that such an esteemed man befriended me." He suddenly chuckled. "But we also had a... reciprocal relationship."

"What do you mean?" Jane asked.

"I make friends readily and converse easily, but he does not. The close friends he had made at Cambridge had graduated, so he found it easier to be around me when put into those situations where he knew few people."

"And what did he do for you?" Elizabeth asked.

Mr. Bingley hung his head. "This does not speak well of me." He paused and drew in a breath. "I found some classes difficult, and he tutored me." He looked at Elizabeth with a grimace. "I hate to admit that I find reading very tedious, while he, being an avid reader, had to encourage me."

"So, you helped him socially, and he helped you with your studies," Jane smiled at him. "I can see why the two of you became such good friends."

He nodded. "To me, the friendship I have with him is deeper than with anyone else I have ever known – even more than family or friends!" He then let out a long sigh. "I think that is why I am so disappointed he will not be coming to the wedding." He looked up with a wistful smile. "He is the one person I wanted to be there." He squeezed Jane's hand, and his smiled widened. "Other than you, my dearest, angel! Other than you!"

Chapter 18

Once there was a break in the winter weather, Darcy returned to London with Georgiana and her companion, Mrs. Annesley. He remained but a few days to make certain she was settled in and to attend to some business. He then left for Portsmouth to visit his uncle, the Earl of Schorleon, and his family.

He had not visited their estate in four years, as it was so far south. He often saw them when they came to London, and they occasionally made the journey to Derbyshire to stay at Pemberley. He was eager to see them and hopefully put a certain lady – and a certain upcoming wedding day – out of his mind.

He would have preferred that Richard be there as well, for he greatly enjoyed his cousin's company. But as a colonel in the army, many responsibilities fell under his purview. Darcy knew that with their annual trip to Kent at Easter to visit their Aunt Catherine already on Richard's schedule, he would likely not be able to get away again.

He leaned his head back in the carriage as he pondered what Richard would have said to him regarding Elizabeth. Would he even have told him about her? He absently shook his head as he gazed out the window. His cousin was as discerning as Georgiana and would likely have noticed something was wrong.

Darcy could imagine his laughter as he teased him about his heartbreak. *"So, the steadfast, staid Darcy has a broken heart, does he?"* He would likely ask, *"What kind of young lady is this who touched your heart, yet showed little interest in a gentleman of grand fortune and consequence?"* Knowing Richard, he would add, *"A gentleman who is also exceedingly handsome and turns the head of every lady in the ton!"*

Darcy groaned as he recollected the many times his cousin had feigned despair over the unfair advantage he had over him. *A lot of good that advantage had been in winning Elizabeth's heart.* He drew in a deep breath and let it out in a groan. It was apparent those things meant little to Elizabeth. Perhaps that was one reason he was so frustratingly attracted to her.

He began to impatiently tap his fingers on his leg. If Richard were there, he would know how to make him laugh, and perhaps laughing at his foolish heart was what he needed.

Unfortunately, he knew his aunt and uncle, and especially Richard's older brother Robert, would not provide the levity and distraction he so needed right now. His uncle was the brother of his late mother and Aunt Catherine. Darcy always considered him more like his mother in his kindness and compassion, but occasionally a streak of his aunt's domineering personality would raise its ugly head.

He decided he would remain a month and then return to London before going on to Kent with Richard to see his aunt and cousin Anne. He always dreaded the trip, but going with his cousin had always made it a little more tolerable.

~~*

When Elizabeth was not occupied with the plans for Mr. Bingley and Jane's wedding, she found herself contemplating what he had said about his friendship with Mr. Darcy. She could not pinpoint why she could not put that gentleman out of her mind, but she felt that in one area, at least, he had improved in her estimation. The times he had stood off by himself was not so much that he was disgusted with the people in the neighbourhood, but because he was not well-acquainted with them and therefore, it was not easy for him to converse with them.

She recollected how he had been at Mr. Bingley's side on several occasions when they entered a roomful of people. It was Mr. Bingley who readily struck up the conversations. She shook her head as she considered this. How could it be that a man of wealth and consequence did not have the ability to converse with others just because he did not know them well?

It certainly was a question that begged to be answered. Despite that, she still could not forgive him for trying to influence his friend or for treating Mr. Wickham as he had.

Mr. Wickham! She wondered about that gentleman. Perhaps once the wedding was over, she would walk with Kitty and Lydia into Meryton and see for herself. She smiled and found herself looking forward to it.

The day of the wedding finally arrived, and there could not have been a lovelier ceremony or a more beautiful couple. Mrs. Bennet, of course, took all the credit for the dress, food, decorations, and even for the beauty of her eldest daughter.

Elizabeth could barely contain her pleasure at the joy and happiness that radiated from both the bride and the groom. Charles steadfastly held onto the hope that his good friend would show up for the ceremony, despite what he had said in his letter. But he did not.

It appeared that Mr. Bingley's sisters were now resigned to the marriage and extended Jane a warm welcome into the family. Jane told Elizabeth that Mr. Bingley assured her that by the time they returned from their wedding journey, Miss Bingley would be in London with the Hursts.

After the wedding breakfast, the couple departed, and Elizabeth breathed a sigh of relief that all had gone well. But she suddenly felt a tinge of regret that she would no longer have her sister by her side to talk to, share her hopes and dreams with, or to stay up late into the night solving all the problems of the world – or at least of their neighbourhood.

She had missed her sister a great deal when she had been in the Lake District but then reminded herself that Jane would be only three miles away, an easy walk for her. Jane had assured her that she could visit her at Netherfield at any time of the day. *But not late at night,* Elizabeth said to herself with just a little remorse.

~~*

At the beginning of the second week of Darcy's visit in Portsmouth, the family received distressing news.

The earl remained calm as he gathered his family to him. "I

have just received word that Richard was injured. I do not know…"

"Injured!" his wife exclaimed. "How serious is it?" She began fanning herself, and her husband led her to a chair to sit down.

"I do not know the particulars; it does not say. It only says he is being brought to the hospital at Portsmouth."

"At least he will be close by," Robert said.

His father nodded. "But he likely will not arrive for few days."

"Is there any way we can find out what happened or what his injuries are?" Darcy asked, consumed by a great sense of dread regarding Richard's condition. He knew now that he must remain as long as needed for him and his family.

The earl shook his head. "I will try to find out." He drew in a breath as he raked his fingers through his hair. "They will notify us when he arrives at the hospital."

The earl began to pace restlessly. "I hate the thought that he might be suffering."

"Or not knowing what kind of care is he receiving." The countess grasped her husband's arm, bringing him to a halt. "Do you think there have been physicians looking after him?" She let out a mournful sigh. "I have heard such horror stories."

"We must hope and pray his injuries are not severe. In the meantime, we must wait for word of his arrival."

The atmosphere in the home was subdued and dismal for the remainder of the day. It was apparent to Darcy that everyone was as worried as he was. His uncle attempted to reassure everyone, especially his wife, that worrying would not help and they must have faith, but Darcy could see that the strain of not knowing added creases to his face, increased his restlessness, and caused his glum silence.

Darcy was content to sit in silence and found it difficult to even comprehend what he would do without his cousin. Despite trying to convince himself that Richard was strong and healthy and would recover completely, there was a thin thread of trepidation that he might not. When he finally went to bed that night, he tossed and turned with worry.

It was not until nearly midnight, with sleep still evading him, that Darcy realized the date. It was the thirteenth of February, and by now, Elizabeth and Bingley were married. He was surprised he had not thought of it at all, although he was certain it was because of the concern he felt for his cousin.

That realization added to the constriction of his chest. He found it difficult to breathe and felt completely helpless in his inability to aid his cousin or to eradicate the strong and enduring feelings for Elizabeth that seemed integral to his very being.

Darcy sat up in bed and dropped his head into his hands, rubbing his throbbing temples. His stomach was in knots, and he took a few deep breaths as he stood and walked over to the dresser.

He picked up a decanter of brandy and poured himself a drink. Lifting the glass into the air, he said, "To you, my friend. May you and…" he swallowed as his throat was suddenly dry. "May you and Elizabeth find great joy and contentment in your marriage." He downed the drink and closed his eyes as the burning liquid travelled down his throat. "You both deserve great happiness."

He returned to his bed and sat down upon it. Now that they were married, he would make every attempt to put thoughts of her aside. He had another, greater concern now, and that was the recovery of his cousin.

~~*

Cold, frigid temperatures and snow kept the Bennet ladies homebound for the next month. When at last there was a slight warming and the snow began to melt, there was hope that a trip into Meryton would be possible soon. Elizabeth did not think the day could come soon enough for her; she so wished to be outdoors. Her two youngest sisters were not making it easy, complaining of nothing to do or wondering how the officers were coping without them.

When the roads were finally walkable and sunshine provided a much-needed warmth, Kitty and Lydia set off for Meryton. Elizabeth, however, chose to go to Netherfield. Charles and Jane had visited twice since returning from their wedding journey, but there had not been an opportunity for just the two sisters to talk. She set off, hoping to spend some time alone with Jane.

Elizabeth walked part of the way with Kitty and Lydia.

"How can you not want to go into Meryton?" Lydia cried. "Imagine how much the officers will have missed seeing us!"

"I thank you, Lydia, for enlightening me on the officers' loss, but I have greatly missed Jane."

"All the more for us!" Lydia exclaimed with a laugh and took Kitty's hand as they set off.

Elizabeth shook her head, wishing the two of them were not so eager to throw themselves at the officers. She had to admit she would like to see Mr. Wickham again, but that was due more to what she might find out from him about Mr. Darcy.

She gave a slight shrug of her shoulders and set off towards Netherfield.

Jane was delighted to see her sister and welcomed her with open arms. Elizabeth was pleased that Mr. Bingley was meeting with his steward, giving the two of them time to themselves.

The sisters sat down, and Elizabeth took Jane's hand. "It is so good to see you. I have missed having your calming presence at home."

"I have missed you, as well." Jane said earnestly. "I have seriously considered making up a room just for you." She chuckled softly. "Do you think Mr. Bingley would mind?"

Elizabeth laughed, and with a teasing glance, said, "Jane, do you not recollect I already have my own room here, for I had to stay here when we had a bad storm?"

"Perhaps if you linger long enough, it will begin to rain or snow and you can stay overnight again. I am certain Charles would not mind."

They both laughed, and then Elizabeth grew serious. "Has he heard anything from Mr. Darcy?"

Jane shook her head. "No, and he believes he offended him in some way. He is certain of it because the letter he received from him in reply was so brief." She let out a sigh. "I have tried to reassure him that surely cannot be the case, but I do not know if he is convinced." She paused for a moment and then added, "He has always sought his friend's advice, and he wonders if he ought to have done so before asking for my hand."

Elizabeth huffed. "Oh, Jane, I am glad he did not! Mr. Bingley is perfectly capable of making his own decisions without consulting first with Mr. Darcy!"

Jane took her sister's hand. "Lizzy, I do not think he wanted to ask for his permission to marry me but to ask for his blessing."

Elizabeth pursed her lips. "But if Mr. Darcy had refused to give it, or worse, admonished him not to marry you, what would he have done?" She felt that familiar burn of anger towards Mr. Darcy rising within her.

"I know he loves me, and he would have made every attempt to convince him of that." Jane tilted her head. "You seem very suspect of Mr. Darcy's character. Why is that?"

Elizabeth shrugged. "I was able to observe him much longer than you were. I was in his company and…" She shook her head. There was no need to confess to Jane what Wickham had told her. Mr. Darcy was, after all, her husband's good friend. "Well, I am certain Mr. Darcy has no ill will towards your husband, and the two will see each other soon."

"I hope so, Lizzy. I hate to see him so downcast over it."

~~*

Despite the mild days that followed Elizabeth's visit with Jane, she no longer had a reason to venture into Meryton with the hopes of seeing Mr. Wickham. For when Kitty and Lydia returned from their walk into the village that day, they returned distraught with the news that Mr. Wickham was singling out Miss Mary King, who had recently come into the neighbourhood to live with her uncle. Apparently, she had recently received a fairly large inheritance, which made Elizabeth somewhat suspicious of Wickham's motives.

She began looking forward to the trip to Kent with her father. While she was not anxious to spend a large amount of time in Mr. Collins's company, she looked forward to seeing how Mary was doing as his wife and mistress of the parsonage. She was also curious to meet Lady Catherine de Bourgh and her daughter.

The day before they were to depart, Elizabeth visited Jane, and they spent the time talking about Mary and how she might be doing. They recalled she had taken only a few things, and Jane asked Elizabeth if she would mind taking some of her older gowns to give to her. Charles had been most gracious in having several new dresses and gowns made for her.

Elizabeth was delighted to do that.

As they talked, the subject of Mr. Darcy came up again.

"Has there been any word from him?" Elizabeth asked.

"No, but that reminds me. Charles mentioned that in the years he has known Mr. Darcy, he always goes to visit his aunt in Kent at Easter."

Elizabeth was taken aback. "He does?" A quaver crept into her voice, and she felt her heart pound.

Jane nodded excitedly. "You will likely see him! Lizzy, perhaps you will be able find out if something happened that will explain his silence and absence."

Elizabeth could not define the feelings she was experiencing. Were they the result of looking forward to seeing him or dreading it? Perhaps she was nervous that she would actually discover why he did not come to the wedding and it would only serve to reinforce the anger she had against him. She did not know, but this suddenly increased her anticipation of going. She actually thought his presence might provide her with a pleasant diversion. But then, again, he might not even come.

~~*

As Richard's family waited for news of his arrival at the hospital, Darcy informed them that he would remain with them as long as needed to assist in his cousin's recovery. He would even stay through what would have been a trip to see his aunt over Easter in the middle of March.

Four days later the family received word that Richard had finally arrived at the hospital. The family readied the carriage for the hour journey.

"I shall travel in my own carriage," Darcy said. "I plan to stay at the hospital with him so you can return home each evening."

The countess took his hand. "Thank you. That will mean a great deal to him."

They anxiously set out for the hospital, wondering how Richard was faring. The earl had not been able to gain any further intelligence about his son's injuries. When they arrived, they were directed to his bed, and the family hurried to his side.

Darcy looked down with concern at his cousin, who was thrashing about in delirium. He heard his aunt moan, and when he looked at her, noticed she had grown pale. He hurried to her side and caught her as she began to collapse. He assisted her to a chair, and her husband began to fan her with his handkerchief.

A military officer came by and gave an account of the incident to the family.

"We were returning from the continent after a successful campaign, but as we rounded the southern tip, we were surprised by French warships." He slowly shook his head. "We were hit several times and lost fourteen men. Seven other men were brought in today with Colonel Fitzwilliam, with injuries ranging from severe lacerations to crushed limbs."

"What is the extent of Colonel Fitzwilliam's injuries?" Darcy asked.

"He is one of the fortunate ones who survived. He has a major laceration in one leg that extends from his calf down to his foot and a broken bone in the other leg." He grew sombre. "As long as he survives the fever and delirium, there is every possibility he will recover." The officer turned his head to look at the patient. "Unfortunately, these injuries may prohibit him from continuing his military duties – at least on the field." He looked at the earl and the countess. "He is an excellent officer and was tending to the injured when we were hit again, and that is when he sustained his injuries. You can both be proud of him."

"Thank you, sir. Are those the extent of his injuries?" the earl asked.

The officer shook his head. "He has other minor injuries, but his leg injuries are the most severe. Unfortunately, the laceration has become infected, and the resulting high fever is what is causing the delirium."

The officer continued, "The physicians here are doing everything they can for him and will keep you informed. From similar injuries I have seen, I suspect he will be here at least a week to ten days and then will be allowed to return home to fully recover." He shook his head. "It is likely to be a long recovery."

"Thank you. We greatly appreciate it," the earl said.

A physician came in a short time later and gave more information to the family. "Colonel Fitzwilliam's break was very typical, and I do not foresee any difficulty in his recovering, although he may not have as much mobility as he did before." He drew in a long breath. "Before he was brought here, the physician with the regiment was able to set the broken bone in his leg. Right now, he has a wood cast to keep it immobile while it heals, and we need to keep an eye on his wounds."

"How long do you think the fever will continue?" the countess asked. "How soon before we are able to talk to him?"

The physician pressed his lips into a thin line and gave a slight shrug. "The fever and delirium might stay with him a week to ten days." He looked down at his patient. "Then again, it may end sooner or perhaps last longer."

"Thank you." Darcy turned to look at his cousin. "He is strong. I am certain we will soon see improvement."

"Once he begins to become aware of his surroundings, he will be in great pain, so we will give him laudanum, as well as some heavy drink to deaden the pain. That may add additional days to his being unresponsive. At that point, however, you will know he is recovering."

After spending the day at his side, his family decided to return home before dusk fell, while Darcy insisted he would remain at his cousin's side. They tried to convince him to return, as well, but he would have none of it. If there were any changes in Richard's condition, he could send a note to them to return to the hospital.

He stayed that night and four more, attempting to sleep in the chair next to his cousin's bed. He saw little improvement, but on the sixth day, Richard's fever lessened, and he began to stir. The next morning, after getting something to eat, Darcy returned to his cousin's side. He found him sitting up in bed; his eyes were open, and he was looking around.

"Well, this is certainly a shocking surprise!" Richard laughed. "What brings you here?"

"You brought me here, my good cousin, and I have been here over a week. Your family ought to be here shortly." He placed his hand on Richard's shoulder, giving it a squeeze. "We have been worried about you. It is good to finally see you awake."

Richard shook his head. "Ha! It is only a minor wound!" He smiled at a young lady who came in to change the dressing on his leg.

"You only consider it minor because you are under the influence of laudanum!"

"Yes, I feel very little."

As the nurse pulled away the wrapping, he winced briefly at the pain as it tugged the skin, but then his eyes twinkled. "I felt that, but it is not often a man gets such fine treatment from a beautiful young lady."

The young lady said nothing, but her cheeks warmed in a rosy blush. When she stepped away to treat another patient, Darcy gave a quick shake of his head.

"A broken bone is not a minor wound, but it was also the infection that set in that had us worried." Darcy frowned. "You have been here a week, and all that time you have been delirious. You were not even aware that your family and I were here!" He let out a huff. "And I am surprised you can still flirt in your condition."

"I am not dead, good sir, and as long as I have breath in this body, I shall behave as I always have."

Darcy smiled, fairly confident his cousin was well on his way to a recovery.

"You ought to give it a try. A little smile in a young lady's direction, a kind word or two…" He shook his finger at him. "You may find yourself with a pretty little wife by your side." He thanked the nurse as she stepped out of the room.

Darcy folded his arms. "Or shackled to some foolish young lady, I fear."

"Well, it would be better than nothing. A foolish young lady can still be beautiful." Richard smiled.

Darcy's jaw clenched as he thought of Elizabeth. Could he have attempted to flirt with her? What would her response have been? He gave a shake of his head.

"And she might have a good fortune," Richard added.

"I shall leave flirting and its outcomes to you, thank you."

Fitzwilliam looked around him. "When can I leave this dreadful place?"

"It is likely you shall have to remain until they are certain the infection is completely gone and the bone in your leg is healing correctly." Darcy paused. "It will be a while before you can walk on it."

"I wonder what that means for my military career," he mused.

Darcy dropped his eyes and did not answer.

"I think I know the answer to that by the look on your face." Richard's lips turned down in a frown. "I had not planned on this."

Darcy pressed his lips tightly together. "I want you to know, Fitzwilliam, that I intend to stay with you as long as needed."

"What about your visit to Aunt Catherine? You know I will not be able to join you."

"Your injuries are a perfect excuse for me not to go. You know I detest those visits. You are the only thing that keeps me sane while I am there."

"Ha!" Richard said, and then gave a groan of pain. "She will not be pleased."

"I cannot help that," Darcy replied.

"So, you are truly not going?"

Darcy pursed his lips. "I want to make certain you are completely well before I even return to London." He shook his head. "The doctor has said your recovery could take another month or more. No, I will definitely *not* be going."

Chapter 19

Elizabeth's journey to Kent with her father went without mishap or annoyance. They knew each other well enough to know when conversation was desired or silence was preferred. Elizabeth spent the quiet times reading, working on needlework, or looking out at the beautiful landscape they passed.

"So Lizzy," her father said as they neared the small village of Hunsford. "We are almost there. What are you most looking forward to? Intelligent conversation with your brother-in-law or being intimidated by his patroness?"

Elizabeth chuckled. "I am not certain intelligent conversation with him is possible, although perhaps Mary has worked a little magic on him and made some improvement."

Mr. Bennet huffed. "I truly doubt that, but then, if you lead him to the subject of some biblical passage, doctrinal issue, or Lady Catherine de Bourgh, I am certain we might get a few sensible words from him."

Elizabeth's eyes lit up. "Actually, I am eager to meet Lady Catherine."

"Lizzy, are you truly?" He shook his head. "In her letter, Mary confessed she had been frightened of her, at first."

She chuckled. "Yes, but considering how Mr. Collins endlessly praised her and her daughter, how could I not be eager to meet her?" She looked up at him with a teasing smile. "In her letter, Mary said we can expect to dine there at least once."

"Oh, dear," Mr. Bennet said as he jutted his chin. "Do you suppose we shall meet her expectations?" He shook his head. "Or shall we fall short?"

Elizabeth shrugged. "It matters not to me; after three weeks are passed, I shall be gone."

Mr. Bennet patted his daughter's hand. "Yes, my dear. That is true, but let us remember that Mary does not have that option. Let us be on our best behaviour so she will remain in Lady Catherine's good graces."

"Do you think we shall be able to behave properly?" Elizabeth asked with a mischievous smile.

Mr. Bennet laughed. "What could we possibly do to make her angry, eh Lizzy?"

Elizabeth turned to gaze out the window. Perhaps inquiring about her nephew's engagement to her daughter?

~~*

They arrived at the Hunsford parsonage in late afternoon and were welcomed by both Mary and her husband. Elizabeth was a little disappointed in her sister's appearance; she looked as plain as she had before Mr. Collins came to Longbourn. She let out a soft sigh as she realized this was likely what Mary preferred and thus was content now that she was married.

The parsonage was very nicely fitted up for the couple. Mr. Collins was eager to show them the changes Lady Catherine had made to the home so it would be better suited for a clergyman and his wife, and Mary seemed to take great pleasure in that role.

They were introduced to John and Jocelyn Malone, who had been long-time servants at Rosings, but were sent to the parsonage to help the single maid once Mr. Collins had married.

"Did Mrs. Collins inform you that we have a son who lives in Hertfordshire?" Mrs. Malone inquired of Elizabeth and her father.

"No, do you get to see him often?" Elizabeth asked.

"Not as often as we like." Mrs. Malone said. Her smile was warm, and Elizabeth liked her immediately. She was an older lady who seemed to be perpetually happy, humming as she performed her duties and occasionally singing when she thought no one was listening.

Later that day, when Mr. Collins was outside showing Mr. Bennet the garden, Elizabeth thought it was the perfect opportunity to give Mary the dresses Jane sent along for her. Mary, however, hesitated to take them.

"Elizabeth, these dresses are far too elegant for a clergyman's wife. I cannot take them."

"Mary, they are not too elegant, and you will take them." She smiled. "You should see the dresses Mr. Bingley had made for Jane. Now *those* are elegant!"

Elizabeth could see a glimmer of admiration in her sister's expression and said, "Perhaps, if you feel the parishioners will think you are too concerned with vanity, you can wear them solely for Mr. Collins – or when you are invited to Rosings."

Mary nodded. "I suppose I can do that."

"Yes, and if you wear them often enough, they shall soon seem old and worn, and will be perfect for every occasion." Elizabeth had to stifle her smile.

"Yes," Mary said as she nodded her head.

Elizabeth picked up a rose-coloured dress. "In fact, if we receive an invitation to Rosings, I think you ought to wear this one."

"Do you really?" Mary asked.

Elizabeth took her sister's hand. "Mary, I am certain Lady Catherine will appreciate that you are acknowledging her rank by wearing one of your finer gowns when you visit."

Mary slowly nodded. "Yes, I believe she would." She called for Mrs. Malone and asked her to take them to her bedchamber.

"Of course, Mrs. Collins. My, these are so pretty. I cannot wait to see you wearing them."

Elizabeth liked Mrs. Malone even more.

They rested for the remainder of the day, and the following day Elizabeth asked if she could walk about. There was a beautiful park, a grove dense with trees, and an inviting wooded area. She was advised to return in a timely manner, for they were to have tea with Lady Catherine de Bourgh and her daughter later that day.

Nothing pleased Elizabeth more than strolling about in a place she had never seen before! She enjoyed it even more so because Mr. Collins had begun to agitate her. She felt sorry for her poor father, who seemed nearly ready to join her on her walk, despite his never having cared much for the exercise.

She decided to walk in the grove, where budding trees and the first bloom of wildflowers beckoned her. She breathed in the fresh air and looked up at the sky, which was a deep blue, dotted with white puffy clouds moving across the sky on a slight breeze. It could not be more perfect.

At length, she came to a small rise on the dirt path she had taken, and when she climbed to the top, she stopped abruptly. Just ahead of her she saw a most delightful sight. A small section of the path was lined with birch trees, which formed a canopy over it. Tall grasses on either side were dotted with the bluebells beginning to bud, as well as some yellow and orange wildflowers. She hurried over to the path, and when she reached the part shaded by the trees, she leaned against one of the tree trunks. It was a sight pleasing to her eyes. The fragrance of the flowers teased her nostrils, and a choir of birds sang their harmonious melodies as they built their nests or tried to attract the attention of another bird.

Elizabeth could have stayed there all day, but recollected the admonition to return in time to go to Rosings, so she returned to the parsonage, where she freshened up and changed. She now felt ready to meet Lady Catherine de Bourgh and her daughter. When she came downstairs to join her sister and Mr. Collins, she was delighted to see that Mary was also prepared to see Lady Catherine. She was wearing the rose-coloured dress she had brought to her from Jane.

As they walked to Rosings, Mr. Collins spoke endlessly about the home, what Lady Catherine expected, how to act in her presence, and the fact that, under no circumstances, should anyone contradict her.

Mr. Bennet turned to Elizabeth with a smile and a single lifted brow, a sure indication that he was issuing a challenge to her to see which one of them could bring down the ire of this woman first. She gave a quick shake of her head. It would not do to irritate this forbidding lady – at least on their first visit to her home.

When they stepped into the manor, she knew from Mr. Collins's enthusiastic descriptions, to look for all the chimneys, windows, cornices, imported area rugs, and fine tapestries. To Elizabeth's delight – and horror – it lived up to his verbose narrative.

Everything was exquisite — almost to the point that it was smothering. There was simply too much. Was it possible that every time Lady Catherine stepped out of her home she returned with something new? Was it her intention to fill every empty space? Was there even an empty space remaining that could hold something new? Heaven forbid that all this had filled the home for centuries with no one having the desire to remove any of it.

They walked through a long, wide hall on plush oriental rugs lying on a highly polished wood floor. The window coverings were made from heavily textured, dark-coloured fabrics that were barely open, letting in a minimal amount of sunlight. Elizabeth fought the urge to pull them open further to allow the brilliant sun to enter and light up the oppressive rooms.

They were brought into a large sitting room, where darkness reigned, prompting Elizabeth to blink her eyes several times to allow them to adjust. She heard a woman's commanding voice before she was able to discern her figure sitting to her right.

"Ah! Mr. and Mrs. Collins! You have arrived and brought your guests! Do come in and have a seat!"

Mr. Collins bowed and thanked her profusely. "It is such generosity you bestow on us, Lady Catherine. We appreciate the invitation to take tea with you and thank you wholeheartedly." He bowed again.

"Yes, yes; now, Mrs. Collins, you must make the introductions."

Mary did as she was instructed, introducing her father and sister to Lady Catherine and her daughter. It was only when Miss Anne de Bourgh was introduced that Elizabeth noticed the frail young lady sitting in a dark corner of the room. To the Collinses and Lady Catherine, her quiet presence there did not at all seem unusual. But to Elizabeth and her father, an exchanged glance indicated they were thinking the same thing. Why was a young lady in her late twenties, the daughter of an esteemed woman, hiding in the shadows? And Elizabeth wondered how it could be true that Mr. Darcy was expected to marry her.

She pushed these thoughts aside, and the usual small talk ensued. They spoke of the journey, the roads, and the weather, interspersed with praises for the home. Those compliments came primarily from Mr. Collins, whose pointed glances at his guests indicated he expected them to agree with him.

Since Mary had already apprised Lady Catherine of every aspect of their family in the past three months since moving just across the lane, most of the conversation was about the de Bourgh family and Rosings.

At length, as they were enjoying refreshments, Lady Catherine looked at Elizabeth. "Mrs. Collins informed me that you are acquainted with my nephew, Fitzwilliam Darcy."

"Indeed, I am," she replied. "My sister is married to his good friend."

"I see," she said with narrowed brows. "He and my other nephew, Colonel Fitzwilliam, are to come soon. They enjoy their Easter visit here every year."

So he will soon be here, Elizabeth thought. "I am certain he enjoys coming to see you and your daughter." Elizabeth hoped for some word from her confirming the engagement between him and Miss de Bourgh, but Lady Catherine said nothing more.

At length, as they were preparing to leave, a letter was delivered and brought to Lady Catherine. She took it and looked down. "Oh! Speaking of my nephew! The letter is from him!" She excitedly opened it, but the smile on her face quickly disappeared. "No!" She shook her head repeatedly. "No, no, no! This cannot be!"

"Lady Catherine, what is wrong?" Mr. Collins asked. "Has something dreadful happened? Is there anything I can do for you?"

Elizabeth watched as the woman's face grew red with fury, and she wondered what Mr. Darcy could have said to make her so angry.

Lady Catherine finally looked up and realized everyone was watching her. She cleared her voice. "My nephews are not to come! Richard has been injured, and Fitzwilliam has chosen to remain with him until he is fully recovered!" She stood up and began to pace about the room. "This is not to be borne!"

Mr. Collins clasped his hands and shook his head. "How grievous this is! How serious are Colonel Fitzwilliam's injuries?"

He shuddered. "Will he survive?"

She stamped her foot. "It cannot be terribly serious, as he is now recovering at home."

"For that, we are grateful," Mr. Collins said.

Lady Catherine shook her head. "But if that is the case, there is no reason why Fitzwilliam should not come! This is extremely vexing!"

Elizabeth looked at Miss de Bourgh to see her response to this news. There was nothing in her expression or demeanour that gave any indication that her disappointment was as severe as her mother's.

Lady Catherine suddenly squared her shoulders, and her expression grew stern. "I know what I must do!" She turned to the others in the room. "It is late, and I regret that you must depart." She rang for a servant, who appeared promptly. "Please show our guests out."

When they stood and thanked her for tea, she followed them out of the parlour but then turned to walk down the hallway in the opposite direction.

As they returned to the parsonage, Elizabeth and her father walked behind Mary and her husband.

"What do you suppose the great woman is going to do, Lizzy?" he asked. "Do you think she will write to that proud nephew of hers demanding that he leave his cousin on his deathbed and come directly?" He turned and looked at her. "What is this reluctant smile, my daughter? Do you regret that he will not be coming?"

Elizabeth shook her head. "No, indeed!" She attempted to laugh. "I would have enjoyed watching him interact with Miss de Bourgh, however."

"Ah, yes. From what I have seen of the proud Mr. Darcy and the meek and frail Miss de Bourgh, they will certainly make an interesting match." He laughed and shook his head. "I would imagine they will spend their days as husband and wife saying absolutely nothing to each other."

Elizabeth murmured an affirmative, but in her mind, she recollected the many intelligent conversations *she* had had with him. She shook her head, trying to reconcile his ever taking Miss de Bourgh for his wife.

Her father continued. "We saw the extent of Lady Catherine's ire tonight, did we not?" He shook his head. "I am glad we heeded Mr. Collins's advice and did not contradict anything she said."

"Yes!" Elizabeth said. "But there were times I could see in your face that you wanted to."

"I believe I saw that look on your face, as well," he said with a chuckle.

~~*

The next day Mr. Collins waited impatiently for a summons from Rosings, but none came. He fretted whether he ought to pay an uninvited call, but decided against it.

Meanwhile, Elizabeth continued to explore the grounds on her walks.

She walked towards the woods but did not wish to get lost and so did not venture too far into them. She also walked down to a nearby stream, before deciding the tree-lined path was her favourite of all.

On the third day, they bid Mr. Bennet farewell as he prepared to return to Longbourn.

"I shall return in three weeks," he said. "I shall enjoy hearing my son-in-law preach the Easter sermon." As Elizabeth hugged him and wished him a safe journey, he said, "You know I am curious about this whole affair with Lady Catherine and her nephew. You must write directly when you find out what she did." He kissed her forehead. "And if Mr. Darcy does come, please delight me by giving a faithful narrative of how he behaves around Miss de Bourgh."

"You know I will," she said with a smile.

As the next two days brought rain, Elizabeth remained indoors. Mr. Collins spent those days at the church, so she and Mary had some time alone together. She was delighted when her sister wore one of Jane's morning dresses, without her even suggesting it. Elizabeth smiled and merely told her that she looked lovely.

The following afternoon, as the skies were clear and the paths dry, Elizabeth eagerly set out on a walk, deciding to return to the tree-lined path. As she walked down the lane that separated the parsonage from Rosings, she noticed a young lady walking in the gardens. An older lady sat on a nearby bench.

Thinking it was Miss de Bourgh and her companion, Mrs. Jenkinson, Elizabeth decided to walk over and greet them. Perhaps she could engage her in conversation and find out something about her. She might not be able to get her to speak about her engagement to her cousin, but perhaps she could discover there was more to her than what she had seen the other day.

As she drew closer, however, she realized it was not Miss de Bourgh. The young lady looked up, and Elizabeth saw that it was a very pretty young lady with a sweet smile.

"Good day," the young girl said as Elizabeth approached.

"Hello! I thought perhaps you were Miss de Bourgh, but I can see now that I was mistaken."

The young lady smiled. "It is understandable. We are similar in height."

Elizabeth searched her face, seeing a vague familiarity in it. "Forgive me for disturbing you."

The young girl smiled and shook her head. "Think nothing of it. Do you live around here?"

"No. I am visiting my sister, Mary, who recently married the clergyman, Mr. Collins. They are living at the parsonage just across the lane." She paused and said, "Forgive me for introducing myself, but I am Miss Elizabeth Bennet."

"It is a pleasure to make your acquaintance, Miss Bennet. "I am Lady Catherine's niece. My name is Georgiana Darcy."

Chapter 20

Elizabeth was taken aback and hoped that the young girl had not noticed her surprise. She felt a tremor pass through her as she considered her brother was likely here, as well. "Miss Darcy, it is a pleasure to make your acquaintance."

"Thank you," she replied softly.

"I… we understood that your brother had changed his plans and he was not coming. Has your cousin healed from his injuries so that the two of you could now come?" Elizabeth placed her hand on her throat and could feel her heart racing.

Miss Darcy shook her head. "My cousin is still recovering at his parent's home, where my brother remains. They are not only cousins, but are as close as brothers, and Fitzwilliam could not bear to leave him."

"I see." Elizabeth's pounding heart slowed, and she was uncertain whether it was relief or disappointment that he was not here and would likely not come.

"I beg your pardon," the young girl said. "I do not mean to take up your time. Were you on your way to see my aunt?"

Elizabeth shook her head. "No, I enjoy walking and was going to the grove."

Miss Darcy's nose crinkled. "Alone?"

Elizabeth softly chuckled at the recollection of Mr. Darcy asking the same thing, but also what he had said about not wanting his sister to do such a thing. "Yes, it is a very bad habit I have."

Miss Darcy looked back at the other woman. "Mrs. Annesley – she is my companion – is not a great walker. I love to walk. When I am at Pemberley, my brother and I walk often, as the weather permits." She bit her lip. "Would you mind having someone to walk with you? I will ask Mrs. Annesley to see if she approves."

"I would be delighted to have you join me."

As the young girl hurried over to her companion, Elizabeth considered this a most fortunate circumstance. She looked forward to discovering whether she was at all like her brother.

Miss Darcy returned with a wide smile on her face. Her companion walked alongside. "She has agreed to allow me to walk with you but first wished an introduction."

After Miss Darcy introduced them, Elizabeth assured the older woman that she would take good care of the young girl while they walked.

"I only request that she return within the hour," Mrs. Annesley said. "Lady Catherine is having afternoon tea and demands punctuality."

"I shall return her to you promptly." Elizabeth offered the young girl her arm, and the two walked away.

There was silence between them at first, and then Elizabeth asked, "When did you arrive at Rosings?"

"Late yesterday afternoon."

"Lady Catherine told us that your brother's plans to come had been cancelled due to your cousin's injury, but she did not mention that you would be coming."

Georgiana looked at Elizabeth. "I had no plans to come at all. My aunt arrived in London two days ago and insisted that I return with her for Easter, as my brother could not." She paused. "She was not pleased that he cancelled his visit."

"She went to London and talked you into coming?"

A troubled look crossed the young girl's face. "She claimed that my brother wholeheartedly approved the scheme, and the next thing I knew, she was having my bags packed." Miss Darcy let out a long sigh. "She is not my guardian, but she sometimes acts as though she is, and I knew not what to do." A small wince appeared. "I do not think I could ever defy her, especially when she is angry and has her mind made up."

"Lady Catherine put you in a difficult situation, but at least she had consulted your brother."

"I thought she had, but now I am not certain. When we arrived yesterday, she insisted I write and tell him I had come to Rosings." Miss Darcy let out an exasperated sigh. "I sent him a letter early this morning."

"I see. Are you and your brother close?"

Georgiana chuckled. "Despite our age difference and the fact that he is my brother as well as my guardian, we are extremely close."

"You are fortunate. I have heard frightful stories of guardians – whether a relation or not." Elizabeth smiled. "He is not particularly severe in his expectations, then?"

Georgiana laughed. "He certainly has high expectations and can be demanding, but... in a loving manner."

Elizabeth tilted her head. "What do you mean?"

Georgiana pursed her lips. "I know he loves me and wants what is best for me. If he dislikes something I have done, he will let me know." She looked up at Elizabeth earnestly. "But he has never gotten angry at me, even when..." She paused and shook her head. "He has always treated me with kindness and compassion, even when I do not deserve it."

"It sounds like he is an ideal brother. I do not have any brothers. I only have four sisters."

Miss Darcy sighed. "I would like to have had a sister."

Elizabeth stopped and looked at her. "Perhaps someday you will, when your brother marries."

"Perhaps. But if he does marry, I worry that I may not have sisterly affection towards her."

"I am certain you shall." Elizabeth was disappointed the young girl did not say anything about his marrying Miss de Bourgh.

They walked on a bit further in silence, and then Elizabeth said, "You said you walk at Pemberley. Have you often walked here at Rosings?"

"No, I rarely come here. I believe I was ten when I was last here. My brother and I did walk, but I remember very little."

"Then if you do not mind, I shall lead the way. Come, Miss Darcy. There is something I want to show you before we turn back."

They passed a variety of trees that had an abundance of new green leaves, while others were still barren from the cold winter.

Some wildflowers had begun to bloom, and Georgiana was delighted to see a few bluebells dotting the landscape.

A small unkempt path separated high grasses on either side. The sky above was a deep, rich blue with an occasional cloud hurrying past. The weather was mild, and a slight breeze stirred the leaves and grasses.

They approached the small ridge Elizabeth had found previously, and when they reached the top, the young girl gasped.

"Look!" she said, pointing towards the tree-lined path. "I have never seen anything like it. It is beautiful!"

"Shall we walk to it?"

Miss Darcy nodded excitedly.

As they reached the path and walked underneath the trees, the air suddenly cooled, and Miss Darcy tucked her arm further into Elizabeth's.

"Your reaction to seeing this was the same as mine," Elizabeth said. "Despite loving to explore new paths, I would be content to spend the remainder of my days in Kent strolling under the shelter of these trees." She let out an admiring sigh. "I believe it would remove any vexations one was experiencing. Do you not think so?"

"Oh, yes!" Miss Darcy breathed in deeply. "Everything smells so fresh."

Elizabeth nodded. "It is like heaven itself."

They walked to the end of the tree-lined path and then turned around, standing still as they looked back. Georgiana sighed. "I like this place and could willingly waste my time in it."

Elizabeth laughed. "I see you read Shakespeare! *As You Like It*, if I recollect correctly."

"Yes, that is correct, but then I almost expect the fairies from *Midsummer Night's Dream* to jump out and dance around us."

"We must keep on the lookout for them," Elizabeth said with a soft laugh.

Miss Darcy looked up at Elizabeth. "Miss Bennet, would you mind if I joined you on a walk every day?" Her eyes lit up in a smile, but then it quickly faded. "You might not want me to accompany you, so please tell me if you would prefer I not. I do not want to be a bother if you wish to be alone."

"I would be delighted, Miss Darcy." She tilted her head. "Do you think your brother would approve?"

"I do not think he would mind. He loves walking so much himself."

"Indeed, he does," Elizabeth replied.

A look of surprise crossed Miss Darcy's face, and then she laughed softly. "It sounds as though you are acquainted with my brother."

Elizabeth quickly turned her head away and then looked back. "As a matter of fact, I am."

"May I ask how you know him?"

Elizabeth drew in a deep breath. "He was visiting his friend last year. Our paths crossed on a few occasions." Elizabeth turned to her. "Are you acquainted with Mr. Bingley?"

Miss Darcy nodded her head. "Indeed, I know him and his sisters fairly well."

Elizabeth smiled. "My sister married Mr. Bingley just this past February." Elizabeth watched as the girl's cheeks grew pink, and her expression turned sombre. "Miss Darcy, is something wrong?" She felt a pang of regret, wondering whether the young girl perhaps had hoped to marry Mr. Bingley, herself.

"No, I am merely... surprised that you are acquainted with my brother and that you are Mrs. Bingley's sister."

"I am."

"My brother spoke of her," she said softly.

Elizabeth discreetly rolled her eyes, imagining what he may have said, knowing how he disapproved of her and her family. "Did he?" she asked.

"Yes. He said he greatly admired her."

"Admired her?" Elizabeth asked incredulously. "Now I have to admit that *I* am surprised, for he barely knew her."

"Oh, but he... he must have known her well enough to have formed such a favourable opinion of her! In fact, he told me he believed Mr. Bingley had made an excellent match."

Elizabeth was astonished he would have spoken so highly of Jane. She wondered whether he was merely being polite to his sister and had not told her his true opinion, or perhaps Miss Darcy was being polite and not telling her what he actually said. She shook her head, unable to comprehend how Mr. Darcy, who was adamant against his friend's forming an attachment with *her*, would approve of his marrying her sister. There was also the matter of his refusing to attend the wedding.

"Would you tell me about your sister?" Miss Darcy asked.

Elizabeth laughed. "You want to hear about Jane?"

Miss Darcy nodded.

"Jane is certainly beautiful," Elizabeth said. "She has always been considered the prettiest lady in our neighbourhood."

"My brother knows the value of a person goes far beyond their outward appearance." Miss Darcy chuckled. "He must have seen other things in her. How else would you describe her?"

"She is the kindest and most generous person I know, but…" Elizabeth paused. "This is all so curious. I do not know how your brother knew my sister well enough to have formed such an opinion of her."

Miss Darcy shrugged. "He must have recognized those qualities in her."

"Well," Elizabeth said with a resigned sigh, "I must own that your brother is a very good judge of character."

"That he is, Miss Bennet. And he is not only a very good judge of character, he is the best example of one who is respectable, principled, and honest in his *own* character and actions." The young girl smiled as she spoke. "I know of no one finer, and there are times I wonder if I will ever be as good as he is."

"I am certain, with such an example as your brother, whom you care for exceedingly, you shall be just as good as he is."

"I hope so," she said softly.

Elizabeth looked up and spotted Rosings. "We are almost back with more than enough time to spare," she said. "I have truly enjoyed sharing my walk with you."

"As did I," Miss Darcy said.

Elizabeth turned to her. "Miss Darcy, I know Mr. Collins and my sister would be delighted to make your acquaintance. May I introduce you?"

"It would be a pleasure," Miss Darcy said.

Mr. and Mrs. Collins were indeed delighted to meet Miss Darcy. Elizabeth did not think Mr. Collins would ever cease his babblings about the honour of being introduced to her and how much he had heard about her. Elizabeth was grateful they had the excuse of getting Miss Darcy back to Rosings in time for tea.

Elizabeth and Miss Darcy slowly walked back to the garden where they had begun their walk. As they approached the large stone steps to the house, Mrs. Annesley came out to greet them.

"Did you enjoy your walk, Miss Darcy? You are not too fatigued, are you?"

"On the contrary! I enjoyed it very much, and Miss Bennet said I could join her every day that she walks."

Mrs. Annesley looked at Elizabeth. "If it is no bother, I know she will appreciate it."

"It is no bother," Elizabeth said. "Shall I call for you at three o'clock tomorrow afternoon?"

Miss Darcy nodded. "I will be waiting."

As Elizabeth walked back to the parsonage, she pondered her encounter with Miss Darcy. The young girl was quiet and reserved – much *like* her brother, but she had a sweet disposition – *unlike* her brother. She was not at all what she had expected, and when the young girl had talked about her brother, at times it seemed as though she was speaking of someone other than the Mr. Darcy Elizabeth had met at Netherfield.

Elizabeth determined Miss Darcy must either have an idealized perception of her brother, especially in reference to his being principled and honest, or all his dealings with Mr. Wickham had been kept from her.

Elizabeth found herself looking forward to their walk on the morrow. She wanted – no needed – to hear something about Mr. Darcy that would confirm her opinion of him. She was not certain whether the young girl even knew anything about it, but she was determined to find out what had occurred between him and Mr. Wickham!

~~*

Richard's condition had improved sufficiently enough to be released from the hospital, and he was recovering at home. While there were still moments of pain, the wounds were healing well, and it was believed he would make a full recovery.

Darcy was able to see more of his cousin's lively disposition return, but that also meant he had begun mercilessly teasing him.

"So, Darcy," Fitzwilliam said early one morning. "How do you suppose our aunt took the news that you and I were not coming for Easter? I assume you wrote to her."

"I did. She certainly could not expect you to come, and as for me, I truly do not care what she thinks." He shook his head. "We can always go another time."

Fitzwilliam winced in mock pain. "I am not certain I will ever be recovered enough to make that long trip. I fear it will be up to you to visit without me from now on."

"Hah!" Darcy scoffed. "As if I would do that!"

"What? Is my esteemed cousin not man enough to stand up to Aunt Catherine? Do you tremble in your boots in her presence?"

"I do not, but you know I have little patience for her."

"Well, you are fortunate this year to have escaped your duty as her nephew. You could have gone, you know."

Darcy mutely nodded.

"And she likely is aware of that. I am not on death's bed just yet, and I am certain my parents have written to her telling her I am recovering nicely."

"So be it," Darcy said. "What is done is done. She has likely already received the letter telling her I am not coming."

"Ah, so that explains it."

"Explains what?"

"I heard some ghastly shriek the other day that sounded a great deal like her."

Darcy let out a breathy laugh. "Fortunately, there is nothing she can do about it." He shook his head. "She will not travel this far from Anne." He paused briefly. "At least I hope she will not."

"You will miss Anne, however. I am certain of that."

Darcy leaned back in his chair and looked up at the ceiling. He knew his cousin liked to tease him about Anne and their supposed engagement, but that was one topic he greatly disliked being teased about. He only shook his head.

"All right, then. She is likely to miss you."

Darcy shrugged. "Of that, I am not at all certain."

Fitzwilliam studied him. "Tell me, Darcy. Are things all right with you? Ever since coming here, you have seemed downcast."

Darcy shook his head. "You would not expect me to be carefree and jovial, considering your injuries, would you?"

"No, I could understand those sentiments when I was in the hospital, but I am now much improved. I shall be up and about in no time. Yet, you seem..."

Darcy drew in a breath and looked away.

Fitzwilliam's brows pinched together in thought. "If I could guess, I would say you have a broken heart."

Darcy turned sharply to him. "That is absurd!" He stood up and turned away. *My cousin knows me too well!*

Fitzwilliam lifted a single brow. "Do you want to talk about it?"

"I do not want to talk about anything at the moment. You either try to marry me off to Anne or accuse me of having a broken heart. I will have none of this!"

Fitzwilliam lifted both hands in surrender. "I beg your forgiveness, Darcy. You know I care about you, and sometimes the only way I can get you to talk about something that is bothering you is to tease it out of you."

"I appreciate that, but you can rest assured I am well. There is no need to worry about me."

A servant walked in and approached Darcy. "A letter has arrived for you, sir."

"Thank you," he said.

"Is it from our aunt?" Fitzwilliam asked.

Darcy shook his head. "No, it is from Georgiana. I wrote to her about a week ago, and she is probably inquiring how you are faring."

Darcy opened the letter, and as he read, he felt a shudder of disbelief, followed by the heat of anger surge through him. His jaw tightened, and he stood up. "No! How dare she?"

Fitzwilliam reached out and grabbed Darcy's arm. "Has Georgiana done something? What has she done?"

Darcy could barely talk he was so upset. He raked his fingers through his hair. "Aunt Catherine had the audacity to go to London immediately upon receiving my letter and tell Georgiana she had to return to Kent with her!" His jaw clenched as he looked at his cousin. "Aunt Catherine told her I wholeheartedly approved of her going!"

Fitzwilliam sat up quickly, but then quickly fell back down. "The insolence… oh, that was painful!"

"Are you all right?"

Fitzwilliam nodded his head. "Yes. I just need to remember I am still healing."

Darcy looked at him with frustration. "I cannot let Georgiana remain on her own at Rosings. Lady Catherine will wreak havoc on her." He shook his head. "Whether our aunt used sheer force of will or a blatant lie to get her to go, poor Georgiana probably felt that she had to agree." His head dropped. "She will have no one there to shield her from our aunt's tirades.

"Georgiana is stronger than you think, Darcy, but I will understand if you feel you need to go to her."

Darcy stared at the letter, trying to decide what to do.

"If you are debating whether you ought to stay here with me or go to her, you know my answer. Go! I will not recover any quicker if you remain here. I have good care. Your sister needs you."

"Yes. Yes."

A small smile appeared on Colonel Fitzwilliam's face. "While you are there, you might consider asking Anne for her hand. Marriage, I understand, is the best remedy for a broken heart."

Darcy grumbled something unintelligible and then told his cousin he would repair to his chambers to think on it. He would decide in the morning whether to go.

As he readied for bed, he thought back to his cousin's comment. He had hoped to keep any indication of his feelings for Elizabeth from him. Obviously, he had failed miserably.

When Darcy had first learned of Fitzwilliam's injuries, he had been burdened with concern for his recovery; sleepless nights were attributed to worry. He thought little of Elizabeth.

Now that his cousin was well on the road to recovery and home from the hospital, Darcy's thoughts had turned to her again. He tossed and turned at night as she invaded his thoughts. If he slept, she was there in his dreams. Would it ever cease?

~~*

Darcy awoke the next morning and slowly sat up, shaking his head. After another night of little sleep and unregulated thoughts, he realized there was no conquering his affection for Miss Elizabeth Bennet, no matter how much time and distance there was between them. Even the fact that she was now married did nothing to dispel his deep regard!

He lowered his head into his hands as he considered what he was going to do. At some point in the night, while sleep evaded him, he decided to go to Kent. He would not leave Georgiana defenceless against his aunt. But it was the other matter that plagued him. By going to Kent, it could all be remedied. He lifted his head slowly. Yes, he knew what he must do.

He called for his valet and waited, rather impatiently, for him to appear. When Sumner entered, Darcy said, "Pack all my bags and have my horse and carriage ready. I will be departing for Kent once I have had breakfast."

"Yes, sir. I shall inform the driver to ready the horses and carriage, and then I shall return to pack for you."

"Thank you."

Darcy fought for the composure that had eluded him these past four months. Fitzwilliam was correct. Once he asked Anne for her hand and they were married, Elizabeth would be banished from his heart completely – and forever!

Chapter 21

It had been a sleepless night for Elizabeth as she pondered what Miss Darcy told her about her brother.

Did he truly approve of Charles and Jane's marriage? While she could not imagine anyone disapproving of Jane, she was quite certain he and Mr. Bingley's sisters did not consider *her* good enough, let alone excellent. How could he have determined that about Jane, when he had barely become acquainted with her? Was his opinion of Jane based solely on her beauty, and because of that, he felt she was an excellent match? She shook her head. "I had really not thought him to be so shallow as that," she said softly.

All day, Elizabeth looked forward to her walk with Miss Darcy. She was even able to endure the foolishness of Mr. Collins while he sat with them before leaving for the church, and the subsequent quiet once he left. Mary had never been a great talker, and there were times Elizabeth felt her sister wanted to be left alone. Elizabeth was grateful for her needlework and the books she had brought to read.

That afternoon, with Mr. Collins from home and Mary resting in her room, the only companion Elizabeth had was the ticking of the small clock on the mantel. She looked up at it frequently, waiting eagerly for the hours to pass until she could set out for her walk. On several occasions she urged the passing of time with a whisper. "Mr. Clock, you are being quite slow this afternoon. I am certain it has been more than ten minutes since I last checked the time."

She thought about what she might learn from the young girl as they walked. She would have to be guarded, for she did not want to overwhelm her with deeply personal questions that she had no right to ask and Miss Darcy might feel uncomfortable answering. But there were things Elizabeth wished to know and hopefully, she would discover the answers.

There had been no invitation to Rosings since Miss Darcy had arrived, and Elizabeth wondered if they had seen all they would of Lady Catherine and Miss de Bourgh. She did not mind, however, as she much preferred the young girl's company over that of the other two ladies.

At three o'clock she informed Mary that she would be taking a walk. She hurried across the lane to Rosings and entered the garden. Miss Darcy was not outside, and Elizabeth wondered if something had happened to prevent her from being able to join her. Even more so, she wondered if she should go to the door to ask for her.

Elizabeth decided to sit on one of the large stone benches at the edge of the garden. She would be out of anyone's way, but she could watch for Miss Darcy to step out. As she waited, she looked around at the garden. It was not particularly pleasing to her eyes, for, although there were flowers, there were many severely trimmed shrubberies that took prominence. Straight walkways jutted out from the house and traversed along its length. Despite being meticulously pruned, she felt the overall look of the garden was much too rigid.

Just as she was about to set off by herself, she noticed Miss Darcy step out and glance about her. Elizabeth immediately stood up and waved, and a smile appeared on the young girl's face. She hurried over.

"Oh, Miss Bennet, pray forgive me. My aunt insisted that I spend time practicing on her pianoforte." Her words poured out. "I complied for a time, although she never seemed pleased. I was finally able to slip away when she went to rest." She turned to Elizabeth with a rueful smile. "That is why I was late."

Elizabeth took her arm, saddened by the distressed spirits the young girl was exhibiting. "I did not mind waiting. Shall we go to the canopy of trees again?"

Miss Darcy blinked away tears and nodded silently.

They walked in silence for a short distance, and Elizabeth wondered whether the young girl would want to talk at all. She waited to see if she could talk about something other than what might have just occurred between her and her aunt.

Finally, Miss Darcy said, "I never seem to struggle through music pieces when I practice on my own, but for some reason, when my aunt is hovering over me, I fumble and falter through the piece. I hit the wrong keys or play in the wrong tempo." She took in a ragged breath. "My playing only gets worse as she reprimands me that I do not practice enough to be proficient." She let out a sigh. "If only my brother were here, he would know what to say to her."

Elizabeth gave Miss Darcy's arm a slight squeeze. "It is unfortunate we have people in our lives that do not see things the way we do."

"I cannot help but wonder if she demands it from me because Anne never learned to play. I would much prefer if she just listened to what I played and not criticize it so."

"I have not had an opportunity to converse with Miss de Bourgh. Are the two of you close?"

Miss Darcy's eyes grew wide. "She has never been one who converses a great deal. She…" Miss Darcy paused. "I think her mother is so outspoken, she speaks for Anne. Or perhaps, Anne feels she has no need to speak."

"That is unfortunate," Elizabeth said. "Conversing is how we get to know people better."

Miss Darcy nodded and turned her eyes away. "I do not always know what to say to people." She gave a quick shrug. "At least until I feel comfortable around them."

Elizabeth took the young girl's hand and patted it. "You seem to be doing quite well with me. And I take that as a compliment."

"A compliment?"

"I hope that means you feel comfortable around me."

The young girl smiled. "Oh, I do. I find your company very pleasant, Miss Bennet, and I enjoy talking to you."

"Thank you very much. I am enjoying your company, as well. And please, call me Elizabeth."

"I shall, and please call me Georgiana."

Elizabeth took her hand and squeezed it. "I shall, Georgiana."

The young girl continued. "My brother is much like me. He can talk easily with those people with whom he feels comfortable or whose company he enjoys, but finds it difficult to make idle conversation with those he does not know." She stopped and sighed. "Our reserve may be a familial trait, but my brother is also in a position where he has found that many people have ulterior motives when it comes to him. People either want to make his acquaintance, hoping he will use his influence for them in some way, or they want something from him directly. His reserve has been a way in which he deals with this."

"I see," Elizabeth said as she slowly nodded her head. She had not even considered how difficult it might be for a man in such an exalted position in society.

Georgiana chuckled. "Especially the ladies. He has to be very careful so as not to unwittingly give a lady any wrongful encouragement. He rarely singles out a lady to converse with her beyond the basic civilities, for fear she will take it as an indication of his interest."

Elizabeth's throat was suddenly dry, and she swallowed hard, pondering this. She thought about the times she had been with Mr. Darcy and he so readily talked with her. They actually conversed quite well together.

The two walked a bit further in silence, and then Georgiana asked, "Could you tell me a little more about your sister?"

"My sister?" Elizabeth was surprised she wished to know more about Jane. She laughed, however, and teasingly asked, "Which one?"

"The one who is married to Mr. Bingley. I know you said she is very pretty, kind, and generous. What else is she like?"

Elizabeth tilted her head and looked at her. "Do you truly want to know more about Jane?"

Miss Darcy nodded.

Confused, but willing to oblige her, she said, "Jane is exceedingly patient with everyone, and her compassion knows no limits. She never speaks unkindly of anyone, and in fact, I am certain she thinks poorly of no one."

Georgiana smiled. "She sounds delightful."

"Yes, and I love her dearly. We are very close, despite our differences."

"Differences?"

"Oh, yes! I tend to speak my mind most readily, whether good or bad. And I..." Elizabeth drew in a breath. "I have been known to judge a person's character too critically based on my first impression of them."

"I am just the opposite," Georgiana said haltingly. "There have been times I have not judged critically when I should have."

Elizabeth pressed her lips together in a small smile. "There is probably good and bad to both those traits." She pointed ahead. "Look, there is our canopy of trees."

They reached the shaded refuge, and a smile adorned Georgiana's face. "I feel better already," she said softly.

"As do I," Elizabeth said. She was fond of Georgiana and enjoyed spending time with her. She was also beginning to see that some of the things she had thought about Mr. Darcy had been completely wrong. But there was still Mr. Wickham.

At length, as they walked slowly along the path arm in arm, Elizabeth said, "I understand that we have another mutual acquaintance."

"Do we?" Georgiana asked.

"Yes," Elizabeth said, wondering if the young girl might know of — or reveal — the circumstances he had spoken about. "The militia came to our village and there was a young officer who, I understand, was well acquainted with your family."

"What was his name?" she asked.

"Mr. George Wickham."

Elizabeth immediately felt Georgiana shudder. When she turned to look at her, she saw that her face had grown pale and she had covered her mouth with her fingers and turned away.

"Miss Darcy." Elizabeth placed her hand on the young girl's shoulder and could feel her trembling. "Is something wrong?"

She waved her hand through the air, but said nothing as a few sobs escaped.

"Miss Darcy... Georgiana! Please tell me what is wrong. Is there anything I can do?" She retrieved a handkerchief from her pocket and reached around to hand it to her. She had certainly not been expecting this reaction from her.

Elizabeth allowed Georgiana a few moments to calm herself, and she was grateful when the young girl turned back to look at her.

She wiped her eyes and then asked, "Did he... did he say anything about... us?"

Elizabeth took in a deep breath and slowly nodded her head.

Georgiana let out a sob. "Oh, I am so ashamed!" she cried.

Grasping her hands, Elizabeth said, "Georgiana, there is no reason for you to be ashamed. It was all your brother's doing."

Georgiana shook her head. "But... no, my brother stopped Mr. Wickham and me... and me from..." She did not seem able to finish.

Elizabeth suddenly realized she and Georgiana were talking about two different things. And what was it Mr. Wickham had done? She shuddered and could only guess. She knew not what to say to her.

Finally, Georgiana stammered, "He told me... he told he loved me and... and wanted to marry me. He said we should elope, that it would be best." She shook her head. "You must think me terribly foolish."

Elizabeth pulled her into her arms and stroked her head. "No, Georgiana, I do not. You are young, and he knew he could deceive you into thinking he loved you."

Georgiana took in a few faltering breaths. "I should have known better. When my brother came and confronted him, he laughed and said he only wanted my fortune." She buried her head against Elizabeth's shoulder and sobbed.

Elizabeth was stunned. This was certainly not the information about Mr. Wickham she was expecting. Could he have deceived *her* in his accusations against Mr. Darcy? And should she confess that Mr. Wickham had not shared that information concerning her?

"Did he... did he share this with others in the neighbourhood?" Georgiana was shaking as she looked up at Elizabeth. Pain and regret filled her countenance. "I would hate to think that others knew about this."

Elizabeth drew in a deep breath. "He did not, Georgiana. In fact... he did not mention this at all."

Georgiana slowly blinked. "Oh," she said softly, her cheeks blushing again. "But you said he told you about us."

"Yes, but I thought you were asking whether he said something about your family, which he did, but more particularly, about your brother."

Her shoulders sank. "Oh. I wish I had not said anything, now." She walked over to one of the trees and leaned against it.

Elizabeth went to her and took her hand. "Please do not worry about it, Georgiana. It is between you and me. I promise not to tell anyone."

The young girl looked off into the distance and then back at Elizabeth. "I do feel as though I can trust you."

"You can. I hope you know you can."

Georgiana smiled weakly. "What did he say about Fitzwilliam?"

"He told me his father was your father's steward, and that your father had promised him a living when it became available."

Georgiana nodded. "That is true."

Elizabeth raised a single brow in surprise. "He also said that when your father died, your brother refused to honour that promise and did not bestow the living when it became available."

"No!" Georgiana said with a look of distress crossing her face. "That is not what happened at all!"

"Can you tell me what really happened?" Elizabeth asked gently.

"He informed my brother that he no longer wanted to be a clergyman." She let out a soft huff. "In truth, Elizabeth, he had no right to be a clergyman; his behaviour and character is so dissolute." She wiped at another escaping tear. "He asked to be compensated in money, which my brother paid him. He spent a great deal extravagantly, and then gambled the rest of it away. He later came back asking for more. *That* request was denied."

Elizabeth shook her head. "He certainly knows how to twist the truth!" She stamped her foot. "Deceitful man! I do not think anyone in town is aware of his character. Your brother said nothing."

"Fitzwilliam likely did not mention it for fear that Mr. Wickham might... he might..." Georgiana closed her eyes as she drew in a breath. "That he might retaliate and reveal what happened – or almost happened – between us."

Elizabeth shook her head, thinking she must get word home about his character so Mary King's family could take proper measures to protect her from him. He obviously was a man solely interested in a young lady's fortune.

"Georgiana, I know you must regret what you told me, but I consider it a blessing. I will not mention anything of what you told me to my family, but I must send a letter home at once warning them about him. He has recently become engaged to a young girl in the neighbourhood who is to receive a fairly large inheritance. They must be made aware of his true character."

Georgiana nodded. "Yes, you certainly must. If my confession saves another young girl, it is worth it."

They turned back and walked silently. Elizabeth knew Georgiana was upset from her earlier encounter with her aunt as well as confessing her indiscretion to her. On the other hand, *she* was reeling from the information the young girl had given her about her brother, as well as Mr. Wickham's behaviour and lies. How could she have been so wrong about Mr. Darcy?

When they reached Rosings, Georgiana turned and took her hand.

"I thought when I had to come here without my brother, it would be terribly distressing and I would not have anyone here that I could talk to." She smiled and squeezed Elizabeth's hand. "You have no idea what our walks have meant to me. Shall I see you tomorrow?"

Elizabeth nodded. "You shall." When Georgiana turned towards the house, Elizabeth said, "Thank you, Georgiana. That means a great deal to me."

Georgiana smiled and then walked away.

Elizabeth stood motionless as she watched the young girl walk towards the house and then step inside, disappearing from her view. She did not move as she considered all she had learned. It was certainly not what she had expected to hear.

She slowly spun around on the path, kicking up some dirt as she did, and then walked slowly over to the bench upon which she had been sitting earlier. She sat down again to consider all this new information. Had she been completely wrong about Mr. Darcy?

Had her initial impression of him wrongly influenced the way she viewed him?

Her hand went over her heart as she suddenly felt a softening of her opinion and her feelings towards him. As she slowly walked back to the parsonage, she suddenly realized that in their conversations, their interests, and their intellects, they were quite similar. She shook her head. But their stations in life were quite different. Whatever feelings of affection she now felt for him, she could never expect him to even consider returning them. For that, she felt a slight tug of regret in her heart.

Chapter 22

When Elizabeth returned to the parsonage, she immediately wrote a letter to her family, advising them about Mr. Wickham. She hoped it would arrive in time for measures to be taken to ensure Miss King's protection from him. Mary was resting, so she asked Mr. Malone if he could arrange to have it sent it off directly. He assured her he would see to it.

Elizabeth was quiet in her own thoughts for the remainder of the day and the next. Rain had moved in around midnight and settled over the area, preventing Georgiana and her from taking a walk the following day.

As she sat in the quiet of the parsonage, listening only to the ticking of the mantel clock as well as the rain pattering on the roof, she found it difficult to order her thoughts.

She chided herself for the stubbornness she had displayed in refusing to acknowledge the good in Mr. Darcy. She had been so deceived – by Wickham and by her own misjudgements – that she had not realized what an excellent man he truly was.

At dinner, as Mr. Collins gave an endless summary of his day at the church, and Mary smiled and made an occasional encouraging remark, Elizabeth's mind was elsewhere. She felt a headache coming on, and as soon as they had finished eating, she excused herself and went up to her room.

She walked over to the window and looked out at Rosings. From her vantage point, she could barely see its tall spires through the trees. The rain, though not heavy, cast everything in a grey shadow, blurring it to her eyes. She walked back to her bed and sat, slowly lowering her head to the pillow.

She had come to Rosings with a wrong assumption about Mr. Darcy's character. Upon meeting Lady Catherine, her first impression of her had confirmed that assumption. She had believed them very much alike in their officiousness, their intolerance of anything contrary to their opinions, and their feelings of superiority. She had even supposed that Pemberley was as dark and dreary as Rosings.

As she had grown to know Georgiana, however, a light had begun to appear in the dark thoughts she had been harbouring against the young girl's brother. It was a light that — through her — had revealed both his true character and her own folly. She shook her head. Yet while Miss Darcy claimed her brother thought Mr. Bingley had made an excellent match, there was still the matter of his trying to persuade his friend from favouring *her* with his particular attention.

Elizabeth shrugged. Perhaps Mr. Darcy truly disliked her. But then…

Elizabeth's thoughts were interrupted when Mary came to the door. Elizabeth invited her in, and she entered and sat down.

"Mr. Malone told me you requested an urgent message be sent home. I wondered what prompted it."

Elizabeth drew in a breath as she pondered what to tell her. She realized she should tell her about Wickham's proclivities, but she would not implicate Miss Darcy in any part of it other than passing on the intelligence about him.

"Mr. Wickham, as you may recollect, was the son of the late Mr. Darcy's steward. Miss Darcy and I were talking about him, as I knew he was a mutual acquaintance of ours." She paused and pressed her lips together. "Miss Darcy informed me that he is not a man to be trusted, has a tendency to gamble away his money, and seeks out women who have a fortune, hoping to charm them into thinking he is someone he is not." She closed her eyes and then looked at her sister. Particularly *young* ladies."

Mary's eyes widened. "He is engaged to Miss Mary King, is he not?"

Elizabeth nodded. "That is why I wrote the letter. Since she is to receive a fairly large inheritance, he most likely heard about it and singled her out."

"Oh, dear! He sounds like a despicable character."

Elizabeth let out a huff. "Yes, but one who can readily charm an innocent woman." She looked down and ran her fingers across the intricately sewn quilt that covered her bed. "Even I..." She paused and shook her head. "Even I found myself enjoying his engaging personality. Little did I know..."

"I cannot help but think about Lydia and Kitty. They were also quite taken by him."

"Soon everyone will know of his true character and they all shall remain safe."

Mary folded her hands into her lap. "I hope so," she replied softly. "I know, Elizabeth, that you must think my husband foolish at times..."

"No, Mary, I..."

Mary put up a hand to stay her. "Please listen to me. I know he has some oddities that may not be appealing to others, but he is a good man. I am very pleased to have found such a man to love and support me. I hope you know how blessed I feel."

Elizabeth smiled and took her sister's hands. "Mary, I could not be happier for you."

Mary looked down. "Perhaps there is something that might make you even happier for me." A wide smile appeared. "I have been resting a lot recently, and..."

Elizabeth suddenly squealed. "Mary! Might you be having a little one bouncing around here in the near future?"

Mary nodded. "Yes, I have been quite tired of late, and I do believe we are on our way to starting a family!"

Elizabeth leaned over and hugged her. "I am so happy for you! What does your husband think about it?"

"He is delighted," she said. "Absolutely delighted."

~~*

The next morning, after a restless sleep, Elizabeth awakened to a bright, sunny day. Her headache was gone, and there was nothing more she wanted to do than be alone with her thoughts. Unfortunately, Mr. Collins had no intention of going anywhere, and his endless observations on everything threatened to bring on another headache. She decided there was no reason she could not walk alone now and then again later with Georgiana.

She had breakfast, read a little, chatted with Mary a little longer than she had anticipated, and then left the parsonage just before noon. Without Georgiana, she was able to walk briskly, and she set out for the tree-lined path.

She was looking forward to having a time of reflection away from her sister and Mr. Collins. She had to admit theirs was a good match, and she had to laugh at the way Mary often corrected her husband. It was apparent she had ideas about marriage and what a husband and wife should and should not do, and was not afraid to speak her mind. She shrugged as she considered that Mary had never been afraid to speak her mind at Longbourn, either. Happily, it appeared Mr. Collins was more receptive to her admonitions than anyone at home had ever been.

"And they are to have a baby," she said to herself. "Oh, Mary, this baby will bring you so much joy!"

As she approached the lane that separated the parsonage and Rosings, she saw a horse tied to a post in front of the stately home. "They must have a visitor," she remarked to herself, and then walked on.

~~*

It had been a gruelling two days of travel for Darcy, who left Portsmouth the morning after finding out that Georgiana was at Rosings. He had said farewell to Richard and his family and set off, riding as fast as his horse could tolerate.

The pounding of the horse across road and meadow exacerbated his anger towards his aunt and solidified the resignation he felt in having to ask for Anne's hand – to rid himself of the anguish and loss he felt in losing Elizabeth to his good friend.

He stopped briefly in London to rest and get an account from his housekeeper as to what had happened when his aunt had come. He was furious to discover she had assured them he knew she was coming to remove Georgiana to Rosings.

When he reached Rosings in the early afternoon that second

day, Darcy dismounted his horse and studied the imposing edifice in front of him. His stomach was knotted as he considered what he must do, but there was nothing else to be done. His feelings about his imminent actions were as unpleasant as the grime that covered him, after the day's ride. He would freshen up and then go face Anne, the woman who would soon be his wife. He only hoped he could do that before Georgiana knew of his arrival. She would not be pleased.

When he entered Rosings, he informed the butler that he did not wish Lady Catherine or Anne to know of his arrival, but would go first to his chambers. He asked that a bath be drawn. He looked forward to being free from the dirt and grime that clung heavily to him, but he knew there was nothing to be done about the decision that weighed just as heavily on him.

As he walked behind a servant who carried his bag, he could barely lift his eyes. He knew this opulent place would soon be his, but he could not feel any gratitude. It was too ornately decorated for his comfort and preference, and he knew as long as Lady Catherine was alive, she would insist it remain untouched. He wondered if Anne felt the same.

He stopped. Did he even know how Anne felt about anything? He had always taken such pains to avoid giving her false encouragement about the engagement their mothers wished for them, that he had barely talked to her.

He arrived at his chambers, and when he entered, he breathed a sigh of relief that he had not encountered anyone. While he was eager to see his sister and would apologize for the position in which their aunt had placed her in bringing her to Rosings, he was not certain what he would say to her of his intentions.

He quickly bathed, dressed, and then prepared to go to Anne.

When he stepped out of the room, he heard a familiar voice behind him.

"Fitzwilliam!"

Darcy spun around and saw Georgiana rushing towards him. He put out his arms to embrace her when she rushed headlong to him. He was grateful to see her, yet wished it had been after he had seen Anne.

"What are you doing here? You did not tell me you were

coming!"

He kissed her cheek and said, "I could not bear to think of you here without me. I have a difficult time handling our aunt, and I could not imagine you having to endure her on your own."

Georgiana gave him a reassuring smile. "It has not been that bad."

"You are too polite to say anything negative about her." He looked around. "Is she here?"

"No," Georgiana replied. "She left a short time ago and said she would be gone for most of the afternoon."

Darcy let out a sigh of relief. "I am glad to hear that. Is Anne here?"

"Of course, Anne is here. Why?"

Darcy paused as he pressed his lips tightly together. "I... I need to speak to her."

Georgiana's eyes widened. "Brother, I do not like the look on your face. You are contemplating something that is not to your liking."

Darcy shook his head. "I am sure you are imagining things. I..."

"No, no! Please tell me you are not going to ask for her hand in marriage. Please do not do this!"

Darcy drew in a breath and stepped back. He could not lie to his sister, especially when she would find out soon enough. "I am, Georgiana."

Her eyes instantly filled with tears. "But you do not love her. You have never loved her, and you know this is wrong!"

"Georgiana, it is something I owe my mother and hers." Did he really feel that way? He reached out his hand and took hers.

"No!" she cried, as she pulled her hand away. "You know what it is to love! You once loved someone!"

"Love has not worked out for me."

"But surely there is someone else! Please think about this!"

"Georgiana, I have been thinking about it constantly for the three days since I decided to come here and ask for her hand. As my horse galloped across fields and through towns, forded rivers and jumped stiles, my mind weighed every possibility. This is for me, a man at the age of eight and twenty, the right decision. Please understand."

Georgiana threw herself into his arms. "I do not fully understand, Fitzwilliam, and I am certainly not pleased, but I shall support you if you feel this is the only choice you have."

"Thank you." He held her tight and then pulled away. "It shall all work out well, Georgiana. It is for the best."

Her eyes filled with tears and she began to shake. "You say it is, but... but I wonder if you truly feel that way." She shook her head. "You cannot feel that way!"

Darcy's mouth grew dry, and he had to force a smile. "Trust me, my dear sister. This is the way it must be."

He watched as she spun around and hurried away. Could he even trust himself with this decision? The heavy weight inside of him just grew heavier.

~~*

Elizabeth was about halfway to the tree-lined path when she heard a noise and turned. She saw Georgiana hurrying towards her with her head down.

Elizabeth quickly realized she was upset. The young girl's hands were fisted, and she shook her head vehemently. She had almost reached Elizabeth when Georgiana looked up and her eyes widened in surprise at seeing her.

"Oh, pray forgive me. I did not see you." She quickly wiped a tear that trailed down her cheek.

"Georgiana, is something wrong? Is there anything I can do?"

Georgiana shook her head. "No. There is nothing wrong with me, other than my frustration at my brother, for he is about to do something very foolish."

Elizabeth tilted her head. "Your brother?" she enquired with a nervous laugh. "Did you receive a letter from him?"

Georgiana swallowed and looked up. Elizabeth saw the pain in the girl's face. It was apparent she was greatly burdened by something.

"What is it? Did he write and tell you something that has upset you?"

She mutely shook her head and then softly whispered, "No, he just arrived at Rosings."

"He is here?" Elizabeth's stomach flipped.

Georgiana crossed her arms and let out a huff. "Yes, his arrival was unexpected, but he is about to..." She shook her head. "I do not understand him."

"Well, we must assume he knows what he is doing. Sometimes it is difficult for a young person to understand something an older person does."

"But he is..." She took Elizabeth's hand. "Oh, Elizabeth, I must tell you something, but you must promise me that you will not tell your sister. It would make things uncomfortably awkward between my brother and her and Mr. Bingley."

Elizabeth's brows lowered in confusion. "What is it that I cannot tell my sister? Georgiana, I do not understand what my sister has to do with Mr. Darcy."

Georgiana's shoulders rose and she let out a shaky breath. "My brother has been heartbroken for the last four months." Georgiana wiped her eyes and looked intently at Elizabeth. "I know I ought not be saying this, but he was in love with your sister. The one who married Mr. Bingley."

Elizabeth suddenly laughed at such an absurd notion. "Pray, forgive me, Miss Darcy, but certainly you must be mistaken. I highly doubt Mr. Darcy was ever in love with my sister."

"No, he was. He told me about how he struggled with his feelings, because his good friend had such strong feelings of attraction for her. He told me, himself. I saw him shortly after receiving Mr. Bingley's letter informing him of their engagement and upcoming marriage. He was quite distraught."

Elizabeth's eyes widened. "In love with my sister? No, this cannot be!" She shook her head, unable to comprehend this. "Georgiana, as I said, the two barely knew each other. She is beautiful, I admit, and has often attracted a gentleman's attention because of her great beauty."

Georgiana waved her hand. "No, he has never been tempted only by a lady's beauty. He told me she was witty and intelligent, and he greatly enjoyed their conversations."

Elizabeth lowered her brows in confusion as she thought back to those times when the two had been in company. "I suppose they could have conversed at the Netherfield Ball as they danced, but I hardly think they had an opportunity on any other occasion to really talk."

She took Georgiana's hand. "I truly do not understand how this could be. My sister had been in the Lake District for most of the time your brother was at Netherfield and only returned home just before the ball Mr. Bingley gave."

Georgiana tilted her head and looked at Elizabeth in confusion. "But he said he greatly admired the young lady Mr. Bingley had grown attached to and despaired because he felt she was better suited for him than for his friend. He even tried to talk his friend out of the affection. He felt his friend was not good enough for her."

Elizabeth winced, and a shudder ran through her whole body. She could barely breathe and suddenly felt inexplicably weak.

Georgiana's eyes were wide as she tried to convince Elizabeth of her brother's affection for her sister. "I recall explicitly he said she was an avid reader, loved walking, and knew how to play chess. They even watched an evening thunderstorm together."

Elizabeth gasped and walked over to lean against a nearby tree. She did not feel as though she could trust herself to stand up on her own.

"Oh, my," she said.

"Elizabeth, what is it?"

She closed her eyes. "I... It was me. At first, Mr. Bingley had singled me out with his attention. My sister did not come back from the Lake District until almost two months after we had met. When the two of them met, they took an instant liking to each other. By that time, I had realized that Mr. Bingley was not suited for me." She could barely form another thought.

"Did you quote Shakespeare to my brother?"

Elizabeth slowly nodded.

"Oh, my! *You* are the one he fell in love with! And you did not marry Mr. Bingley! Oh, Elizabeth, this is wonderful!" Georgiana clasped her hands and smiled. She then looked back towards Rosings. When she turned back, her face had gone pale. "No, no, no! This is terrible!" She grasped Elizabeth's hand. "Please, excuse me! I must get back before it is too late!"

Elizabeth watched the girl as she ran back to the house. She felt as though a blindfold had suddenly been removed from her eyes with what she had just learned. She could barely fathom that Mr. Darcy had grown fond of her – even loved her. When she had overheard him discouraging Mr. Bingley, it was because of his admiration for her and his realization that she and Mr. Bingley were not well-suited for each other. She had discovered that herself, but assumed he felt she was not good enough for his friend. Her heart pounded as she looked towards the house, wondering why Miss Darcy was in such a hurry to return. And why was she worried about being too late?

She could barely move as she considered this. It grieved her to know this esteemed gentleman had loved her, and she had treated him despicably. The light that had revealed his true character the other day was now a brilliancy that she could barely look upon. It had been incomprehensible to her when she had discovered he had thought well of the match between Charles and Jane, and his opinion of her had been so favourable. But this! She began to walk slowly back to the parsonage.

As she passed Rosings, she looked towards it. He was here! The man who loved her was here! Her eyes widened. How was she to face him or treat him, knowing what she did now? Her hands began to shake, but she suddenly felt a surge of elation as she found herself looking forward to seeing him again. Was it too late? Would his feelings still be the same?

She shook her head, unable to think rationally at all. Suddenly all she could see was his tall form and confident walk, his dark eyes looking at her with a slight sparkle, and an occasional smile in her direction. She could hear his mellow, baritone voice and soft chuckle. Elizabeth gasped and clasped her hand across her heart. How could she not have realized it? It was suddenly very clear to her. She was in love with Mr. Darcy.

"Is it possible to realize you are in love with someone when you are not even with them and have not seen them for months?" she asked aloud. "If not," she added, "is it possible that I have been in love with him all this time but refused to admit it?"

She shook her head and hurried her steps, walking on legs that felt very unsteady, as she returned to the parsonage.

Chapter 23

Georgiana ran, most inelegantly, back to Rosings, but cared little who saw her. She had to return before her brother went in to see Anne! Her tears flowed as she considered what she must tell her brother, and how much more difficult it would be if he had already asked for Anne's hand. Knowing how important honour and integrity were to him, if he had already asked her, he would never break the engagement, no matter the circumstances.

She stopped just outside the front door and tried to catch her breath. She wiped her eyes, but knew they were likely red from her tears and would fool no one. She smoothed her hair and then stepped inside, seeing the footman.

"Do you know where my brother is?" she asked, casting her eyes away from him.

"Yes, miss. He is up in his chambers."

"Thank you." Georgiana hurried up the stairs, grateful for the slightest hope that he had not yet gone to the drawing room to see his cousin. When she reached his door, she knocked.

"Come," he replied from within.

"Fitzwilliam!"

Darcy's eyes narrowed at he looked her. "Georgiana, what have you been doing? You are positively dishevelled!"

"I had to hurry back to you. You cannot ask for Anne's hand!"

Darcy rested his hands on Georgiana's shoulders. "Georgiana, we have already discussed this."

"No, you do not understand! Have you already gone to her? Have you seen her and offered for her?"

Before he could answer, there was a shriek from below. "Oh,

Anne! This is wonderful! I knew he would fulfil his duty! You are to marry Fitzwilliam!"

The two looked at each other upon hearing Lady Catherine's outburst.

"There, you have your answer," he replied with little emotion.

"Oh, Fitzwilliam, this is terrible! Simply terrible!" She threw herself against him, burying her head in his chest. She shook as she began to sob.

"It was the only option I had," Darcy said softly, stroking his hand over her hair.

She pulled her head away and looked up. "No! No! It was not your only option! She is here! Elizabeth Bennet is here!"

Darcy's face coloured, and he looked confused. "You mean Elizabeth *Bingley*?" His voice faltered as he said her name.

She grasped his hands. "No, Fitzwilliam. I mean, yes, she is here, but Mr. Bingley did not marry Elizabeth; he married her sister. He married Miss Jane Bennet! Elizabeth has been here with her other sister, Mary, who is Mr. Collins's wife. She did not marry Mr. Bingley." Her words poured out of her mouth so quickly, she could only hope she was making sense.

"I do not understand," Darcy said, a crease forming between his brows.

Georgiana took several breaths and pulled away. "Elizabeth is here visiting her sister, and she is *not* married to Mr. Bingley!"

Darcy spun around and grasped the back of a chair to support him. He was quiet for a few minutes. "She is not married?" He suddenly bent over, and Georgiana hurried to his side.

"No, she is not. Fitzwilliam, are you all right?"

He nodded mutely. "So, Bingley did as I feared he would do. Miss Jane Bennet was very pretty, but I only met her twice and had no idea that his affections had shifted. I hope… I hope Miss Elizabeth was not terribly distressed by his actions."

"Elizabeth does not seem to have any ill feelings towards him. She said she came to realize he was not well-suited for her. I do not think she suffers from a broken heart."

"How do you know what a broken heart looks like?" Darcy asked with a pained smile.

Georgiana placed her hands on her waist. "All I have to do is look at you!"

Darcy said nothing. He held himself still, propping himself up with his arms on the chair.

"You must go to Anne and tell her it was a mistake. Tell her..."

"Fitzwilliam!" Lady Catherine strode in. "You have done your mother and I such an honour by asking for Anne's hand. Our greatest wish was for you to marry, as well as join our two estates." She came to his side. "I knew that the two of you were destined to be together." She clasped her hands tightly. "I have sent for Mr. and Mrs. Collins to take tea with us later today so we can discuss the details." She turned to leave. "I did not tell them. I wanted the announcement to be a surprise. Oh, this will be a grand wedding! There is so much to do!"

Before she stepped out, Georgiana asked, "Will Miss Bennet be joining us?"

Lady Catherine stopped and pondered this. "I imagine she will come, as well." She looked at her nephew and smiled. "They shall be elated!" She turned and walked out.

Georgiana grasped her brother's sleeve. "You must do something!"

Darcy lowered himself into the chair and leaned his head against the back. "It is too late, Georgiana. I cannot go back on my offer." He slowly turned and looked at her, taking her hand in his. "Besides, Miss Bennet has never had a good opinion of me. She thought I was rude, officious, cruel, and..." He waved his hand in the air. "None of that matters. What is done is done." He turned away from Georgiana and drew in a deep breath.

"I cannot imagine that Elizabeth has such a poor opinion of you as that." She suddenly gasped. "How did you come to know her opinion? Did she tell you?"

Darcy shook his head.

"Did someone tell you she thought that way about you?"

"It matters very little who told me."

Georgiana stepped around him and looked up into his face. "It most certainly does matter!" Her face grew sombre, and she asked, "Was it Mr. Wickham?"

Darcy's head shot up. "How did you know he was there?"

"Elizabeth told me. She knew he was a mutual acquaintance, as he told her he was the son of our old steward." She paused. "Fitzwilliam, she also told me what he told her about you, which were all lies. She sees that now."

Darcy drew in a shaky breath. "What did that scoundrel tell her?"

Georgiana told him what Wickham had claimed and how she cleared up the issue with her.

He slowly shook his head. "This might absolve me of some of her poor opinion, but likely not all." He suddenly lifted his eyes. "Georgiana, did you tell her about Wickham and...?"

Her cheeks paled, and a pained look crossed her face. "I did, but I felt... I feel that I can trust her." Her brows pinched together as she fought against a wave of grief. "I truly like her, Fitzwilliam. I wish..."

Darcy put his fingers under Georgiana's chin and gently lifted it. "Even if her opinion of me has improved after finding out the truth of Wickham's lies, I am certain she does not love me." He shook his head. "And as I said, it does not matter now."

Georgiana's shoulders dropped, and a tear rolled down her cheek. "Sometimes, you are too principled for your own good." She was quiet for a few moments. Finally, she said, "If she comes later for tea, do you think you will be able to look upon her with any composure?"

Darcy turned his eyes towards the window. "I do not know, Georgiana. I shall try, but I truly do not know."

~~*

When Elizabeth reached the parsonage, Mr. and Mrs. Collins welcomed her joyously. It was apparent they were both elated about something.

"Oh, Lizzy!" Mary said. "We have been invited to Rosings for tea. Lady Catherine hinted that there was a surprise!"

"A surprise?" Elizabeth smiled. "I think I know what that might be."

"You do?" Mary asked.

"How might you know of her surprise?" Mr. Collins asked, his brows lowered in disbelief.

"I saw Miss Darcy earlier, and she said her brother arrived today. She hoped her voice sounded calm, despite the thunderous beating of her heart.

"Oh, I am certain Lady Catherine is delighted," Mary said as she clasped her hands. "She was so upset when she heard he was not coming."

"Yes, she was." Elizabeth took in a deep breath as she considered she would soon come face to face with him.

"Perhaps we can share *our* surprise with her," Mary suggested. "I believe she will be overjoyed to hear that a little one will soon be added to the residents of the parsonage."

"Indeed, she shall!" Mr. Collins exclaimed.

"I am certain she will be pleased," Elizabeth said. She paused, and then asked, "Mary, do you mind if I go to my room to rest before we go?"

"Certainly not! And now that I know what the surprise is, perhaps I can rest, as well." She chuckled. "I have not been sleeping well lately, and now I will not lie in bed trying to figure out what it is."

Elizabeth was grateful for the opportunity to contemplate her thoughts and feelings in the solitude of her room. She needed time alone for quiet reflection and to prepare herself to face Mr. Darcy with tolerable equanimity. Her stomach was knotted and churning as she considered what it would be like to see him, now that she knew he had loved her. What would he say to her? What should she say to him?

She wrapped her arms about her and fell back on her bed. She smiled as she considered that unfathomable, improbable, and most unexpected revelation.

How could Mr. Darcy have come to love me, of all people? And how could I have been so blind to that love and his true character?

She closed her eyes as she considered it was not just his character that she ought to have comprehended, but their great similarities. She slowly shook her head. Unfortunately, those common interests they shared, their stimulating and intelligent conversation, and any preference for her he might have displayed had all been hidden to her.

She let out a soft laugh. To think that a man of his esteemed position had grown to love her! She sighed and pressed her hand over her heart. She felt the rhythm of its beating and knew that from now on, it would beat only for him.

She suddenly paused and lowered her brows in thought. What was it Georgiana had said as she hurried back to Rosings? She had to get there before it was too late. Elizabeth had been unable to formulate any thought as she watched her leave. Her emotions had been so overpowering, her only thought had been to try to make sense of his loving her.

She swallowed and felt a heaviness begin to press down on her. When the young girl had first come upon her, she had told Elizabeth that her brother was about to do something very foolish.

Elizabeth struggled to recollect what else the young girl said.

Her eyes widened as she realized that Georgiana had then begun talking about his love for Jane – at least they thought it was Jane he loved. This foolish thing he was going to do had something to do with the fact that he discovered he had lost the woman he loved. And that woman had turned out to be *her*, and not Jane.

Elizabeth suddenly felt as though she could barely breathe. Could he have come to Rosings to make his engagement with Miss de Bourgh official? She began to shake.

"No, please, no," she whispered as tears pooled in her eyes. He would not – *could not* – do that. Having spent an afternoon in Miss de Bourgh's presence, she thought how impossible it would be for him to be married to her.

She hugged her pillow tightly to her and rolled onto her side as a tear travelled down her cheek. She let out a shaky breath. If indeed that is what he had come to do, perhaps – hopefully – Georgiana *had* reached him in time and had been able to stop him. But perhaps this is not what was about to happen at all!

She wiped the tears that had trailed down her cheeks and still pooled in her eyes and walked over to the basin. She dipped a cloth into the water, pressing it to her face. The cool moisture felt good, but she knew it was very possible more tears might come. She would think of it no more now. If Mr. Darcy had once loved her, there was no guarantee he still did. She could not cling to a hope of something that might never come to pass. A hope that she had only briefly realized.

~~*

Later that afternoon, Elizabeth was quiet as she and Mr. and Mrs. Collins walked across the lane to Rosings.

Mr. Collins seemed to enjoy his uninterrupted monologue about Lady Catherine's surprise. He pondered that if Elizabeth had been correct, should they still act surprised? Should they inform her they already knew? No, that would never do!

"We must all act very surprised and express our great delight that her esteemed nephew arrived. Yes! That is what we must do!"

Elizabeth did not wish to hear his nonsense. She was conflicted. She wanted to see Mr. Darcy again with eyes that saw him as he truly was and with a heart that now loved him, but she also feared for what might no longer be. Her thoughts were on that first moment when she would see him again. How would she act? How would he?

Her hands began to tremble as she considered the depth of feeling she now had for him. She could not have imagined even a week ago having such a different opinion of him – and such a change of heart. She swallowed hard as she wondered what the next few moments would bring.

She knew he would not be able to display outwardly any affection he might still have towards her. How would she know whether his feelings were still the same? How would she let him know her feelings had considerably improved since she last saw him?

She blew out a breath as they took the large stone steps up to the front door. As they waited to be let in, she closed her eyes, feeling the quickening of her heart, and steeled herself for what was about to come.

~~*

Darcy stood in the parlour with his sister, aunt, and his recently affianced cousin. He was at the window that overlooked the front garden, but restlessness overtook him, and he began to pace. After taking several turns about the room, he returned to the window to gaze out. When he saw Elizabeth with Mr. and Mrs. Collins walking the long drive that brought them to the front door, his heart sputtered. He gave his head a frustrated shake, as he realized asking for Anne's hand had done nothing to stem the tide of his feelings for her.

He fisted his hands and contemplated the moment when she would step into the room. If only his sister had not told him she believed Elizabeth's feelings were more favourable towards him, having improved when Georgiana denounced Wickham's lies and gave her a positive account of his own character. He smiled softly at Georgiana's devotion to him. She had no idea what she had been doing in talking to Elizabeth about him. He gave his head a brisk shake. But it was all for naught!

He closed his eyes as Elizabeth disappeared from his view and knew the moment he had been looking forward to – and at the same time dreading – was about to take place. He swallowed, gave his coat a tug, and turned when they heard the voice of Mr. Collins as the group approached.

Darcy stole a look at Anne, who sat quietly with her hands folded in her lap. Her mother had brought her forward, to sit on a settee in the centre of the room. He looked at the open seat next to her and clenched his jaw as he knew that was where he was expected to sit. He found it more difficult to look at his sister, who he knew was fighting back tears. It grieved him that she felt the loss of what could have been as deeply as he did.

When the arriving party stepped into the room, his eyes were drawn first and foremost to Elizabeth. She was looking straight ahead, and then when her eyes turned to meet his, a small smile appeared and then just as quickly disappeared. She averted her eyes to look at Lady Catherine, who greeted them with a satisfied smile on her face.

"Come, have a seat. I am delighted you were able to come on such short notice. You will find me in a most pleased and ecstatic state this afternoon, as you can see my nephew has finally arrived." She cast a glance at Darcy and then turned back to the others. "I believe you are acquainted with him, as well as his sister, who I know has paid a call at the parsonage."

There were nods of affirmation. Elizabeth turned to smile at Georgiana, but when she turned to him, she seemed unable to meet his eyes. This was quite different from the beaming smile Mr. Collins now wore on his face and the serene smile Mrs. Collins had on hers.

"Oh, esteemed sir," Mr. Collins said. "It is a joy and privilege to see you again. We were so pleased to make your sister's acquaintance and are delighted you have now come just in time for Easter. How is your cousin? We heard he had been injured."

"He is improving, thank you." Darcy's mouth was dry, and he felt barely able to talk. His eyes turned to Elizabeth, and he felt as frustrated as he had been in Hertfordshire, when Elizabeth was so close to him – and yet so far. Then it had been due to loyalty to his friend; now it was due to a pledge he had just made.

"I know Lady Catherine must be pleased you came," the parson said with a quick bow of his head.

Lady Catherine looked over at Darcy with an indulgent smile that he did not return. "He has made me the happiest lady in all of England, I dare say." She then turned back to the others. "Not only did he surprise me by showing up when I had not expected it, but there is something else, as well."

She motioned to Darcy. "Come, take your seat beside my daughter."

Darcy felt as though he were trudging through mud as he walked over to take the seat beside Anne. There was such heaviness in his chest, he thought he would soon be unable to take another breath. He looked briefly at Elizabeth, who had her eyes averted and cast down. He could have sworn she looked paler than he had ever seen her.

"There is another surprise that occurred today." She clasped her hands. "It is something I have been waiting to occur for a long time."

"Tell us, Lady Catherine," Mr. Collins said enthusiastically. "We are all anticipation to hear this news, are we not?" He turned to Elizabeth and his wife; Mary was the only one who nodded.

"Well, I shall keep you in suspense no longer. Today, my nephew asked for my daughter's hand in marriage! Anne and Fitzwilliam are to be wed!"

Chapter 24

Elizabeth felt the room begin to spin, and she grasped the armrest of the chair in which she sat. She could not look up, for she feared that all the grief, regret, and disappointment she was feeling would be evident on her face. Fortunately, everyone's attention was on the engaged couple, save for two people. She knew Georgiana and Mr. Darcy were gazing at her.

Mr. and Mrs. Collins bestowed upon them wishes of great joy. Elizabeth made an attempt to smile, but the turmoil inside her made it an impossible feat. She knew she was expected to offer her congratulations, and at length, she looked at Miss de Bourgh and said, "I wish you... both... the greatest happiness." She hazarded a glance at Darcy, and their eyes briefly locked.

"Thank you," Darcy said with a quick nod of his head.

"Now that the engagement is settled, we must make plans." Lady Catherine turned to Mr. Collins. "This must be the grandest affair Hunsford has ever witnessed; nay, all of Kent. You must..."

Elizabeth found it impossible to attend to her words. She was grateful she was not required to and wished she could ask to be excused.

Her grief was so overpowering, she could do nothing to disguise it. Georgiana's glance passed from her to her brother, and back again. Elizabeth readily detected tears in the young girl's eyes.

It was apparent, as she became aware of the conversation again, that Lady Catherine was doing all the talking and planning. Mr. Collins nodded his head and agreed to everything, but the engaged couple said very little. Elizabeth could not help but wonder just how much – or how little – Miss de Bourgh desired this marriage.

At length, tea and refreshments were brought in. Elizabeth did not feel that her stomach would be able to tolerate anything. It was in a knot, and in addition, she knew conversing with anyone would be an impossibility.

Elizabeth's hand trembled as she picked up her cup of tea. She bit her lip as she grasped the handle tightly, hoping it would not spill. A tremor shook her when she looked up into Mr. Darcy's eyes. She struggled to take in a breath, feeling her chest tighten.

Conversation about the wedding continued, mainly between Lady Catherine and Mr. Collins, and Elizabeth wanted nothing more than for this day to be over. She looked forward to going back to the parsonage and crawling into bed. How she wished she could fall into a sleep that would remove this all from her mind and she would waken in the morning with the resolve to forget the tumult of emotions that overpowered her today.

Elizabeth attempted to partake of some cake, but she soon found it difficult to look upon anything with interest. Everything seemed unappealing to her taste, despite the praises coming from Mr. Collins. Lady Catherine continued to speak about the wedding and what she would expect to see done.

When talk of their wedding journey came up, Lady Catherine suggested some wonderfully romantic and secluded places. Elizabeth experienced such a headache that she did not think she could remain, and when there was a pause in the conversation, she said, "If you would please pardon me, I am feeling quite ill and ask that I may be excused." She shook her head slowly and struggled to push herself up from the chair. "Please forgive me... but I must take my leave."

Mr. Collins sent her a warning look, accompanied by a firm shake of his head. "But surely, my dear sister, Elizabeth, you cannot be..."

Elizabeth hurried out of the room without waiting for Mr. Collins to finish or anyone else to speak.

When she stepped outside, she drew in a shaky breath of fresh air. She stood still a moment, trying to determine where to go. She knew she could escape to her room at the parsonage but thought the tree-lined path would better help compose her feelings. She also knew that if Mary were to return to the parsonage shortly, she would immediately come to her to ask how she was feeling.

Propelled by tears and raw emotion, Elizabeth made her way through the grove to the tree-lined path. She felt she could walk there blindfolded, as she had walked there so many times. This was a benefit, since she could see little through her tear-filled eyes.

The sun was drawing near the horizon, painting the clouds vivid colours of red, pinks, and oranges. She barely noticed this, however, as her thoughts were too heavy to appreciate such beauty.

When she finally reached the path and came under the shelter of the birch trees, she collapsed shakily against the trunk of one of them. The tumult of her mind was painful. Her legs felt numb and unable to support her. She slid down to the ground and leaned against the trunk of the tree. Her head fell back, and her hands trembled as she brought them up to her heart, so broken by what she had just found out.

That Mr. Darcy had been in love with her for so many months! That she had but recently comprehended that he was a man worthy to be loved by herself, only then to discover he had become engaged to his cousin!

Elizabeth had no idea how long she sat there. Her eyes were closed, and she felt the air begin to grow cooler. But it was not that which stirred her. She heard the clatter of horse's hooves approaching.

She turned and opened her eyes, holding her hand up to shade the sun, which was now resting just above the horizon. She gasped and attempted to rise to her feet as she saw Mr. Darcy draw near on a horse.

It seemed like a dream as she watched him easily dismount the saddleless horse and walk towards her in that same easy stride she had so often seen. But there was something else. It was quicker. Was it urgency? Was it nervousness?

"Mr. Darcy," she said, shaking her head as he drew near. "You ought not to be here." She held onto the tree to help steady her as she rose to her feet.

"I know," he said, his eyes searching her face. "It was probably not wise, but I..."

Elizabeth quickly turned away and folded her arms tightly about her. "You...you are now..." She shook her head, unable to finish.

"Please allow me a few moments of your time. I do not intend to remain long."

"How did you know I was here?" Elizabeth stole a glance up at him.

"After tea, Mr. Collins asked if he could go to the library to look for some books. I rose to join him, and as I did, Georgiana whispered to me that you had most likely come here."

Elizabeth inclined her head slightly towards him. "In our short acquaintance, she has come to know me well." His close presence stirred her.

He paused and drew in a breath. "She knew I would want to talk to you."

Darcy's chest rose as he took in a deep breath. His lips pursed tightly as he looked about him. "Once I had escorted Mr. Collins to the library, I excused myself, claiming I had some business to attend to."

"I see." Her attention was focused on the birch tree that she leaned against, and she absently picked off some of the bark. She knew if she looked in his eyes, she would not be able to breathe.

"Miss Bennet, I have much I would like to say to you, but there are several things preventing that conversation. First, if we are seen lingering here, your reputation might be compromised." He took in a deep breath. "Secondly, my feelings prohibit me from forming a coherent thought, and finally, coming here to speak to you when I am engaged to another goes against every principle that has been ingrained in me."

From the corner of her eyes, Elizabeth saw him pull out some folded paper. "Will you do me the honour of reading this letter?"

Elizabeth swallowed hard and quickly wiped away a tear as she reached out and took the letter, not considering the lack of propriety in the situation. Her hand shook as she looked down at it.

"I wrote this earlier, when my sister informed me of your being here after I had..." Darcy shook his head and swallowed hard. "I had no idea if I would have the opportunity to present it to you." He paused. "Miss Bennet..."

Elizabeth held up a hand. "Please say no more, Mr. Darcy." She tightly closed her eyes, hoping to rid them of the pool of tears threatening to spill.

"I wish there was something I could say or do…"

Elizabeth looked up as a tear escaped and rolled down her cheek. Mr. Darcy slowly lifted his hand and gently wiped it away with his thumb, caressing her cheek with his fingers as he did. Elizabeth shuddered and felt her breath catch.

"Please go, Mr. Darcy. It is not proper for you to be here with me, and it serves no purpose."

Darcy lifted his eyes from her and seemed to focus them on the horizon. "You are correct, but I felt the need to talk to you one last time." His brows furrowed, and he slowly shook his head. "I cannot begin to know what you are thinking or feeling at this moment, but it grieves me to know - by evidence of your response to the announcement of my engagement – that you have been deeply hurt."

"It is not your fault, Mr. Darcy. You have only acted in a manner that was dictated by what you believed to be true."

He drew in a long breath. "I feared that Bingley would be the one who hurt you." He looked down, but lifted his eyes to her. "Despite doing the very thing I dreaded he would do, in shifting his affections to someone else, I regret it was not him who brought you grief, but me." He shook his head. "I am very sorry."

Elizabeth tried to gather her thoughts. "Mr. Darcy, there is nothing to be done now. I shall recover, as the affection I felt for you has been of a short duration. If you do not mind, I should like to be alone."

Darcy clenched his jaw and gave a quick shake of his head. "I hate to leave you here in this state. The sun will soon set, and it will grow dark quickly."

"There is no need to worry about me."

Darcy's eyes narrowed, but a small smile appeared. "You know how I feel about you walking alone. I would not want anything to happen to you."

Elizabeth let out a breathy huff, accompanied by a brief smile. "Yes, and you also know my propensity for getting into predicaments. I promise I shall be careful."

"Please allow me to escort you back." He took a step forward.

Elizabeth put out her hand to stop him, pressing it lightly against his chest. "If you insist, allow me to leave before you. You can follow at a distance." She shook her head. "It would not be prudent for anyone to see us together... especially now."

Before she could remove her hand, Darcy quickly placed his hand over it, pressing it against his heart. Looking about him, he said, "This place has always been a type of refuge for me when my aunt's expectations and demands overburdened me. I would come and sit underneath these beautiful trees or pace back and forth underneath the leafy glade." He drew in a breath. "I am glad you found it to be so, as well."

Only a sliver of a smile appeared on Elizabeth's face, as his words only served to bring about a stronger feeling of regret. She felt unsteady on her feet and was not certain she would make it back to the parsonage in her unhappy state.

Darcy took her hand, brought it slowly to his lips, and kissed it. "May God be with you," he said as his voice quivered with emotion.

He walked slowly to his horse and mounted as Elizabeth began taking the path slowly back to the parsonage. As she walked, she knew he was far enough behind so as not to arouse any suspicion, but close enough to keep his eye on her. When she reached the lane that took her to the parsonage and him to Rosings, she knew he would set off toward the stables.

At length, she glanced back and saw him heading away from her. She kept her eyes on him until he disappeared behind the hedgerow. As he did, the last of the sun dipped below the horizon.

~~*

Elizabeth felt grieved beyond anything she had ever experienced before. She would treasure in her heart, however, the fact that Mr. Darcy had come to seek her out. She held his letter tightly in her grasp, and when she reached the steps of the parsonage, she glanced down at the back of her hand. She could still feel the pressure of his lips upon it. She slowly brought it up to her lips, closed her eyes, and tears spilled out through her lashes.

When she stepped in, she stopped to wipe her eyes. As she did, Mrs. Malone hurried over to her.

"You have come alone, Miss Bennet?"

Elizabeth nodded. "Yes, I was not feeling well. I shall be up in my room."

"Yes, ma'am."

Elizabeth's breaths were shaky as she sat down on a chair and unfolded the letter with trembling hands. She began reading.

Miss Elizabeth Bennet,

Be not alarmed, madam, on receiving this letter, by the apprehension of its containing any sentiments of love from a man recently engaged to another. I write without any intention of paining you, compromising myself, or tempting the two of us by dwelling on wishes which, for the happiness of both, must be immediately forgotten. You must, therefore, pardon the freedom with which I request your attention.

I am writing this letter to you after speaking with Georgiana who informed me that I had been under a great misapprehension. I believed that Bingley had married you, only to find out he had instead married your elder sister. I also discovered Georgiana had unintentionally made you aware of the depth of my feelings for you, thinking she was talking about your sister. You, however, eventually comprehended the truth. This news came to me after I had asked for my cousin's hand in marriage, as both her mother and my own wished. As a man of principle, I now cannot break this engagement to Anne.

I want you to know, Miss Elizabeth, that I had not been long in Hertfordshire, before I saw, in common with others, that Bingley preferred your company over any other lady in the country. While I considered you to be an extremely acceptable match for him, I doubted he would be the same for you. Bingley has not your intelligence, quickness, nor interest in the same passionate pursuits, such as walking, reading, and playing chess. I feared you would quickly grow weary of him. While contemplating this, I began to strongly feel that in those areas where you and Bingley differed, we were much alike. These traits I saw in you are something I greatly admire and seldom find in a lady. Those times I had the honour to walk with you, dance with you, and talk with you, made my partiality for you grow, as did my struggle, for I could never betray my friend by trying to engage your heart while his partiality for you continued to grow. As I had seen him in love many times before, I hoped it would soon end as the others had. I could only hope that you would not be hurt if he behaved as I thought he might. I left Hertfordshire before seeing that that is exactly what happened when he shifted his affections to your sister.

As to the other matter that my sister confessed having shared with you, she is confident of your trust, and I have no doubt of your discretion. For that I am eternally grateful.

Miss Elizabeth, I know not whether I will have the opportunity to present this letter to you or if there is even a need to give it to you. If you are reading this, you will know that I went against my principles and the dictates of society by handing this letter to you – especially when I am engaged to another. I am aware that you may not accept it or, if you do, you might not read it. As Georgiana often tells me, at times I am too principled for my own good, but that is a deeply ingrained part of me.

I want you to know, Miss Bennet, that you are an exceptional young lady, and from my heart I wish the best for you. You have so much to offer a gentleman, and I plead that you will only consider one who is as intelligent as you, and is as kind and generous as you. I hope he will be someone who will enjoy your clever conversation, join you in the pursuits you enjoy, and take delight in your lively personality and fine eyes.

I will only add, God bless you.
Fitzwilliam Darcy

A tear drop fell and smudged part of his name. She quickly dabbed it, hoping it would not spread the ink any more than it already had. She let out a sob and fell back onto the bed, placing the letter upon her heart. She curled up and wished no one would disturb her for at least a month.

A few moments later, however, there was a knock at her door, startling her.

"Yes?" she said as she quickly wiped her eyes.

"A letter has arrived for you, Miss Bennet." It was Mrs. Malone.

"Thank you. Can you just leave it outside the door?"

"Certainly."

Elizabeth waited until she heard her footsteps fade away down the hall. She slowly opened the door, took the letter, and quickly closed the door behind her. She looked down and recognized

Jane's handwriting.

"Oh, Jane, how I need you right now." This was the best thing that could have happened after suffering so much the past few hours. She knew that reading how Jane and the rest of the family were doing would improve her spirits.

She sat down and began to read the letter, but the joy and delight she had anticipated, quickly disappeared.

My dearest Lizzy,

I hope you are well and enjoying your time with Mary and her husband. We miss you dearly! Unfortunately, I have some news that may distress you. It has to do with Lydia.

"Lydia!" exclaimed Elizabeth. "Now what has she done?" She looked back at the letter, blinking away the tears that lingered.

Father received your letter warning us all about Mr. Wickham. He immediately went to see Miss Mary King's uncle, and the young girl was quickly and expediently rescued from his clutches. But Lizzy, this did not sit well with Mr. Wickham, for you see, he had recently asked her for some money to help pay the gambling debts he had accrued in Meryton. When that source of money evaporated, he became desperate. He went to, of all people, Lydia, appealing for help.

Oh, Lizzy, what he asked her to do, I cannot comprehend, but that she did it is even more inconceivable. He asked her for some of Mother's finest jewellery so he could sell it in exchange for money to enter some high-stakes games. He assured Lydia his winnings would be large, and he would be able to buy back the pieces of jewellery before anyone discovered them missing.

Mother, however, noticed some pieces of jewellery gone one morning when she was dressing for church. According to Father, the whole household was in an uproar, and Kitty finally confessed the whole thing to them, as Lydia had confided in her what she was going to do.

Wickham did not win in these games as he had hoped, and was in no position to buy the jewellery back. Our family was not, either. Mother is terribly distraught, Father is furious, and Lydia continues to grieve for 'poor Wickham.' It has since been discovered that not only does he have debts with some of the tradesmen in Meryton, but also debts of honour with his fellow officers. It is altogether distressing, and Mr. Wickham has left the neighbourhood.

I wonder if there is any way you can come home early. I cannot continually go to Longbourn, and I certainly do not wish to spend my nights away from Charles, although I did the first night I heard of this.

Please consider it. I know Father would welcome your presence back home. I hate for you to come home earlier than you had planned, but I hope you will consider it.

Your dearest sister,
Jane

Elizabeth let out an anguished cry and dropped her head back. This was altogether too distressing. She was grateful that her warning was heeded and Miss King was safe, but Lydia's foolish and unpardonable actions were difficult to comprehend.

"Oh, Lydia! How could you?" Elizabeth said as her hand dropped into her lap. Her tears began to flow again.

"Lizzy? I knocked, but apparently you did not hear me."

Elizabeth looked up to see Mary peeking through the door. "Mary, pray, forgive me. Do come in."

"Are you feeling better?"

Elizabeth closed her eyes and shook her head. "Oh, Mary, something terrible has occurred at home. I need to return directly." She extended the letter towards her sister. "Here, read this."

Elizabeth watched her sister's eyes grow wide as she read Jane's letter. When she finished, she looked up. "This is dreadful! I cannot imagine Lydia doing such a thing!"

"I cannot either, but she has." Elizabeth drew in a breath. "I need to leave on the morrow. I can travel post. It is a short distance."

"Oh, I wish I could accompany you, but in my condition…"

Elizabeth waved her hand. "There is no need for you to concern yourself. All will be well."

"I am certain my husband will be able to find someone from the church to take you as far as Bromley, and I will see if Mr. and Mrs. Malone would like to travel with you. I will feel so much better knowing you have someone accompanying you. They have wanted to visit their family in Hertfordshire, and this will be the perfect opportunity. I think we will be able to get by without them for a while."

"Thank you, Mary. I greatly appreciate it."

Once Mary spoke with her husband, he set about settling the details. Mr. Collins found a parishioner willing to drive Elizabeth and Mr. and Mrs. Malone to Bromley, where they would board a post chaise for the remainder of the journey. The Malones dispatched a note to their son, apprising him of their journey, and giving him the location of Longbourn and an approximate arrival time, so he could send his carriage to pick them up.

Later that evening, Elizabeth went to her room, sat down in the chair near the window, and looked out into the dark void. That was exactly how she felt. She had cried so much, she believed there were no more tears left to shed. She stood up shakily and shuffled to her bed, very nearly falling into it. She pulled the coverlet over her and buried her head in her pillow, hoping – although not confident – that she would get some sleep.

~~*

Several times during the night, Elizabeth pounded her pillow, wiped her eyes, or rose from her bed to pace. Her thoughts and feelings were in a tumult, and she knew not what upset her more. Was it Lydia's behaviour or the loss of Mr. Darcy? She tried to tell herself she never had him to lose, for once she came to know of his love for her and realized she loved him, he was already betrothed to his cousin.

It was a futile endeavour at trying to sleep, and when the sun began to lighten the sky the next morning, Elizabeth had managed only a few hours of rest. She hoped she would be able to sleep in the carriage on her way home.

The thought of being home and in her own bed appealed to her; however, knowing the circumstances she would encounter when she arrived distressed her. At least she would have Jane to give her the steadiness she would require, both from what she would encounter there and what she had encountered here.

As the carriage was loaded and prepared for their departure, Elizabeth kept glancing towards Rosings, wondering whether she might see Mr. Darcy again. She would have particularly enjoyed seeing his sister, but they likely knew nothing of her departure. She doubted Mr. Collins would inform his patroness of his youngest sister's disgraceful behaviour. She conceded, however, it would have been difficult to face either of them, and she resigned herself to having formed an acquaintance with both, only to have them both snatched away.

As Elizabeth sat with Mary in the parlour awaiting her departure, Mary remarked, "I had hoped to tell Father our news when he came, but since he will not be coming, I give you leave to tell him and Mother. While I will likely not travel before the baby is born, I hope to be able to make the trip home afterwards."

Elizabeth smiled. "I shall be delighted to give them the news, which, in turn, shall delight them. I think they will welcome such wonderful intelligence."

"I hope they shall."

Later that morning, as the carriage drove away, Elizabeth stole one last longing look at Rosings. Not that the place held anything dear to her, but two of the occupants currently inside would always have a place in her heart.

Chapter 25

Elizabeth and her pleasant companions, John and Jocelyn Malone, settled in for the short ride to Bromley. She had enjoyed Mr. Malone's teasing spirit and Mrs. Malone's ever cheerful demeanour at the parsonage, and she was glad for their company. She assured them they would be welcome to stay at Longbourn as long as necessary as they waited for their son's arrival. They thanked her, saying they hoped his arrival would coincide with theirs.

Mrs. Malone was quite pretty for her age, but she had become rather frail recently and helped with the duties in the parsonage only as needed. When Elizabeth and her father had come, she had assisted the maid in her duties.

As the carriage passed Rosings, Mrs. Malone commented, "I was certainly surprised to hear that Mr. Darcy finally asked for Miss de Bourgh's hand." She shook her head. "I never believed he would do it."

Mr. Malone leaned forward in the seat. "Do you think he loves her?" He looked at Elizabeth as if he was addressing her. "Do you think Miss de Bourgh ever received love letters from Mr. Darcy?"

At his words, Elizabeth unwittingly reached for her reticule, in which she had placed the letter Mr. Darcy had presented to her. While not typical of a love letter a heroine in a novel might receive, she would always treasure it.

Jocelyn sent her husband a scolding glance. "Do not speak such nonsense, John. You and I both know this was a marriage of duty, not of love." She looked at Elizabeth and asked, "What do you think, Miss Bennet?"

Elizabeth clenched her jaw, and she fought back tears as she picked up her reticule and placed it on her lap. She glanced down at it and said, "I... I did not know her... either of them very well."

At Bromley they switched to a post chaise without any difficulty and thanked the driver. The Malones quickly realized that Elizabeth was not in a mood to converse as they travelled. She was fairly certain her red, swollen eyes indicated she had not only spent a good amount of time crying, but that she was also fatigued. She rode the remainder of the way either reading or resting. The clamour of the carriage moving along the rough road prevented her from getting a sound sleep, but the pleasant sound of Mrs. Malone's humming helped soothe Elizabeth's distressed spirits.

They finally arrived at Longbourn, and the driver helped them out of the carriage. Their luggage was unloaded, and the carriage departed.

Seeing that the Malones' son had not yet arrived, when they came to the house, Elizabeth gave instructions for the couple to be shown to a guest room where they could freshen up and asked that food and drink be brought to them. She then inquired where she could find her family. Elizabeth knew her arrival would be a surprise, but hopefully, a welcome one.

She hurried to the parlour where she had been directed and asked that her father be summoned to join them. When she stepped in and greeted them, everyone looked up in surprise.

Jane hurried over to her, and the two sisters flew into each other's arms.

Jane drew back and grasped her hands. "I am so glad you have come home!"

"Oh, Lizzy! It is so good to have you home. I have been so...so..." Mrs. Bennet seemed unable to continue.

"I apologize for not sending a note ahead, but I wanted to get here as soon as possible."

Mr. Bennet walked in. "So, Lizzy, you have returned. It is good to have you home." He gave her a quick hug. "Did you travel alone?"

Elizabeth shook her head. "No. Do you remember Mr. and Mrs. Malone? They accompanied me." She turned to the others.

"They were servants at the parsonage, and their son should be on his way here to pick them up. They are now freshening up in one of our guest rooms." Noticing Lydia's absence, she asked, "Where is Lydia?"

"She is in her room, defiantly claiming we have made this a much bigger incident than she believes it was." Mr. Bennet shook his head in disgust, but took his daughter's arm as they walked. "You look as though this has taken a heavy toll on you," he whispered. "I am grateful you wrote to us about Wickham, and I deeply regret that one young lady in our household disregarded the warning."

Elizabeth gave a slight shrug. "Thank you, Father. I am doing better now." She could not even allow herself to think about what had brought on her deepest grief.

They all sat down, and Elizabeth drew in a breath, clasping her hands. "Tell me all that happened."

"Oh, Lizzy!" Mrs. Bennet cried. "It was shocking! I was getting ready for church and pulled out my jewellery. I immediately noticed several pieces missing, including my mother's diamond and sapphire brooch."

Elizabeth's eyes widened. "That was your nicest piece of jewellery!"

She nodded and began to fan herself. "I was terribly distraught!"

"How many pieces did you discover were missing?"

"At least five. I grew fearful that perhaps someone had come into the house and taken them!" She shuddered. "I cannot believe they are gone!"

"Your mother's cry alerted us all to the fact that something was wrong, and we hurried up to find out what had happened." Mr. Bennet gave a solemn shake of his head. "It was Kitty who informed us that Lydia had given the pieces to Mr. Wickham to help him pay off some debts he had with local merchants, as well as some honour debts with some of the officers."

Elizabeth looked at Kitty. "I am certain that was difficult for you to do, as you and Lydia are so close."

Kitty's face was downcast. "I should have said something sooner, and I regret that I did not try to talk her out of doing such a thing."

"Apparently, he claimed that he had a high stakes game he was going to be part of and he was certain he would win the money back and more, buy back the jewellery, and return it before anyone noticed." Mr. Bennet cradled his jaw with his hand. "I do not have to say that he was not successful at those games, and I would wager – although right now I abhor any gambling – that his debts have increased and the jewellery is lost forever."

"Ohh!" Mrs. Bennet cried. "I shall never be able to replace many of those pieces."

Elizabeth patted her mother's shoulder to comfort her. "We shall do everything we can to find out where your jewellery is and try to get it back."

"I hope so, but oh, I think it will be impossible!"

"How is Lydia?" Elizabeth asked. "Does she at all regret her actions?"

"She still thinks the jewellery will be returned and believes everyone has condemned Mr. Wickham too harshly," Jane said softly.

"But he was always such a fine gentleman!" Mrs. Bennet declared. "I know he had every intention of returning it."

"Mrs. Bennet, if you believe any man can guarantee his winnings as he gambles away his money or someone else's belongings, you are…"

"Father," Elizabeth spoke up, shaking her head. "I am certain Mother only wishes for her jewellery to be returned."

Mr. Bennet let out a groan and began to walk out. "I shall be in my study if anyone has need of me."

"Before you leave, Papa, I do have some good news to cheer you."

"Oh, we do need good news!" Mrs. Bennet exclaimed.

"Mr. Collins and Mary will be adding to their family in a few months."

Mrs. Bennet waved her handkerchief. "I am to be a grandmother? Heavens, I can scarce believe it!"

"Are we old enough to be grandparents?" Mr. Bennet asked, his expression allowing a smile. He reached up and grasped a strand of his hair, pulling it out. Looking down, he said, "Yes! I do have a few grey hairs, so I believe I can be one!"

"Oh, Mr. Bennet, I am certain I do not have a single grey hair, but I will still be delighted to be called grandmother."

Elizabeth was glad she could bring a little joy into what was otherwise a distressing situation.

Mr. and Mrs. Malone's son arrived, and before they departed, Elizabeth introduced them to her family. The Malones thanked them for the use of the guest room, and Elizabeth thanked them for accompanying her on the journey. They then took their leave.

Elizabeth took Jane's arm, and they followed them outside so Elizabeth could meet their son.

After the introduction was made, the carriage pulled away, and they waved goodbye.

Elizabeth turned to Jane. "Tell me, Jane, how do you think everyone is coping?"

"Mother is quite upset," Jane said. "But I know it is difficult for her to be completely angry at Lydia; you know she has always favoured her."

"Yes," Elizabeth agreed. "I could readily see that." Elizabeth scuffed her foot across the ground. "And Mother does not seem to truly recognize Mr. Wickham's character. Lydia does take after her."

Jane turned to face her. "Lizzy, you look..." She shook her head. "You look quite distressed over this. How did Mary and Mr. Collins take the news?"

Elizabeth smiled. "Mr. Collins was upset, but Mary was able to calm him by suggesting Lydia is still young." Elizabeth's brows lifted. "But she came to me later, expressing her great disappointment in Lydia, regret for her dishonest behaviour, and her hope that things are resolved quickly."

"But are you certain you are doing well?"

"I am... Oh, Jane, there is so much I need to talk to you about, but now is not the time. I do not think I can talk about some of the things that happened in Kent, since I do not fully comprehend them." She took Jane's hand. "But fear not, we shall talk. Please do not worry about me."

"I shall try," Jane said.

As they walked, Jane told her how she and Charles were faring, which helped lighten Elizabeth's heavy spirits. It was good to see that someone was happy, despite her concern for all that had occurred at home. At length, Jane said she had to leave, and she stepped up into the carriage that had been waiting for her.

Elizabeth waved goodbye, feeling a sudden surge of regret. This was the first time since Jane had married that she wished that her sister still lived at home. She was grateful she was just three miles away, but oh, how she longed for her constant company.

As the carriage began to pull away, Jane stuck her head out of the window. "I forgot to ask you if you saw Mr. Darcy at Rosings."

At the mention of his name, she felt her face flush and her hands tremble. "I did, but… he only just arrived yesterday."

"You will have to tell me all about it later!" Jane waved and then pulled her head back in.

Elizabeth shook her head. She was grateful she had another day to prepare before talking to her sister about the love she unexpectedly found and just as suddenly lost.

~~*

Elizabeth spent some time walking around Longbourn's small garden as she prepared to return to the house. She knew that any tears she shed could be attributed to Lydia's behaviour, but she would prefer not to be shedding tears for a particular gentleman while discussing her sister.

She finally stepped back in and went to her father's study. When she knocked, he bid her enter.

"Well, Lizzy, now that we are alone, tell me your honest thoughts."

"I am deeply grieved over what happened. It is difficult to think that even with my warning, Lydia was deceived by him." She looked down at her father's desk and picked up a large stone paperweight. As she ran her hands over the smooth surface, she drew in a deep breath. "What is his standing with the militia?"

Mr. Bennet began tapping his fingers on the desk. "The only crime committed in this was that of Lydia stealing." He shook his head. "Wickham's intentions towards Miss King were certainly questionable, but she willingly accepted his offer of marriage. Many men have to marry for money, but she is young, and fortunately, her uncle used some persuasive argument to help her see sense and break it off." He shook his head. "And as for his gambling, many of the officers gamble, but he obviously found himself seriously deep in debt and could not repay it." He folded his hands and looked at her. "He gave up his commission and left. No one knows where he is, and I, for one, do not care, as long as he is no longer in the neighbourhood!"

"I am so angry with Lydia! In addition to stealing, I would add the crime of ignoring the warnings I sent and then not being at all repentant of her actions." She closed her hand tightly about the stone she held.

"She is young," her father said. "But she ought to have known better."

Elizabeth looked up and searched her father's face. "I know how deeply upset Mother is. How are *you* handling this?"

Mr. Bennet's eyebrows rose as he pondered this, and he let out a long huff. "I regret that I have not taken the time to properly discipline my two youngest daughters and bring them up to be respectable young ladies. There is hope for Kitty, and I can only hope and pray Lydia will learn from this." He forced a smile. "But apart from my regret, disappointment, and having to endure a wife who cannot always see things as they truly are, I am well."

Elizabeth turned over the stone in her hand to study it, and then replaced it upon the desk. "Do you think Lydia will see me?" She bit her lip. "I wonder that she might be angriest with me for sending that letter exposing Mr. Wickham's true character."

Mr. Bennet pursed his lips and looked up. "You might go to her, Lizzy. See if you can talk some sense into her. She will not listen to any of us."

Elizabeth reached across the desk and took her father's hand. "I think I shall." She smiled. "Perhaps a little later, however, when I am not so angry."

~~*

Elizabeth first went to her own room to think about what she would say to Lydia. She wanted to shake some sense into her, help her to see what she did was wrong, but also to reassure her that she still loved her. She was certainly disappointed in her but loved her despite her actions.

After a time of composing both her feelings and her thoughts, pondering what might be happening at Rosings, and wiping away a few tears, she stepped out of her room and walked down the hall to Lydia's room. When she knocked on the door, Lydia issued an order, "Go away!"

"Lydia, it is Elizabeth. May I please speak with you?"

"No! I do not want to speak to you or anyone else!"

"Please, Lydia. I want to hear what you have to say about what happened."

There was silence, and then Elizabeth heard the shuffle of feet and the latch turned. Lydia did not open the door, but unlocked it so Elizabeth was able to step in. Lydia was turned away from the door and sitting at a desk, her head resting on her arms.

"Hello, Lydia."

The only response she received back was a moan.

"I know everyone is upset and likely have not allowed you to say much in your defence. Can you... do you think you can tell me what happened?"

Lydia spun around. "I am sure everyone told you how foolish I was in listening to Mr. Wickham and believing him after having received your... your letter."

Elizabeth pressed her lips together and drew in a deep breath. "I had hoped to enlighten everyone to his true character."

"But he was always so friendly, so gentlemanly!" Lydia fisted her hands. "Everyone makes mistakes!"

Elizabeth reached for Lydia's clenched hand, but she pulled it away.

"Lydia, unfortunately, there are some men who know how to make themselves appear proper and considerate... and gentlemanly, when in truth, they are anything but those things."

Lydia shook her head. "He only needed a little help so he could pay off his debts!"

"There are no guarantees in gambling. You ought to know that."

"He said it was going to be an easy win."

"I am certain he did."

"You are just like the others! So against him!"

"Lydia, do you remember how much I enjoyed his company? I found him quite amiable. I had no idea the depth of his deceit." She drew in a breath to calm herself. "Deceiving others has been a part of his life for many years."

Lydia swallowed hard and said nothing. Tears pooled in her eyes. "Do you think Mamma and Papa will ever forgive me? I do not know how we will ever get Mamma's jewellery back." She shook her head. "I just took some pieces and did not know how much she treasured her mother's brooch." She let out a sigh. "I just thought it looked like one of the finer pieces of jewellery I could take."

Elizabeth clasped her hands and looked away, wondering what else she could say. She had to force herself not to raise her voice, as Lydia might order her out if she became angry.

"Do you know one of the main reasons Mother and Father are angry?"

"No."

"You have only made excuses for what you did and have never apologized. We must take responsibility for our actions, recognize them for what they are, and hopefully, grow as a result of what we learned from them. You are still young, but you can learn from this."

Lydia said nothing, and Elizabeth waited. When she did not seem inclined to say anything more, Elizabeth stood up. "Just think about what I told you, will you?"

She started for the door, stopped, and turned back to her sister. "There are times when it is difficult to learn a lesson, especially when we are stubborn about realizing the truth of something." She paused and drew in a breath. "But what is worse is realizing too late you were wrong. Trust me, I have learned that lesson the hard way." Elizabeth tried to smile. "I still love you, Lydia. We all still love you."

~~*

The next day, the tension in the household grew considerably less. Lydia nervously came downstairs, made her apologies to her mother and everyone else, and promised she would never do anything like that again. That seemed to appease Mrs. Bennet, but Mr. Bennet was not satisfied until she promised to have nothing more to do with any of the officers, particularly Wickham if he were to return. She reluctantly agreed. Kitty was grateful for the restored position of her youngest sister, who was also her closest friend.

Elizabeth looked forward to another visit from Jane. She hoped Jane would come to Longbourn, for she knew if she went to Netherfield, Charles would question her about Mr. Darcy. She did not think she could talk about him and maintain her composure with Charles. It was going to be difficult enough talking to Jane about him.

Jane arrived in the early afternoon, and Elizabeth went out to welcome her. She told her that Lydia had finally left her room and had apologized and that she was now on fairly good terms with everyone.

"I knew she would. It took her a little time because she is so young, but I knew she would."

Elizabeth shrugged. "It took a little persuasion on my part, but she did do it on her own."

"How is Mother? Is there any possibility of retrieving her jewellery?"

Elizabeth shrugged. "It would take a great amount of money. We do not even know who has it or if that person has already sold the pieces. With Mr. Wickham gone..." Her voice trailed off. Elizabeth tugged on Jane's arm. "Jane, I do need to talk with you. Can we step outside after you speak to everyone?"

"Of course."

They entered the parlour, and Jane greeted her family. They talked for a while before she and Elizabeth stepped back outside and walked to a bench quite a distance from the house.

Jane chuckled. "When we come to this bench, Lizzy, I am quite certain you do not want anyone to overhear our conversation."

"You are correct, Jane. It concerns a most extraordinary thing that happened at Rosings, but when I tell you, you must not tell anyone... even your husband."

Jane gasped. "You want me to keep something from Charles?"

"Only part of it. It has to do with Mr. Darcy."

"Oh, yes! You said he came to Rosings! Did he tell you why he did not come to the wedding?" She covered her mouth. "Oh, it was something terrible, was it not?"

Elizabeth let out a long sigh, wondering if she would be able to tell Jane what happened without becoming emotionally distraught. She took her sister's hand, drew in a deep breath, and proceeded to tell her all that happened, including finding out that Mr. Darcy loved her.

When she had finished, Jane stared at her in astonishment. Her mouth had long been agape, and her eyes were wide with wonder. "Mr. Darcy loved you all the time Charles was paying particular attention to you?"

Elizabeth forced a smile and shook her head. "I do not know at what point he fell in love with me." She drew in a hitched breath. "But there is more, Jane, and I can barely think about it without copious tears falling. I fear talking about it might become impossible."

Jane grasped her hands. "What is it, Elizabeth? What happened?"

"I came to realize I loved Mr. Darcy, as well, but at the moment I realized it, he was... he was..." She looked down; her only movement was the shaking of her shoulders.

Jane wrapped her arms about her sister, a tear falling as she did. "Lizzy?"

Elizabeth drew in a breath to compose herself. "Mr. Darcy was under the misapprehension that I was the one who had married Charles, and the only way he knew to rid himself of any feelings he still had for me was to abide by the wishes of both his mother and his aunt, and..." Elizabeth began to tremble, and tears filled her eyes as she looked at her sister. "Oh, Jane, he asked Miss de Bourgh to marry him." She closed her eyes and dropped her head.

Jane leaned her head against Elizabeth's. "I am so sorry. Is there nothing that can be done?" She shook her head. "He knows now, does he not, that Charles is married to me and not you?"

Elizabeth nodded. "He does, but nothing can be done. It would be wrong of him to break off the engagement. He is such a principled man, that going back on an offer of marriage would be something he would never do."

Jane shook her head slowly. "Oh, Lizzy. I never really got to know him, but I know Charles thinks very highly of him. I am so sorry." She took her sister's hands. "And here you had to come home to the disaster we were facing when you were confronting such disappointment yourself."

Elizabeth shrugged. "I am glad I had to come home. I needed to be away from him." She did not tell Jane that he had come to talk to her after his engagement was announced and had presented her with a letter. It would serve no purpose but to put him in a bad light.

A noise drew their attention, and they saw someone arrive on horseback.

"I wonder who that is," Jane said.

Elizabeth stood up so she could get a better view. "I believe something is being delivered. A package of some sort." She took Jane's hand and pulled her up. "Come, let us go see. I could use a diversion."

When Jane and Elizabeth entered the house, they were surprised by an uproar. Hurrying into the parlour, they discovered their mother crying with joy.

"It has been returned! My jewellery has been returned!" She held up the brooch that had belonged to her mother and pressed it to her lips, kissing it.

Chapter 26

"Your jewellery has been returned?" Elizabeth's eyes were wide and her smile genuine. How did this come about?"

Mrs. Bennet waved her hand through the air. "I do not know, but that is not important! I have all my jewellery back, including my mother's brooch." She looked at Lydia with her brows lifted. "I am certain that fine Mr. Wickham was able to buy it back."

Elizabeth and Jane exchanged looks of dismay, but it was Lydia who replied. "I do not think so, Mamma. I do not think a man like him cares at all about someone else's jewellery."

Elizabeth allowed a small smile, thinking it took a great deal for Lydia to say that.

"Oh, it matters not!" Mrs. Bennet cried, shaking her head. "All I care about is that it has been returned!"

Mr. Bennet stepped in demanding to know what all the commotion was about.

"Someone just returned my jewellery! Oh, Mr. Bennet! Is this not wonderful?"

Elizabeth thought for a moment that perhaps her father had arranged for someone to find out where it had been and buy it back, but from his pinched brows and twisted mouth, she could see he was just as perplexed as everyone else.

"Who did this?"

"We do not know, Father. It was delivered by a messenger."

"What did he say when he delivered it?"

Mrs. Bennet shrugged. "I do not think he said anything about where it came from. He only handed the bag to the footman and said it was to be delivered directly to me." She hugged the pieces of jewellery to her bosom. "I do not care how they were found or who did it; I am just elated that I have these pieces again."

Mr. Bennet glanced at Elizabeth and shook his head. His frown displayed just how much he disagreed with his wife, but he left the room without saying anything else.

"I am going to go put these back directly so I don't lose them again."

Things grew quiet as she stepped out of the room.

Elizabeth looked at Lydia. "Do you have any idea how these could have been returned?"

Lydia shook her head. "I did not even know who he had sold them to. Whoever returned them had to know who had them – or found out where they were."

"Well it is quite odd," Elizabeth said. "I cannot help but wonder if we will suddenly be expected to pay someone for their work and expenses to get these back to us." She looked up at Lydia. "We do not even know how much money Mr. Wickham received for these pieces." She slowly shook her head. "And I would imagine the amount to buy them back was even more."

She looked warily at Jane. "While this is a pleasant turn of events for Mother, I wonder if Father is worried about the same thing."

"I cannot imagine someone delivering the jewellery without first asking for payment if they expected it," Jane said.

"That is what makes this so odd," remarked Elizabeth.

Jane was eager to return to Netherfield to tell Charles all that had happened. She and Elizabeth hugged their goodbyes, and Jane assured her that Charles would do what he could to help if they were required to pay.

"Let us hope it does not come to that," Elizabeth said as Jane was helped into the carriage.

"I shall come by again tomorrow sometime around noon."

Elizabeth smiled. "Thank you, Jane." She laughed. "And thank Charles, as well, for allowing you to come so often."

They waved goodbye, and Elizabeth returned to the house and the sanctuary of her room.

~~*

As was the norm for her mother, now that her jewellery had been returned, all was well – at least until the next vexation. Lydia was as confused as everyone else about the unexpected appearance of the jewellery, and when her mother offered any compliment to Mr. Wickham – no matter how slight – Lydia refuted it.

This pleased Elizabeth, and she hoped Lydia had truly learned a valuable lesson from the experience.

She spent the next morning reading, as she waited for Jane's visit. She was surprised, then, when the carriage arrived early. She had been reading in the drawing room, which looked out over the front drive, when she saw the carriage.

"Oh! Jane has come early!" She looked to the door, eager to see her, but instead of Jane, a footman came in and presented a letter to Elizabeth.

"Mr. Bingley's driver asked me to present this to you," the footman said.

"Thank you."

She quickly opened it and began to read.

Lizzy,

My plans have changed. Could you please come to Netherfield as quickly as possible. Please take our carriage and do not walk!

Jane

Elizabeth smiled. She was eager to get away, so she went directly to her parents and told them she was going to Netherfield. It would be good to see Charles again, as well as being a welcome change.

As she rode the three miles to Netherfield, she suddenly realized she would be walking into the same rooms where she had encountered Mr. Darcy on several occasions. She thought particularly about the night the two of them briefly watched the thunderstorm together. It was when Georgiana mentioned that incident that she realized he loved her and not Jane.

She felt another tremor pass through her, and she drew in a

deep breath, hoping she would not succumb to tears as those recollections, accompanied by a surge of feelings, surfaced.

She arrived at Netherfield wondering what had prompted Jane to change her plans but knew it could be something as simple as Charles having a slight cold. She knew Jane would not wish to leave him if he was ill. Perhaps since the crisis at Longbourn was over, she felt she could remain at home.

When Elizabeth entered the house, she was directed to the parlour.

"Thank you," she replied, but just as she turned to walk in that direction, Jane came out with outstretched arms.

"I am so glad you were able to come." She took Elizabeth's arm.

Elizabeth chuckled. "Jane, why are you holding my arm so tightly?"

"Trust me," was all she said.

"Jane, what is going on? Why did your plans change?"

Jane shook her head. "Just hold onto me tightly."

Elizabeth stopped. "Would you please tell me what has happened? Your behaviour has me concerned."

A small smile appeared. "You shall find out soon enough."

"Jane, you are being very mysterious." Elizabeth laughed. "Or perhaps I should say you are being mischievous, and neither are like you at all!"

They stepped into the parlour, and Elizabeth saw Charles sitting in a chair across the room. He jumped to his feet when she entered.

"I am so glad to see you, Elizabeth. Jane and I have both missed you exceedingly!" He wore his typical wide smile.

"It is good to see you, as well, Charles. I hope you are…"

Elizabeth stopped as a figure who had been sitting in the chair facing away from her rose and turned towards her just as Jane's arm tightened about hers.

"Hello, Miss Bennet." Mr. Darcy looked at her with a small smile, but a look of apprehension also appeared on his face. "I hope you are well."

Elizabeth felt she would have fallen if not for the fact that Jane was holding onto her arm with all her might. She drew in a shaky breath and made an attempt to return his smile. "I am... I am well, thank you. And you?" she felt and heard the quaver in her voice.

"I am well, thank you."

"Come, Lizzy, let us sit down." Jane escorted her to the sofa, their arms still locked together.

Elizabeth's mouth was dry, and she looked from Mr. Darcy, to Charles, to Jane, and then back to Mr. Darcy.

"I... I am surprised to see you. What brings you to Netherfield?" She hoped she sounded calm, but she strongly doubted it, as she felt every nerve in her body was shaking.

Mr. Darcy leaned forward and clasped his hands together. "I was remiss in not attending the Bingleys' wedding and came to offer them my congratulations."

At the mention of their wedding, she flinched. She did not think she could bring up the topic of *his* wedding and how the plans were proceeding.

"I see."

It was quiet for a few moments, and then Charles said, "He surprised us last night when he arrived. We were not expecting him, but he was certainly welcome." He looked at Darcy and smiled. "But the surprise in arriving was not the only surprise." He nodded his head towards his friend. "Are you going to tell her, or should I?"

Elizabeth looked from one to the other, a puzzled look on her face. "Tell me what?" she asked, just as Jane's arms tightened about her again.

Darcy's eyes locked with Elizabeth's. "My engagement to Anne is ended."

Elizabeth's eyes widened, and her jaw dropped. Her hands trembled despite being clasped tightly together. "It... it is ended?" She shook her head. "How can that be?"

Charles jumped to his feet. "It is a rather long story, and as he related the whole of it to Jane and me last night and answered all of our questions, why do we not step outside for a leisurely walk?" He looked at his wife. "Come, we shall lead the way."

Jane stood and walked to Charles, taking his arm. The two swiftly left the room.

Elizabeth felt the loss of her stronghold and refuge with Jane's departure. How would she be able stand on her own two feet, let alone walk with Mr. Darcy at her side? She looked at him as he rose from his chair and walked over, extending his hand.

"Shall we?"

She met his gaze as his hand closed around hers and pulled her up. She was grateful when he tucked her arm about his, for she did not think she would be able to stay upright, let alone walk.

As they stepped outside, he said, "Knowing your inquisitive nature, I would assume you have some questions."

Elizabeth shuddered, not knowing where to begin. She continued looking forward and asked, "I do. Is your sister here?"

Darcy laughed. "That is your first question? Is my sister first and foremost on your mind?"

Elizabeth pressed her lips together. "I fear at this moment, I do not know what to ask, but I would like to know."

"The answer to your question is no, she is not here. She and Mrs. Annesley departed for London by carriage when I set out to come here."

"I see." A sly smile appeared, and she looked up at him. "I fear before we get to the pressing matter at hand, I would also like to inquire about your cousin – your cousin who was injured. Do you know how he is doing? You said at Rosings that he was improving."

Darcy drew in a deep breath. "My cousin, Colonel Richard Fitzwilliam, was recovering well when I left him. It is doubtful, however, that he will be able to continue serving in the army, as he always aspired to do."

"I am sorry. Does he know what he will do?"

"I am not certain. He does not want to be a burden to his family or his brother, with whom he does not get along well. I have always told him he is welcome at Pemberley, but I know he does not want to be indebted to anyone." Darcy stopped walking and turned to Elizabeth. "I wrote to him last night to tell him where he can reach me so he can apprise me of how he is doing, and… and to acquaint him with what transpired at Rosings."

Elizabeth swallowed, and her heart pounded. She could not look at him and turned to begin walking again. "About that, I do have a few questions." She shook her head to rid herself of her unravelled nerves. "Did *you* call off the engagement with Miss de Bourgh?" She did not know what she wished him to say, she only knew she dreaded whatever it was he might tell her.

"No, I did not."

Elizabeth looked up at him stunned. "Miss de Bourgh called it off?"

They walked a short distance before he stopped and turned to her. "Not quite."

Elizabeth sent him a questioning look. "I fear I do not understand."

He pressed his lips tight. "The day you departed for Longbourn, we were sitting in the parlour at Rosings. Anne said little as she worked on some stitchery. Her mother was doing what she had been doing the night before, making plans for the wedding without consulting either one of us." His shoulder's lifted as he drew in a deep breath.

"Anne finally looked up and told her mother that there was no need to make any more wedding plans as she had never agreed to my offer of marriage."

Elizabeth's eyes shot up. "She never agreed?"

Darcy slowly shook his head. "She then turned to me and asked if I recollected what she had said to me after I asked for her hand."

"Did you remember?" Elizabeth asked.

Darcy took her hand and nodded. "She had said, 'My mother shall be so pleased.'"

"That was all she said?"

"Yes. Anne never agreed to marry me." He squeezed Elizabeth's hand. "There was never a consent and therefore never an official engagement!"

"But her mother must be furious!" Elizabeth's heart pounded. "She will certainly not accept such an excuse."

"She was furious, but Anne was insistent that she could not marry me and would hear nothing more about it. My aunt insisted she would be disgraced by calling off the engagement, but Anne did not care."

Elizabeth's eyes widened. "Why?"

Darcy shook his head slowly. "She said she had no reason to

fear what others would think of her because she had lived with derision her entire life. She was adamant that she had no intention of marrying someone just because it was expected of her." He shrugged. "She also reminded us that it was only Mr. and Mrs. Collins — and you, of course — who had been made aware of the engagement. No announcement had been made. Other than the servants, who would be dismissed immediately if they talked to anyone about it, no one else knew."

"Why did she not say something the night before, when we were all at tea?"

"Here is where I do not have all the details. I strongly suspect Georgiana had some part in this, informing her that I was... that my affections were attached to another."

Elizabeth felt her cheeks warm at his admission.

"I am of the opinion Georgiana said something before you and Mr. and Mrs. Collins came for tea, and Anne must have been watching to see if there was any evidence of mutual admiration between us."

"I am certain she must have readily seen how I felt when the announcement was made. I was terribly distraught, as I had just spent the previous two hours contemplating how a man like yourself could have... could have fallen in love with someone like me, and then... consequently... realizing my own depth of love for you." She felt him squeeze her hand.

"Needless to say, once Anne made her declaration that she would not marry me, I made arrangements for Georgiana and Mrs. Annesley to return to London. I had all our belongings packed and my carriage readied. My sister, however, could not take her leave until she visited you at the parsonage to say goodbye." He shrugged his shoulders. "I also suspect she wished to inform you about the termination of the engagement."

Elizabeth looked away. "And she discovered I had departed for home."

He slowly nodded. "Mrs. Collins informed my sister that you had left and why. I believe the only reason she told her was because of our connection with Mr. Wickham." He glanced down at her. "Georgiana was terribly distressed, but grateful for the intelligence, which she then related to me."

"Then you sent her to London so she would not have to endure Lady Catherine's wrath about the broken engagement, and you decided to come here?"

He nodded. "I saw them off in my carriage and immediately rode here on horse."

Elizabeth's brows pinched together. "That all took place the same day I left?"

Darcy again nodded.

Elizabeth tilted her head as she bit her lip. After a moment, she said, "Mr. Darcy, that means you have been here longer than we suspected. Charles said you only arrived last night."

Darcy swallowed hard.

Elizabeth closed her eyes as she gathered her thoughts. "It is interesting that just yesterday my mother's jewellery was returned. Someone found it and must have paid back what Mr. Wickham owed for its return, but we had no idea who that was." She looked up at him. "Would you happen to know anything about this?"

He took both her hands in his and squeezed them. "I..." He drew in a deep breath, letting it out slowly. "I own I did some checking with the other officers. If Mr. Wickham had still been in Meryton, I would have gone directly to him, but it is probably good for him that I did not confront him. I was glad to hear he was gone, and I was able to secure the names of some merchants in Meryton who had loaned money to the officers in exchange for valuables. I discovered who had your mother's jewellery and bought it back."

Elizabeth could barely think of what to say to him as she pondered his earlier actions done solely to remedy her family's situation, as well as the actions he was presently exhibiting, as his fingers gently caressed her hands. She could not help but wonder, however, if he was stroking her hands intentionally or if it was because he was feeling nervous, much as she was.

She finally said, "Mr. Darcy, my family owes you a great deal for your kindness. Let me thank you now for them. You did not have to do this."

"How could I not?" He stopped and faced her, enclosing her hands in his. "I would prefer that your family not know. They might eventually determine it was me, but for now, I would ask that you not say anything. As far as they are concerned, I only arrived late yesterday."

"Do Charles and Jane know?"

He nodded. "Yes, Jane was able to deduce the whole situation much like you did." He chuckled. "I tried to talk my way out of it with her, but she was too clever. I knew there was no way I could keep it from you, so I did not try."

Elizabeth smiled. "I will not tell my family, but I warn you my father is also very clever. Once he discovers you are here, he will be convinced you were involved in the return of the jewellery and will insist on paying you back."

Darcy tilted his head. "Which I will refuse, of course."

"He will not understand, nor will he be pleased."

"He shall hopefully understand in due time."

The look he gave Elizabeth assured her of his continued love and admiration for her. He cupped her face with his hand. "My dearest, loveliest Elizabeth, while I cannot ask for your hand so soon after the dissolution of my engagement to my cousin, I do pledge to you my abiding love and devotion, and assure you that I have every hope of making you my wife – if, of course, you will have me."

Elizabeth smiled. "I can think of nothing that would make me happier."

Chapter 27

Darcy took Elizabeth's arm again, and they resumed walking. "I would imagine most women would wish to hear declarations of love spoken first from the mouth of the gentleman, rather than to hear it from someone else – a sister, for example."

Elizabeth smiled and then chuckled softly. It helped ease the nervousness she felt.

He continued. "As Georgiana has already unwittingly and unknowingly declared my admiration for you, there is nothing to be done about it."

"She had no idea it was me," Elizabeth said. She turned her head away and then looked back nervously. "And neither did I."

"No, because I could not have made known to you my true feelings while I was at Netherfield. It would not have been right, and I might have destroyed a strong and loyal friendship if I had attempted to persuade either of you out of your attachment." He cleared his throat. "As much as I wanted to."

"Ah, but you did attempt to do that." She pursed her lips and looked up at him. "On several occasions, you tried to make me see how little he and I had in common. Then the night I stayed at Netherfield, I came downstairs for my book and overheard you and Miss Bingley try to convince him I was wrong for him."

Darcy closed his eyes briefly and looked up, shaking his head. "I regret you heard that. Miss Bingley was, indeed, not pleased with your family, fortune, and connections. She has always wished to improve her rank by being aligned with someone in an elevated position in society. She had the same intentions for her brother, however little Bingley desired it." He turned to Elizabeth and took her hands. "As for my words, both to you and him, I feared your differences in intellect and interests would make an incompatible match. I felt he was not best suited for *you*, and that was the reason I spoke as I did."

"As Georgiana informed me."

Darcy's jaw tightened. "My faulty thinking was in believing I was doing you both a favour. I had resolved, however, that I would not display my feelings for you as long as Bingley favoured you."

"And you had no idea that the day you left, his affections had already begun to shift to Jane." Elizabeth pressed her lips together and then asked softly, "Why did you leave?"

Darcy drew in a deep breath. "I did not think I could remain any longer because of the depth of my admiration for you and my anger towards Wickham." He shook his head. "I was a man in great turmoil."

"Something I knew nothing about until Georgiana revealed it."

"I hope my sister did me justice in declaring the depth of my admiration."

Elizabeth tilted her head and looked up, meeting his intense gaze. "What did she say? I could barely recollect her exact words in such a state of bewilderment as had come upon me. All I comprehended was that you had fallen in love with me and had become deeply grieved when you thought Charles and I were to marry."

"Leave it to my good friend and his terrible letter writing abilities to lead me to that misapprehension. All I could decipher were the first few lines, giving me the date of the wedding and that he was marrying Miss Bennet." He exhaled a groan. "I assumed he meant you."

Elizabeth silently shook her head.

"I once believed you thought ill of me, but my dearest sister informed me that much of your dislike was due to one man's intentional deceit."

Elizabeth looked down, feeling a great deal of shame in believing Wickham's lies. When she looked up, she saw such a look of compassion in his eyes that her breath caught. "I was under a great misconception concerning your character, I confess." She looked down and rubbed her hands together nervously. "Some of it was due to his lies, but much of it was due to my own stubbornness in only believing things that would reinforce my wrongly formed prejudice against you." She slowly shook her head. "For that, I was wrong and I apologize."

"I am far from perfect, but I am grateful my sister has such an elevated opinion of me that she was able to help you see there was a slice of goodness in me."

"She is a dear girl, but as she expressed such praise for your honest and principled character, at first I thought that either she must be shielded from your officiousness, or she so highly idolized you, she could not see who you truly were."

"And yet you came to believe her."

Elizabeth chuckled. "I did, and I feel as though she and I have forged a close friendship."

Darcy straightened and closed his eyes. When he opened them, he smiled. "I am grateful she is so dear to you, as she is very dear to me."

Elizabeth looked up, feeling a deep sense of love and admiration for him. She tilted her head and with a mischievous smile said, "I would imagine a gentleman such as yourself would prefer to have a young lady fall completely in love with him at their first meeting, think highly of him no matter what, and refuse to believe any and all lies about him." She cast her eyes down. "I regret that I came to realize I truly loved you when we were not even together. I had not seen you in over four months."

Darcy took her hand and searched her face. "I cannot tell you how I have longed to hear those words from you." He chuckled and shook his head. "And I truly care not how or when your love for me came about, only that it happened."

Elizabeth gave him a reassuring smile. "I do love you, Fitzwilliam. With all my heart."

~~*

The couple returned to Netherfield almost an hour after Jane and Charles had returned. Darcy knew not how long he ought to wait before officially asking for Elizabeth's hand, but he thought a month sounded sensible. He knew he loved Elizabeth, but her love had only blossomed recently and having had very little interaction with him, he wished to spend as much time with her as possible so she would know for a certainty she loved him and wanted to marry him. He vowed to himself to display only the most kind, humble, and generous conduct, which he admitted would be easy around her. It grieved him that she had believed him officious and cruel. He wanted no trace of those things in his life.

Elizabeth had been correct in declaring her father would quickly determine it was Mr. Darcy who had paid for and arranged for the jewellery to be returned. It took him a while longer, however, to realize it was due to Mr. Darcy's love and admiration for his favourite daughter. Mrs. Bennet, on the other hand, did not seem interested at all in determining who may have been involved in returning it and took his frequent presence in their home as being due to his friendship with Mr. Bingley.

Lydia became more placid and pensive, which seemed to suit Kitty. When the officers were removed to Brighton, both girls saw them leave without too much regret.

~~*

About a month later, when the Bingleys and Mr. Darcy were visiting Longbourn, a letter arrived from Charlotte, which Elizabeth read to the others.

Dear Lizzy and family,

I hope you are all doing well. Jacob and I have settled into married life, and I am thoroughly enjoying living in the Lake District. While I miss my family immensely, I look forward to having them visit in another month. We had planned to come down to Hertfordshire, but another more pleasant and important event is preventing it. We shall be increasing the number in our family just before Christmas. What a blessed Christmas gift this will be!

I am delighting in taking on the responsibilities of having my own home. Mrs. Marshall readily relinquished this duty to me, but has been extremely helpful when I have questions. We all seem nicely suited together.

Please write and let me know how you are all faring. Lizzy, I miss you and Jane so much and hope that perhaps you are making plans to come up to the Lake District with your aunt and uncle later this summer so we can see you.

Give my love to all!

Yours,
Charlotte

"Oh! Is that not the best news! First, we hear about Mary and Mr. Collins, and then Charlotte and her husband!" Mrs. Bennet directed a pointed glance at Jane and Charles. "I suppose another announcement ought to be made fairly soon!" She wiggled in her chair.

Elizabeth could see the distressed look on Jane's face and decided to quickly change the subject. "I suppose I ought to write to Charlotte and enlighten her to events that have transpired since she married Mr. Marshall." She looked at Mr. Darcy and smiled. "I have wondered myself if my aunt and uncle will want to take me on a tour of the Lake District."

Mr. Darcy suddenly rose to his feet. "Miss Elizabeth, if you would oblige me, I would very much like to step outside for a walk. Would you please join me?"

Elizabeth smiled. "I would be delighted to."

She looked at Jane. "Do you and Charles wish to join us?"

Jane shook her head wearily. "No, I think we would prefer to stay here, but you both have a lovely walk."

They stepped outside, and Darcy drew in a deep breath. "It is a lovely day, is it not?"

"It is, Mr. Darcy."

He looked at her and lifted her chin up with his fingers. "We are no longer in your mother's presence. You may call me Fitzwilliam."

She obliged him with a nod. "It is a lovely day, Fitzwilliam."

They began to walk, and he made a suggestion. "Would you mind walking to the stone bridge again?"

Elizabeth laughed. "Are you certain that is where you want to go? On two occasions there I ended up in quite a predicament."

Darcy laughed. "I do not think there is any predicament in which you might find yourself from which I would not be able to rescue you."

"Is that your intent?" Elizabeth slipped her hand around his elbow and wrapped her fingers about it. "Do you actually hope I shall end up with a twisted ankle or lose a shoe to the stream's current so you can rescue me?"

Darcy pressed his lips together as if pondering her question. "It does sound appealing." He took her hand and enclosed it within his hands. "I believe... I hope that you would be more amenable to allowing me to carry you back home now than you were then." He lifted a single brow. "Would that be correct?"

Elizabeth chuckled as they took a turn on a small road that would set them in the direction of the bridge. "While the prospect of your carrying me is not at all distasteful – in fact, I think it would be quite pleasant – I hope you do not have anything planned that will end in my being hurt solely so you can carry me."

They walked quietly for a while, and then Darcy asked, "Would I need a reason?"

Elizabeth looked up at him curiously. "What do you mean?"

Darcy shrugged. "Do I need a reason – like a twisted ankle or a lost shoe – to carry you in my arms?"

"Mm," she murmured with a smile. "You are clever, my dear Fitzwilliam. I am certain you can come up with a decent reason."

There was silence between them as they enjoyed the landscape about them. Elizabeth occasionally pointed to a beautiful patch of flowers, a deer or raccoon scampering away, or a small home in the distance. As they passed those homes, she told him who lived there and what she knew about them.

They soon came to the stream and walked along the shore to the bridge. When they reached it, Darcy led Elizabeth to the centre, and they looked out over the water.

"So this is where you lost young Mr. Goulding's love."

Elizabeth vehemently shook her head. "No, this is where Jane lost his love." She shrugged. "Although I can only assume he admired her, as every other young man in the neighbourhood did."

He chuckled and shook his head.

Elizabeth looked up. "What do you find humorous?"

Darcy's brows pinched together in thought. "It is not so much humorous, as it is that Mr. Bingley also fell in love with your sister because of her beauty."

"Do you think that was his only reason? Jane does have many commendable qualities."

Darcy braced his arms on the bridge's wide ledge and looked down at the water rushing beneath them. "Fortunately, she does. Bingley did well to marry her." He drew in a deep breath. "But you know I felt it was wrong for him to have singled you out as swiftly as he did and then abruptly shift his attentions to your sister."

"And you know *my* feelings on the matter. I had realized quite early on that he was not suited for me."

Darcy suddenly turned and looked down at her. "If you had discovered early on that he was not suited for you, why did you not make your sentiments known to him? Why did you wait so long?"

Elizabeth winced and looked away.

"Elizabeth? What is it?"

She began to shake her head. "You will think me silly, immature, and quite… vindictive."

He tilted his head, and a crease appeared in his forehead. He nodded for her to continue.

"When I overheard both you and Miss Bingley discouraging Charles in his particular regard for me and…" She closed her eyes and let out a huff "Despite realizing he was not someone well-suited for me, I decided I would continue to make the two of you suffer a little longer for your officious meddling. I took every opportunity to speak to the two of you about my admiration for him, while hoping I was not encouraging him in that regard." She stole a glance up at him and grimaced when she saw the scowl on his face. "You must think me horrible."

Darcy stood erect and placed his hands upon Elizabeth's shoulders, turning her so she now faced him. "What I regret the most, Elizabeth, is that you overheard us, and, while my reasons were very different than Miss Bingley's, you took my meaning as being made in the same spiteful spirit." He then took her hands in his.

"I know that now." She smiled as she watched him slowly lower himself to the bridge. Her eyes widened, and her heart began to pound fiercely.

When he got down on one knee, he said, "My dearest, loveliest Elizabeth. You have made my world a much grander place just by your presence. I love your joy, your enthusiasm, your energy, your intelligence, your wit…" He shook his head. "I could go on and on, and I know that if my heartfelt hope is realized, I shall continue to grow in that deep, abiding love for you. Elizabeth, would you do me the honour of consenting to become my wife so I can have you by my side now and for always?"

Elizabeth's mouth was suddenly dry, and she fought back tears of joy that were threatening to spill. "Fitzwilliam, my love for you, although of a shorter duration than yours, is as strong and will be as enduring as yours. I will gladly become your wife and I look forward to walking through this life together with you."

"Elizabeth Bennet, as you have now made me the happiest of men, there is nothing you can say or do that will upset me. Indeed, I am so happy, I could kiss you!"

Elizabeth lifted a single brow. "Do you need another reason to kiss me?"

"Apparently not," he said with a smile.

He pulled her close and wrapped his arms about her. As she looked up, he met her lips with his, and Elizabeth was suddenly unaware of anything but the close presence of the man she dearly loved.

He lifted his head slightly but tightened his hold on her. "Elizabeth, I…"

Elizabeth smiled and whispered, "Shh," and lifted up onto her toes to press her lips to his again. All thoughts of time and space, friends and family, past encounters and future hopes disappeared for those few short moments.

At length, Darcy stepped away. "I have already spoken to your father, and he was going to inform your mother whilst we were out today."

"That is… that was a very good idea." She felt dizzy and grasped the ledge of the wall to help steady her. When she was finally able to order her thoughts, she said, "I would also suggest you wait until tomorrow to venture into our home. I am certain my mother will need at least one day to get over the shock – with the help of her smelling salts." She looked up at him with a teasing smile. "My mother will be so pleased."

Darcy's brows pinched down over his eyes, and he gave her an admonishing shake of his head. "I shall allow her to be pleased, since you have already agreed to my offer." His face softened in a smile. "I shall wait until tomorrow, Elizabeth."

She placed her hands against his chest. "Do you remember when we were at the tree-lined path and I put my hand on your chest only to have you capture it in yours?"

"Vividly."

"I wanted so much for you to kiss me." She shook her head. "And not just my hand. I knew it would be wrong, but I do not think I have ever wanted anything more than I did at that moment."

Darcy closed his eyes and nodded his head. "I only wish I could have."

He wrapped her in his arms again and kissed her soundly. It was only a brief kiss but ardent in its intensity. When he released her, she again steadied herself by putting her hand onto the bridge.

The next thing she knew, Darcy had swept her into his arms, and she was being carried off the bridge.

"My good sir, what are you doing?" Elizabeth asked.

"Carrying you, as you see."

"Why? I am not injured in any way. What if someone were to see us?"

"If someone were to see us, I would tell them that you became quite unsteady on your feet and were unable to walk without assistance."

"I was not unsteady."

"You can try to convince me otherwise, but I readily saw that you put your hand on the edge of the bridge for balance – twice!" He looked down at her and smiled. "Besides, you would not allow me to do this when I came upon you after you lost your shoe, and you must know that I really wanted to."

"Shocking! Mr. Darcy, I cannot believe this from the man whose sister claims him to be so principled and upright."

"Elizabeth, if I had been without my horse, it would have been impossible for you to have walked without your shoe. I would have certainly offered you my boot, but I fear it would not have served you well." He nodded his head for emphasis. "My only other option would have been to carry you. Yes, I was willing – and desirous to carry you."

Elizabeth smiled and put her arms about his neck, resting her head against his chest. She was pleasantly surprised at how secure and comfortable she felt in his arms.

They continued on in companionable silence, and at length, Elizabeth lifted her head. "There was another reason I waited so long to begin discouraging Charles in his admiration."

"Truly? What was that?"

"Mr. Collins."

Darcy came to a halt, looked down at her, and laughed. "And how did my aunt's clergyman influence this decision of yours?"

"Kitty and Lydia overheard him talking to Mother, telling her that he had come to Longbourn to select a wife from among us." With her fingers, she began to twirl the hair along his neck.

"Miss Bennet, you are evoking two completely different responses in me, and while I prefer one over the other, I would suggest you refrain from your pleasant attentions to my neck and finish telling me about Mr. Collins."

Elizabeth smiled. "Pray, forgive me."

Darcy shook his head. "There is no need to ask for forgiveness. I shall, at some later time, request that you continue." He leaned over and kissed her lips. "Now, what is this about Mr. Collins?"

Elizabeth drew in a breath. "My mother conveniently informed him that Jane and I were practically engaged to Mr. Marshall and to Charles. As much as I detested the gossip going around about us, at that moment I was grateful. It was then I decided to help Mary get Mr. Collins to notice her. She was practically in love with him from the moment he arrived at Longbourn."

"I am grateful, then, for everyone's part in staving off what might have been a distressing situation for you and Jane." His head and shoulders shook. "I cannot imagine how that might have turned out."

"I am glad you understand."

"Now on to the other matter."

Elizabeth looked up at him. "Other matter? What would that be?"

"Walking alone." He looked at her sternly. "I fear we need to get this one matter settled before we marry and set out for Pemberley. It is far too hazardous for you to walk unattended. There are ridges you could slip down, lakes and streams you could fall into, and of course, a heavily wooded area in which you might get lost."

Elizabeth lifted her head. "Are you telling me you will not allow me to walk unaccompanied at Pemberley?"

"You have proven yourself to be quite adept at finding yourself in predicaments when out alone. I know of at least four instances."

"And I can guarantee that those are the only instances that have ever occurred." She let out a huff. "Who am I to walk with if you are from home?"

"If I am from home, I would hope you would be with me. But if you are not, Georgiana would be delighted to accompany you." His shoulders rose. "And if neither of us can accompany you, there is always Winston."

"Winston? Who is Winston? I assume he is an older gentleman, for I do not think you would approve of me walking with a young man."

Darcy shook his head. "He is not very old."

"Then there must be something wrong with him. I imagine he is not particularly handsome."

"He is actually quite good looking."

Elizabeth's brows pinched together. "And you trust him to accompany me?"

"Winston is very loyal. I trust him implicitly."

"Well, this is certainly unexpected."

"There is one thing, however…"

Elizabeth rolled her eyes. "I knew there would be something."

Darcy's brow crinkled mischievously. "When you are with him, he might like to have his belly scratched." He paused, and a smile appeared. "In fact, he will likely hurry on ahead of you and beat you to the top of the ridge, jump into the stream or lake while he is waiting for you to catch up, or lead you back home if ever you are lost."

Elizabeth tilted her head as she looked up at him. "I have a suspicion that Winston is not a person."

Darcy smiled. "You are correct. He is my dog. And if ever anything happens to you while you are out alone, send him home. When he is seen without you, he can lead someone back to you."

Elizabeth chuckled. "You have thought of everything."

"Yes, because I know you well, my dear, and I know you would never promise to walk unattended. The land around Pemberley is – you may believe me to be prejudiced – some of the most beautiful in all of England. I would hate for anything to happen to you as you go out exploring it – which I know you will want to do."

Elizabeth leaned up and kissed him again. "Thank you for caring about my well-being."

Darcy set her back down to her feet and wrapped his arms about her again. He lifted his head and said, "I shall always care about your well-being, Elizabeth. You are dearer to me than life itself."

Chapter 28

As plans for the wedding began, it was all Elizabeth could do to keep her mother from becoming frantic over every little thing. She often claimed a fainting spell was about to come upon her, or she fretted that nothing would be ready in time for the wedding. Elizabeth also did everything in her power to keep her mother away from Mr. Darcy when she was in one of her agitated moods. Elizabeth had to continually assure her that she and Mr. Darcy wanted little expense put into the wedding and wedding breakfast, and there was no reason for her to get distressed over it.

There were certain things, however, that Mr. Darcy insisted upon taking care of himself. He wanted Elizabeth's wedding dress and her trousseau to be made by the finest modistes in London. A trip to town with Jane and Charles allowed Elizabeth to be reunited with Georgiana, be introduced to a few of Darcy's close acquaintances, and to visit a millinery shop that had always served the Darcys well. It was at this shop that he told Elizabeth he would spare no expense and wanted her to select only the finest materials for her wedding gown and trousseau.

When they had first arrived in town, Elizabeth questioned Georgiana on her part in Anne's announcement that she had never accepted Darcy's offer of marriage.

Elizabeth took her hand as they sat next to each other in the parlour. "Tell me, Georgiana," Elizabeth said. "Did you use some persuasive language in convincing Anne to break off the engagement?"

Georgiana blushed. "I own that I had spoken to her at great length the evening my aunt announced their engagement. I told her everything, explaining my brother's feelings for you and his grave misunderstanding." She looked down and shook her head. "I knew my brother would never break the engagement, but what Anne told me surprised me."

"What did she tell you?"

"She said that as she had watched the scene unfold earlier that day, she had suspected there was something between the two of you that she did not fully understand. She thanked me for making the situation clear and told me I need not worry."

"Do you think she really had never accepted his offer?"

Georgiana bit her lip. "I do not know. I was as surprised as everyone else when she made that declaration the next day, and once that happened, I never had the opportunity to clarify it with her. I have wanted to write to her, but I know her mother would never allow a letter from me to reach her hands without her first reading it."

Elizabeth let out a long sigh. "I hate to see families torn apart like this. I hope Anne will not suffer too greatly from her mother's anger."

Georgiana squeezed Elizabeth's hand. "She has suffered so much already. I am not certain how this has affected her and will continue to affect her, but I hope that she will somehow, someday find contentment."

Darcy was delighted with the friendship his two favourite ladies had developed in Kent and that continued to grow in London. While they were very different in temperament, he knew, without a doubt, that Elizabeth would be good for Georgiana, as she would become more confident with her by her side.

Charles and Jane stayed with the Hursts at their London home but spent most of the time with Darcy and Elizabeth. Jane enjoyed accompanying her sister to choose her gowns, fabrics, and accessories. Under other circumstances, Elizabeth would have chosen to be frugal in her selections, and it took Jane to remind her of the need for only the finest as the wife of Mr. Fitzwilliam Darcy.

As they shopped, Jane confessed that she and Charles had spent many hours with his sisters trying to explain how the engagement between her and Mr. Darcy came to be. Caroline refused to believe it was due to anything but Elizabeth's arts and deceptive allurements, but they assured her it was not.

Elizabeth stayed in Cheapside with the Gardiners, and they were delighted to finally meet Mr. Darcy. They had heard a great deal about him through their niece's letters. Mrs. Gardiner enjoyed talking with him about growing up so near Pemberley in the small village of Lambton and how she had always admired his family.

Darcy greatly enjoyed this couple, finding them both fashionable and well-mannered. He knew once he and Elizabeth were married, the Gardiners would be relatives he would truly enjoy getting to know better, and he would wholeheartedly welcome them to Pemberley.

After several weeks in London, they finally returned to Hertfordshire with Georgiana accompanying them. It was only two weeks before the wedding, and Elizabeth had a beautiful new trousseau with which to begin her new life as Mrs. Fitzwilliam Darcy.

~~*

Four days before the wedding, as Jane and Elizabeth spent time together at Netherfield, Charlotte and Jacob Marshall surprised them with a visit. After a joyous greeting, Mr. Marshall joined Darcy and Bingley in the billiard room while the ladies gathered in the parlour.

"I am delighted you were able to come!" Elizabeth reached for Charlotte's hands. "I did not think you would make the journey in your condition."

"I would not have missed it for anything!" She looked at Jane. "I am so sorry to have missed your wedding, but as we had barely returned to the Lake District after our wedding, it was impossible."

Jane grasped their friend's hand. "There is no need to apologize. We understood perfectly."

"Let me send for Georgiana. She is in her room resting." Elizabeth started to rise, but Charlotte put up her hand.

"In a while, if you do not mind," Charlotte said. "I would like some time alone with my good friends. It has been too long."

The ladies sat down, and Elizabeth felt a swell of joy as she considered all that had transpired to bring the three of them to this place. Charlotte then expressed a similar thought.

"Can you believe that a little over six months ago, none of us would have ever expected to be married to – or marrying – the gentlemen in the billiard room?"

Elizabeth laughed. "Not only would I not have imagined it, I would not have desired it in the least!"

"But I think everyone is perfectly suited to the other," Jane said.

Charlotte squeezed her friends' hands. "Jacob and I are so much alike as we are both so practical." She looked down and pressed her lips together. "I knew, as we were dancing together at the Netherfield Ball, that he was a gentleman I could admire." She let out a small chuckle. "I knew he had the disposition of a man who would be so well-suited to me." She shook her head. "I did not know what to do about it, since, at that time, we were all expecting an announcement between Jacob and you, Jane."

"And how I struggled with my thoughts and feelings for Charles," Jane said. "They had been formed a few days earlier when he came to visit Elizabeth while she was out walking."

Elizabeth laughed. "Yes, and on that walk, I encountered Fitzwilliam." She drew in a breath and let it out in a sigh. "While you two ladies were well on your way to falling in love with those gentlemen, I was still being stubborn about my feelings towards the proud and officious *Mr. Darcy*, although…" She pressed her finger to her lips. "I do believe my feelings for him that day began to improve – slightly." The two ladies joined Elizabeth in laughter.

"But seriously," Charlotte said. "Jacob and I view everything in our married life in a very practical manner." She gave a shrug. "We could not be better suited."

Jane then spoke. "And Charles and I both consider kindness and generosity to be very important."

Elizabeth leaned in toward Charlotte. "They shall never have an argument, I can guarantee it," she said with a laugh.

"And what about you and Mr. Darcy?" Charlotte asked.

"Oh, dear," Elizabeth pondered as she pressed her finger to her lips. "I believe we shall be ardent in all we do, whether it is walking, talking, reading, playing chess, or sitting together quietly."

The ladies continued to talk, and Elizabeth was quite surprised when Charlotte brought up the subject of a woman's wifely duty. "We have a very special word for it," she said. "No one knows what it is, so do not even attempt to try to talk me into telling you." Smiling, she said, "It is a very practical word." She laughed and looked at Jane. "Do you have one?"

Jane blushed and swallowed. "I had not thought that much about it, but yes, as a matter of fact, we do."

Elizabeth was surprised to hear such a notion and was actually grateful for the information she received from her friend and sister that afternoon, which was not at all like what she had heard from her mother. At one point in the discussion, the three ladies could not stop laughing.

When the gentlemen joined them, they asked what all the laughter had been about.

"We are ladies," Charlotte said. "We shall never tell you!" She then winked at Elizabeth and Jane.

~~*

Another visitor arrived two days before the wedding. As final touches were being made to Netherfield's ballroom for the wedding breakfast, a visitor arrived and was announced at the door. The gentleman wore a soldier's uniform but was using a crutch to walk.

"Colonel Richard Fitzwilliam to see Mr. Darcy," the footman said.

Darcy jumped to his feet. "You came! I am so glad you were able to make it!"

"Richard!" Georgiana exclaimed, hurrying to his side and disappearing in his large arms as he wrapped her in a tight embrace.

When Fitzwilliam released her, he took a few faltering steps towards Darcy, who had met him halfway, and the two embraced. "I would not have missed this for anything," he said.

"Come, I want you to meet Elizabeth and some of her family." Darcy extended his hand towards Elizabeth, allowing his cousin to set a slow pace. "Elizabeth," he said, as he came up to her. "This is my cousin, my friend, and someone whom I greatly respect and depend on."

Elizabeth smiled warmly. "It is a pleasure to finally meet you, Colonel Fitzwilliam."

He shook his head. "None of this formality. It is Richard to you. We are now family." He gave a shrug. "Well, almost, and besides, my days as a colonel are numbered."

"I am sorry to hear that," Elizabeth said.

"As am I," Fitzwilliam said forlornly. But he quickly smiled. "But sometimes things become clearer to you when you are faced with an adversity."

Elizabeth grasped his hand. "I hope things work out for you in a way that ensures your happiness."

"Thank you! I think they shall."

Fitzwilliam was then introduced to Charles and Jane, who invited him to come in and have a seat, while Jane called for the maid to bring refreshments.

They talked as tea and cake were served, and it was apparent that Colonel Fitzwilliam greatly enjoyed Elizabeth's company. Several times in the conversation he looked at Darcy, giving him a nod of approval.

At length, Darcy asked, "Does your family intend to come for the wedding?"

Fitzwilliam shook his head. "No, they were unable to make it. I am here on their behalf... and on behalf of... of my betrothed."

Darcy's eyes widened, and he stood. "Fitzwilliam, you are engaged? When did this happen? How did this happen, and more importantly, who is the young lady?" Darcy looked down at his cousin with an expression of astonishment.

"I know it seems sudden, but the *who* in question is what became surprisingly clear to me, as I mentioned earlier."

"Fitzwilliam, of whom are you speaking? I cannot recall your mentioning any young lady recently who had penetrated your heart enough to ask her to marry you."

"I will tell you as soon as you sit back down." He waited for his cousin to oblige him before he continued. "I think you will be even more astonished by the identity of this young lady than over the fact that I am engaged."

Darcy eyed him warily. "Fitzwilliam, what have you done?"

"There is no need to worry. It makes perfect sense. The letter I received from you telling me what had occurred at Rosings got me thinking in a way I had never before considered."

Georgiana's face grew pale. "Richard, please do not tell me you…"

Fitzwilliam lifted a single brow and began to slowly nod his head.

Darcy's eyes narrowed. "What did you do?"

Elizabeth tucked her hand through his arm. "I believe your cousin went to Kent."

Fitzwilliam smiled. "Indeed, I did. I went and asked for Anne's hand."

Darcy stared at his cousin and was momentarily at a loss for words, seemingly only capable of shaking his head. Finally, he asked, "But, why?"

"Look at me," he said, waving his hand over his frame. "I can barely walk. The only career I ever sought and was trained for has slipped through my fingers." He looked away, staring at the wall across the room. "I have never desired to be a burden to my parents, and especially my brother." He turned his eyes to Darcy. "You know how incompatible we are." He chuckled, clasped his hands, and looked down. "My ability to make a decent living has dropped dramatically due to my injuries."

"But Fitzwilliam, this is ludicrous!"

Richard put up his hand to silence Darcy. "How can you say that? It is no more ludicrous than you doing the same thing. In fact, I spent days considering it, and, you may be surprised, I even prayed about it. While you, Darcy, made the same decision hastily and with very little thought." Fitzwilliam's face grew sombre. "We both did it for the same reason."

"My reason was very different than yours!"

Fitzwilliam shook his head. "No, my good cousin. Our reasons were very much the same. We were both desperate." He gave a nod in Elizabeth's direction. "You were desperate to put this lovely lady out of your heart and mind, and I…" He gave a shrug. "This will allow me to be master of my own home. Our aunt is growing old, and in the past few years, she has asked more and more for our advice. Hopefully she will allow me to step into the role, while ensuring Anne is well cared for."

"But you do not love her!" Georgiana protested.

"In a way, I do. Not in the way you are thinking, Georgiana, but I do love and care for her deeply." He turned back to Darcy. "Aunt Catherine became enraged with you when she heard of your engagement to Miss Bennet. She was, therefore, certain there had been some sort of coercion on your part to make Anne give up the engagement." He lifted his brow and smiled. "You can thank me for taking away some of her indignation against you. Not all, mind you, but some."

Richard took a sip of his tea. "Now, we have talked enough on that subject. I would like to get to know the future Mrs. Darcy, if you do not mind."

~~*

The morning of the wedding, the households of Longbourn and Netherfield were busy with their guests, who filled every room. Extra servants had been brought in to take care of the family and friends who had travelled to Hertfordshire for the celebration.

Darcy found it difficult to stand still as Sumner meticulously dressed him. He was impatient and eager for the ceremony and wedding breakfast to be over. He looked forward to riding away from all those who had come to witness their nuptials. While grateful for those who had made the journey, he wanted only to be sitting beside Elizabeth, stealing a kiss, looking into her eyes, caressing her hands, and running his fingers through her hair. He drew in a breath.

"Steady, sir," Sumner said, as he attempted to tie his neckcloth.

Darcy grunted.

"May I say, sir, that I believe you and Miss Bennet will be very happy."

"Thank you, Sumner."

He nodded. "If I may speak for the staff at Darcy House, they were delighted with her, and I am certain the Pemberley staff will be, as well."

There was a knock at the door, and it immediately opened. "How are you doing, Darcy? Are you ready for the best day of your life?" Fitzwilliam hobbled in slowly and patted him on the shoulder.

Darcy smiled. "I have been ready for a very long time."

"Well, I will be taking notes. I am certain you know our aunt's propensity for wanting to do everything her way. I shall present her a list of what I do and do not want for Anne's and my ceremony. She will crumple it up and throw it away, but I shall at least make an attempt."

"I am certain you shall, Cousin, and I am even more certain, that *that* is exactly what *she* will do."

~~*

Elizabeth's family gathered around her at Longbourn as she came downstairs with Jane and her Aunt Gardiner at her side.

"My, you look beautiful!" Mrs. Bennet declared.

"You shall make Darcy proud, my dear Lizzy," Mr. Bennet said with a chuckle. "As if he needed another reason to be proud."

Elizabeth closed her eyes and smiled. "Thank you. You are all too kind, but I am truly too nervous to be thinking about any of that!"

Jane took her hand. "There is no reason to be nervous."

Elizabeth drew in a deep breath. "I keep trying to tell my stomach that." She looked around at everyone she loved dearly. "You cannot imagine how I feel, knowing that I will be so far away. I will miss each and every one of you, and I assure you that every time we come to town, a side trip to Hertfordshire will be mandatory!"

"I will hold you to that, Lizzy!" Mr. Bennet declared. "If I hear word that you have been in town without making the short trip here, I shall be most displeased!"

"As will I." Mrs. Bennet waved her handkerchief through the air. "My third daughter to marry! And to such an esteemed gentleman." Her shoulders waggled. "I do not know how I ever came to deserve this!"

"You did nothing, my dear," Mr. Bennet said. "It was all Lizzy's doing."

"Well, it will be Lizzy's *un*doing if we do not get her to the church," Mr. Gardiner said. "Shall we go?"

~~*

Darcy stood at the front of the church as the time drew near for the ceremony to begin. Colonel Fitzwilliam was at his side.

"Are you certain you want to go through with this?" the colonel asked. "I can always snatch you away, and no one will be able to find you."

"I am certain, and you shall do no such thing," Darcy whispered.

Fitzwilliam chuckled. "I had a feeling you would say that, and I would not have stood at your side if you had replied any other way!" His shoulders rose as he drew in a breath.

"And you?" Darcy asked quietly. "How will you answer that question at your wedding?"

Fitzwilliam glanced down and then back up. "I... I will..."

He was interrupted when Darcy nudged him to be silent. Elizabeth and her father stepped into the centre aisle of the church and proceeded to walk towards them. All Darcy could do was smile, a wide smile that was reserved for only the happiest of times. This was, indeed, the most joyful moment of his life.

When Elizabeth stepped up to him and took his hand, his only thought was to squeeze it. He heard nothing of what the clergyman said, but only saw Elizabeth's love and admiration gazing back at him through her fine eyes and beaming smile. His mouth was dry, and he could only hope he would be able to recite his vows without stumbling through them. If only he could be as calm as Elizabeth seemed to be.

~~*

Elizabeth was grateful that she was on her father's arm as she stepped into the church and began walking down the aisle. She needed his strength to support her. Not that she was frightened of what this day would bring, but she had so much emotion ready to burst within her. As she reached for Darcy's hand, the light squeeze he gave it was enough to bolster her strength as she came and stood next to him. She smiled up at him and was rewarded with one in return, unlike any she had ever seen. While it soothed and pleased her immensely, her anticipation of their coming together as man and wife was such that she felt it could not happen soon enough, and she wished he could somehow bestow upon her the calm and serenity he seemed to be exhibiting.

Despite the length of the ceremony, before each was aware of it – after the clergyman's message, his charge to the couple, the vows being recited, the ring placed on Elizabeth's finger, and prayer – the pronouncement was finally made. They had come into the church as two separate individuals, and they were now leaving joined together as one in holy matrimony.

Epilogue

The wedding of Fitzwilliam Darcy and Elizabeth Bennet was not the finest ever witnessed in the county of Hertfordshire, nor the neighbourhood of Meryton, nor even held in Longbourn church. But it was certainly exceptional in that the bride might have worn the finest gown, married the most esteemed gentleman, and would be calling her home one of the most illustrious manors in all of England.

As Darcy and Elizabeth rode to Netherfield for the wedding breakfast, he was very impatient to finally kiss his bride in the privacy of the carriage.

"I almost took it upon myself to kiss you in front of all the wedding guests." He reached over and cradled her hand in his. "While it would have been most shocking, I actually considered it."

Elizabeth smiled. "I would certainly have welcomed it, my dear, but I believe I would have been the most shocked of all." She brought his hand up and kissed it. "You are far too reserved to exhibit such behaviour in front of so many people."

"True," he said. "But the thought did cross my mind."

He wrapped his arm about her shoulders. "How long are we required to remain at the wedding breakfast?"

Elizabeth tilted her head as she looked at him. "Would you mind clarifying your question?" She laughed. "I do not know whether you are asking, that as the bride and groom, what is the proper amount of time we are required to remain or..." she paused. "Or... what is the shortest amount of time before I give you leave to... leave."

Darcy leaned over and kissed the top of Elizabeth's head. "You know me well enough to know I do not do well in these situations."

"All you need to do is stay by my side, my dear. I shall introduce you to those in my family and friends in this neighbourhood with whom you are not well-acquainted, and you will only be required to do the same with your family."

"You make it sound so easy, but I love you for being thoughtful."

"Now, with that understanding behind us, I think I can freely say we shall stay for several hours, at least." Elizabeth teasingly lifted her brow.

"Several hours?" Darcy's face grew grim. "I had not thought…"

"No, I imagine you did not."

"We want to travel while it is still light, and we have a journey of several hours to take us to the inn."

"Hmm," Elizabeth said softly. "The days are longer now, so I think we should be fine." She shot him a mischievous smile. "Unless you have other reasons for wanting to get away from the wedding breakfast in a speedy manner."

"Of what are you accusing me?" he asked, placing his fingers under her chin and lifting her face towards his.

"Oh, I have my suspicions."

She had barely spoken the last word when his lips claimed hers in another kiss.

When he finally pulled away and set her back down on the seat as they pulled up to Netherfield, Elizabeth said softly, "I think perhaps the longest I shall be able to endure the wedding breakfast is one hour."

Darcy smiled. "I shall keep my eye on my pocket watch and let you know when the hour is up!"

~~*

The newly wedded couple spent three hours at the wedding breakfast. It would have been impossible to eat the meal and greet all their guests in a shorter amount of time. Darcy finally gave up pulling out his pocket watch and giving a nod in its direction whenever his bride looked his way. While he would have preferred to set off for the inn immediately after the ceremony, he enjoyed talking with his family and friends and getting to know some of Elizabeth's family and acquaintances better.

At length, as they said their final thanks and goodbyes just before taking their leave, Colonel Fitzwilliam came up to them, holding out a letter. "I want to give you this from Anne," he said. "She said to give it to you once you were married. I have no idea what it says, but I believe she is wishing you great joy."

"That is very kind of her," Elizabeth said. "I do hope we can see her again soon."

"You shall get an invitation to our wedding. Her mother might not approve, but I am of the opinion there are times when you must go against the advice of your elders."

Elizabeth smiled. "Yes, I can certainly understand that." She took his hand. "Thank you, Richard. And I would like to wish you great joy, as well."

He pursed his lips and nodded. "Thank you. I greatly appreciate that."

The married couple climbed into the carriage and were sent off with waves and cheers of congratulations.

Darcy let out a long sigh and dropped his head back as they pulled away. "I thought we would never leave."

"It would have been difficult to have departed any earlier. There were too many people to greet."

Darcy huffed. "I was ready to leave two hours ago. I finally gave up checking my pocket watch, since you completely ignored me."

Elizabeth chuckled. "I did no such thing." She snuggled her head against his chest. "And now it is to be only us. No family, no friends, and no interruptions."

"That sounds delightful," he said softly, kissing the top of her head. When he lifted his head, he saw Elizabeth was looking up at him with an inviting smile and sparkling eyes. "*You* are delightful." He kissed her lips and then laughed.

"What do you find so humorous?"

He shook his head. "When Bingley believed himself to be

falling in love with you..."

"*Believed* himself in love? I protest! He *was* very much in love with me."

Darcy put his finger up to Elizabeth's lips. "If he *had* been in love with you, he would not have shifted his affections so readily. Now if I may continue." When Elizabeth said nothing, he said, "I gave a rather harsh reprimand to him for always calling you and everything else he liked *delightful*."

Elizabeth smiled. "Have you now changed your opinion on the use of that word?"

"I was not so much against his using that word, but angry that he could use it in reference to you." Darcy gazed at her intently while shaking his head. "Every time he said it, whether it was about you, the neighbourhood, or some dish served at dinner, it reminded me how envious I was of him because you seemed to have a continued and growing admiration for him, despite what I perceived as great differences in your personalities and interests. That afforded me little pleasure."

Elizabeth fingered his neck cloth. "I now regret the anguish I caused you. While at the time I wanted you and Miss Bingley to believe my affections were strongly attached to him because neither of you wished it, I had no idea you had such strong feelings for me." Her fingers slowly went up and caressed his jawline. "I was acting rather foolishly."

"As was I," Darcy said, clasping her hand in his and bringing it to his lips.

"And I am glad you no longer have such an aversion to the word delightful."

Darcy looked at her curiously. "Why is that?"

"Well, I would suppose you are looking forward to a most delightfully diverting evening once we arrive at the inn."

Darcy's eyes widened. "Delightfully diverting evening? To whom have you been talking? Not your mother, I would suspect."

Elizabeth laughed. "Indeed, my mother did give me my wifely duty talk, but no, it may surprise you to hear that Charlotte told me a great deal more than I ever thought she would." Elizabeth shook her head. "But have no fear, she is very practical, you know, and was very tactful in all she said."

"Is that what you ladies were laughing about when we came from the billiard room?"

"Indeed, it was. Both Charlotte and Jane told me they have special words they use with their husbands regarding this… matter." She laughed. "I had no idea couples did this."

"What were their words?"

Elizabeth shook her head and shook her finger at him. "I have not an idea. One is not allowed to tell someone else what their word… or words are."

"I see. It sounds as though you have put a lot of thought into this."

A smile lit Elizabeth's face. "I have. And you cannot tell anyone – even Richard – our words. It is to be only used between us!"

"So it is to be a kind of code word, is it? When we are out, I might say to our hostess, 'Thank you for the evening. It was certainly a delightful diversion.' You would then know what is on my mind."

"I suppose that is how it is done."

Darcy smiled. "Well, then, I do look forward to a delightful diversion this evening." He wrapped his arms about her and leaned over and kissed her. He had intended for it to be a light, brief kiss, but when Elizabeth began to entwine her fingers in the hair at the nape of his neck, he lifted her up and pulled her onto his lap, his lips remaining on hers for quite some time.

~~*

After three days of travelling and just as many delightfully diverting nights, the blissful couple drew near Pemberley.

Elizabeth could barely contain her excitement as Darcy began pointing out the woods, a stream that they would follow all the way to the house, and off in the distance, the ridge that stood behind Pemberley. If Elizabeth had been at all envious of Jane having gone to the beautiful Lake District, she no longer felt that way. The grounds surrounding her home were beautiful, and as they made a turn in the road, the manor itself was suddenly visible through the window.

Elizabeth gasped and could not pull her eyes away from the

manor, as well as its reflection in the lake in front. The water glistened as the sun danced on the slight ripples caused by a steady breeze. Darcy put his arm about her shoulder.

Very softly, he said, "I have always hoped I could share this home with someone I love, who loves me, and who would also appreciate Pemberley in all its beauty."

Elizabeth could barely formulate a word. It was difficult for her to fully comprehend that this place was now hers. Pemberley was her home. She slowly shook her head. "I have never seen a more beautiful place so delightfully situated." She reached up for his hand, which had begun to rub her shoulder, and gave it a squeeze. Turning back to him, she said, "I love you, Fitzwilliam Darcy, and I look forward to exploring all of Pemberley while by your side. I promise I shall never grow tired of you or this place."

Darcy leaned over and kissed her just as the carriage came to a stop at the front door. He drew back and rested his forehead against hers. "And I shall endeavour, my dearest, loveliest Elizabeth, to do my best to continue to earn and keep your full devotion."

They were silent for a moment, until there was a knock at the door.

As it opened, Elizabeth saw servants hurrying out to the front of the home and lining up to welcome them. She tilted her head. "Do you think your staff shall be pleased with me?"

Darcy laughed. "They will not only be pleased, but delighted, as was the staff in London." He smiled. "I look forward to introducing my main staff to you, and I am certain they are looking forward to meeting you, as well."

Once they stepped out of the carriage, Elizabeth was introduced to the staff who helped in the running of Pemberley, including Mrs. Reynolds the housekeeper, Mr. Jones, the steward, and Mr. Baker, the butler. Darcy then called over another servant and whispered something to him. The man hurried off as Darcy continued with a few more introductions.

When the introductions were concluded, Elizabeth knew she would not remember all their names and would need several reminders. She hoped they would be patient with her as she learned their names. Hearing a slight commotion, she turned and saw a beautiful, large black and white dog greeting her husband excitedly. His tail wagged rapidly, and he seemed to be doing everything in his power *not* to jump up on his master.

"Is this Winston?" Elizabeth asked, as she took her husband's arm.

"Yes, it is, but he is so excited to see me, he is having a bit of difficulty obeying."

"He is beautiful. What kind of dog is he?"

Darcy shrugged. "A mix of springer spaniel, retriever, and most likely a few other sporting breeds." He looked at Elizabeth and smiled. "But you will not find a kinder, more loyal, or obedient dog."

Elizabeth bent down and stroked his coat. "I like him very much." She let out a sigh as she straightened up and looked around her. "I like *everything* very much!"

Once that greeting was over, Winston remained obediently at his master's side as they began walking towards the house. "Are you ready to see your new home?"

Elizabeth nodded. "I could not be more ready."

~~*

Although Elizabeth would have been content to remain at Pemberley and never leave, they returned to London for a short stay before going to Kent for Fitzwilliam and Anne's wedding. While in London, they visited the Gardiners, and plans were made for her aunt and uncle to make a trip to Pemberley later in summer.

While in Kent, they chose to stay with the Collinses, as did Georgiana. Anne would have welcomed them into her home, but her mother was still displeased that Darcy had become engaged to Elizabeth Bennet so shortly after Anne broke off the engagement.

When they were in the presence of Lady Catherine, she often made remarks about how pleased she was that Richard was marrying her daughter, as he was her favourite nephew, and she would have despaired had she married anyone else. These comments were usually accompanied by glares at her other nephew.

Elizabeth got to know Anne a little better, and it appeared she was quite content to be marrying Richard. He treated her with love and respect, and Anne told her she believed they had a fairly good chance of happiness, as long as her mother allowed Richard to be the master of Rosings.

Elizabeth also met Richard's family, who welcomed her warmly into their family.

After the wedding, they travelled to Hertfordshire to visit her family for a few days. While there, Jane told them the exciting news that she was with child, and Mrs. Bennet's attention was then turned to Darcy and Elizabeth, with the hope that they would soon make their announcement. Of course, once Mary and Jane's babies arrived, a mere announcement would not compare to actually holding the baby in one's arms. While Mary's baby would not be as readily available for Grandmother Bennet to hold, Jane's would be an easy distance of three miles away.

Despite having to leave her family, and especially Jane, Elizabeth was ready to return to Derbyshire. She was delighted to call Pemberley home, for she had her own stream, lake, woods, and a small ridge behind the house to climb. She looked forward to exploring more of it with her husband, Georgiana, Winston, and, hopefully in the near future, with a little one she suspected may have begun to grow inside of her. With a husband whom she loved and admired and who loved and admired her, she could not be happier. While chance and circumstance had intervened in the beginning to keep them apart, the same had conspired to eventually bring them together.

THE END

ABOUT THE AUTHOR

Kara Louise grew up in the San Fernando Valley in Southern California, but now lives in the suburbs of St. Louis, Missouri with her husband, and their ever-changing number of dogs and cats. Their son and his wife and their two precious granddaughters live nearby.

Other books by Kara Louise:

Darcy's Voyage

Only Mr. Darcy Will Do

Assumed Engagement

Assumed Obligation

Master Under Good Regulation

Drive and Determination

Pemberley Celebrations: The First Year

Pirates and Prejudice

Mr. Darcy's Rival

and

Peculiar Engagement

~~*

www.karalouise.net

KARA LOUISE

CHANCE AND CIRCUMSTANCE

Made in the USA
Middletown, DE
12 May 2018